The Devil's Anvil

MATT HILTON

The Devil's Anvil

HODDER &
STOUGHTON

First published in Great Britain in 2015 by Hodder & Stoughton
An Hachette UK company

1

Copyright © Matt Hilton 2015

A CIP catalogue record for this title is available from the British Library

Harback ISBN 978 1 473 61003 3
Trade Paperback ISBN 978 1 473 61002 6
Ebook ISBN 978 1 473 61001 9

Typeset in Plantin Light by Hewer Text UK Ltd, Edinburgh
Printed and bound by Clays Ltd, St Ives plc

Hodder & Stoughton policy is to use papers that are natural, renewable
and recyclable products and made from wood grown in sustainable forests.
The logging and manufacturing processes are expected to conform
to the environmental regulations of the country of origin.

Hodder & Stoughton Ltd
338 Euston Road
London NW1 3BH

www.hodder.co.uk

The one is for Sue Fletcher

'Keep your friends close but your enemies closer.'
– Michael Corleone (paraphrasing Niccolò
Machiavelli), *The Godfather Part II*
Mario Puzo and Francis Ford Coppola

I

'Keep your head down this time, Billie, and don't move. They won't see us if you stay still.'

There were three men in a GMC Suburban hunting us, two in the front and one in the back. The bottle-green SUV was canted on its chassis, the right side sitting in a deep rut in the road where it crested the hill, the other wheels on the grass embankment. One of the men held something to his face, the glint of moonlight off lenses betraying a set of night vision binoculars. He scanned the road and the forest on both sides. His friends relied on their unassisted vision as they checked out the road both front and back.

They couldn't see the woman or me.

Wilhelmina 'Billie' Womack was scrunched in a hollow in the forest floor, with a stack of broken twigs piled in front of her offering further concealment. I was ten feet away, crouching behind the bole of an ancient fir tree. A storm had torn down the upper half of the tree during a previous season, and the tangle of its brittle branches hid me from the watchful eyes of the hunters in the Suburban.

'Where are the others?' Billie whispered. 'What if they're moving in behind us, Joe?'

'It's always a possibility, but I won't hear them if you keep talking. Do as I say, keep still and stay silent.'

Billie was a spirited woman, not someone who ordinarily took orders lightly. But I was glad to find that this time she knew I was speaking sense, and that it was best to keep her head down.

The Suburban didn't move. The men inside continued to search the woodland, but none of them was looking our way. The road before them wasn't an easy track to negotiate, not even for an off-roader. Best-case scenario was if they reversed back the way they'd come, took another route through the forest. Yet it seemed they weren't ready to give up on the hunt. I listened. Distantly I could hear another engine, alternately revving and petering out as a second SUV pushed its way along another trail. The terrain was hilly, densely forested, and though there was no way of pinpointing the direction of the second vehicle it sounded far off and of no immediate concern. A helicopter kept buzzing overhead, but the canopy was too thick for its crew to see us. More worrying were the searchers on foot who for all I knew could be close.

Occasionally I heard the crackling of twigs, but again the sound was distant. Didn't mean that a more accomplished stalker wasn't nearby. My friend Rink could move through this forest without setting a foot wrong or leaving a distinct track, and there were plenty of trackers as skilled as him, some more so. Truth was, the people hunting us were more capable than many. They didn't rush trying to flush us out; once they'd got in position, they were controlled and methodical in their search. Someone guiding them was laying down a search grid and sooner or later they'd stumble on to our position.

I was armed, albeit lightly, with a SIG Sauer P226 and a folding knife. But those that sought us came with heavier armament: rifles, automatic pistols. It was serious artillery to bring down an unarmed, untrained woman. Our only advantage was that those chasing Billie didn't realise who was with her. The only person who could have told them about me was in no position to do that. He was lying at the bottom of a ravine with a broken neck.

The man with the binoculars swept the ground before us, but continued past without being alerted to our presence. He must have said something, because the driver brought the Suburban forward a few yards. The big car tipped like a seesaw as it negotiated its new position, but it inched forward again. Then, once out of the deepest ruts, the driver steered it down the hill and so close that I could smell the exhaust fumes that plumed from the tail pipe.

'They're going to see us . . .' Billie's voice was high-pitched, fraught with anxiety.

'Hold your position. They're not aware of you, and things will stay that way unless you move.'

'Please, Joe,' Billie said. 'Don't let them take me.'

'I won't,' I promised.

My pledge might have rung empty to her. Billie had come to me for protection, and in her mind that might mean firm and resolute action, not hiding like rodents in a burrow. But I was one man against many, outgunned and outmanoeuvred, and her best hope for safety was that we'd go unnoticed by the hunters. I was itching to do something more telling than crouch behind the fallen tree, and if it had been only my life on the line I'd have probably gone for broke. I bit down on the urge to shoot it out with the men in the SUV.

They passed us by.

I sighed as the Suburban jounced a route along the trail and headed up the next incline. I followed the big car's progress, seeing it through drifting rags of blue smoke that hung in the cold moonlight like will-o'-the-wisps. As it crested the next rise it paused again as the men inside checked the terrain for any telltale signs.

Billie adjusted her position so that she could check where the car was and I heard the crackle of twigs beneath her elbows. The sound was a faint rustle at most, but in the stillness of the forest she might as well have jumped up and down, waving her arms and yelling 'Over here!'. A corresponding crackle alerted me to the location of something moving through the brush. I hoped in that fraction of a second that it was merely a forest creature, startled by our proximity, but knew our luck was out.

Twisting round, I brought my SIG to bear on the man who'd risen from a dry watercourse about twenty feet behind us. He was wearing cammo fatigues to help blend with the forest. It seemed a lot of trouble to go to when hunting a townie like Billie, as did the rifle the man aimed. The only saving grace was that my movement surprised him. He'd been stalking the woman, closing in on her, and was up until that moment unaware of my presence. He was no weekend warrior though, and my presence gave him only a split second's pause. He swung his rifle on me even as I shot at him.

Our bullets must have crossed midway; because I was knocked back against the tree at the exact same time he folded over my round in his gut. I'd been hit higher up; attesting to that was the way in which my body was spun by the impact and my left arm swung out to compensate. I smacked up against the tree, and then fell on my side, landing badly because my arm wasn't able to break the fall. The initial shock of being shot was bad enough, but the pain hadn't hit yet. It would come and when it happened it would be debilitating. Had to stop the hunter before he could turn his attention on Billie. I fought to a good shooting position, even as the man cursed and struggled with the bolt on his rifle. In his shadowed face, his eyes rolled white and his teeth flashed. His concentration was on me as he fired and the impact on my left shoulder made me jerk the trigger of my SIG so that my return shot missed. Blackness edged my vision, and I barely saw the man take an extra step forward, firming his rifle against his shoulder. A hot wetness was pooling in my shirt and my breath hitched in my lungs. So this is it then, I thought, the place I'm going to die?

I pushed the thought aside. I'd reconciled myself to violent and uncompromising death long ago, also resolving that when the time came I wouldn't lie down and give in to the inevitable.

'Bastard,' I snarled as I squeezed my trigger again and again.

The rifleman's gun flashed, but my hearing had compressed to register only the rush of blood through my veins. He danced a jig, a dark crimson halo puffing around him as my bullets struck repeatedly. I felt the solid thud of his round slam me, and the strength required to pull my trigger fled.

The smell of cordite wafted past, replaced by the coppery tang of spilled blood: whether the gunman's or mine I couldn't be sure.

My hearing was still muffled, and a heavy fog descended through my field of vision. Billie clawed herself free of her foxhole, began crawling towards me. I showed her my empty palm. Droplets of blood peppered the back of my hand.

'Leave me,' I said. 'Go back the way we just came. Try to get to the road.'

Perhaps the words were only in my head, or she was more spirited than I'd already thought, because she didn't run away. She went down on her knees beside me, and I realised I was lying on my back, peering up at her. She'd found my knife. Her hair whipped round her face as she slashed and stabbed in an arc around her, her voice screeching a challenge.

'I . . . I'm done. Get away before the others come.'

Between killing the rifleman and Billie grabbing my knife, I must have passed out. I'd lost time. There were already men standing around us, pitiless in the way they aimed their guns down at us both.

Billie shrieked something at them, lunging with the knife.

One of the silhouetted figures grabbed her by an elbow and yanked it away. She fought to break loose. Her captor struck her across the face and she slumped. I tried to struggle up, but if anything only my astral form moved, because I wasn't going anywhere. My arms were numb, as were my legs. My body felt as heavy as a mountainside. Only my eyelids had the ability to move, but even that strength was slipping away.

Someone crouched close by my side. A hand roughly patted me down, checking for other weapons. I'd no idea where my SIG was.

'So who the hell is this guy?' a voice asked, the words coming to me as if from a great distance.

'Doesn't matter now,' said another. 'Finish him, Danny.'

My lids flickering, I tried to face death.

I saw the metallic gleam of a gun barrel.

A flash.

That was all.

2

Days earlier...

Billie Womack loved her home. It was a ranch-style, two storeys, with a peaked roof and stone chimney stack at one end and a flower garden out front. A porch ran the length of the front of the house, with a pitched roof to sluice off the frequent rain showers, or for depositing the accumulated snow during the winter months. Beyond the house was an old double-width garage, a reclaimed barn from the days when farming was the primary occupation in the region. In the garage she kept her father's ancient Chevrolet pick-up truck and her smaller runaround, a VW Jetta SportWagen, as well as a quad bike for when she needed to get around her land on maintenance chores. The house stood on a spit of land above a pebble embankment marking the southern shore of a lake known locally as 'Baker's Hole'. A stream plumed from the higher hills to the south of the house, disappeared beneath the access road, then wound a narrow path past her front garden and emptied into the lake. Tree-capped hills dominated the horizon whichever way she looked.

She'd inherited the house and fifteen acres of land on the southern side of the lake years ago, but never tired of standing on her porch viewing the changeable hills as each successive season passed. She recorded the passage of time with the hues of each season, painting them in oils and acrylics, occasionally in the sombre hues of charcoal and pencil when her mood plummeted from longing to regret. She was certain her daughter, Nicola, would have loved her home too, but Nicola was no longer there to appreciate it.

These days her paintings were Billie's main source of income. She'd earned herself a name in the art world, and occasionally sold her creations to buyers over the Internet, but most she sold to tourists from a boutique gallery she ran in the nearby town of Hill End, Washington State. Her artwork was a reason she'd held on to her dad's old pick-up, as temperamental a vehicle as it was: carting her easel and paints and all the attached paraphernalia around wasn't easy in her Jetta, particularly when she went off-road to capture the scenery from a higher vantage point than the lakeside. On occasion she used the back of the pick-up as a platform on which she erected her easel, usually when the ground was thick with snow or boggy from rainfall.

She'd used the pick-up to get to a high point on the western hills, from where she could barely make out the roof and chimney stack of her house in the distance. On most days she'd have had no view of her home but today the weather was clement. Although the sky was pale grey, the clouds were insubstantial and very high. A little of the sun's heat made it to the valley floor, but it wasn't warm enough to shed her coat and boots yet. She was painting the undertones on to canvas; readying a landscape view she'd later take indoors and finish by memory in the attic bedroom she'd converted to a studio. It was important that she lay down the basis of the painting, not so much that the detail was exact later on. She took delight in inventing facets of her artwork that did not exist in the real world, and also by leaving out those that did. In that way she could paint the same scene over and over but each would be unique. Her current work showed the rock-strewn shore of

Baker's Hole, the still waters stretching half a mile to an undulating forest. For undertones she was using a sepia palette. But then she dipped her brush in the cadmium red and directed a single vertical stroke near the water's edge. That was where Nicki would stand in the finished painting. Nicki featured in all her paintings without exception. It was her way of keeping her daughter's memory alive.

In her paintings Nicki's features were always left blank. It wasn't through lack of trying that Billie couldn't bring to mind her child's face, and she had no desire to do so wrongly. She had any number of photographs of Nicola, digital and regular, but refused to refer to them for inspiration. The featureless girl had become her trademark and she preferred things to remain like that. She doubted she could have done her daughter's beauty justice anyway.

She wasn't maudlin as she applied the red paint to canvas. Nicola had been dead more than four years, the first raw flush of grief behind Billie now. When she thought of her daughter these days it was with a smile, and not the soul-devouring rage that once drove her to slash at the canvas with charcoal.

Finished for now, she stepped back, measuring the proportions of her creation, judging angles and depth, the play of shadow and weak sunlight, and she nodded in something approaching satisfaction. Never full satisfaction, because like all artists she was never confident that her creations were as good as they could be. It would do, she told herself, and washed out her brushes. She loaded her kit in a purpose-built lock-box, and placed it on the back of the pick-up with her collapsed easel. The canvas she set on the passenger seat for safety. After a half-dozen turns of the ignition key the old pick-up started, belching blue smoke. Driving back down the hillside, she took it slowly, and not just because she barely trusted the vehicle to complete the journey; she had no wish for the still-wet canvas to fall against the dashboard and smear.

A narrow track wound between trees, before the woodland opened up to the valley and lake. Birds broke from the tree line, startled to life by the sputtering growl of Billie's vehicle. The engine noise and the cawing of birdlife carried far across the still waters, before echoing back from the line of hills. Billie part-squinted at each high-pitched call of the birds, sensing that if they continued it would herald the onset of a migraine headache. She had no desire to retire to a darkened room to stave off the pain and nausea, so instead elected to wind up her window and block the shrieks. She urged the pick-up along the road, seeing again her lovely house heave into view. The rise and fall of the road made it impossible to see all of the property in one go, and at first she could only make out the gable, the chimney stack and the garage; then when only a quarter-mile from home she saw something that was out of place.

'Who's that?' she wondered aloud.

Parked in front of her house was a gunmetal-grey sedan car. Occasionally she received visitors, but they were few and far between. Generally it was a neighbour who called by, or someone interested in purchasing her artwork having been guided to the house by Hilary Bartlet, who worked part-time at Billie's shop in Hill End. She wondered if this latest arrival had come in search of a particular piece of art, or to commission work, because the grey car wasn't a vehicle she recognised. Billie craned to make out a figure inside it, but from this distance the windows were opaque, as blank and formulaic in colour as the car's paintwork.

A man of similarly bland colours was standing on her porch.

That of itself wasn't surprising. Someone who'd made the effort to drive all the way out to Baker's Hole might decide to wait for her on receiving no reply when they knocked. Even as she figured the visitor had come to such a decision, he straightened and spied back at her. The man then turned briefly, and from the way he snapped his attention back on the approaching pick-up she guessed he'd hailed someone else. She followed the direction in which he'd turned and saw a second man walk out from the front of her garage. For obvious reasons, Billie experienced a twinge of concern. Hilary wouldn't have sent these men to Billie's house like this, not to the home of a single woman out in a remote corner of the hills. There was no formula to spotting an art lover, but Billie doubted the men in suits and raincoats were the type to while away the hours in any gallery – other than a shooting gallery. They looked like cops, or maybe FBI.

Billie fumbled her cell phone from her coat pocket and checked for missed messages. There were none. Hilary would have warned her if the men had been at the store enquiring after her whereabouts. She put the phone away. She didn't take her foot off the gas. Momentarily she considered bypassing her house, keeping going until she was in Hill End, where she would feel less intimidated by facing the strangers. But what if she was worrying about nothing? The appearance of the men – cops, FBI agents or whatever – might have nothing to do with her former life. And, if it had, trying to run wouldn't make any difference. Better to face things than have the grey car chase her along the valley.

She slowed, then pulled the Chevrolet into the drive. By now the first man she'd noticed was leaning on the porch rail, smiling faintly as she drew up alongside the sedan. His friend had stalled midway between the garage and house, and looked mildly embarrassed that he'd been caught snooping where he'd no right. She gave him a disapproving squint through her bug-encrusted windshield as she turned off the ignition. The engine continued to sputter a few beats after she withdrew the key.

As she climbed out of the pick-up, she looked at the two men in turn, before settling on the one on the porch. It was obvious from their manner that the one on her porch was the senior, in age and in rank. She directed her question at him. 'Who are you people, and what the hell do you think you're doing trespassing on my land?'

On the porch, the man adjusted his raincoat so that Billie got a look at the official shield clipped to his belt. 'We're looking for Wilhelmina Womack.'

'Why?'

'I'm Agent Brandon Cooper. I need to speak with her concerning her husband.'

Billie scowled at the man. 'Why would a federal agent be asking after a dead man? You do know that Richard died?'

The agent snorted, before approaching the steps and moving down them at a leisurely pace. Billie waited. She folded her arms, a defensive posture. On her right forearm was a smudge of paint which she rubbed at with her opposite thumb, then allowed her arms to swing down by her sides. She felt awkward and knew that the agent would recognise her ill ease.

'Mrs Womack,' he said as he came to a halt in front of her. He was taller than her, slight of build, a man with neat grey hair, but he carried the faintest buzz of beard growth on his chin. She guessed that the agents had driven through the night to reach her home this morning. 'Can we speak candidly and cut to the chase? You are Wilhelmina Womack?'

'Billie . . . but I don't need to answer your questions. I've already been through all this with the police, so I'll ask you to leave.' She pointed at their car.

Neither man budged.

'Go on, get the hell out of here,' Billie demanded. 'And don't come back without a goddamn warrant.'

'Why would we need a warrant?' asked Cooper. 'I only want to speak with you.'

'Show me that shield of yours.'

Cooper grunted at her attitude, but flicked back the front of his coat.

'How do I know that it's official? For all I know you guys are weirdos who seek out lone women while pretending to be federal agents. A badge like that, I could buy one of those at Toys R Us. Any other form of identification?'

For the first time Cooper's look of smug satisfaction slipped. He dug in his breast pocket and brought out a leather wallet, flicking it open and holding it close to Billie, who studied an ID card inside it in detail.

'Satisfied now?' Cooper asked.

Billie checked his face against the photograph ID on the card. 'Why would an ATF agent wish to speak to me about my deceased husband?'

'Wouldn't you rather we went inside? It's a bit cold out here, don't you think?'

Billie folded her arms: to hell with looking defensive. 'We're not going inside. I'm fine where we're at; if you don't like it, then you're free to leave.'

Cooper glanced once at his fellow agent, turning his mouth up at one corner in a sour smile of acceptance. 'It could take a while,' he said.

'I haven't much to say about Richard. We ended on very acrimonious terms ... and that was before he killed our daughter.'

Cooper appeared momentarily knocked off-stride by her bluntness. He again glanced at his colleague, this time indicating that he return to the sedan. 'I'll handle this, Ray. You may as well stay warm.'

'This is your show, Brandon,' said the other agent and turned away.

Cooper pushed his wallet inside his coat pocket, and then flicked a hand towards the lake. 'If you're unhappy about going inside, will you walk with me? It was a long drive over from Seattle, and I'm feeling every mile in my bones. Do you mind taking a stroll down by the lakeside?' After a moment he added: 'I can see why you'd live out in these hills. It's beautiful here.'

As the younger agent climbed inside the sedan, Billie brought an extra coat from the passenger seat of her pick-up. It was through stubbornness that she'd refused to go inside, and now she was regretting it. While painting she hadn't felt the cold, but down here where a chill breeze blew off the lake she found that she was trembling. Then again, it was more to do with Cooper's loaded words than the low temperature, so it would probably make no difference. She shrugged into the coat, and then indicated that Cooper lead the way. His patent leather footwear wasn't conducive to walking along the rocky shoreline, but it had been his decision to go that way, and his discomfort gave her some slight satisfaction.

Ripples of water sloshed on the pebbles along the shore. A recent storm had thrown leaves and twigs on to the lake surface; now they were piled in a small drift a foot or so higher up than the waterline. Cooper walked, using the mound of flotsam as a route marker, keeping it always at a pace to his right. Billie moved along, a step behind his left shoulder. A couple of hundred yards further on Cooper halted and stared across the lake to where the hills on the far shore shimmered in the breeze. He exhaled, long and slow, purging some of the weariness of the journey from his bones, but also, Billie thought, girding himself for what was to come next. She also settled her gaze on a point on the distant shore, and nodded to herself.

'Has Richard been in touch?'

Billie blinked a couple of times in confusion, but it was a waste. Cooper was still watching the far shore. Billie shoved her hands into her coat pockets. 'What? Like via an Ouija board or something? Are you forgetting he's dead?'

Cooper's shoulders rose and fell an inch. He still didn't turn towards her. 'His body was never found. I know that you filed to have him recognised as deceased, and your petition was granted, but that's not the same as us discovering his corpse.'

Images flashed across Billie's vision of a vehicle plummeting from a bridge, with her daughter Nicola inside, screaming in terror all the way down to the shocking collision. It was easy to imagine the terrific impact of the car as it slammed hood first into the river: from the height it had fallen, it would have been akin to striking concrete. She saw the structure of the car collapse, roof and doors bursting open like a rotted fruit, the windshield smashing to glittering atoms as frothing water cascaded inside to force Nicola from her seat. She thought of her unconscious daughter expelled by the displacement of pressure, to tumble and turn in the dark, freezing water, until finally she'd been caught by the clinging tree roots a quarter-mile downstream, to perish from her injuries and hypothermia. Nicola had not drowned, but it was easy for the investigators to assume that had been Richard's fate. They thought that the freezing waters had claimed him, sucked him down to some deep, dark place beneath the boulders from which the subsequent police dive team had failed to discover him.

'You suspect that Richard's still alive somewhere?' she said, her voice a raspy whisper. 'How could he have survived the fall, or being swept along by the freezing water? Our daughter Nicola died. He did too.'

'That's assuming that he was still in the car when it went off the bridge.' Cooper finally turned and faced her. His features had taken on a hangdog expression. 'I know it's not something you wish to contemplate, but he could have jumped clear before the car went through the balustrade.'

'That isn't what the police investigation concluded. They said that the car was moving at speed when it hit, it had to be to smash through the barriers, and that – even if Richard had jumped clear and survived – he'd have been severely injured. There would have been signs to show where he struck the ground: blood, clothing fibres, scuff marks, those kinds of things.'

Cooper gave a noncommittal shrug. 'It sounds as if they took the lazy approach to me. Just because they didn't see the obvious doesn't mean that more subtle indicators weren't there. I dug into the police report, and also others on file concerning the same bridge. The fact that the safety barrier had been damaged by a previous collision seems to have escaped the investigating officers, or they simply discarded it as being unimportant. It suited them to believe that both Richard and Nicola were in the car when it crashed. But it's easy to conclude that the car wouldn't have needed to be travelling as fast as they assumed. In fact, a car driving at as little as twenty miles per hour would have had enough force behind it to break through the previously damaged barrier. Your husband could quite easily have jumped clear at the last moment, without leaving any trace on the asphalt.'

'If that was the case, wouldn't Nicola have jumped as well?'

'Not if she was incapacitated in some way. There were bruises on her face, as you may recall from the County Coroner's report, sustained before she died. Now the lazy thing is to assume that your daughter suffered her injuries when the car struck the river, or while she was being carried along by the floodwaters . . .' Cooper allowed the suggestion that Nicola's bruises had been delivered at the hands of her father to hang, urging Billie to come to her own conclusion.

She shook her head angrily.

'It's something you have to consider,' Cooper said. 'Your belief was that your estranged husband snatched Nicola, after you refused him access to her during the divorce proceedings. You also believed that he drove the two of them to their deaths out of some bitter sense of revenge. In other words, if he couldn't have his daughter, then neither could you. But what if his reason for taking her was for an entirely different reason?'

Tears stung Billie's eyes, but she refused to allow her emotions to overwhelm her. 'That's ridiculous. Despite everything, Richard loved our daughter. I can accept that out of torment and irrationality he might – on the spur of the moment – drive them off the bridge in some misguided act of desperation. But no, I'd never believe that he'd set out to purposefully murder Nicola so that he could . . . what? Disappear? Why would he do that? Where was the gain? Our divorce was acrimonious, and he was contesting ownership of my family home, but disappearing like that would simply mean he'd end up with nothing. In fact, if anything, without having to split everything, not to mention the payout from his life insurance policy, it made me a relatively wealthy person. Isn't that the exact opposite to what you'd expect from him?'

'Not if he was attempting to disappear completely, without fear of ever being hunted down. Believe me, Billie, he stood to be far wealthier that way than taking half of your combined assets.'

'How? What in God's name are you talking about?'

'You didn't know about the cash Richard stashed away in offshore accounts then? Hmm, I can tell by the look on your face that this is all news to you.'

'I hadn't the faintest clue,' Billie said. 'How much are we talking about here?'

Cooper pulled a notebook out of his coat pocket and opened it to a page marked by a blue ribbon. Billie doubted that he needed to refresh his memory; Cooper's actions were designed to add gravitas to the announcement. He turned the notebook towards her. 'Count the zeros, Mrs Womack. And, before you ask, no I haven't forgotten to add the decimal point.'

Staring at the open page, Billie totted up the zeros as instructed. Before she'd even finished she was shaking her head. 'No. This can't be right. There's simply no way possible. My ex-husband didn't have access to *that* kind of money.'

Cooper merely raised his eyebrows.

Billie shook her head.

'It's true, Billie,' Cooper said. 'Your husband disappeared with more than eighty million dollars.'

3

It was evening in Tampa. Most Brits – as I once did – tend to think that it's always hot in Florida, but not so. There'd been a bit of a cold spell, and for the first time in ages I'd dressed in blue jeans, a navy sweatshirt and black leather jacket. I could still feel the nip in the air, and shivered involuntarily as I walked towards where Rink had parked his Porsche Boxster. It was out of sight of the main strip in an otherwise deserted parking lot.

'Any movement?' Rink had wound down the window and leaned out with one elbow dangling over the door. He too had foregone his usual bright attire to pull on a dark-coloured jacket that he'd zipped up to his throat.

'Not a thing,' I said. 'I'm beginning to think that Redmond's worrying over nothing.' What were the chances of a repeat of the two previous weekends' burglaries tonight? Pretty slim, I thought.

'Who knows? But chances are they see his place as a soft target and will try again.'

'Hope they come soon,' I said. 'Don't know about you, Rink, but I don't fancy hanging around all night. It's bloody freezing out here.'

'Lovely and warm in here.' Rink offered a grin.

'Don't rub it in.' I scrubbed my palms vigorously on my opposite upper arms.

'I thought you Brits were supposed to be used to the cold?'

'Been a while since I was home,' I reminded him. 'I'm turning into a snowbird like you, Rink. We're growing soft in our old age.'

'Speak for yourself, brother. I'm toasty.'

'Care to swap places?'

'Nope. I'm claiming executive privileges. My car, my warm spot. Don't forget you're just the hired help.'

He was kidding. He was the owner of Rington Investigations, but as far as the day-to-day business went we were full partners. He just enjoyed taking the mickey at my discomfort, the way I would have if our roles were reversed.

'I'm going to take another walk around the block,' I said, 'check on the back lot while I'm there.'

'Gimme a shout if you need me.' Rink scrunched down in the heated seat, getting comfortable as he buzzed up the window. He gave me a shit-eating grin all the while. I shook my head in disbelief and his grin only broadened.

I walked away, feeding my hands into my jacket pockets. It wasn't cold enough for ice, but it was as near as damn it. Putting a bit of energy into my walk warmed me up, and also gave me a little cover as I headed around the block. Who'd think I was on a stakeout when it looked like I was in a hurry to be elsewhere?

Jerry Redmond had sought our services after thieves had targeted his business premises two weekends in a row. The Tampa PD had reassured him that they'd send a squad car by his warehouse to keep an eye on things, but they'd also made the same promise last week and had missed the second burglary. Through two nights and the four hours this evening that Rink and I had been in the area we'd never seen a patrol car. Didn't surprise me; there were more important things for the cops to concentrate on than protecting fridges, freezers and washing machines. To be honest, there were probably better things for us to be getting on with but a job was a job. The economic downturn meant that you had to take whatever work came your way. Redmond's cash would help keep Rington Investigations in the black as much as payment from any other job.

It was mundane employment, but employment all the same.

I didn't look like a nightwatchman. I could pass as a worker on his way home from a late shift, so if the burglars happened to notice me wandering around the streets it wouldn't concern them too much. They'd only need wait for me – a potential witness – to leave the immediate area and they could be in and out of Redmond's Electrical Supplies as quickly as they had on those two previous occasions. That's if they ever turned up, but it looked like another no show was on the cards. I was starting to think that Redmond's fears were unwarranted, and the thieves knew that three times was the charm that would get them captured and had moved on to robbing someplace else.

So I was a little surprised when my cell phone vibrated in my breast pocket.

'They're here?' I asked without checking that it was Rink on the other end.

'Nope,' Rink said. 'These guys are on foot, and I doubt they intend carrying away the appliances on their shoulders.'

'So what's the problem?' It wasn't unknown for small groups of guys to wander through the neighbourhood on their way home from the bars across town.

'They're stalking a couple of old folks,' Rink said. He didn't elaborate and didn't need to.

'Where?'

'Comin' your way, brother.'

'How many?'

'Four. I'm out of my car and on their tails.'

'OK,' I said, 'I'm heading back to you.'

'Best be quick, they're making a move now.'

Rink cut the call.

I started running.

This was more the kind of service to law enforcement I preferred.

My walk had taken me around two corners of the block, and though it would take me no more than thirty seconds to run back, it was plenty of time for a group of muggers to pounce. If it weren't for the fact that Rink was closer, I would have been more concerned.

I slowed at the final corner, approaching it at a quick walk. At the last moment I actually came to a full stop, hidden from view. I could hear muffled voices. Some were harsh and commanding, others meek and pleading. Obviously Rink hadn't arrived on the scene yet. Probably waiting for me to show. I rounded the corner, keeping my head down and my hands in my pockets: just an ordinary guy on his way home. I pretended not to notice the tableau playing out twenty feet away, but was taking in the details in a quick sweep.

There were four men, as Rink had said. Three of them stood in a semi-circle, hemming in the fourth man, who had cornered an elderly couple in the recessed doorway of a building. The three were actively intimidating the old couple while the other man took their possessions from them. No hint of a weapon. Perhaps the quartet hadn't deemed it necessary to show one when the threat of violence was enough.

The thug nearest me noticed my approach.

He was a tall guy with a spray of acne across his chin, maybe in his mid-twenties and by the look of things the eldest in the group of muggers. I wondered if he was the leader. Not that it mattered. He would be the first to go down if I had my way. The tall guy knocked elbows with the man nearest him, and both turned to me. The second man gave me a hard look, flicking his head and ordering me to cross the road. I played dumb and continued towards them.

'Hey, dickweed,' the skinny one said, 'keep fucking moving.'

I only then lifted my head and feigned noticing them for the first time. I took my hands out of my pockets quickly, showing them my empty palms. By then I was barely ten feet from them.

I caught a beseeching look from the old man trapped in the doorway. He had a protective arm across his wife's body, trying to stop the gang from taking a ring off her finger. I couldn't spare him a look of support for fear those blocking me noticed. Instead I forced a fearful expression on my face, made a garbled apology and began to divert away from the group.

Just then I noticed Rink loom into view as if he'd materialised out of nowhere.

He gave no warning as he shot a stiffened palm into the ear of the third man in the semi-circle. His strike was blindingly fast, and the mugger was already on the way to the floor before he had time to groan. The man who'd flicked his head at me heard his pal go down and turned towards Rink with a look of surprise, just in time to catch Rink's head-butt on the bridge of his nose. He too began a graceless fall to the sidewalk.

In the meantime I wasn't standing idle.

I adjusted direction with a subtle pivot of my feet and was within the tall guy's reach before he thought to ward me off. I snapped the 'V' of my thumb and index finger into his throat with enough force to make him gag then, before he could suck in his next inhalation, closed my fist around his windpipe. I felt the cartilage popping. I gave him a brief squeeze, and it was all it took to drop him on his arse, thinking he was dying.

The man trying to take the old woman's wedding ring was so intent on his task he was unaware that people other than his gang now surrounded him. Rink glanced at me, and I shrugged, allowed him to go for it.

Rink grasped the collar of the man's jacket and yanked backwards, where a foot sweep took him entirely off balance. The mugger fell on his back, becoming entangled with the limbs of his pals. Rink stood over them all, his features a mask of disdain while I turned to check on the elderly couple.

'Let's get you out of the way,' I said to them.

'They've got my wallet and watch,' the old man croaked, 'and my wife's necklace.'

'Don't worry, we'll get them back for you,' I promised, as I steered the couple out of the doorway and towards the corner. 'Are you OK, did they hurt you?'

'We're OK, just shaken up. I thought they were going to . . .' The old man looked horrified at the prospect of what might have been. Then his look was aimed at his wife, ashamed that he hadn't done more to protect her.

'The important thing is that you're both all right. You don't have to worry about these young punks anymore.' I quickly checked what was going on. The four muggers had rearranged their positions so that they were in an orderly line on the ground. One of them was unconscious – the first guy to be hit – and was blissfully unaware of his friends sitting alongside him. One of them was trying to staunch the blood flowing from his nostrils, the next attempting to straighten out the kink in his trachea, while the uninjured man was the only one capable of showing any defiance. His ballsy attitude lasted only until Rink stepped in and slapped his mouth shut. Even from the corner, and under dim street lighting, I could see a bruise pop out on his jaw. The tough guy mugger was suddenly a weeping overgrown brat. Rink barely gave him any notice as he brought out his cell phone and hit 911.

I kept an eye on the group, but also reassured the old couple that they were safe.

'Thank you,' the old woman said. She was a short, wide-hipped lady, with grey curly hair. Reminded me of my mother, albeit she'd have easily been ten years older.

'No problem,' I said.

'Really, son,' the old man said. 'You have my gratitude. If you and your friend hadn't come along I don't know what I'd have done.'

'You did the best thing possible in not giving them any problems. If you'd tried to fight they'd have hurt you. All's well that ends well, right?' I gave him a surreptitious wink.

'Thank you, thank you,' he said and wanted to shake my hand. It was unwise to compromise myself by accepting his handshake, but Rink had everything under control. He'd finished his phone call, summoned the cops to clear things up, and was now standing over the group, willing them to make a false move. None of them took up the challenge, and little wonder. Rink's big, built like a pro fighter. He's also mean-looking when he sets his jaw so tightly that an old knife scar on his chin practically glows against his tawny skin.

I approached. 'Cops on their way?'

'Yup.' Rink wasn't amused. 'We're going to be tied up giving statements because of these assholes.'

'At least it gets us out of this bloody cold,' I said. 'And with the police activity there's no way the thieves will try their luck at Redmond's tonight.'

'Then it'll only mean we'll be back here again next week.' Rink made sure that the muggers – the conscious ones – heard him. By the way they hung their heads they wouldn't be plying their trade around this neighbourhood again.

My run, followed by the brief scuffle, had done me a world of good. I was feeling much warmer. And, unless the warehouse thieves were more reckless than I gave them credit for, our work was probably done. Not a bad result in my estimation. But still, I was ready for a job that I couldn't complete in first gear. The slight buzz of adrenalin I'd experienced from kicking the muggers' arses only made me crave it all the more. Who knew that things would grow more exciting within the next few days?

4

Billie Womack couldn't concentrate on her art.

After her visit from the ATF agents she'd tried to occupy her thoughts with carting her canvas and materials inside and up to the attic room she'd converted into a studio. She'd set the unfinished painting of Baker's Hole and the surrounding mountains on the easel, inserted a CD in the music system, and then perched herself at the ready to add new layers to her work in progress. However the brush had yet to be dipped in the acrylic paint. She merely stared at the ochre shapes on the canvas, unable to focus on them, let alone bring them to life. The bold red slash she'd earlier applied was the only thing to catch and hold her attention, even if for only brief and fleeting moments.

Finally she stood up and walked to the CD player positioned on a windowsill. The music CD – old-school jazz – had played out without her taking in any of the tunes and was now part of the way through its second revolution. Billie turned it off. The silence was noisier than when the soft strains had filtered unnoticed through her subconscious. She rubbed a hand over her face, and swore softly, then peered out of the window, the view allowing her to see all the way across the lake where her gaze settled on the distant shore. Momentarily she thought she saw a flash of red dashing along the shoreline below the trees, and she blinked in confusion, her pulse responding to the stimulus. It took her another moment to realise that the colour from the painting had etched its memory in her retina and she was only experiencing a ghost image.

A poor metaphor, she thought.

She turned from the window and left her studio, making her way downstairs to the kitchen where she immediately headed for the fridge. Inside was a bottle of wine she'd opened in celebration at selling her most recent work of art to a collector from Seattle. She poured wine into a tumbler she found resting on the drainer next to the sink. Any other time she'd have chosen a more suitable glass, but what the hell! This wasn't a celebratory drink; she only needed the alcohol. After swallowing the wine in two long gulps she reached again for the bottle, but forewent the glass and elected to carry the bottle with her as she went outside and sat on the chair on her porch.

Evening was descending.

It was cold out on the porch and luckily she had been so distracted that she hadn't taken off her coat from earlier. She pulled up her collar and snuggled down in the rocking chair, pulling her feet up under her. She drank directly from the bottle.

Eighty million dollars.

Billie couldn't visualise what such a figure amounted to if the dollars were stacked one on top of the other. But Agent Cooper hadn't actually said that Richard Womack had stolen such a large amount in cash, but that he'd siphoned it off to some untraceable account – maybe many accounts – somewhere offshore. Such an unimaginable amount of money gave credence to the fact that Richard had staged his own death, allowing him to disappear into obscurity from where he could enjoy his ill-gotten wealth. According to Cooper, Richard had sacrificed his own daughter in his plot to disappear without a trace.

The ATF agent was wrong.

Billie and Richard's divorce had been acrimonious. By the end there were only two aspects of their marriage that they could agree on: they had grown to hate each other, but they both loved their daughter. Despite Richard being narcissistic, a conceited son of a bitch and a philanderer, Billie had never doubted his love for Nicola. He'd been petitioning for full custody for Christ's sake! Why would he do that if only to murder her during his disappearing trick? Cooper had a singular take on things: by sacrificing his beloved daughter it added more plausibility to his own supposed death. Richard had proven to be both incredibly manipulative and supremely self-motivated when it came to embezzling the multi-million dollar sum, to a point where he would not wish to hand any of it away, not even to his child. Agent Cooper believed that Richard Womack was a sociopath, with no love for anyone but himself and his needs.

Nicola had been killed, that fact wasn't in dispute. She'd been stuck in the car when it went over the bridge, but it had nothing to do with Richard wanting a clean break so he could keep all the money to himself. Why would he need to murder his daughter, Billie asked the agent, when he could as easily have deposited her back with Billie and then staged his death on the return journey?

Something troubled Billie more than Agent Cooper's insistence that Richard was behind Nicola's death. It wasn't his suggestion that Richard might actually have survived his plunge into the torrential river. The agent was concerned that those whom Richard had stolen from might also have come to the same conclusion. The way Cooper saw things, she could be paid a visit by people who didn't have the same hopes for her well-being as the ATF did.

Billie dipped her hand in her coat pocket and pulled out the card Cooper had handed her.

'Joe Hunter,' she read out loud. On the reverse of the card were the handwritten name and a telephone number. Billie turned it over. As she'd expected, Agent Cooper's details were printed on the front. He'd suggested that she contact Hunter in the event that his skills might prove helpful.

She'd asked who Joe Hunter was. 'Is he an ATF agent like you?'

'No. He's a private operator.'

'A bodyguard?'

'Among other things,' Cooper had said. He'd glanced back at the house to where Monaghan sat in the sedan car. 'Look. I'm going out on a limb here. I wouldn't ordinarily hand out the details of a private operator like this, particularly when you'd expect my agency to offer you any protection necessary. But, you must understand, uh, Billie, that there are some of my colleagues who think that you are complicit in your ex-husband's crimes and that you should be brought in for questioning.' He'd warded off her concerned look. 'I don't think that, but there are some that do. Now, hopefully I'm way off mark and trouble will never come to your door, but in the event that it does, well . . .' He'd indicated the card in her hand. 'Call Joe Hunter.'

'There's something you're not telling me, Agent Cooper.'

Cooper had pursed his mouth in confusion.

'You didn't drive all the way out here on the off chance that something might happen. You *expect* something to happen.'

Again Cooper glanced back at his colleague. He'd weighed the pros and cons of telling her the truth. Finally, he'd decided that forewarned was forearmed, and it was after all his purpose for driving out into the boonies. 'I'm tasked with finding your ex-husband – *if* he's still alive – and recovering the money that he stole. But it has come to my attention that I'm not the only one looking. One of the accounts that Richard tapped to the tune of almost thirty million dollars was in the name of a shell corporation belonging to some pretty dangerous individuals. We've started another investigation into those behind Procrylon Inc., and through our endeavours discovered that they are making enquiries of their own. An ATF agent looking into Procrylon was recently compromised, and subsequently turned up dead. We've no evidence to say those behind Procrylon murdered my colleague, but I'd be a fool to ignore what common sense tells me. If they're prepared to murder a federal agent, then they won't shy away from hurting others to get what they want. It's why I fear that you might become a target.'

'But I don't know anything.'

'I have your word on that, Billie, but that's all they'll have too. I'm willing to take it at face value, but they might not be as accommodating.'

Billie snapped the card against her thigh, and then put it away in her pocket.

Cooper was most likely scaremongering. Despite his reassurances that he believed she knew nothing about the theft or Richard's disappearance, his words were thinly veiled. He thought that she was involved. Perhaps not willingly, but how could her Richard have conducted his criminal affairs without her at least suspecting something? Cooper intended instilling panic in her in the hope that she'd try to contact her ex-husband and lead the ATF to him.

Or was that paranoia speaking?

What if Cooper's intentions were honourable after all and she did indeed require protection from the men hunting Richard?

She took out the card again and stared long and hard at it.

5

'Well, brother. I vote we call it a night.'

Rink was at the wheel of his Porsche, but this time I was sitting in the warmth alongside him.

'Only complete idiots would try another burglary now,' I said by way of agreement.

'Let's roll.' He took off so quickly I'd bet that twin strips of rubber were etched on the road.

The cops had been and gone, taking the bunch of muggers with them; some of them detouring via an emergency room so the thugs could have their wounds tended. The elderly couple, Gino and Muriel Bidinotto, had given their statements and again profusely thanked Rink and me for intervening on their behalf, before they were escorted home by a duo of uniformed officers. A detective I'd come across before, Holker, had taken down our version of events. Holker didn't exactly have any love for me – though he did owe me for helping clear up a previous homicide investigation of his – but he had begrudgingly thanked us for our public-spirited work then sent us off with a gruff warning about curbing our excessive use of force. Personally, I thought that the gang had gotten off lightly. Then again, he could have been referring to the last time we'd worked together. Holker was the kind who wasn't very sympathetic to my cause; when pushed on it he'd said, 'Hunter, you know where "sympathy" lies in the dictionary, don't you? Right between "shit" and "syphilis".'

'Well you've given me plenty shit in my time,' I'd said.

'I'm happy to be of service. Now fuck off.'

Nice.

That was the way with some cops. They couldn't publicly admit that they appreciated my style of doling out law and order, even if they wished they could take off the gloves now and again. But that wasn't really Holker's problem with me. I was sure he was envious of my relationship with his detective partner, the lovely Bryony VanMeter, who'd been more open with her thanks in bringing down a murderer. Holker – I thought – carried a torch for Bryony, but it was not reciprocated. Maybe he saw me as a rival for her affections, when really he shouldn't. Our relationship had cooled after only a few short weeks, and though we'd remained friends, there was no hint of romance left. Bryony was more interested in her career, and don't let it be said that I'd stand in her way: dating a suspected vigilante wasn't conducive to career progression within Tampa PD.

'Fancy a beer before turning in?' Rink didn't take his eyes off the road as he headed towards his place at Temple Terrace. 'One of those wussy Coronas you're so fond of?'

'I'd prefer a coffee,' I said. 'Something hot that'll shift the cold from my bones.'

'I've a Mister Coffee at my place. You can watch me drink beer while it brews.'

'I could do with one now.'

'How do you ever sleep?'

'Why do you always ask? I must be immune to caffeine.'

'Definitely addicted.'

Rink had that right. 'See if you can find a convenience store, will you?'

It was just another mundane night for us private eye types. Then my cell phone tinkled and I dug it out of my pocket.

Caller unknown.

I hit the button and waited.

'Hello?'

It was a female voice, but not one that I recognised.

'Hello? Is this, uh, Joe Hunter?'

'Who's calling please?' I wished to remain noncommittal. It was my personal cell the call had come through on, not the one linked to Rington Investigations.

'I got this number from a . . .' The woman paused, choosing her words. 'I got it from a mutual acquaintance. Brandon Cooper said that you could help me.'

Brandon Cooper? I couldn't immediately place the name. I mouthed the name at Rink.

'ATF,' he reminded me.

I'd never learned Special Agent Cooper's first name, the reason why mention of it had thrown me. Cooper had been part of a Bureau of Alcohol, Tobacco, Firearms and Explosives task force I'd come in contact with during a bust on some arms dealers a couple years earlier. At the time, Cooper had been tasked with regulating firearm commerce in and around Tampa, through targeting and arresting violent offenders in possession of unlawfully held guns. Out of gratitude for me saving his arse from a methed-up perp with a hatchet, he'd allowed my owning an unregistered SIG Sauer P226 to slide, and had even given me further hints on how to confound ballistics reports. It was good of him, considering that the ATF was also actively involved in the NIBIN programme, providing support in tracing firearms to state and local law enforcement investigators through the National Integrated Ballistic Information Network. He wasn't exactly corrupt – not as far as I knew – just more appreciative of my assistance than the likes of Detective Holker.

I vaguely recalled giving Cooper my private cell number, but this was the first time he'd ever used it. Or, more correctly, passed it on to someone who needed to contact me.

'Who am I speaking with?'

'You *are* Joe Hunter, right?'

'I am.'

'I'm Billie Womack.'

There was a moment while neither of us spoke. I formed the impression that the woman regretted making the call now. But that wasn't it.

'I'm sorry for calling at this late hour,' Billie said. 'It has just occurred to me that I don't know where you are and it could be the middle of the night. If I've placed your accent correctly, you're British, right?'

'Yeah, but don't worry, I'm not in England. I'm in Florida.'

'Florida? Still, you're three hours ahead of me . . .'

'You didn't wake me. I'm a bit of a night owl.'

'Too much coffee,' Rink muttered.

Ignoring him, I urged Billie to continue. 'You said that you needed help.'

'Well, yeah, uh, that's the thing . . .'

I heard the unmistakable sound of swallowing. There was a slight slur to Billie's voice, and I took it that her nightcap was that bit stronger than the one I was looking forward to. She'd just taken another slug to gird her for what she was about to divulge.

'I might be in danger.'

'Might be?'

'That's the thing. I don't know if the threat is for real.'

'Tell me about it.'

She related how she might or might not be the target of men seeking her ex-husband, Richard Womack. 'My husband died more than four years ago: why would anyone come after me now?'

'It's a fair point. Brandon Cooper encouraged you to call me?' I had the sense that Cooper wasn't the hysterical type, and even if Billie Womack had no real sense of the danger she was in, I accepted that he did.

'He seemed . . . *concerned.*'

'Where are you, Billie?'

'I'm at home.'

She was stating the obvious, and it took another prompt from me to get the details out of her. She lived in a house near some lake called Baker's Hole in Washington State, way across country in the furthest corner from where I presently sat in Rink's car.

'I can be with you by later today,' I said.

'But you don't even know if my problem is genuine yet.'

'You said you might be in danger. Whether or not the threat is real, we can't take the risk. I'll grab a few things and get the next available flight.'

Beside me Rink had grown quiet and still.

'When Cooper gave you my number, did he also leave you his?'

Billie read a number and I memorised it.

I then checked the details of Billie's address.

'Is there anyone at home with you?'

For a moment Billie paused. She didn't know me from Adam, and was obviously afraid to admit as much to a complete stranger. Her silence answered my question for me.

'I need you to go somewhere where you are in the company of someone you trust. You have my number. Call me when you're there and I'll meet you. We can take things from there.'

'You're prepared to fly across country without the full details?'

'Do you want my help?'

'Uh, yes.'

'Then do as I ask. Go stay with a friend and call me when you're there. By the time I arrive I'll have all the details I need.'

'OK.' Billie didn't know what else to say. There was another swallow.

'Billie? Make that your last drink. You need to get moving right now.'

'You do think I'm in danger then?'

'I'm not trying to frighten you. Hopefully there's nothing in the threat as you say, but I trust Agent Cooper's judgement. Go now, Billie. Rest assured I'm on my way.'

I hung up.

Rink had stopped the Porsche outside a convenience store. It was an open-all-hours type from where I'd previously enjoyed the occasional grab-and-go drink.

'Do you still have time for that coffee?' His expression of resignation wasn't for my caffeine addiction.

'I've a feeling I'm going to need it. And more besides.'

6

Special Agent Brandon Cooper looked ten years older than the last time I saw him. But since then he'd been stuck beneath the nigh-on perpetually dull skies of the northern state of Washington for upwards of two years and had lost the healthy tan he wore while based at the ATF field office in Tampa. He was sallow, a bit grey around the gills, and had lost much of the lustre from his hair and eyes. Wearing a charcoal suit and tie with an off-white shirt added to his monochrome appearance.

I sat opposite him in a diner on Western Avenue, Seattle, a block from the waterfront of Puget Sound: any view of the water was blocked by a viaduct and the Seattle Ferry Terminal buildings. I wasn't much more colourful than Cooper, having donned my usual attire of black jacket on black jeans. My only concession to the colour palette was the brown of my short hair, my bluish eyes, and a small yellow motif on my T-shirt: you had to look closely at the motif to tell it was Homer Simpson's face, proclaiming his trademark utterance of 'D'oh!'. The shirt had been a present from Rink after he'd reconciled himself to my hasty decision to head off on my latest errant crusade to save a damsel in distress. His words, not mine. Rink had expected me to scowl and throw the shirt back at him, but I liked it. I liked Homer. He was the kind of guy whose off-kilter wisdom I appreciated, and he was often as rash in his decision-making as I was.

Cooper didn't comment on my shirt, but I caught him checking it out, and we shared a wry smile before we'd shaken hands in greeting. Then he led me to a booth in the corner of the diner he'd chosen for our meeting. The retro diner was part of a chain based upon the one frequented by Fonzie and the gang in that old TV show *Happy Days*. I almost expected to find Pat Morita serving behind the counter, but instead a team of less-than-exuberant college kids whose modern hair-cuts didn't quite fit the scene manned it.

'You want anything to eat?' Cooper asked.

'I'm good. I ate on the flight over. Just coffee for me.'

Cooper gave our order to a bored-looking girl who only showed any sign of life while jamming our check under the condiments. She then fell back into slouch mode to return to the counter.

'Kind of spoils the "caught in amber" effect when the staff don't get into character,' Cooper noted.

'The music creates enough ambience for me.' From a replica Wurlitzer jukebox came the dulcet tones and pound-ing piano of a Fats Domino number. I checked out the memo-rabilia on the walls: there were signed photos of some of the diner's famous patrons, a couple of old guitars, a saxophone, and even a rhinestone-covered jumpsuit purportedly worn by Elvis Presley. It wasn't up to Hard Rock Café standards, but I appreciated the place. I guessed that Cooper had brought me here with that in mind having talked about our shared taste in vintage styles of music while on stakeout.

'Tell me about Billie Womack,' I said.

'Directly to the point as usual, Hunter? What, no "How are you these days?"; no "How's the family doing?"'

'You have a family?'

'Nope.'

'So tell me about Billie Womack.'

Cooper grinned. 'I forgot how funny a guy you were.'

The thing was, I wasn't trying to be funny.

Cooper took a look around, a habit for anyone in his game. He appeared satisfied that none of the costumed kids were eavesdroppers. 'I took a chance calling you in on Billie's behalf. It kind of works at odds with my current investigation.'

'She told me about how you're looking into the disappearance of a huge sum of cash: that isn't usually in the ATF's remit either.'

'Ordinarily you'd be right, but not this time. The missing cash is related to the commission and resale value of illegal explosives. To make a case against those behind Procrylon Inc. it'd help to have the tangible cash in evidence: it holds more weight with a jury than any paper or digital trail we can present.'

I'd never heard of Procrylon Inc., and Billie hadn't mentioned them in her brief summation of her problem. 'What's their game?'

'Procrylon? They're a shell set-up, a dummy corporation, a blind for another company which primarily supplies explosives to the mining and demolition sectors. They develop and manufacture polymer and acrylic "safe" casings and carry boxes for high-explosive components. Through Procrylon they serve another sector of the market. I think you can guess where I'm heading with this . . .'

'Some of their product has been siphoned off to paramilitary and terrorist groups?'

'The casings make the explosives largely undetectable to the usual security equipment, so you can see how some extremists would have orgasms about getting their hands on them. Procrylon, as you might imagine, are making a tidy sum through their black market dealings. The ATF would like to present the evidence of these deals but alas Billie Womack's husband Richard threw a wrench in the works when he stole their ill-gotten gains. With the evidence going missing it kind of derailed our plans to bring a case to court.'

I didn't comment.

Our lacklustre server returned and plonked down our drinks. Cooper had also ordered himself a turkey club sandwich. It was huge, and it sat between us like an insurmountable barrier. The girl looked at us looking at the sandwich, perhaps waiting for an ecstatic response. We both glanced up at her at which she shrugged and slouched off.

'Billie told me that her husband died years ago,' I finally said. 'Why the sudden interest in this case again? How is it that you think Billie might be in imminent danger?'

'Billie didn't say?'

'I didn't push her on anything. I preferred to come directly to the source.' I took a sip of my coffee. It was just the way I enjoyed it, black with no added frippery.

'A colleague of mine who was digging into Procrylon was recently murdered. His death was made to look like a typical mugging, but nobody believes that story. His death was too timely, too *convenient* to be anything but murder. It coincided with a sighting of a man believed to be Richard Womack.'

'Billie's dead husband? Yeah, she mentioned that you're convinced that he faked his own death. He's been spotted? For real?'

'He was picked up by a facial recognition program at Seattle-Tacoma Airport a little over a week ago. Because I'd had him red-flagged, a report came through to the ATF field office. The match wasn't as concise as I'd like, but I've seen the video footage and am certain that it really is Billie's husband. He'd grown a beard, styled his hair differently, but enough unique points were met for it not to be anyone but Richard Womack.'

'Why come back now?'

'Perhaps he's worried Billie's in danger, too, and wants to warn her.'

'This is the same man who supposedly sacrificed his own daughter to add credibility to his own death. You really think he'd care enough to warn his ex-wife that she was in danger?'

Cooper wasn't telling the entire truth, I knew. He also knew that I knew. But he wasn't going to admit anything.

'There are plenty other people you could've contacted to protect Billie,' I said. 'Why me, Cooper?'

'I was impressed by your capabilities the last time we worked together.'

'You can stow the compliments. I know why you had Billie get me all the way out here. You want a deniable asset in place, but someone you can trust to alert you should her husband come calling. Why not put an undercover ATF agent in place?'

'We already lost one undercover agent, and it'd be easy to assume that we've been compromised.'

'You think this Procrylon outfit has a mole inside the ATF?'

'It's a fair assumption. That's why I need you, Hunter. Someone they know nothing about.'

'You mean someone who answers only to you.' I eyed him steadily, wondering about his private agenda.

Teasing some turkey from his sandwich, but not going as far as eating anything, Cooper considered my words. Finally he nodded, but it was an almost undetectable dip of his chin.

'I trust you to do the right thing,' he said.

There was no admission, but he wasn't fooling me. Perhaps Cooper did care enough for Billie Womack's welfare to bring in protection for her, but it came with the caveat that I contact him immediately if Richard really had come back from the dead. Fair enough. I'd no loyalty to a thief who might very well have murdered his daughter; my loyalty was to his ex-wife, whom I'd already as much as sworn to protect. Call me suspicious, though – Cooper wasn't engendering any loyalty in me either. It was apparent that he was playing me, but that was the way of most federal agents I'd come across, so I wasn't surprised. I wasn't about to walk away from a woman in trouble just because Cooper had another agenda in mind. Truth was, Billie *was* in danger. Cooper knew more than he was letting on, and that also meant that he had a very tangible reason for fearing for her life.

'Did you bring the items I requested?'

Cooper finally dry-swallowed some of the turkey from his sandwich. He considered the mayonnaise bottle, reached for it but withdrew his fingers. He pushed the plate aside and rested his knuckles on the table. He met my gaze, and this time he was forthright with the truth. 'They must not come back to me, Hunter. If they do, I'll be finished. So will you for that matter.'

I winked. 'You can trust me to do the right thing.'

'Good enough.'

Because I'd flown here, I didn't bring any weapons from Florida. In the past I'd used a special dispensation notice to transport a firearm, but that was while I was working on a retainer contract with the CIA. This time I enjoyed no such luxury, so I'd pressed Cooper to bring me the weapons I required. Being engaged in 'the regulation of firearm commerce through the targeting and arrest of violent offenders in possession of unlawfully held guns' had its perks: it meant that Cooper had access to an available stash of throwdown weapons.

His agreement to supply me with the tools to do my job, not to mention his foresight in warning me to dispose of them correctly when I was finished with them, also confirmed that the threat to Billie was real. I wished he'd be more specific, but

I'd had all the information I was going to get from him . . . for now. Cooper stood, picking up the tab and waving over our server.

I finished my coffee while he paid the girl, adding a generous gratuity she'd failed to earn.

'Would you like your sandwich to go?' the girl wondered, eyeing the barely touched mountain of bread, meat and salad.

'I'll swap it for another of these,' I said, holding out my cup to her. 'To go, please.'

Then, with my replenished drink in hand, I followed Special Agent Cooper out to his vehicle to see what treats he'd brought me. There were more than I expected.

7

Situated between a store selling collectable vinyl records and a gift shop that appeared to hold the monopoly on cheap video and photography equipment, Billie Womack's art gallery was a thin wedge of red brick, a single plate-glass window and door, and more class than both neighbouring establishments combined to the power of ten. Despite the two tatty shops, Hill End, Washington, was the type of town I loved. Surrounded by forest and hills, and bordered on two sides by a forked river that perpetually foamed over boulders in its descent to the point where the rivers converged again a mile west of town, it was picturesque. There was a proliferation of Victorian-era bridges, metal arches and stanchions buried deep into the bedrock. The dwellings and business establishments were primarily Victorian as well, a mixture of timber and brick, painted in pastel shades. If not for the satellite dishes and modern vehicles parked on the roadsides, you could be forgiven for thinking you'd taken a trip back to a quainter time.

I was happy to note that the major chains hadn't moved in on the main square, and that family-run establishments still held sway, even in the current climate. Though it was off the beaten track, Hill End attracted enough tourism to save the town from going under. As I moved towards the gallery from where I'd parked my rental car, I had to skirt an Asian couple flouting common sense to stand in the centre of the street to

snap their vacation photographs. I wondered if the man had
newly purchased his camera from the cheap store next to
Billie's gallery, as he fiddled wildly with the contraption before
he was happy with his shots. His partner, probably his wife,
didn't lose her pose or her cheesy grin despite how long he
took setting up the perfect shot. When I glanced in the direction he was aiming and saw a dramatic skyline of snow-topped
mountains I understood the attraction. I'd grown to love
Florida in the years I'd made it my home from home, but it
was a nice change to see a bit of countryside with some
elevation.

Habit prompted me to take a last look around before I
entered Billie's shop. There were dozens of pedestrians out on
the main strip, an equal number of motorists, but nobody that
caught my attention, certainly nobody who struck me as a
Procrylon-sponsored killer. I went up three steps to the front
door and pushed inside. A bell above the door announced my
arrival. I expected to smell paint and white spirit, but the
aroma was redolent of scented candles: cranberry, I thought.
The showroom was small, narrow, and every available space
was filled with canvases. Billie Womack shared some of her
gallery space with other artists, but perhaps seventy per cent
of the paintings bore her trademark image of an indistinct
figure in a red coat standing at lakeside. Having learned that
Billie was a talented artist I'd searched for images on the
Internet, both of her and her work, so I immediately recognised the woman sitting behind a counter in the far right
corner.

Billie wouldn't have been able to find anything about me via
a similar search, certainly not a picture, but when she looked
up from what she was busy with I caught an immediate crin-
kling of her eyes as she studied me intently. She even went as
far as mouthing my name as I walked towards her.

'Yeah, I'm Joe Hunter.'

She stood up from a stool. Not that it made much difference to her height, which barely topped five feet. She was slim, but there was strength in her forearms. I saw the ligaments move as she stretched out a hand flecked with paint in myriad colours to greet me. Her skin though proved dry and warm to the touch.

'Pleased to finally put a face to the voice,' she said.

'Hope it doesn't disappoint? People tend to expect Kevin Costner when they hire a bodyguard.'

She smiled briefly, and then swept a hand over her hair, patting down a stray lock. Her hair was a blend of grey and brown, cut in an easy-to-maintain style. A paint-splattered blouse hung loose over jeans and boots. She had a tight, fit body: a wilderness girl, despite being in her late thirties. 'Who am I to complain?' she said in a self-deprecating manner. 'I guess I'm not of the star calibre you're usually employed to protect.'

On my arrival in Seattle, and prior to meeting Brandon Cooper, I'd called Billie on her cell. I'd already explained that I wasn't usually engaged in close protection work, not in the way that an outsider would recognise or understand. I'd protected people, or tried to at least, but I was no bodyguard. Still, it was a tag she was happy with, and I suppose was what I'd signed up for when accepting the job.

Billie appraised me. The top of her head came up to my collarbones. I looked down into clear lavender eyes. It took a moment to realise she was wearing tinted contact lenses. They loaned an unnatural sheen to her eyes, but couldn't hide the fact that some of the spark had gone out of her. I wasn't sure if it was through grief, or through fear.

'I'll do my best to keep you safe,' I said.

'Let's hope that there's nothing in Agent Cooper's concern.'

'We'll know soon enough.' If Cooper was correct and Richard Womack had resurfaced, at much the same time an undercover ATF agent was murdered while investigating his case, then it made sense that Procrylon might have a sudden interest in Billie. To be fair, I was never the most patient, and part of me hoped that Procrylon would show their hand soon. Another part hoped that it was all smoke without the fire and Billie would never again be troubled by the misdeeds of her husband. She'd suffered enough through the loss of her daughter without handling a personal threat.

Billie sat on the stool. I noted that she had a work in progress on a small easel behind the counter, but couldn't tell what she was painting. She saw me craning for a look.

'I don't usually work here, but I followed your advice and came where I felt safest.'

'I hoped that you'd have other people around you,' I pointed out.

'My assistant Hilary just stepped out. She'll be back in a few minutes.'

'Do you get many visitors to the gallery?'

'Passing trade only. Most of my artwork is sold online these days.'

'Is it regulars you get or mainly tourists?'

'A bit of both.'

'So you wouldn't immediately be alerted to a stranger?'

'Not normally but I think I've been on high alert since Agent Cooper's visit. There was a guy this afternoon who struck me as . . . uh, odd.'

'In what way?'

She thought for a moment, then crinkled her nose in distaste. 'It wasn't so much anything he said or did, it was his odour. He stank of mould, or rotting vegetation. I actually lit a few scented candles to clear the air after he left.'

'There's a lot of forest out there; maybe he was a worker, a tree feller or something?'

'Wrong type, and he didn't strike me as a regular hiker or camper, either.'

'Describe him to me.'

'I can do better than that. Follow me.' She was up off the stool and heading for a door at the back of the shop. I went after her, my heels loud on the wooden floor. The door frame was misaligned, and the door didn't fit neatly. When Billie pushed it open it barely made two feet of clearance before it wedged against a stack of boxed items. 'We're a bit cramped for space back here,' she said. 'You'll have to squeeze in.'

Billie sat on an office chair before a cluttered desk on which sat an old computer monitor. The air was crisp with ozone, and the hard drive blipped and blooped merrily beneath the desk. I moved into the narrow gap behind her as she played her fingers across the keyboard and a feed from a CCTV system came up onscreen. The screen was divided into four equal-sized quadrants but the bottom two were blank. The top left screen showed a view of the sidewalk outside the store, at too tight an angle to see anything but the tops of heads and shoulders of passers-by. The second image, the top right, covered the interior of the gallery. The image came from a fisheye lens, so that everything near the camera bulged and enlarged, while to either side objects curved and shrank the further away they were.

'Not the best CCTV that money can buy,' Billie muttered. She ignored the exterior view and brought up the interior one so that it filled the screen and didn't look as skewed. Billie began keying in commands and I watched a date/time stamp rotate backwards at speed. I watched us retreat from the office then stand at the counter, before I walked backwards out of the shop. Billie sat at the counter. A woman backed into the store, spoke with Billie, before making a weird reverse trip around the gallery, untidying as she went. Billie shook her head, keyed in another command and the recording speeded its backwards journey. A young couple backed into the store, danced around in the aisle, then backed out again. An old woman came in, went out. A man in a suit followed – or actually preceded her visit – then a young mother with a child in a stroller. No one left with a painting or even spoke with Billie or her assistant. Then there was a length of time – corresponding to a couple of hours – where nobody but Billie or Hilary was in view. I watched as Billie unlit some candles and knew that we were nearing the point where her unsavoury visitor had called. Sure enough, Billie shuffled in her seat, anticipating the man's arrival. When he appeared he was almost a blur as he backed into the shop, hung about, then backed out again. Once the image of the shop was clear of him, Billie hit buttons and the recording first halted, and then began to advance at normal speed. 'He should come into view any second now.'

I leaned in, my thighs brushing the back of Billie's chair. On screen I saw the door open. It was at the far left of the fisheye scene, so at first the figure was small and indistinct. But he moved further inside the shop and perused some of the paintings on view. He glanced down the gallery towards where Billie sat. The man then moved closer and I got a good look at him. There was nothing remarkable about him, nothing to make him stand out in a crowd. He looked to be aged in his late twenties, not tall, not built, just your average guy. His hair was short, combed neatly right to left. He was wearing a dark red ski-style jacket over a black shirt and jeans, boots too. He could have been a hiker or camper, except that his clothing looked too new. The neatness of his clothes – even showing creases where they'd recently been folded and packaged – was at odds with the odour that Billie claimed had come off him.

The man positioned himself in front of an easel, but I could tell he was looking over it towards where Billie sat at the counter. Even when Billie's assistant, a good-looking young woman, passed him, he didn't pull his gaze from Billie.

'He was taking a lot of interest in you,' I said.

'Maybe he was star-struck at seeing a famous artist at work,' Billie quipped.

Onscreen the man turned his head aside, and it was because Hilary had walked by him again. He was averting his gaze, avoiding any contact. As Hilary moved towards the counter, her face was scrunched, and she gave a discreet wave of her hand under her nose. I watched as the onscreen Billie lifted her head and looked directly at the man. He reacted exactly as a guilty man would: he began to scrutinise the paintings with far too much interest, his facial expressions and body language exaggerated. Then he made a show of looking at his wristwatch, and moving for the exit as if he'd just recalled he had an urgent meeting elsewhere.

'I thought he was a shoplifter,' Billie said.

I ignored her words, still watching the screen. I noticed a shadow in the far right of it that hadn't been there earlier. 'Can you bring up the other screen and rewind it to the same point?'

'Sure.' Billie did as asked, and the image on the monitor was replaced by the view of the sidewalk.

'He didn't leave immediately,' I said, pointing out the obvious. The smelly man hung about outside the shop, peering in through the window. He'd positioned himself so that he wasn't obvious to anyone inside, watching Billie through the narrow gaps between paintings in the window display. I watched the clock on the screen and saw that he hung around for another seven minutes. Perhaps he'd have stayed longer but another man approached him. This man was older and wore a suit.

They spoke for a few seconds before the suited man beckoned the other away and they disappeared offscreen.

'Fast-forward the picture,' I said, and Billie complied.

Sure enough, after two hours of no customers a young mother pushed a stroller inside the shop, leaving shortly afterwards. Then the man in the suit came back. He entered the shop. Billie went to switch views, but I touched her wrist. 'Hold on.'

Smelly Man reappeared and took up his earlier position, peering in through the gap in the window display.

'They're working together, all right.'

Billie looked up at my words, frowning.

'Let's have a closer look at the suit,' I said, and Billie switched screens.

Viewed in real time, and with the knowledge in hindsight that the suited man and the smelly one were in cahoots, it was apparent that he too was taking too much interest in Billie as she worked unaware of him at her painting. He was only in the shop for a minute or so, but in that time I could see him weighing and calculating his options and coming to some sort of decision. He went outside, and a quick change of screens showed him walk away with his pal. Just before they disappeared from view, the suit pulled out a cell phone and began keying buttons.

'Can you bag me something up?' I asked.

'What for?'

'They were definitely watching you, Billie. Stands to reason they might still be watching now. They'll have seen me come inside, but that isn't unusual. If I stay much longer, it may arouse their suspicion and they'll come to take a closer look. I'd rather they didn't know I was here for you yet, so it's best I look like a satisfied customer. I've probably been inside too long to have only been browsing, and will look more natural if I leave carrying something.'

'I understand,' Billie said. She flicked at the buttons and checked that neither of the men was out on the sidewalk now, spying inside. 'It's all clear.'

We moved into the gallery and while Billie bagged up a picture frame, and packed out the bag with some bubble wrap, I moved towards the front and peered out through the window. Pedestrians wandered by, cars passed, followed by a truck. Then a figure loomed in the doorway, and pushed inside. The bell tinkled, announcing the newcomer's arrival. I didn't flinch. I recognised the young woman as Billie's assistant, Hilary. She was carrying paper cups of coffee, and a paper sack containing fast food. She smiled at me the way shop assistants do at strangers. I wondered if Billie had already told her about me, or if she'd kept things close to her chest, but I didn't have time to explain. I returned to Billie, followed by the young woman, and collected my bag.

'The two of you had best lock the door behind me,' I said. 'Eat out here in plain sight, OK. Make it look like any other normal day, just in case the spies return.'

'Where will you be?' There was a note of trepidation in Billie's voice, eliciting a worried exclamation from a confused Hilary.

'Nearby. Don't worry. Just don't let anyone inside before I come back.'

There were questions building in Hilary, who looked from Billie to me then back to her boss, but I hadn't time for them. I took it that Billie hadn't mentioned I was coming. She could explain everything while I was gone. I walked away, lugging my pretend purchases, and as I did so I pulled out one of the handguns supplied to me by Brandon Cooper and concealed it behind the bag, holding it tight alongside my thigh.

Billie followed. She flipped the sign on the door to 'Closed'. I gave her one last reassuring nod, then went outside, and heard her throwing bolts. Immediately Hilary began asking questions, but I didn't linger. I headed across the road to where I'd parked my rental car and got in, placing my SIG on the passenger seat and placing my faux purchases on top of it, then pulled out and drove north: I had to make things look as natural as possible. I'd spotted Smelly Man leaning against a street lamp at the intersection only a hundred yards or so ahead.

8

'So they aren't your guys, Cooper?'

'No. I can assure you that there are no ATF agents in Hill End.'

'Is yours the only law enforcement agency looking into this case?'

'As far as I know.'

'I could do with confirmation on that: wouldn't like to hurt a cop or federal agent by accident.'

Cooper was somewhere noisy. I could hear a babble of voices, the thrum of traffic, sirens. He definitely wasn't in sleepy Hill End; probably he was still in Seattle. I'd turned my rental car around and come back the opposite way, parking between a Toyota and a delivery truck that was being offloaded at a convenience store. From my vantage, I could see Smelly Man lounging against the street lamp, but didn't have eyes on his partner, if indeed he was still out there. I kept viewing my mirrors as I spoke to Brandon Cooper on my cell, in case the suited man was more counter-surveillance-savvy than his pal and was checking me out. If he was out there, he must be further along the street to the south of Billie's gallery, or maybe inside one of the adjacent properties.

'I'll do some digging and get back to you,' Cooper went on. 'Hunter ... I think it's best that you do *nothing* until I can check things out.'

'You didn't bring me in because I'm the type to sit on my thumbs.'

'OK. I'll rephrase that. Don't *kill* anyone until I can check things out.'

'Don't worry, I'm not going to shoot someone simply for having poor hygiene.'

Cooper had no idea what I was referring to, and I made him no wiser. He hung up and I placed the phone on the seat alongside the other items. Easier to get at when required as was my SIG. Not that I anticipated shooting anyone. Not yet. But I had the sense that the gun might prove an important motivator before long.

Even without Cooper confirming it, I didn't believe that Smelly Man or his partner were federal agents. Neither could I be certain that they had anything to do with Procrylon Inc., but whom else could they be working for? Even if their earlier visits to the gallery had been misconstrued and they were simply star-struck art fanciers it didn't explain why they were still hanging around hours later. They were surveilling the gallery, no question about it. The obvious conclusion was that either they were waiting to get a chance to corner Billie alone, or they were waiting for someone else to show up. Before I'd arrived, and while Hilary had done the coffee and doughnuts run, they could have caught Billie on her own, so my bet was on the second idea. They were watching for Richard Womack. It was possible that they meant no harm to Billie and that their earlier perusals had simply been to confirm that she was in the shop, or that she hadn't smuggled Richard inside by some clandestine means. How long would they remain patient? They didn't strike me as the most professional, particularly the smelly one – getting so close to their target while stinking as bad was an amateur's mistake; it made him memorable and had led to their discovery. Amateurs aren't usually known for their patience, and I figured that they wouldn't wait long before they decided that they could achieve faster results by forcing Richard's whereabouts from Billie. Whether that would come in the form of intimidation or physical assault, they weren't going to get away with it.

I picked up my phone and checked the time. It was mid-afternoon in Hill End. Back in Tampa it would be early evening. Tuesday evenings Rink attended a mixed martial arts club, adding to his considerable karate skills by the inclusion of jujitsu grappling work and some boxing. He'd encouraged me to attend the sessions with him, but I struggled when it came to sport. My instincts wouldn't allow me to tap out of a hold, and I feared that I'd end up with a broken arm or, worse, break the arm of some other poor sap. I respected Rink's self-control, and understood my lack was a weakness in a training environment. But out here in the real world, it was my never-say-die attitude that often saved my arse, and training for sport worried me in case it was blunted by fair competition. Then again, sometimes it got me in trouble, and Rink's calming influence was all that kept me out jail.

'Yo, brother!'

'You OK, Rink? You sound out of breath.'

'I'm good. Just come outta the cage.'

'I can hear you sweating from here.'

'You know me, Hunter, I never break a sweat.'

'Dream on, old man.' The pleasantries over, I asked, 'Are you free to talk?'

'Just gimme a second.' Over my cell I heard congratulations shared – Rink and his opponent extolling the other's skills in ass-whuppery – and Rink moved away from the fighting area to a quiet corner. 'So what's the deal: anything in Cooper's story?'

'I'm looking at a guy casing out Billie Womack as we speak.'

'Good guy or bad?'

'Cooper's checking, but I'm going with bad.'

I told him how the stinking man and his suited partner had both been in the gallery earlier, and how I'd spotted Smelly again outside. 'I'm guessing the guy doesn't have some sort of fungal complaint. Before coming here, I think he was holed up near Billie's place in the hills, maybe hiding out in the woods while keeping an eye on her, using the fallen leaves to camouflage the colour of his clothing.'

'Or he could live in an apartment with a rising damp problem,' Rink said.

'Whatever. He's taking too much interest in Billie for it to be a good reason.'

'You said she's kinda famous among those arty-farty types . . .'

'Already considered and discarded that idea.'

'Not like you to jump to conclusions, brother.' His tone said otherwise.

'I've grown to trust my instincts.'

'So you want me up there?'

'That goes without saying. How soon can you get here?'

'Tomorrow soon enough?'

'It'll have to do.' Earlier I'd given Rink the details of Billie's home address, but added the location of her gallery now. I wondered if it was safer to keep Billie in town for the duration rather than go back to her farm. In town there was less chance that her watchers would make a move on her, therefore it was a safer location. But to find out what their interest in her was I required them to act, and that meant allowing them to follow her home. Also, we had to make sure that her behaviour and habits didn't obviously change: her watchers might deduce she had something to hide and step up their operation. 'We'll be at Billie's farm. Will you come straight there?'

'Will do, brother. You want me to bring Harvey?'

Harvey Lucas was a buddy of ours based in Little Rock, Arkansas. He'd joined us on a few previous jobs where discretion was the order of the day, and the possibility of violence was likely. He'd proved a good man to have at our sides, plus if anyone could research our enemies it was Harvey. But I felt a word of caution whisper its way through my mind. 'Not yet. Cooper's bankrolling this job and hasn't budgeted for three. In fact with us he's getting a two-for-one deal . . . are you happy coming all the way here for little payback?'

'A little's better than nothing, brother. Things are kinda slow at this end. We've still got that contract with Jerry Redmond. It's unlikely it will get hit again, but he wants his premises covered this weekend. I've got Mack and Velasquez on that. I'd just be sitting here contemplating my navel, and you know that's not good for any narcissist's sense of importance, least of all mine.'

'Maybe I can get Cooper to throw a bit more cash our way. He knows as well as we do that a close protection detail takes more than one man.'

'Unless that was his thinking all along,' Rink said.

'You don't trust him?'

'Do you?'

I said nothing.

'I'll go see if I can book a standby flight now,' Rink said. 'Should be with you early tomorrow afternoon. Don't go getting yourself or Billie killed in the meantime.'

'I'll try.'

We hung up, and I made a cursory check of my mirrors. No man in a suit lurked nearby. I sought the smelly man and saw him delve in a pocket of his coat and pull out a cell phone. Exhaling, I sank back in my seat as I focused on him. Not for the first time during my career I wished I'd learned to lip-read. Not that it would have helped because the guy turned his back and began a slow walk up the road, heading towards Billie's gallery, albeit still on the opposite sidewalk. I picked up my SIG and put it in my jacket pocket, before getting out the car and locking it with the fob. I headed in the same direction, using the delivery truck for cover. I paused alongside the cab, and saw the man come to a halt directly opposite the gallery. He was totally unaware of my scrutiny, his counter-surveillance as crappy as his choice in inconspicuous clothing. Who chooses a red coat when they wish to blend with their surroundings?

The watcher stood out like a beacon; he moved from foot to foot as he tried to get a view through the front window of Billie's shop. Even a few of the tourists passing by glanced at him, he was so obvious. His actions gave me pause: was he acting deliberately to draw me out from cover? I checked for his suited pal, or anyone else taking any interest in me. No one stood out. I crossed the street and approached the man. The breeze was blowing away from him, so I didn't catch a whiff of his scent until I was within a couple of feet. Billie had been correct: he stank. It was a mixture of mildew and rotting wood and I considered again the possibility he'd been hiding in the forest near her farm. He was so intent on peeking inside the gallery he was unaware of my presence. I stood a few feet behind him, listening to him as he spoke on his cell.

'I think we're wasting our time here. She's in there taking a late lunch or something, so it's unlikely she's going to leave any time soon. The sign on the door says the gallery stays open until six. Why don't we just come back at closing time?'

His words confirmed that he was waiting to make a move of some type but not that he was dangerous. I couldn't hear the answer, but his body language told me he was on the receiving end of a berating.

'When will you be back, Kirk?' the man demanded. 'I wouldn't mind taking a leak and I can't do that standing out on the freakin' sidewalk.'

I guessed he was speaking to the suit. From his tone of voice the suited man wasn't a superior, just a better-dressed peer. Smelly wasn't happy that his buddy Kirk had left him to stand guard all this time. On the contrary I was. I was also happy to note that his pal wasn't returning in a hurry. It would be so easy to move in close, jam my gun under his ribs and move him somewhere quiet. In fact, I contemplated doing so for a long heartbeat, but decided no. If the man went missing it might draw in his pal, and likely reinforcements, so it was better that I bide my time, consider my next move. Rink would have been proud of me. I moved away and entered a store a couple of units along. I kept an eye on him through the window, while pretending to examine some gifts on a rotating stand. When enough time had passed, I came out the shop again and wandered past him, back to my rental car.

Inside the car I placed my SIG on the seat again and covered it with the corner of the bag supplied by Billie. I took out my cell.

'Billie? Joe.'

'What's happening? Are they still outside?'

'One of them is.'

'What does he want?'

'At a guess I think he's waiting for you to go home.'

'You know, something came back to me after you left. Yesterday, before I rang you? I think I saw the same man down by the lake on my property. I can't be sure, but I caught a flash of red – the same colour as his coat – but I just wrote it off at the time as my imagination. Do you think he's been out there watching me since Agent Cooper was here?'

Billie was astute, no question.

'I've checked with Cooper, he says they're not with him. But that's if he's telling the truth.'

'Why wouldn't he? Oh, yes, I see. He wants Richard and thinks I might lead him to him.'

'There is that,' I said. 'But we won't know until I speak to our smelly friend. Can Hilary take over your duties at the store?'

'I'm sure she will, but let me check.' There was a muffled conversation, and then Billie came back on. 'Yeah, Hilary's happy to take over for a while. What's on your mind, Joe?'

'All I want you to do is come out of the shop, get in your car and drive home.'

'You want me to get the man to follow me?' Surprisingly there was no fear in her voice. If anything she sounded excited at the prospect of a chase. 'Are you going to trap him, find out what he does when confronted? We could probably make him speak if—'

'That's not my intention. I just want to see how he reacts.'

'Huh.' My reply was obviously displeasing.

'It's important that you don't alert him, Billie. Try to act as natural as possible. Don't look for him. He has his eyes on you and won't miss you coming out. Just get in your car and drive home. Don't stop. Even if you see him pull over, don't do anything to let him know you've spotted him. I'll join you at your house, OK?'

'OK. But what if he doesn't follow?'

'He will. I'm sure of it.'

'Give me a few minutes to get my coat and purse and then I'll set off.'

'Great. And don't worry, because I'll be close behind.'

'OK.'

'Billie?'

'Yes?'

'Which is your car?'

'The blue Jetta parked a few spaces up from the gallery.'

The delivery truck had pulled away. I had a clear view along the street and could see the roof of Billie's Jetta over the top of a smaller sports car. 'Got it,' I said.

I waited for less than two minutes. Billie came out of the shop and strode towards her car. She looked determined, bouncing on the balls of her feet, her shoulders a tad stiff, but she resisted taking a look for the smelly man. He, on the other hand, almost performed a pirouette as he turned away to avoid eye contact. He watched her reflection in a store window, and as soon as she pulled the Jetta away from the kerb he jogged across the road and clambered inside a parked SUV. He peeled away and followed close behind Billie. I gave it a few seconds then also pulled out. I didn't fear he'd notice me following because he was so engaged in watching his quarry. Through the back window, I could tell he had his cell phone pressed to his ear. Calling in the suited man.

9

Billie led the way over one of the Victorian bridges at the southwest corner of town, and picked up a road that went deep into a valley. We didn't get far out of town before the woods closed in on both sides. The road hugged the slopes of the northern hills, twisting and turning with each convolution of the terrain. If I hadn't known where Billie was heading it would have made it difficult to follow, but with foresight I could sit back on the tail of Smelly Man without fear of losing her.

I'd never been to Billie's farm. But neither had I been idle on my way out to Washington State: I'd brought up maps on my cell phone, noted the main routes and major features of the landscape. Even so, it's one thing viewing a map, quite another when you're on the ground. Some of the landmarks were hidden by the hills or forest, and it didn't take me long to put aside what I'd learned and concentrated on what lay ahead. One feature burned into my memory was of a long teardrop-shaped lake about midway to Baker's Hole, and I began to look for it, watching for a glimmer of sunlight on water through the trees. On zoom, I'd found that there were a couple of wide layovers opposite the lakeshore, and thought I could put one of them to good use if going with Billie's idea of a confrontation. Maybe I should get to the bottom of things at first opportunity.

Smelly didn't make a move to close the gap on Billie. He hung back, just out of the range of her mirrors, and it confirmed to me that he knew where she was going. It also strengthened my theory that he'd been hiding out in the hills near her farm, and that it hadn't been a trick of her imagination when Billie thought she'd spotted someone in a red coat. I decided to drop the plan I was formulating. Why force his car off the road on to one of the layovers when he would presumably stop before reaching the farm and skulk off to his hiding place?

The teardrop lake seemingly came out of nowhere. I steered round a tight bend in the road, and there it was. On the right the road hugged the lakeshore and I could see the first layover. Billie was already passing it, Smelly about a quarter-mile behind her. I could have sped up enough to catch him at the second pull-off, but I held back. I doubted he had the presence of mind to check if he was being followed, but you never could tell. Then we were all past the lake and heading up an incline to a wedge-shaped pass. Another mile or so further in the next valley Baker's Hole dominated, and Billie's farm sat approximately a mile further on again. Less than two miles before Smelly Man would have to pull over or risk alerting Billie to his presence.

Periodically I checked the road behind. I'd be crazy if I neglected to check my six. It was apparent that Billie's watcher had called his pal and informed him of Billie's unscheduled return home. If I were in either of their shoes, I'd assume that something had occurred to summon her back to the farm. Being that they were awaiting the imminent arrival of Richard Womack, it would be fair to assume that she'd hurried home at his beckoning. They'd be excited by the possibility and Suit Man wouldn't want to miss out on capturing their prey. He'd be coming, and probably quickly to make up for lost time.

There were a couple more dogleg turns in the road, and as I came out the second I was just in time to see Smelly pull into a service trail that disappeared between a small stand of trees towards a ridge line on the hills. In the distance, Billie's Jetta was a blue blur against the mist drifting off Baker's Hole. She turned on her flashers as she approached the entrance to her farm, a conscientious driver.

It was decision time. If I followed the SUV up the hillside I could no longer stay hidden. Also, I trusted that Smelly would come to a halt before long and I'd have to abandon my vehicle on the trail below him. I didn't mind the hike in, but if his suited pal was on his way to rendezvous then he'd come across my car and know that they'd been rumbled. I continued on a few hundred yards and pulled the car off road on to a shoulder lumpy with coarse grass and rocks. If it was Suit Man's intention to carry on towards the farm, then he'd see my vehicle, but I didn't think he would. I inserted my gun in my waistband as I got out the car, zipped my jacket up to my throat against the chill and tracked back to the service road. A check along the road showed no impending arrival of the second man, and I couldn't hear the sound of a distant engine. It meant nothing: the turns in the road blocked any view, and the topography would play havoc with acoustics; for all I knew, Suit Man could be very close behind. I began jogging up the trail. It was muddy going, and the deep ruts showed how often vehicles had come and gone up the trail in the last few days: a lot of times. I arrived at the first bend where the road followed the natural ridge and plunged into the forest, continuing to jog at a parallel to the trail.

The going was easy enough. The trees weren't tightly packed and there was room to move between them without fear of breaking any of the lower branches, though I had to watch for brittle windfalls underfoot. As I'd expected, I came across the parked SUV soon enough. To gain any vantage point on Billie's farm, the guy couldn't drive too high up the trail or his view would be obliterated by the mist coming off the lake, or by the low-lying clouds crowning the hills above. I slowed, walking heel to toe, ensuring that each foot was placed with care as I moved closer to the SUV. I pulled my SIG from my waistband, and held it against my right thigh as I progressed.

There was some condensation on the inside of its windows, but unless Smelly was lying down across the seats, I could tell he was out of the SUV. I moved in, got within spitting distance of the parked vehicle, and made out a fresh set of boot prints in the mud. They led across the road and into the stand of trees on that side. I crossed, placing my feet in the same tracks, and then concealed myself among the trees. I couldn't see Smelly, but decided that he'd have moved towards the farm, not away. I'd progressed barely a hundred yards when I caught a glimpse of red. The young man was squatting on the hill-side, using a fallen tree for cover as he surveyed the farm below through a pair of binoculars. He was so intent on watching Billie, or indeed for anyone else turning up at the farm, he had no idea he was being observed in turn. If I'd wanted to I could have walked up, put my gun to his head and that would have been that.

But the hopeless sap didn't deserve to die. All he was guilty of up until now was keeping an eye on Billie, and being pretty useless at his job. I squatted down, kept him under observation, waited to see how things would play out.

My wait didn't last. Within a quarter-hour I heard the growl of a car engine making its way up the trail. A sticky brake squeaked as the car came to a halt, then it was followed by silence as the engine was turned off. A dull thud announced the closing of a door. Only one person had come out to the observation point, and I guessed that it was the suited man. He cursed and grumbled as he negotiated the muddy trail, and I pinpointed him by his voice as he picked his way through the forest. He'd donned a raincoat over his suit, but hadn't had the sense to change to more appropriate footwear. His shoes would be ruined.

Thinking they were out of sight, out of earshot, and therefore beyond notice, the newcomer called out for his friend. 'Adam, where are you?'

A short whistle hailed him, and there was a flash of red as Smelly beckoned him over to his hiding spot. Their ineptitude was magnificent.

'What kept you, Noah?' Smelly – or Adam as I'd heard him called – said to his friend. I wondered if they were using code-names derived from Genesis in the Bible. Earlier he'd mentioned the name Kirk, so probably not. The suited man's full name was probably Noah Kirk.

'I took another look at the gallery. There was only that hot girl there, but I wanted to check that Billie wasn't leading us away while Womack snuck inside.'

'I take it he wasn't there?'

'If he was, I wouldn't have wasted my time hiking out here in all this crap.' Noah took a desultory look down at his shoes, and wasn't particularly pleased at what he found. 'I'd have grabbed him there.'

Noah's words confirmed everything I'd surmised. They were watching Billie in the hope that she'd lead them to Richard. I'd been hoping to learn more. All right, Noah had just confirmed that they intended grabbing Richard, but what were their intentions after that? My priority was to keep Billie safe from harm, but I had to assume that once they had her husband in the bag, they'd come back for Billie.

I stood and walked towards them. Noah had crouched alongside Adam, peering over the fallen tree at Billie's farm. Neither man heard me coming until I was within touching distance of them. Then they both scrambled up and stood eyeing me like startled deer. Noah was first to get over my sudden appearance. He straightened, and discreetly fed a hand into his raincoat, drawing it aside. I couldn't see a gun, but his body language told me that there was a firearm just out of reach under his coat. I kept my gun hidden too.

'What are you fellas up to?' I played dumb.

'You're the guy from the gallery!' Adam said, catching a confused glance from Noah. To his friend, he said, 'This guy was in Billie's shop earlier. I saw him. He looked like a shopper, but I thought there was something suspicious about him.'

I gave them a steady look, before aiming my gaze past them at the farm in the distance. 'You think that I was acting suspicious? Well, you don't look like a pair of birdwatchers to me. If I'm not mistaken I'd swear you were spying on the woman who lives down there.'

'Well you're not mistaken,' Noah said. Adam, by contrast, stayed silent. I could see from the way he shifted his weight, glanced around, that he was perturbed by my sudden appearance and trying to understand what it meant. Some of the colour had drained from his features, and he was licking his lips, while his gaze skipped from me to the cars out on the road. Signs that he was ready to run or attack, dependent on my next move. Noah nudged the younger man, a warning to hold still. 'But what we are up to is no concern of yours, *fella*,' he went on. 'So I suggest you just walk away and forget all about seeing us.'

'No can do,' I said.

My phrase elicited a frown from Noah. It probably wasn't a common idiom around there.

'Look, pal,' Noah said, and he took a step forward and threw back his coat and suit jacket to show the gun holstered on his hip. 'You're pushing your nose into business you want no part of. Walk away and forget about us. Got it?'

Bolstered by Noah's bravado, Adam stopped licking his lips and took a step alongside his pal, presenting a united front. 'Go on. Get out of here, or we'll make you.'

Maybe if I were a six feet-five man-mountain with an ominous line in quips their challenge wouldn't have been as open, but being an average-sized guy, with no ready answer, they thought me easy fodder for intimidation. I was tempted to bring out my gun, but Noah might draw his weapon and I'd have to kill them. I'd learn few answers if they were dead.

'Let's not be too hasty here, guys,' I said. 'We're on the same side aren't we?'

My comment earned a squint from Noah. Adam licked his lips again.

I feigned incompetent, to get them on side. I leaned in, playing conspiratorial. 'You are here from Procrylon, right?'

Noah's pause was a tad too long. 'Procrylon? I don't know what you're talking about.'

'Oh, come off it,' I said, giving him a grin. 'You're Noah, right? And you're Adam?' I gave Smelly a nod. 'I was told to hook up with you in town, to help out with the surveillance, but, well, I have to admit that I didn't spot you at first. I took a look in at the woman's shop to see if I could eyeball you, but I must admit you were too good for me. I followed Billie back here, and only by chance spotted you turning in here at the forest trail.' I directed my last at Noah. 'I took a chance that I'd find you up here. It's a good vantage point for watching the farm.'

My cover story was paper-thin, but it didn't matter. Neither man had admitted being Procrylon's hired guns, but they didn't have to. Noah's denial was written all over his face.

'I don't know what the fuck you're talking about,' he tried again.

'Look,' I said, 'I know this is probably a bit unconventional, me appearing like this, but our employer wanted a few extra guys on the ground. Sounds to me like they don't trust you to do the job.'

Motherfuckers, Adam mouthed.

Noah gave him a nudge, but his warning was as subtle as a building brick to the side of the head. Noah squared up to me once more. 'Look, mister, I don't know who you are or what you're talking about, but I'm going to say it one last time. I don't know who Procrylon are.'

'You don't have to be secretive with me.' I stepped forward, offering my hand. 'I'm Samson. Perhaps you've heard of me?'

Noah's hand edged towards his gun a fraction more.

I halted, but it was to throw my hands up in feigned regret. 'Look, OK, maybe I made a mistake here. Maybe I shouldn't have introduced myself the way I did, and it's right that you're suspicious. I should've had Procrylon contact you and tell you to expect me. Look, if you want, I can call them now and they can confirm . . .'

Noah shook his head. 'Keep your hands where I can see them.'

'Fair enough, you call them then. Or have your buddy do it.' I directed my gaze at Adam. 'Do you have a cell phone?'

'No,' he lied.

Noah said, 'Look, mister . . .'

'Samson,' I reminded him. 'I'm Samson.'

'Yeah, right, so you said. But I haven't heard of no "Samson".'

'Before this morning I hadn't heard of you either. In fact, I'm guessing your names are codes, right? What is it with those assholes at Procrylon and their Biblical references?' I was still pushing for an admission, and knew I was stepping over the line with the act. But I could also see that I was beginning to disarm Adam with my insistence. He looked at Noah and said, 'Maybe you should call this in. Just in case.'

'You need the number, Noah?' I said.

'I've got a number,' he said, and he offered a sly grin as he pulled out his sidearm. 'But I'm not calling it in. I already spoke to my boss today and nobody mentioned anything about you joining us. In fact, when I asked for a few extra hands they said they had nobody else in the area yet.'

I'd been caught in a lie, but I didn't care. His words were the confirmation I'd been waiting for. Noah and Adam were there on Procrylon's behalf, and that made them a threat to Billie.

Noah lifted his gun and aimed it at my chest. It was a Smith & Wesson six-shot revolver. He was only four feet away. From that range his .45 round would put a nice big hole through me.

'Aah, shit, man,' I said, putting up my hands. 'You got me.'

'Yeah,' said Noah, grinning wider. 'I don't know what kind of idiot you took me for.'

'Y'know,' I said affably. 'Just the regular shit-for-brains-type of hired guns who get lumbered with the scut work before the real professionals arrive.'

Noah didn't know if he should be offended or not. My insult made him pause fractionally while he thought of an appropriate comeback.

While he was still thinking, I moved.

My left palm slapped his elbow; my right swept under and cupped his gun hand. I extended his arm upwards and to the right of my head, safely out of the way. The web of my thumb forced against the hammer so that he couldn't cock the gun, even as I twisted the barrel down and away. His trigger finger caught in the guard as I yanked the gun out of his hand, and I heard the click of the dislocating digit.

Noah let out a wild shriek of pain, but it didn't last long. I rapped him against the temple with the butt of his own gun, knocking him cold. He fell to the forest mulch and lay there motionless, while I turned the revolver in my hand and pointed it at Adam's incredulous face.

'Hmmm,' I said. 'All those lies and they didn't work for any of us, did they? Time to begin telling the truth, Adam.'

10

'I swear to God, mister, we don't mean Billie Womack any harm.'

Adam was sitting on the fallen tree, his hands wedged under his backside, on a promise that if he moved them I'd put a bullet through his knee before he had a chance to stand. He believed me. His eyes protruded from their sockets as he glanced at his fallen companion, then at my gun, then back to Noah again. His pal was rasping softly as he slept. I pushed him with a foot, but he didn't wake; instead he rolled on to his side and opened his airway, so it would do.

'Like I said, I want the truth out of you. You say you don't mean to harm Billie, so why are you here?'

Adam screwed his face tight. I'm not sure if he was thinking hard or he had an itchy nose that required scratching. I was beginning to feel sorry for the guy, and for Noah. I'd knocked the man unconscious, when really I was beginning to suspect that they were no threat at all. All of that bull he mentioned about Procrylon; he'd been bluffing as much as I was. I tapped my SIG against my thigh. The sound was subtle, but enough to cause Adam to sit upright and concentrate on me.

'You haven't a clue who Procrylon are,' I said.

Adam blinked. 'I, uh, Noah already told you that. When you mentioned them a minute ago.'

'He did. But when I suggested calling them, he said he had their number,' I reminded him.

Shaking his head, Adam said, 'Noah said he had a number. He didn't mention this "Procrylon". Don't you get it, mister? With no idea who you were he was playing *you* for information.'

I raised an eyebrow. The old double bluff, eh? Maybe these guys weren't the bozos I'd first thought. 'He thought I was really from Procrylon and wanted to find out who they were.' It wasn't a question.

'Sounds right to me,' Adam said.

'So why were you pissed when I said they'd sent backup for you?'

'Pissed?'

'You called them "motherfuckers" under your breath.'

'I was referring to *my* employers,' Adam said pointedly. 'I thought they didn't think we were good enough for the job.'

I didn't answer. But Adam recognised the inanity of his complaint. He had the good grace to blush.

'Which brings us to the point: who are your employers? You're some kind of private eyes, right?'

I could tell he was fishing for a plausible denial, but when all came to all, it would only cause him further problems. He looked at Noah, who was stirring, pondered if he should wait for his pal to fully recover and let Noah do the talking. I tapped him on the shoulder with the gun barrel. 'C'mon, I haven't all day.'

'Can I ask something first?' he said, showing a bit of backbone.

'Go ahead. I told you it was time for the truth.'

'Do you work for Procrylon?'

'If I did you'd probably both be dead by now,' I said.

A shadow passed over his face. My words had definitely hit home.

'We are private investigators,' he admitted. 'If you let me show you, we're licensed and everything.'

'No need,' I said. 'Just tell me why you're here. I know that you're waiting for Richard Womack to show up. What's your interest in a dead man?'

Adam shrugged, no mean feat with his hands wedged under his arse. 'All we need do is confirm and gather proof for our client that Womack is alive. I swear, mister, that's all we're employed to do.'

'Tell me who your client is.'

'A guy called Chris Frieden.'

So much for client confidentiality, I thought. But then I wasn't complaining at his lapse of professional decorum.

'Tell me about him.'

'He's nobody, man. He's just a broker, an intermediary. He passes us jobs. That's all. He gets the gigs and subs out to me, Noah, and a couple other guys in the business. He takes a cut off the top line, kind of like our agent, y'know? Everyone's happy with the arrangement.'

'So who's his client?'

'I don't know for sure. Some insurance company.' He nodded over his shoulder in the general direction of Billie's house. 'When her husband supposedly died, Billie Womack got richer to the tune of six figures. If it's proven that her husband didn't die, then her claim is nullified.' Looking suitably ashamed of himself, Adam added, 'We are on a percentage return on this. Whatever the insurance company manages to claw back, we get ten per cent.'

I sighed. Not so much at the immorality of their agreement with the insurance company, but at the realisation that we worked in a similar field. But I guess that's the lot of the modern gumshoe: in this tough climate you had to take what jobs you could, however it grated against your sensibilities.

'You must be pretty certain that Richard Womack is alive. If he's dead, where's your payment then?'

'We get a retainer fee, and our expenses are covered.' Adam glanced once at Noah – checking he was still in dreamland – then said conspiratorially, 'To be honest, mister, it gets us out of the city for a while. I'm happy to do a bit of hiking and camping at someone else's expense. I like it out here in the hills; it's kinda like a working vacation for me.'

I checked out his clothing. 'You get those duds on expenses?'

He looked down at his North Face coat and Timberland boots. He didn't have to reply.

'Noah should have decked himself out at the same outfitters,' I said, and Adam chuckled at the idea. Not only were Noah's leather shoes ruined, but now his raincoat and suit were equally muddy. Maybe Noah sensed he was the subject of our humour, because with a drawn-out groan he stirred, before starting wildly and sitting up. His face was level with the barrel of my gun. His eyes almost crossed, focusing on what he believed was the weapon of his imminent execution. He uttered another moan and reared away.

'Take it easy, pal,' I told him. 'It sounds as if we all got off on the wrong foot.'

'You going to kill me?' His head snapped back and forth. 'Where's Adam?'

'Right there.'

Noah followed my gesture and was relieved to see his friend safe from harm. He looked back at me. 'You knocked me out, you son of a bitch.'

'I did. The alternative was that I shoot you. Think I made the wrong decision?'

He was still sitting in the dirt. More mud had adhered to his clothing. His hands were brown with muck and leaf mulch, but it didn't matter because he touched his head, seeking the source of the pain. He let out a cry and looked goggle-eyed at his extended index finger. It stood off at a right angle. 'Holy Christ! Look what you did to me!'

'You did it to yourself by pulling a gun on me,' I pointed out.

'Hell, it's broken!'

I studied the unnatural shape of his finger. 'Hold out your hand,' I told him.

Noah stuffed his damaged hand under his opposite armpit. 'No way.'

'Look, pal. If I intended hurting you, I'd be hurting you. Understand? Now hold out your hand, I haven't all day.' I offered my left palm, beckoning him to comply.

'Do it,' Adam cajoled his friend. 'This guy really ain't all that bad.'

Noah shot Adam a look of incredulity. It was understandable: he was the one with the thumping headache and grotesque hand, muddy and covered in crap, while Adam sat pretty in his brand new hiking gear. Still, I wasn't kidding when I said I didn't have much time. The longer I wasted here with these two amateur detectives, the longer Billie was at risk from someone who did mean her harm. I clicked my fingers. 'Let me see your hand.'

'You broke it,' Noah groaned. 'I need to see a medic.'

I waited a few seconds, just staring at him. My mouth was set sternly, I guess, because he grimaced at me. But eventually he took out his hand from his armpit, studied it, then turned his face away as if in disgust. Slowly he began to extend it. I waited no longer. I grasped his finger in my left palm and folded a fist around it, gave a hard jerk and let go. Noah howled, but the sound was quickly curtailed when he realised that I hadn't torn the finger off. He held his hand in front of his face, studying it, surprised to find everything in the correct place. He made a tentative attempt at a fist, hissed, unfolded his fingers, then tried again. It was easier second time. He blinked in astonishment.

'You'll be fine. First chance you get, strap your index finger to the middle one, give it some support, otherwise it might pop out of joint again.' I tossed his revolver down on the forest floor. 'And don't try to pick that up with your right hand. Put it away with your left.'

He looked at the gun, up at me. 'I'm not a complete idiot,' I told him and allowed the bullets I'd emptied from the cylinder to trickle from my hand. 'You won't need those, I'm not sure you'll be firing a gun any time soon. You'll have some tenderness in the joint for a few days, but if you take things easy with it your finger should be fine.'

'Why'd you care?' Noah huffed.

'I don't. You know, there's a lesson in this for you. Unless you're prepared to shoot, don't go drawing your weapon.'

Noah scowled. He checked for where I'd put my SIG. It was in its carry position at my lower spine, and he couldn't see it for my clothing. But he knew it was there, and most likely that I'd been holding it ready when I'd walked up on them. 'Could say the same for you,' he pointed out.

'Oh, worry not. I was prepared to shoot. I just didn't have to.'

My last was an insult I hadn't intended, but it was too late to retract it without losing my position of dominance. I wondered if Brandon Cooper would be proud of me for restraining my killer instinct. I was pretty sure that Rink would be.

On the fallen log, Adam stirred. 'Is it OK for me to move my hands now? Seeing as we've straightened out our misunderstanding.'

His friend wasn't so sure. As far as he knew, I was some guy working for Procrylon who'd almost busted his head, dislocated his finger, then, for some reason unknown to him, reset it. Perhaps so I could dislocate it all over again.

'You can move, but don't go getting fresh,' I warned Adam.

Relieved, he took out his hands and worked some blood flow into them. The skin on his hands was the same pattern as the bark on the tree, only much paler. He quickly rubbed at the end of his tickly nose with a palm, squinting in relief.

Noah took my relaxing of the rules as permission to stand. He used the fallen tree for support. Adam offered a helping hand, but Noah shrugged him off. 'I'm not totally useless,' he growled, but to me he was trying to convince himself rather than his friend.

'Sit down before you fall down,' I told him. He still looked cross-eyed from the smack round the head. He perched himself unsteadily alongside Adam. 'We've established that you're not the bad guys. For the record, neither am I.'

Noah touched his head, unsure of the sincerity of my statement.

'That's the thing,' Adam said. 'You know who we are, but you haven't explained yourself. Are you just a friend of Billie Womack's or something else?'

'Can't I be both?'

Apparently Adam wasn't that sharp when it came to a subtle response. He frowned, trying to figure out what I meant.

To speed things up, I decided to be more forthright. 'I'm looking after her.' I eyed them pointedly. 'Some strange guys have been following her around recently.'

Adam glanced at Noah, and had the grace to appear abashed.

'He doesn't mean us,' Noah told him. 'He's talking about this "Procrylon" outfit.'

'How long have you been here?' I asked.

'Here in the woods?' Adam wanted clarification.

'Baker's Hole, in town.' I swept our surroundings with an all-encompassing gesture. 'Since leaving the city.'

'Three days,' Adam said.

Noah clucked his tongue at the looseness of Adam's.

'What?' Adam raised his palms. 'You'd rather he beat the truth out of us?'

'Doesn't look like he touched you,' Noah pointed out. 'Yet.'

'I only want to know if you've noticed anyone else hanging around,' I reassured them.

Noah rubbed his fingers over his scalp, wincing at the pain – whether in his hand or his head I couldn't be certain. Then he made a quick gesture towards Billie's house. 'Couple of days ago some guys turned up and spoke with Billie. They looked official. Feds maybe.'

That would have been Brandon Cooper and his colleagues. Cooper had told me they'd come to the farm and spoke to Billie. That was when he'd suggested she get in touch with me. 'No one else?'

'Just you,' Noah said.

I wasn't wholly surprised. Their surveillance skills left something to be desired. I paused, peering out across the valley to where the farm buildings crouched alongside the lake. It was growing cooler and mist was beginning to rise off the water. Soon it would veil Billie's house. Anybody could be out there watching and I'd be none the wiser, but for one thing. I got that prickling sensation that I was in somebody's crosshairs, something I'd experienced many times in the past. When I was in the army I'd grown to believe in what was sometimes termed Rapid Intuitive Experience: the fabled sixth sense. It was nothing to do with psychic ability, just a throwback to the natural instincts we all had when we were still prey to larger animals. It warned of impending danger, and right then my hackles were raised. There was someone out there much more dangerous than Noah and Adam, and I felt that they'd show themselves soon.

I I

Billie had poured herself a glass of wine. Probably not a good idea, but I didn't say anything. If she'd reached for the bottle for a top-up I'd've diverted her, although the alcohol might help calm her. She was livid that her insurance company had the temerity to disbelieve her claim was lawful, and to send investigators to spy on her.

'They're not the only ones who believe that your husband might still be alive,' I reminded her. There'd been a high profile case back in Britain a few years ago when a supposedly drowned canoeist was found to be alive and well and living off the proceeds from a life insurance claim lodged by his wife. I supposed there were other claimants who had got away with similar ploys in the past.

'I buried my daughter,' she said, her voice cold. Her statement didn't prove the point that Richard was dead, but to her it was all that mattered. I could see her eyes glittering and it had little to do with the small amount of wine she'd consumed. Feeling a little uncomfortable, I perched myself against her kitchen counter. Billie was sitting at her large table. Once it had accommodated an entire family; now the table was far too big for a single woman. She looked like a tiny child sitting in her dad's chair.

'I think they're the least of your problems,' I said, trying to take her mind off her dead child. 'If you made the claim in good faith, I'm not sure there's anything they can do to get the money back even if Richard does turn up.'

'Do you think I care about the money?'

Judging by the basic, faded furnishings that surrounded us, I took it that Billie didn't enjoy the most extravagant lifestyle. Her belongings appeared to have been collected from various sources, primarily yard sales and thrift stores. Except, I reminded myself, she was an artist and shabby chic was probably more to her taste. For all I knew her furnishings came with a 'retro' price tag, and were more expensive because of it. Plus her home and adjoining land must have been worth a packet.

'I make enough from my art to live off,' she went on, as if having to prove her point.

I attempted another diversionary tactic. 'You mind if I have a drink?'

'Wine?' She lifted the bottle.

'Water will do. Or coffee if you have it.'

Without answering she got up from the table and joined me alongside the counter. She began spooning grounds into a coffee maker. 'How strong do you like it?'

'Strong strong.'

'Do you think there's any truth in it?'

'In what?' She wasn't talking about coffee.

'About Richard being alive.'

'To be honest I've no idea. You seem pretty certain that he's dead. That's good enough for me.'

'Is it though, Joe?' She stopped what she was doing and stared at me.

'I don't know what you mean.'

'Sure you do. There's a reason Agent Cooper encouraged me to contact you.'

'He trusted me to protect you,' I said.

'But there's more to it, isn't there?'

Billie wasn't a fool. And I wouldn't insult her intelligence by lying. 'He asked me to watch out for you, but, yeah, he also asked that I watch out for Richard. I've to give him a heads-up if he shows his face.'

'Priority?'

'You. Always,' I said. 'If he is still alive I honestly don't care what happens to Richard. If what I hear is right and he killed your daughter, then to hell with him.'

'It is right.'

'Then I'm here for you.'

Billie nodded, but from the way she hugged herself she wasn't convinced. 'You don't know me. You don't owe me anything, and vice versa. Yet, listening to you, you sound as if you're prepared to go beyond the call of duty on my behalf.'

I just looked at her. She hadn't exactly asked a question, but I got her meaning. 'You're wondering why,' I eventually offered.

She continued preparing my coffee, using her silence to obtain the information she was seeking.

'I used to be in the military,' I said, but that was nowhere near enough for her. 'I volunteered for a special unit and spent fourteen years there. At the time it felt right: I was saving people. But to do that I'd to also kill, and now when I look back I'm not sure that everything I did was as honourable as I thought at the time. I'm not proud of some of the stuff I did back then. You might say that since I left the unit I've been trying to make amends in some way. I want to help people who need my help, and to do that I will risk my own neck. I'll fight for them,' I lowered my voice for my final words, 'and kill for them if necessary.'

'You're trying to make amends by following the same exact lifestyle? The same violent path?' Billie grunted out a humourless laugh.

'No. As hard as it is for you to understand, it isn't the same now. Back then I was acting under orders. I didn't question them. I was a good soldier.' I offered my own humourless laugh. 'The difference now is that I'm steered more by my moral compass. I choose who to help . . . who to hurt.'

'What gives you that right? You choose who to hurt! God!'

'I phrased that poorly,' I admitted. 'What I meant to say was that these days I haven't got some self-serving hierarchy pointing me at targets; these days I choose to help people in need and only hurt those intending them harm.'

Billie's features were flat, emotionless, as she absorbed my words.

'I guess I'm not too good at explaining myself,' I said.

She shook her head. 'No. It's not that. I understand what you're saying. It's just that I'm surprised how alike we are.'

'You seemed disturbed by what I was telling you.'

'I was. No, I am. But you don't disturb me. I realised that – given the chance – I'd do exactly the same. If my husband is alive and does make the mistake of showing his face I'm pretty certain that I'll be his judge, jury and executioner. Without hesitation. For what he did to our daughter I'll gladly shoot him dead, or smash in his head with the heaviest object to hand.'

Pouring coffee from the jug, Billie watched me for a reaction. She didn't get one. When you talk about killing from your moral standpoint, you can't be judgemental of others without sounding like a hypocrite. I took the offered mug, and nodded gratitude. Perhaps Billie took my gesture as a seal of agreement because she smiled, and immediately changed the subject.

'When did you last eat?'

It was back when I was in Seattle. Far too long ago, I understood. My stomach growled its own agreement.

'I can make you something if you like,' Billie said. 'There are some leftovers I can warm up.'

'Please.'

She went to her fridge and began rummaging. While she was engaged in the task of cooking something up, I went through to the living-room window and peered outside. Dusk had settled in, but even with the lowering of night's shade and the mist building over the lake the view was still spectacular. For the last few years I'd been living on Florida's Gulf Coast near Mexico Beach, working mostly in Tampa. As much as I enjoyed the warmth and the beauty of the coastline, my heart always longed for a rugged mountainous skyline, forests and lakes. It very much reminded me of home. As a young man I regularly spent time in the wilder areas of Scotland, or in the Cumbrian Lake District. I could imagine myself living at Baker's Hole, or somewhere like it. I turned and looked through the open doorway and watched Billie pottering around. She glanced briefly my way, and offered a smile. I smiled back at her, before she moved out of view. I could imagine myself living in a place like this with some female company, I thought.

Billie Womack wasn't a classical beauty. But then again neither was I. She was pretty though, and looked younger than I knew she was. Perhaps it was the boyish way she wore her fair hair, the dimple that showed when she smiled lopsidedly, the way in which she bounced slightly on the balls of her feet when she walked, but I found her quirky looks and slightly spiky mannerisms more attractive than the faux beauty presented in movies and celebrity magazines these days.

We were alike in many ways.

We each carried a burden of loss. Billie had lost a daughter, and had been vilely betrayed by her husband, and she probably hurt constantly. Though my grief was different, at its base it was similar. I'd been in a couple of short-lived relationships recently, and though I occasionally thought about both, missed them, I didn't still yearn for Imogen or Kirstie. Both women had gone on to enjoy happy, trouble-free lives, and were the better for me being out of them. I hurt when I thought about Kate Ballard. We'd barely begun our relationship when a murderous bitch acting on behalf of an enemy snatched her from me. I see Kate's murder as my major failing, and often wonder how my life would have turned out if I'd been better at my job. More than Kate even, I missed Diane. She wasn't dead, but we had divorced, and the decision to do so hadn't been mutual, just necessary for her. Diane had remarried, and was enjoying her new life, and yes, it too was all the better for me being out of it.

I returned my attention to the window, and the view beyond. In the reflection on the glass I was aware of Billie passing to and fro across the kitchen. I watched her, sure that she was unaware of my perusal. I caught her pausing in the threshold and casting lingering glances at me, appraising looks that told me she was equally satisfied that I was as unaware of her interest. I allowed myself to enjoy the little game. Adjusting my vision slightly I could see my own face reflected back at me, and I noticed that I was wearing a sad smile. With some effort I straightened my face. I'd no right thinking about Billie in any way other than as someone I was employed to protect. In other words, I should keep my mind on my job.

I searched beyond the window.

Again I experienced that sensation of being watched.

I knew that Noah and Adam were probably still out there somewhere. Because of the mist their original position on the hillside would be a fruitless lookout, and I supposed they'd moved closer despite my friendly warning to back off. I had no real right ordering them away; like me, they had a job to do. But I'd told them that if Procrylon's people were indeed here then they might not be as affable. Despite getting off on the wrong foot with those guys, I held no animosity towards them. In fact, I felt mildly responsible for their safety and hoped that they didn't get caught in the crossfire.

Perhaps I was assuming a lot. There was no proof that Procrylon's hired guns were here, other than that Brandon Cooper had said they would be coming. But Cooper was certain, and for that reason so was I. The point being, he knew a lot more than he was letting on. Earlier I'd admitted to Billie that Cooper was using me as his eyes and ears on the ground. That contradicted what I'd told her about me now acting solely under the guidance of my moral compass. Except I'd been telling her the truth when I also stated that she was my priority, contrary to what Cooper wanted.

I wondered how soon Rink would arrive.

One man can't effectively protect another person; it doesn't matter what level of skill or experience you possess. I wasn't superhuman, and despite my over-indulgence in caffeine I had to sleep some time. At a minimum it took two people to stand guard around the clock, and more was better. The only good thing I could think of about our current predicament was that if a team did come for Billie, then they wouldn't wish to kill her. What good was she to them dead? They would want to learn what she knew of Richard's whereabouts, and then would prefer to keep her as bait to draw him to their trap. But again I was assuming a lot. There was so much I didn't know about this case that I felt hamstrung.

While she finished preparing our meal, I went out to the rental car and fetched the extra items I'd requisitioned from Agent Cooper.

When I returned to the kitchen, Billie had laid out plates on the table. At its centre was enough food to feed us five times over. Billie was seated in the same chair as before and she offered me the place directly opposite. I noticed she'd refilled her wine glass, but I'd been too distracted to put her off. I didn't comment, just took my place and waited for her to raise an eyebrow as my permission to eat. I ate, and it was good food, and it would be a shame for any of it to go to waste. Hell, I was hungrier than I'd realised.

As I was spooning down a third bowl of thick meaty stew, Billie retrieved the coffee jug and gave me a refill. She also put aside her wine glass and filled a second cup for her. She tipped it towards me in salute, smiling faintly, as if she'd guessed that I preferred she remain alcohol-free for the time being. 'Cheers,' I said, and returned the salute.

'You want dessert?' She looked over at the fridge.

'No thanks. I'm full. Don't think I could eat another bite.'

'You don't have a sweet tooth, then?'

'I prefer savoury stuff. Meat, mostly. I'm a bit of a carnivore, I'm afraid.'

'Finish off that stew, it'd be a shame to waste it.' There was still a ladleful in the casserole, and despite my protestations I offered little resistance when she reached for it and piled the rest of the meat and vegetables in my bowl. 'You look like a man who appreciates home cooking.'

Most of my life I'd existed on canteen food, military rations or what could be downed on the hoof. But she was correct: I did enjoy some home-cooked food when it was on offer. Her stew reminded me of a recipe my mother used to serve up back home in the north of England. We called it hotpot; I'm not sure what the equivalent was here in Washington State, but was too busy spooning it down to ask, and besides it would have been rude to speak.

'Had enough?' Billie ventured when I'd finished.

'More than.' I chuckled. 'Hell, you must think I'm a glutton.'

'There's nothing wrong with having a healthy appetite. I'm pleased it's finished, otherwise I'd have been eating leftovers for a week.'

I wondered that – even after all this time – she found it difficult catering for only one whereas before that she'd fed a family. Perhaps it was just her way to prepare food in quantity and save some for later, when a convenient dinner was required. Way out here in the hills she wasn't in a good position to telephone for home delivery. Then again, I had to consider that she'd prepared the food especially for me after I'd agreed to come. We hadn't broached the subject of where I was going to stay yet, but we both knew that there was only one answer to that.

'I don't want to put you to any more trouble. I'm happy to sleep on the couch,' I said.

'I wouldn't hear of it. I have a spare room upstairs. You're welcome to it.' Her words were delivered as if she'd practised them, but I noted a fleeting shadow darting behind her features as if she felt a little uncomfortable making the offer to a relative stranger. 'Just don't go getting any funny ideas.'

'I'd prefer to be down here, if that's OK,' I said. 'I'm not much use as a watchman if I'm tucked up in a comfortable bed upstairs.'

Billie shrugged, as if she cared less for my comfort. I wondered whose room she had offered me. To be honest, I didn't want to invade the space that she thought should belong to her daughter. 'It's early yet, but when you're ready you can help fetch down some blankets.'

'Sure,' I agreed. 'In the meantime, let me help you with the dishes, then there are some things I want to acquaint you with.'

She knew I'd brought the stuff from the car, and she craned her neck to peer through the open door into the living area, but I'd piled the gear out of sight on the settee. 'I'll just load up the dishwasher. Help yourself to more coffee if you like.'

I helped take the dishes to the machine. Then I refilled my cup, and hers too. We carried them to the living room where Billie stopped and blinked in surprise at what I'd brought indoors.

'Are they bulletproof vests?'

'They're not infallible, but better than nothing,' I said, lifting up the smaller of the two antiballistic vests. They weren't military issue, weren't even law enforcement issue, but were enough to stop most small arms fire. 'This one's yours.'

Billie looked torn by indecision. She looked from the vest to me and then back again. 'You're really taking this threat seriously, aren't you?'

'I'd be remiss if I didn't. Here, try it on for size. Don't worry, it's adjustable.'

'You're joking, right?'

I held the vest out for her.

'Lord! It's heavy.' Billie almost sank to her knees as she took the vest. It was heavy, but she was overreacting for effect.

'Once the weight is distributed it's not too bad. You'll get used to it in no time.'

I helped her into the vest, then cinched the Velcro straps at the sides. She looked tiny, the vest riding up almost to her throat. She test-thumped her chest. Grimaced. 'I felt that.'

'It only stops the bullet from penetrating; it doesn't do an awful lot to dispel the kinetic force. There are better vests on the market, but I'm afraid these were all I could lay my hands on at short notice.' I moved behind her, adjusting the vest, lengthening the straps over her shoulders so it settled a little lower down. The vest was designed to offer most protection from a bullet to the centre mass. If a round struck her in the throat or gut, or even under the arms, then it would be 'Goodnight Irene'.

Billie went to a mirror and admired herself. She grinned unabashedly, enjoying the dressing up. It took her a moment longer to realise the severity of having to don protection, and she sobered rapidly. 'How long am I expected to wear this thing?'

'Until I know it's safe enough not to.'

'When will that be?'

How long is a piece of string?

12

A sound roused me from sleep. It was faint, distant, and came and went as the mountain acoustics played with it: the thrum of an engine. The road past Baker's Hole wasn't private, and this wasn't the first car to pass in the last couple of hours. On those occasions I'd woken from my slumber too, listening as the vehicles passed the farm and continued along the lake's shore road and further into the hills. I wasn't immediately concerned at this latest sound, but I got up from the settee, piling the blankets at one end. I was still wearing my jeans and Homer T-shirt, and I quickly pulled on my boots and began lacing them. A bulletproof vest identical to the one Billie had taken upstairs with her was propped at the end of the settee. Ordinarily I went without protection, choosing manoeuvrability over the safety blanket of heavy Kevlar, but I had to make a good example if I expected Billie to wear hers. I slipped into the vest – as I had on those other occasions when cars approached – and pulled the Velcro snug. Out of habit I checked my SIG, then placed it at its carrying position at my lower back. I pulled on my jacket to conceal the vest and gun as I approached the front window. Billie had drawn the drapes earlier, but standing to one side I could see through the gap between the curtains and frame, without anyone outside spotting me. My angle allowed me to look towards the road, but in the wrong direction from which the vehicle approached.

While I'd prepared, the engine sounds had grown louder and more consistent now that there were fewer obstructions. The pitch of the engine changed as the car slowed. It was still out of my line of sight, so I went quickly through the living space and into the kitchen. I left off the lights, but there was some faint illumination cast by the LED from the microwave cooker's display panel. It wouldn't pick me out to anyone watching from outside. Staying in the shadows, I moved round the table and positioned myself so I could look out of the window at the side of the building. A few hundred yards away there was a dim glow in the mist. The engine sound stopped. A moment later the dull glow blinked out as the headlights were switched off.

I thought briefly about Noah and Adam, if it was in fact either of them in the car, perhaps moving to a better vantage point to watch the farm – but I doubted it. I had that prickly sensation up my spine and I could taste iron in the back of my mouth.

Judging distance was difficult in the mist, but I guessed that the car had come to a halt a couple of hundred yards before the entrance to Billie's farm. Having driven by there earlier, I knew that a wire fence separated Billie's property from the road, but it was an insubstantial thing and wouldn't prevent anyone from climbing over it. They need only then cross an untilled field to approach the back of the house. There could of course be an innocent explanation why someone would stop their car there, perhaps to relieve themselves by the road-side or to make a phone call, or something equally mundane, but it wasn't a chance I was going to take. I headed upstairs and softly rapped on Billie's bedroom door.

She mumbled something, and without waiting I slipped inside, just as she reached for her bedside lamp.

'Don't turn it on,' I whispered.

'What?' Billie's eyes were huge – I could see the whites reflecting the glow of a digital alarm clock. Just about then she possibly regretted allowing a strange man to stay in her home with her.

'There's someone outside,' I explained. 'Don't alert them by switching on the light.'

Billie sat up in bed, holding the sheets around her. My eyes were adjusted to the darkness and I could see that she had worn a sweatshirt to bed. 'Where's your vest?'

'I took it off; it was too uncomfortable to sleep in.' The bedclothes slipped away as she swung out her legs, clad in leisure pants. She pushed her feet into a pair of slip-on pumps. The vest was on the floor.

'Put it back on,' I said.

She paused, staring at me in the darkness. Likely she believed I was overreacting, but that was fair. Perhaps I was. But perhaps I wasn't. She bent for the vest.

'When you're ready, go to the room we talked about.' I didn't wait for her to agree to my demand, because she might argue. Leaving her like that gave her no option. Earlier I'd discovered the studio where she painted, in the corner of which was a walk-in closet. At the back of it a concealed trap-door allowed access to a crawl space under the eaves. It wasn't an infallible hiding place, but it would slow any searchers down before they discovered her. I went downstairs, where the kitchen door and windows were all locked – part of the routine of securing the house before we'd gone to sleep – and headed to the front door. I was confident that nobody could have got from where they'd parked the car to a position where they'd see me exit in the short space of time I'd been upstairs. Pulling the door to behind me so that it locked, I moved around the blind side of the house, then jogged across the yard to the barn. I skirted it, so that I was still out of sight of anyone who could now be approaching across the field from the road.

The mist offered me cover. The same could be said for anyone approaching the farm. The advantage I had was that I was expecting them; they wouldn't be expecting me, and certainly not outside. I moved from the barn to an old stockade now bereft of livestock and crouched alongside a rusty trough. A corner post and the trough helped disguise my shape in the mist. Glancing up I noted that the sky was cloudless, and stars twinkled back at me. No moon though, it was yet to rise. I wasn't in danger of being picked out by an errant moonbeam. I waited, breathing steadily to calm my pulse, my chin dipped against my jacket collar. I ensured that I breathed into the fabric, because my breath was condensing and might also give me away to an alert watcher if I allowed it to plume like a smoke signal. I took out my SIG, held it against my thigh. Waited.

A soft scuff to my left brought me round.

I'd miscalculated the direction from which the person would approach the farm. They'd taken a more circular route across the field – perhaps growing confused in the mist – and now approached from a wider angle. Taking things slow and easy I lowered myself to my haunches. Ten feet out a figure moved past, wraithlike, featureless. I could make out enough to determine it was a burly male figure, and his attention was on the back of the house, not on my position. Something glinted wetly in the blanketing mist. Whether it was a weapon or a breaking-and-entering tool didn't make much difference, it spoke of ill intent as much as his stealthy approach. I could easily have moved in on him from behind, stuck my gun in his back and ordered him to drop it, but I wasn't positive that the intruder was alone. A single car could comfortably hold up to five individuals, and I was certain that the man would not have come without help. This wasn't about spying on Billie's home, waiting for her supposedly dead husband to do a Lazarus, but something else. As Agent Cooper had feared, Procrylon had decided that the best way of finding Richard Womack was to lean on his wife.

A clatter came out of the mist to my right. It caused the first figure to halt, to crouch down as the man scanned for danger. He must have been in a position to spot his colleague through the mist, because he gave a wave of his hand, his palm down, demanding caution. I narrowed my eyes, trying to discern movement in the direction he'd gestured. I made out another form, but this one was too distant to decide if it was man, woman or beast. I fully expected it to be the former.

Try not to kill anyone, Cooper had cautioned me. Up until now I'd managed not to. But I now wondered how to play this. It was apparent from their approach that these interlopers meant to grab Billie while she was unaware. They'd come during the night, probably armed, and it was highly likely they intended forcing their way into the house to grab her from her bed. Could I stop them without using lethal force? And if I did, then what would be the consequences? My immediate belief was that they'd only return, and in greater numbers. My instinct was to drop them, then sink them out there in the lake. Leave Procrylon wondering what had become of their attack dogs while I moved Billie somewhere more defendable, and with more backup.

But I couldn't just go in shooting. What if these people were no more dangerous than Noah and Adam had proved and I made a huge mistake? It was time, I thought, to hang on and see how things played out before resorting to the kind of violence I had used on other occasions.

I watched the nearest man drop to a crouch. He responded exactly as I would have if caught out in the open when hearing the noise. Another car engine purred as it made its way along the valley towards the lake. The guy looked for his pal in the gloom, and then reached for something on his belt. He pulled out a cell phone and hit buttons. The screen glowed, but he didn't speak, so I guessed he was sending some prearranged message instead, perhaps giving the all clear.

While he was distracted I moved away, concealing myself in the creeping blanket of mist as I headed along the side of the house to the front. Happily, I noted that the house was in full darkness, and there wasn't the faintest sound of Billie moving within. By now she should be hidden in the crawl space. From beyond the house came the sound of the engine as the latest vehicle approached. I had to consider that this car would pull directly into the yard at the front of the house: those guys lurking out back were only there should Billie make a run for it. They weren't my immediate concern. Earlier I'd moved my rental car into the barn, alongside Billie's little blue Jetta and a stack of galvanised steel barrels. Her battered old Chevrolet pick-up was parked in the yard. To all intents and purposes anybody making only a casual perusal would suspect there was no one but Billie at home. I hoped to keep things that way until I had a better idea of the new visitors' intentions. I hurried across the yard and stationed myself at the back of the pick-up, and had to bob down as a vehicle swung off the road and down the short track to the farm. Its headlights made the mist milky. I had no clue what kind of vehicle it was yet or how many occupants were inside. Part of me hoped that Rink had arrived early, but I knew it wasn't him. He would have called ahead to warn me.

As the vehicle pulled into the yard, it turned to avoid hitting the pick-up, and from behind the headlights materialised a large, bottle-green van. Two figures sat up front. There was no way to see into the cargo area from my position, but I doubted there was anyone inside. I took it that the van's purpose was for transporting Billie out of here beyond sight of any prying eyes. The muscles in my jaws bunched. The van stopped and a moment later two men got out. Both were in their thirties, of wiry build, with that bearing that picked them out at a glance as ex-military. The driver was wearing spectacles, perched on a nose that looked as if it had been broken a few times over the years. His skin was pale and blotchy. His pal was similarly coloured, with the same short-cropped fair hair. His nose had been broken too, but not as profoundly as the first man's. They looked enough alike to be brothers.

They didn't draw any sidearms as they first peered up at the house, then in silent agreement headed directly for the front door. It didn't mean that they weren't armed, only that they didn't deem it necessary to show their hand yet. I was conscious of the gun in my hand as I watched them from over the back of the pick-up.

Drop the fuckers!

My instinct was to do just that, but I stayed my urge to put out their lights before they could threaten Billie. I waited, trusting to our plan to keep her safer than if I got into a fire-fight with these men. Yes, it went against the grain somewhat, but perhaps patience did come with age as Rink often cheek-ily pointed out.

They stepped up on the porch and paused. Then the one with spectacles craned round and looked directly at me. He couldn't see me clearly for the mist, because I could barely see them now, but I had the benefit of my night vision being more adapted than his. He had just got out the van where the back-wash from the headlights and the display on the dashboard would have affected his. I didn't move; if he did spot me he would take my form for just another bit of the old pick-up. I realised quickly that he was simply checking out the truck, calculating. He turned back and said something too low to hear. His pal stepped forward and tried the door handle. I was glad that I'd remembered to drop the latch, so that it locked behind me when leaving the house. Their actions next would determine how intent they were on finding Billie.

I knew that by leaving her alone in the house it was placing her in a precarious position, but the alternative was that if I was inside when they entered then a fight would be unavoidable. Best I wait outside and see. At the first hint they had discovered Billie's hiding place, I'd go in. We'd organised a course of action earlier: if she thought they'd discovered the crawl space she was to hit speed dial on her cell phone and I'd slip in behind them. If they didn't find her then all well and good. Hopefully they'd leave and we'd have learned that, yes, she was indeed under threat from the criminals seeking her husband.

While the guy in spectacles stood in front of the door, his partner moved along to the sitting-room window, cupping his hands on the glass and peering inside. He couldn't see much for the closed drapes, except for down either side – the same strips I'd used to look out earlier. He shook his head at his pal. The one at the door took out his phone and pressed a button – speed dial – and I was positive that he was calling the men round back for a status update. He spoke too low for me to hear, but I caught his gruff tones, and his apparent dissatisfaction. 'No. Stay there,' he said a bit louder. 'Watch the exits. I'll go in with Danny: if we flush her out she'll have to run your way. Do not let her escape, even if it means bringing her down hard.'

His words were enough for me, answering the question succinctly. Again I was tempted to rise up and plug both those guys on the front porch, but the noise would bring the others running. With the element of surprise gone, the second part of the battle wouldn't be as easy. Not that I feared the fight as much as I did what would become of Billie if I failed to win. I'd already formed the opinion that the two out front were pros, and it stood to reason that the other two would have similar military backgrounds. If they beat me, then they'd realise there was something to protect in the house and their search wouldn't end until they had their hands on Billie.

The man put away his phone. I half expected him to kick his way inside, but he didn't. He took out some tools from his jacket pocket and set to unlocking the door. In less than two minutes he had unpicked the lock; having no experience in lock picking I didn't know if that was a good time or not, but it again told me that they were pros – at least of some type. He opened the door and pushed it gently inward. His pal, Danny, went inside first, and then he followed. Before fully committing himself to the depths of the house, he paused on the threshold and looked again at the truck. He shrugged off whatever was troubling him and went in. My heart beat fast. I waited, nervously listening for the first indication that they'd discovered Billie's hiding place.

13

Clutching her phone to her chest, Billie sat in darkness, under the eaves of the roof. She couldn't remember when she was last in the place, and would be happy if she didn't have to hide in it after this night. She imagined that spiders and possibly even bats shared the space with her, and that was almost as frightening as the thought that strangers prowled through her house seeking her. She could hear them moving from room to room, checking all the conceivable places she might be. They went stealthily, but the old house creaked and moaned to their footsteps. A loose board on the stairs sang out a cry of discomfort as one of the men ascended the steps to the attic. Billie held her breath.

She glanced at the faintly glowing screen of her phone.

Joe had instructed her to hit the call button if she felt she had been discovered. She was tempted to hit the button right then, but forced herself to hold off. She mustn't panic. Joe was positive that these men meant her no immediate harm, preferring to take her prisoner, and they would only hurt her if she attempted to flee them. He'd encouraged her to remain silent, keep hidden and allow them to carry out their search while he saw to her safety. 'That's why I'm here,' he had reminded her.

When he'd handed her the bulletproof vest and made her wear it, when she'd seen the gun he'd armed himself with, she half expected Joe to barricade himself inside the house and gun down anyone trying to break inside. Wasn't that what bodyguards did in the movies? They laid down their lives for the person they were protecting. But she conceded that it made more sense to stay hidden. There was less chance of injury all round, and maybe when these men failed to find her they would go away. But what would happen then? They'd only come back again.

The door to her art studio creaked open. She could almost picture the scene as the searcher peered inside the room. He would move stealthily across the room, checking behind her easel, then perhaps going to the window and looking out towards the lakeshore before returning to poke around behind the canvases propped along the wall next to the closet. The darkness under the door to the crawl space shifted, greyness where before it had been blackness. The closet door had been opened. She held her breath, finger poised over the phone. The grey darkened and she thought the seeker had closed the door again, but as she strained to see she could make out the faintest hint of movement. The person was inside the closet, his feet directly in front of the small door, blocking the dim starlight. She believed she could hear his breathing, but that was probably just the blood coursing through her own veins. There was a soft click as something in the closet was moved aside. Another noise, akin to a knock. Then the greyness was back as the seeker stepped out of the closet and into the studio again.

The muscles in Billie's forearms were aching, and she realised that she'd been posed statue-like as she held off pressing the button on her phone. Her jaws ached from clenching her teeth and there was a dull pain in her breasts from the tension, or from the uncomfortable weight of the vest; she wasn't fully sure. She was too tense to let out her pent-up breath. She feared that she'd hiss like a snake, and the searcher would hear and return to the closet, more intent on finding her hiding place than before. Her lungs were screaming for fresh air, and she forced her breath to leak between her teeth in a series of short exhalations. Finally she sucked in air, and the effort not to gulp caused a tremor to run through her.

Another sound.

This one from further away.

The seeker had left the studio and returned to the short flight of stairs. There was a low murmur of voices and she understood that her hunters were confused by the apparent deserted nature of the house. What would they do now? Would they remain in the house, assuming that she was late returning home, and decide to wait her out? Or would they simply leave as Hunter had figured?

Damn you to hell, Richard!

The curse almost found voice, but she managed to keep it to herself. Nicola had died in the crash. Were they stupid? How the hell could her husband have survived the plunge from the bridge, the crushing impact with the boulders in the river, the raging white water? She'd said earlier to Joe that she'd happily execute Richard given the chance, and she felt no less certain in her conviction now that her husband had brought these men to her home. If she were found, she'd show the invader just how far she'd go to protect herself too. She'd smash her phone into his head, try to jam the broken shards into his eyes if she could . . .

Calm down, she told herself. *You're about fit to burst, and those people will hear you. Do you really think you can fight your way past them with no real weapon? Just use the phone as Joe said.*

It was a struggle to contain her anger, but she managed. She sat in the dark, listening to the soft footfalls in the house. Occasionally she caught a soft clunk or squeak but they were distant. She kept her eyes on the faint grey strip of light at the base of the door, anticipating it going black again. Her hands clenched her phone, one finger poised over the call button. They shook with the effort, and she was positive she'd have trouble straightening her bent finger afterwards. To take her mind off discovery, she thought about her daughter. It didn't matter how hard she tried, she couldn't bring Nicola's features to mind. All she saw was that indistinct figure in red, flitting away from her every time she tried to draw her face to clarity. It was *his* fault: Richard had taken even the memory of her daughter away. And now he'd brought these men to her home. *The bastard!*

Billie felt her breath hitch in her chest, knew she'd made the bitter announcement aloud.

The greyness at the bottom of the door grew black.

'Oh hell,' Billie wheezed under her breath and she stabbed at the cell phone.

The door was pulled open, and she shuffled back as far as she could get. The roof pressed down on her shoulders, constricting her, and she pulled up her knees, ready to kick and flail if that was all that was left to her.

A figure crouched at the doorway, too large to fit easily through it. He leaned in, and Billie saw the glow from a phone he held in his hand. She didn't doubt that it vibrated softly with the incoming call.

'It's all right,' Joe Hunter said, extending a hand to her. 'It's only me. They've gone. You can come out now.'

14

'Pack only what you think's necessary for a couple of nights. Anything else you need we can grab along the way,' I said.

Billie looked at me as if I'd told her we were emigrating to Australia.

'What do you mean? I can't leave.'

'We have to. But only for a day or two, until we know you're safe.'

Billie held up the flats of her palms. 'I can't leave my home. Hell, Joe, all of my work is here. I've a business to run!'

'I'm sure that Hilary can hold the fort for a day or two without you. Surely you take the occasional day off? A vacation? Doesn't she look after the gallery then?'

'She does, but that's not the point. I shouldn't have to run away and hide. I've done nothing wrong, remember?'

'I know. But that doesn't matter to those guys. They're after your husband, and I'm assuming will use any means necessary to find him.' I didn't want to frighten her, but under the circumstances maybe a little fear would do some good. 'They came here with the intention of snatching you. What do you think they were going to do then?'

'Hurt me? Beat Richard's whereabouts out of me?' Her voice was frosty, no trace of fear. 'They'd be wasting their time because there's only one thing I could tell them. Up until yesterday Richard was a rotting corpse as far as I was concerned.'

'But now we know different.'

'No, Joe. We don't. We only know what Agent Cooper told us. How do we know that this man who was spotted was actually Richard? For all we know it's all part of a trick; there's something that Cooper isn't telling us. And even if it were Richard, why would anyone think that he'd come here? This is the last place – and believe me, I'm the last person – he'd want to lay eyes on.'

'Doesn't matter. Those men believe he's alive. Get your things together, we need to leave.' I picked up my meagre belongings that I'd stuffed into a knapsack. Everything else I owned I was wearing. 'Whether Richard's alive or not, whether Cooper is lying to us or not, those men think otherwise. They will come back. I overheard them as much as say so. Right now they think they missed you, perhaps assuming that they can find you in town, but they'll be back. Next time they won't play things as nice and easy.'

'Where are we supposed to go?'

'I'm not sure yet,' I said. 'Just out of here. If we can't call the police, I need to take you somewhere nobody will think of looking.'

We'd already talked about summoning help, and for a change it wasn't me who'd argued against calling the local police. Billie had been dead against the idea, and she still was. 'I've told you, if you call those idiots from the sheriff's depart-ment in Hill End, I know how that will play out. They'll have a poke around, take down my complaint, and when they see no harm's been done they'll leave with instructions that I call them again if anything further happens. They're a bunch of inept fools, trust me.'

'Those men invaded your home, Billie, and if I'm right it was with the intention of doing you harm. Forget the local deputies, we'll call the county police, they have a duty to protect you.'

'No. I won't go to them either, not after they treated me like a suspect in Nicola's death. Don't you see, Joe? If I go to them with this, it will only give them reason to dig up the past again. I was treated badly by them the last time, and I don't need to go through all *that* again.'

Billie looked ready for a fight. In the end she was probably right. Until something major happened, and hamstrung by procedure, the police wouldn't be able to do a thing to help, and by then it would be too late. Plus she'd enough to contend with without being set at the centre of a fresh criminal investigation, where the past would be raked up, opening her already raw wounds.

'OK,' I acquiesced. 'But we're still leaving. Once Rink arrives we'll be in a better position to protect you, but we can't wait for him here.' Billie knew that my friend was coming to help, but also that he wasn't due until sometime the following afternoon. I made a mental note to call and tell Rink we were moving.

Billie fetched a small holdall, but didn't start filling it.

I'd thought about contacting Cooper again, confirming his fears that Billie was a target and demanding he organise protection now that we knew the threat was real. But like it or not, my old ATF buddy had a personal agenda in this, and I knew I was the only protection Cooper was prepared to send. 'C'mon, Billie, you've got your own way, but time's short.'

Leaving her to it, I went outside and stood in the yard. It was still night, still misty. I was confident we could slip away unnoticed but time was growing short. The recent visitors wouldn't give up on the farm easily – if at all. Perhaps one or more of them had stayed behind to keep an eye on Billie's home while the others checked out other locations in Hill End. I eyed her pick-up, and decided it would be best left as it was. I went to the barn and got my rental car and pulled up alongside the old Chevrolet. Billie came outside, surprisingly quicker than I'd expected. She was toting the holdall, as well as a smaller leather bag over her shoulder. After locking the door she walked to my car and piled her belongings on the back seat. She stood for a moment looking back at the house, maybe thinking she'd never see the place again. If I had my way she would, and it would be without fear of anyone else invading it in future. She shook her head, then turned for the front passenger seat.

'Climb in the back,' I advised.

She frowned.

'We might pass those guys out on the road. If you're sitting up front they could see you. Get in the back and lie down on the seats until I give you the all clear.'

She clucked her tongue, but again conceded I had a point. She clambered in, pushing her bags on to the floor, making more room to spread out.

'Comfortable?' I asked.

'Just drive, why don't you?'

'That road there.' I meant the one that circled the lake and into the hills. 'Where does it go?'

'Into the wilderness,' she said without sitting up. 'There's about twenty-five miles of woodland and hills between here and the next town along. It's called Hope End.'

'Unfortunate name for a town,' I said.

'I don't think they considered its double meaning when naming the town. It sits at the western end of Hope Lake, hence the less than imaginative choice.' Billie gave an exasperated laugh. 'Come to think of it, the "end of all hope" connotation didn't come to my mind until you asked: I *hope* it isn't a bad omen.'

'Not if I have anything to do with it.' I was trying to reassure her, but doubtless came across as egotistical and overconfident. She gave another laugh of exasperation. I shut my mouth and drove off without the benefit of lights, because in the mist the glow would give us away.

Earlier when the four searchers had finished at the house, the two that looked like brothers had conversed at the front door. Then the one with spectacles had taken out his phone and spoken to those lurking out the back. Though I couldn't hear clearly enough to make out what was said, from his body language he looked annoyed that they hadn't found Billie asleep in her bed, but was unprepared to give up on the hunt. Slightly louder he'd mentioned going to Hill End. The two had then got in the green van and driven off. I thought I heard the second engine too, but couldn't be certain that the other two men had left. One thing I was sure of was that their vehicle – if it was still at the roadside – was to the left, so I turned right for Hope End.

It was an amateurish miscalculation. I should have realised that once they found the farm empty they'd move their vehicle beyond the entrance. They hadn't left at the same time as those in the van; they'd driven further along the road and positioned themselves to watch for Billie returning home. I saw their navy-blue SUV parked on the edge of the road furthest from the lake. They'd turned it so that they were facing us as we drove towards them. Their lights were off, and so were mine. The only saving grace was that they were watching for Billie's headlights as she returned along the Hill End road and didn't have a great view through the mist, so they didn't see my rental pull out of the farm track and only noticed us as we were almost upon them.

'Keep your head down,' I whispered.

'What is it?'

'Shhh. Can't speak.'

As I drove by the SUV, I restricted myself to only flicking a cursory glance over those inside. I hoped that I'd fool the watchers into thinking me some local, a drunken one at that, returning to my mountain home, without the sense to switch on my lights. It was a long shot, but it was all I could do.

I've trained myself to snapshoot scenes with one glance. That way I can take in detail for later recollection. I did so then. To the lone watcher in the SUV my glance would have looked like a flick of my eyes at most, but I saw enough to tell he was studying me – and my car – with interest. The interior of his SUV was in darkness, but I could still make out a man of solid build and close-cropped hair. His eyes caught an errant moonbeam and they were fixed on my face with laser intensity. Then he began to crane over and I knew he was checking out who was in the back seat.

'Keep down,' I warned again.

'Aw, hell, Joe! I think he saw me.' Billie squirmed around on the seat, and I didn't know if she was trying to get down into the foot well with the bags or if she'd given up the deception. 'I'm sorry, but I couldn't help looking. I think he looked right at me.'

By then we were two car lengths beyond the SUV and moving further away. I checked my mirrors, and saw the man poke his head out of the window to get a bead on us. Either that or he was taking down the licence plate number. Not good. Not good at all.

'I asked you to stay down.' I tried not to sound angry.

'My curiosity got the better of me. I said I was sorry.' Billie didn't sound sorry, she sounded equally angry. 'I wanted to know who it was we were running from.'

'It looks as if we're about to find out.' Behind us the man had switched on the engine. The lights came on automatically. I gave my rental throttle but not too much. I probably couldn't outrun the SUV in a sedan on these mountain roads. I placed my SIG on the passenger seat when I saw the SUV do a rapid turn on the road and follow. 'OK. This isn't working out the way I hoped.'

The SUV powered up behind us.

Headlights flashed, glancing off my mirrors.

Still playing it dumb, I turned on my lights, and offered a friendly wave of thanks out of the window.

Behind me the guy flashed his main beam again, then hit the horn. I sped up, passing the lake; the road began to rise up into the surrounding hills. The SUV came close on our tail, the driver accelerating and decelerating aggressively. His lights flashed, his horn blared.

I braked and pulled over.

'What are you doing?' Billie demanded.

'Seeing how our friend wants to play things,' I said.

The SUV came to a halt. I couldn't see for the glow from his headlights but it was fair to assume that my abrupt stop was the last thing the guy had expected. Grabbing my gun, I was out of the car in an instant and marching towards him. I kept the gun hidden behind my thigh, but I had to be fast and decisive before he thought to call in reinforcements.

'Hey, buddy! Hey!' I acted drunk, loud and slurring my words. 'What you doing blinding me like that, huh?'

The driver didn't reply. Maybe he hadn't seen Billie after all and was now wondering how best to deal with a belligerent drunkard. As I strode up to his door I hoped that he would reach for his phone before he did a weapon. I pressed up close to his window, making an angry face, but really checking out his hands. I thumped the ball of my left fist on the glass. He wasn't easily intimidated. He peered back at me, evaluating, unconcerned by my bravado. Both his hands were still on the wheel. Then he reached and switched off the engine. I stepped back as the door swung open. The guy stepped out. He was taller, and outweighed me by a number of pounds. Younger too.

'Who the hell are you?' His voice was husky. A crescent scar above his right eyebrow was puckered and white against his ruddy complexion. I didn't require the extra details to recognise him as the first man I'd spotted lurking at the back of Billie's house.

I lifted my SIG and aimed at his gut. 'That's exactly what I want to know about you.'

He glanced down at my gun as if it was a peashooter. His mouth turned up at one corner. 'If you're gonna shoot me, you betta make it count. A pissant little gun like that won't stop me from ripping your head off.'

I lowered the barrel so it was inches from his groin.

The corner of his mouth drooped.

'Who are you?' I asked.

'Who are *you*?'

'If I tell you, you're day won't end well. Now come on, I'm not fucking about. Who are you and what do you want?' My promise to Brandon Cooper was weighing heavily in my mind. Maybe the guy read that I was reluctant to shoot, because he just laughed.

'Who's that in the back of your car?' He aimed a finger past me. If he expected me to follow his gesture so he could cold-cock me while I was distracted he was mistaken.

'What's it to do with you?'

'It's Wilhelmina Womack, right?'

'Never heard of her,' I lied.

'Richard Womack's wife,' he went on.

'Aren't they the pop singers?' I said. He looked at me dumbly. 'Womack and Womack? You know them. You look like a man who enjoys his disco music.'

'Yeah, right. Funny,' he said, unimpressed by my humour as much as by my appearance, or my gun. Maybe the same joke had been made a few times during discussions with his pals. 'That's her, all right. I saw her. I want to speak with her.'

'Not going to happen.'

'You're gonna stop me?' He raised an eyebrow. He opened his hands, palms up. It wasn't a sign of surrender; he was readying himself for action.

'Yes.' Now I dropped all pretences at being anything other than what I was. I jammed the muzzle of my gun under his chin, forcing back his head. Now his palms did come up, open, near his shoulders. 'But first you're going to tell me a few things. You're from Procrylon, right? You want Billie to draw out her husband? Well I hope you're a fucking psychic medium, because he's dead. You understand that? Dead. Just like you're going to be unless you get the fuck in your car, drive away and don't look back.'

The man snorted. He craned his neck, disdainful of my gun. Maybe he thought a nine mm slug up through his jaw and into his brain was something to be shrugged off. He even placed the fingers of one hand against the barrel, about the press it away. I shoved it harder into the soft flesh of his neck. 'You're not taking me seriously enough, buddy,' I warned him.

'Why'd I even bother? If you were gonna shoot, you'd shoot. All this talk just tells me that you ain't gonna.'

Sadly he had a point.

'Try me,' I growled.

He craned his neck again. 'Pal, you ain't gonna do nothin'.'
I kneed him in the groin.

Gasping, he went down on his knees, his hands cupping his sore bits. 'Son of a . . .' his words ended in a wheeze.

I shoved the barrel of my gun into the nape of his neck. 'You'd best start taking notice. Now listen up. Up till now you haven't given me reason enough to kill you, but we're getting there. Now stop trying my patience. You're with Procrylon, right?'

'They pay the bill,' he agreed.

'What are you? Merc, hired muscle, what?'

'Private contractor.'

'Same thing,' I said. 'How many guys are you working with?'

'Enough for you to know not to mess with us.'

'Still being the asshole, eh? Well, pal, it's you on your knees with a gun to your head. Doesn't matter how many others you can call on, they aren't going to get here in time to help.' To enforce my point I pushed down hard on the gun. The guy didn't resist. Maybe his mind was still on his damaged balls. Before now he'd been smug, thinking I was all bluff, but now I got a whiff of his scent. He was sweating, the raw stink of fear evident. 'Now listen up. This is how things are going to play out. You leave, you tell your friends to leave. Nobody goes near Billie Womack and we're good. Do anything else and I swear to you; you're entering a battle you're not going to win.'

He let go of his groin to hold out his hands. This time they were palms down. 'You can threaten all you like,' he said. 'Won't mean a damn thing to the Jaegers. They won't turn away from a fight, even if you were Jack-fucking-Reacher.'

'The Jaegers: are those the two brothers you were with at the house?'

He stiffened slightly. Alarmed that I knew about the men in the van? Or maybe he was more surprised that I'd admitted to being at the farm when they'd searched it.

'You should fear them,' he said.

'I don't.'

'Just let me call 'em, and we'll see.'

'Once you're back in your car and driving away, you can call who the hell you want. In fact, do that. And tell them what I just told you.' I grasped his collar and hauled him up, transferring the gun to his eye socket. 'Are my instructions clear enough for you?'

Behind me there was a gasp. Shit! I'd told Billie to keep her head down. But her curiosity had got the better of her again. I glanced quickly at her. She was standing alongside the rental car. The guy spotted her too. He laughed to himself. He was a big man. Solid. On his knees. Nobody of his size should have been able to move as fast. Yet he contradicted everything in a split second. With one hand he butted my gun over his head, with the other he snapped round my right ankle and yanked upward, even as he bounded up. He didn't release my leg and it was snatched off the ground and I'd no way to go but backwards. I tried to realign my gun on his body, but his free hand swept my hand aside and he shouldered me in the chest. I went down on the gritty road. Distantly I heard Billie's squawk of alarm.

I wasn't hurt, not if you discounted my ego. But things were about to change. The man kicked my gun out of my hand. It skittered away across the road. He looked as if he was going to go after Billie, but thought better of it. I was a long way from being out of commission. He reached to grasp me by my jacket front and hauled me up. If I'd tried to fight free of him, he'd have kicked me stupid while I was attempting to scramble up: I went with the flow. He set me on my feet, but kept hold of me. He was bigger, stronger, had the upper hand now that my gun was lying in the dirt across the road.

'Let's just go through those instructions of yours again, shall we?' he said, grinning at my expense. I feigned defeated as he pulled me in close.

'Let's not.' I head-butted him, and felt his nose cartilage collapse under my forehead. He reared back, blood flooding over his top lip, and his eyes screwed tight. He didn't release his hold, but that was good. It meant he couldn't punch me. I butted him again, this time against his left cheekbone. We both fell against his car and the door slammed shut. The man used the body of the car to support his weight, then he swung me round and thrust me over the hood. Pain flared through my lower back, but it was muscle pain; my spine was still intact. I still didn't fight his hold, I actually allowed him to push me further up and as my hips popped over the curve of the SUV's hood, I lifted my legs and braced my heels in his pelvic girdle. I used the power in my legs to force myself out of his grip, but not so far that he fully let go. Immediately I wrapped my left leg over his arms, and bridged up with my hips. The move painfully locked his right arm at the elbow. Now he wanted to let go, but I gripped his right wrist in both hands, allowing no escape, even as I transferred my foot from over his arm to under his chin. He fought to free his left hand to get a good punch at me and it was the moment I was waiting for. I pistoned my leg, kicked his head back, yanking in the opposite direction on his arm.

He grunted in pain, but shook off the kick. He chambered his free arm to power it into my chest.

So I kicked him harder.

There was a crack like a gunshot.

I released his trapped arm and the man slid backwards, no strength in his knees, or anywhere else from the way he flopped in a boneless heap on the road.

'Oh my God!'

I heard Billie's exclamation, and it echoed the words that went through my mind. I slid off the hood and stood over the man. He didn't move. He was too still.

'You've killed him,' Billie said.

'Stay there,' I warned her. Not for one second did I believe the guy was playing possum, but it wasn't a chance I was going to take. I crouched, pushing aside his head so I could feel for a pulse. His flesh was warm, clammy, but there was no life in it. 'Jesus, they make bad guys too brittle these days,' I murmured. My intention had been to knock him unconscious, not snap his vertebrae!

Billie again chose to ignore my instructions. She stood at my shoulder as I checked the guy a second time.

'He's dead.' It wasn't a question.

'Yeah,' I said.

'You didn't have to kill him, but you did.'

'Trust me: I wasn't trying to.' I stood up, frowning down at the mass of inert humanity. 'How many bloody warnings does one man need? I tried to avoid this.'

'This complicates things, doesn't it?'

'Very much so,' I sighed.

I stood looking down at the corpse, hands fisted on my hips. This did indeed complicate matters.

'I suppose we *have* to call the cops now,' Billie said glumly.

Ordinarily she'd be right. His death was an accident; he was the bad guy who'd intended kidnapping a woman. But it'd be me who'd end up locked in a jail cell until things were cleared up. Billie would be defenceless against his friends. 'Go and get in the car,' I said.

'We can just walk away from this?' Billie's stare was locked on the dead man's face. 'What are you planning on doing?'

'What's going to happen is this: you're going to have to start listening to my instructions, and not challenging them. I'm here to protect you, and I can't do that if you're forever second-guessing me. Now go on. Get in the car, and this time keep your bloody head down.'

Billie transferred her stare from the dead man to me. I held her flinty gaze. No more messing around.

She finally pushed her hands through her hair. 'OK. You're right.' She walked away cursing under her breath, but I was happy to note her displeasure was aimed at her husband for placing her in this hellish situation. I retrieved my SIG, checked it over for damage and found it worked fine. I pushed it away in my belt at the back, then bent to deal with the dead man. He was heavy, felt even more so in death, but I got my hands under his armpits and dragged him to the SUV. I then got the door open and hefted him up and into the driver's seat. By the time I was done I was bathed in sweat. I put his hands on the steering wheel, then clasping mine over his used them to twist the wheel sharply to one side. At the edge of the road was a deep gully where a stream poured off the mountainside, under the road and downwards to the lake. The trees on the gully's embankments had been felled in recent years but new growth had sprung up in their place. The saplings wouldn't halt the plunge of the SUV. I was about to turn on the engine and set the SUV on its course when I spotted a cell phone in a holder on the dash. It still glowed from recent use. Actually, for all I knew, it was still turned on and had an open line to the Jaegers. Could my unlucky streak get any worse?

With no other recourse, I started the engine, slipped the gear into 'drive' and stood aside as the SUV began rolling across the road. It dipped off the shoulder, and bumped up again over a small mound of earth. Then it hung there for a long moment, while I considered going and putting my shoulder to it to help it on its way. Maybe the mound of dirt gave way beneath the weight, because in the next instant the SUV plummeted out of sight. It made a lot of noise crashing its way into the depths of the ravine.

15

'I can't believe what happened back there.' Billie rocked forward, her head thrust between the front seats as I drove for Hope End. She spoke so close to my ear I felt her breath on my neck. It was hot. There was a tremor in her voice, but it wasn't through fear or revulsion. Her excitement was palpable.

For my part I felt numb.

I genuinely hadn't intended killing the man. My heel must have struck him just right – or just wrong for that matter – so that instead of the impact knocking him out it had transferred to the fragile vertebrae of his spine. If I'd tried to kill him like that I just bet that the opposite would have applied. The guy had been too full of himself, a grade one ass, but killing him was more than he deserved. But what was done was done. I'd killed many times before, and might be called upon to do so again. I couldn't dwell on his death or it would slow me down if the time came when I must choose a fatal option again. I'd seen other soldiers sickened by violence, who grew reluctant when it came to pulling the trigger, and it was them who ended up in a grave.

'Things weren't meant to go down like that,' I explained. 'I hoped to frighten him off, not send his corpse to the bottom of a valley.'

'He asked for it,' Billie said. Her forthrightness surprised me.

'He was just a guy earning a wage,' I countered.

'If you hadn't stopped him, he would have hurt you. Maybe even killed you. Then where would that have left me?'

Jesus, talk about reverse psychology.

That was the only thing that gave me any sense of peace. But it surprised me to hear Billie say as much. I thought that she'd be horrified to learn that the man supposed to protect her was a killer. On the other hand she seemed excited by the prospect. Except, once she thought about it, and her heart-beat had slowed some more, then I expected she'd see the man's death for the horrible thing it was.

'How far to Hope End?' I asked, trying to focus her mind on something else.

'About fifteen miles. But on these roads it could take half an hour or more.' She rocked forward and back, barely able to contain her fidgeting. 'Do you think we'll make it?'

'We'll make it, I'm just not sure it's a good idea to go there now.' I told her about the cell phone in the SUV and how I suspected that the man had contacted his friends before I'd had chance to confront him. 'They could already be after us.'

She sucked in breath, but again it sounded more like antici-pation than fear. She was thoughtful for a moment before saying, 'They've no chance of catching us before we get to town. Once we're there we'll be able to hide out.'

'They'll find us. To be honest I don't really want to get stuck in a small town with a bunch of mercs. They might not be too particular about who they hurt while trying to find us. I don't want to put anyone else in danger because of what I did.'

'Maybe once they learn how easily their friend was killed they'll back down. It's like you said, they're just guys earning a wage. Who'd want to die for a few dollars?'

She obviously didn't understand the world of mercenaries and soldiers of fortune.

'They won't,' I said.

'How can you be certain?'

'I know their type.'

'Your type?'

I glanced at her. It was enough to see her face was set, her eyes steady as she peered at me from between the seats. I returned my attention to the twisting road, but could still sense her perusal. 'Unlike my type,' I corrected. 'I'd never take on a job that threatened an innocent woman.'

She laughed. It was short and sharp. I'm not sure what it meant. Billie didn't explain. She sat back in her seat, and I was relieved because her perusal had been uncomfortable.

Something struck me as important. 'Is there a more direct route from Hill End to Hope End, or is this the only road?'

'There's another way north of these hills,' Billie said. 'Why?'

I'd followed the road from Hill End to Baker's Hole, travelling more or less south-east. Now we were travelling north-east. I'd driven the two longer sides of a triangle. A direct road from one town to the other would be much shorter. 'How far?'

'Ten or eleven miles at most. Oh!'

Billie had got it too. If the man whose neck I'd broken had given our direction of travel to his friends, our destination would stand to reason. Anyone coming from Hill End could get to Hope End before us. Cut us off.

'We should turn back,' Billie said.

Perhaps we should've, but anyone with sense would send men along that road too, in case we did so. I wondered how many men Procrylon had sent after Billie. I couldn't assume that it was only the four I'd seen. What was it that merc said when I asked how many people were with him? 'Enough for you to know not to mess with us.' I took it that he was referring to more than another three then. Unless the respect he held for the abilities of those Jaeger brothers wasn't as over-blown as I first suspected.

I pulled over at the side of the road. The drop off to our right was steep, wooded, pitch dark.

'What are you doing? They'll catch us if we sit here.'

'I need to check my phone,' I said, digging in my jacket pocket. A quick look at the screen showed me I had no signal. 'Did you bring your phone, Billie?'

'Yes, but out here there's no service.' She leaned over my shoulder, looking at my phone as if to confirm her suspicions. She nodded upwards, vaguely indicating the surrounding mountains. 'Maybe if we were on top of one of the higher peaks, but down in the valleys the signals can't get through.'

'Damn it,' I said. I had hoped to text Rink, give him a status update, then call Brandon Cooper and tell him to get his arse out here to back us up. Now I could do neither. 'OK, we're on our own for now.'

I had my handgun, spare ammunition, and a couple of anti-ballistic vests. We weren't exactly equipped for a full-on fight but that never stopped me before. Except this time I had Billie's welfare to care about. I thought hard, and was only partly content with the idea I came up with. I started the car again and drove. 'You know these hills, right?'

'I know them well enough not to get lost. I regularly go out this way to paint.'

'I take it you don't stick to the main routes?'

'No. I prefer going off-road. The scenery is more dramatic once you get up on the peaks.'

'Good,' I said. 'I need you to think. If you wanted to hide out, where would you go?'

Billie didn't have to give it much consideration. 'There's this cabin. During hunting season people stay there if they're caught out by the weather. Right now I doubt that there's anyone there.'

'Is its location well known?'

'Only by local hunters.'

I mulled things over. Came to a decision. 'How do I get there?'

'Keep going,' she said. 'In about two miles you'll see a trail on the left. It takes you up into the hills a couple more miles, but then we'll have to trek in.'

The cabin sounded remote. An ideal hideout until I could figure out somewhere more appropriate. My initial plan was to shake off any pursuit, lying low while our trail went cold, then in a day or two head to a more populated town than either Hill End or Hope End where I could rendezvous with Rink. From there we could help Billie disappear until things were resolved at this end.

My plan was probably the most ill-thought-out of my life.

16

Less than a mile up the hunting trail I regretted not bringing Billie's Chevrolet pick-up. My rental car was wholly unsuited to the type of terrain we'd to navigate. Hitting a soft patch of earth, turned almost to soup by the frequent rain, the car slid sideways off the road and the tyre went into a ditch. Ordinarily that wouldn't have proved too bad, except that the low profile of the car meant it became wedged on the roadside, and it didn't matter how much power I gave it, all I achieved was to dig further into the mud and ensure the car was well and truly trapped. In desperation I had Billie clamber into the driving seat while I put my shoulder to the trunk and tried to shove us clear, but there was no hope. It would take a tractor or four-wheeled-drive truck to pull us free.

'It looks as if we're walking from here,' I said, wiping spots of mud off my face and shoulders.

'We didn't exactly dress for a hike,' Billie muttered. She was still wearing her sweats and pumps, though she had thought ahead and brought a jacket, mainly because it helped conceal the vest.

'Didn't you pack a sturdier pair of shoes?'

She shook her head. 'I thought we were driving. You said we'd pick up what we needed along the way. Sadly there's a shortage of hiking stores around here.'

I looked up the trail. It was still dark, and the trees concealed most of the sky overhead, but I could see that the trail was humped at the centre, where grass grew between the ancient tyre tracks. 'Try to stick to the middle and you should be fine. I think your pumps will be good for a few miles, but try not to get them wet and muddy, or walking will be hell.'

'You don't say.'

'If it comes to it, I'll carry you,' I offered, but maybe my delivery didn't sound convincing. Billie gave a scornful laugh, shook her head again, and set off without me. I allowed her to gain a short lead before setting off after her, carrying our bags over my shoulders. My gun and ammunition were close to hand. I kept an eye on the trail behind us, checking back at regular intervals, but more than that I listened. At that time there was no hint of pursuit.

Billie wasn't a young woman, but she was fit and healthy. Her lifestyle as an artist suited her, and her frequent treks into the mountains to find new vistas to paint had prepared her well for our walk in the night. The trail sloped sharply upwards, but she walked with that same spring in her step and her breathing was regular. I could feel the pulling of my muscles at each step, and was soon breathing harder. I'd neglected my regular runs these past few weeks and made myself a promise that once this was over with I'd get back to my usual fitness routines. Supposing, that was, that I was still well enough, uninjured or even alive.

About a mile further up the trail I called a halt. Billie stood with her hands on her hips, peering up at the tree canopy. While I caught my breath, I checked my phone for a signal but got none. I swore softly, but it carried to Billie's ears.

'I told you, we need to get up on the peaks if we have any hope of getting a cell phone signal.'

'I just thought it was worth a try.' Really I was concerned that we were stuck out in the wilds and nobody knew where we were. That was good concerning our pursuers, but it also meant we'd no help coming. 'OK, let's get moving again. I want to contact Rink as soon as.'

'Maybe we should've stayed put at the farm,' Billie said, 'and called the police like you suggested.'

'You're probably right.' But that didn't matter now. We were on our own and had to make the best of a bad situation. Shoving away my phone, I followed as Billie again led the way.

Another half a mile on Billie was the one to stop this time.

'Did you hear that?'

All I'd heard was my puffing and panting. I stopped, listening. I didn't hear a thing. 'What was it?'

'Listen.' Billie stood with one finger in the air.

'Shit. You're kidding me?' I could hear the distant whop-whop of rotor blades.

'What're the chances it's them?' Billie asked.

'The way our luck is going, I fear the worst.' The huge sum that Richard stole from Procrylon might warrant the company going to the expense of a helicopter to track down a direct conduit back to the cash. 'Let's hope it's just mountain rescue or something like it.'

Billie stared upwards. 'Sometimes light aircraft pass over, but I've never seen a helicopter here before. And if it was a regular flight what are the chances they'd be flying at this time of night?'

'I don't like it.' I was never much of a believer in coincidence. 'Come on, let's get going. If it sounds as if it's approaching we should get into the trees.'

In the darkness Billie's eyes gleamed, as if this was some exciting adventure and with little inkling of the concern I felt. I wished that I'd paid more attention to Agent Cooper's suspicions about Procrylon, and asked a few more questions to determine their strengths and resources. If the men had access to a helicopter, they might also have the appropriate equipment to conduct a manhunt in the dark. It wouldn't matter if we hid in the trees if they had access to thermal imaging technology, as our body heat would mark us out like flares against the cold, damp forest. I thought back to the bold statement I'd made to the man I'd killed earlier. *You're entering a battle you're not going to win.* Well, if Procrylon had the numbers and resources I now feared, then I'd been a tad ambitious with my prediction.

The sound diminished, which for the moment was a good thing. I encouraged Billie to get moving again, and she went ahead. Now I paid more attention to our back trail than before. If those in the chopper had spotted our abandoned vehicle they could be directing those on the ground up the mountain behind us.

A short time later we came to a fork in the trail. We hadn't heard the chopper for some minutes, but now that we stood deciding our next move I could again make out the distant chop-chop, and below it the thrum of another engine. Bad news. 'Which way is the cabin?'

'That way,' said Billie, pointing up the left trail.

'We go to the right, then,' I said.

Billie gawped at me as if I'd grown a second head.

'If they've got a helicopter, it stands to reason they'll spot the cabin. They'll know that's where we were heading. We go the other way.' I waited for her to understand the logic of my plan.

Finally she nodded towards the right-hand path. 'That way goes out and over the hills. The trail was used by loggers, but not for a while. It disappears after about another mile. After that there's nothing but mountains until you get back to the north road to Hope End.'

'Good. More space for us to lose ourselves in,' I said.

'Or just to get lost in.' Billie scowled.

'Without any hope of backup, our best hope right now is to get lost. We don't want to be found, remember?'

Billie fisted her hands on her hips, refusing to budge. 'And there was I trusting you knew what you were doing.'

'Sorry?'

'When Agent Cooper encouraged me to ring you I thought my safety was going to be in good hands.'

'Thanks for the vote of confidence. I've kept you alive until now haven't I? What do you think might have happened if I hadn't answered your call?'

Billie chuckled. 'Stop being so serious, Joe. I'm only joking.'

I stood there. Was she only joking, though? Fair enough, up to this point I hadn't exactly made all the best decisions, but it was like I said, she was still alive. If I'd not been around when the Jaegers and their pals turned up at the farm, she wouldn't be enjoying her liberty now.

She waved away any concern. 'Come on. Let's get moving then. Going that way does make sense when I think about it.'

'Thank you,' I said. 'I think.'

She grinned, and I was again reminded that she felt that this was some grand adventure. We still stood eyeing each other, Billie wearing that grin. My face felt stern. Billie shrugged, then turned and marched up the right-hand path. Her enthusiasm placed a worm of unease in my guts, the way her excitement over witnessing a fight to the death had. Somehow I felt that Billie welcomed another confrontation, and she didn't care if it was with me or with those chasing us.

17

The helicopter was back, and this time there was no doubting that we were the subjects of a search. The surrounding peaks played havoc with the acoustics, and we had no warning before the chopper hove into view a little over four hundred yards ahead. Thankfully its cockpit was turned away from us as it skimmed over the treetops, and I was able to lunge forward, grab Billie and steer her off the trail before it swung around. We hid beneath a fallen tree trunk while the chopper flew back down the trail we'd just followed. Somebody directed a high-powered flashlight between the trees, sweeping it down the trail, playing it into the woods on either side.

'The idiots are going the other way.' Billie stated the obvious, sotto voce, when there was no need. The racket from the chopper would have covered her voice if she'd blared out at the top of her lungs.

I didn't reply, instead urging Billie further into the woods. We were in the wedge of woodland between the forked trail, and I'd have preferred if we had gone the other direction so we weren't trapped between the two routes. But it was what it was, and it was up to me to change things as best I could. I touched Billie on the shoulder, indicating she should crouch beside a tree. 'We need to get across the road,' I said, 'before they turn round and come back this way.'

Billie gave no argument this time. She nodded, and her body tensed, ready for the run. The chopper was out of sight from our position, but it still thundered nearby. A few hundred yards to our left another engine grumbled, a vehicle moving up the trail towards the hunting cabin. I shook my head, silently berating myself for the poor decisions I'd made. But there was nothing for it. 'Don't run, move slowly, and when we reach the road let me check it's clear first.'

'OK,' she whispered.

Nodding her forward, I stayed slightly behind her, watching behind me through the woods in case anyone had decamped the vehicle and was searching on foot. There was no hint of pursuit between the trees, but you never could tell. We arrived back at the road and Billie crouched by the tree line without bidding. I leaned out a bit further. The chopper hovered like a massive hummingbird against the night sky. The flashlight beam stabbed the darkness, but thankfully in the wrong direction. 'They're at the point where the road forked,' I informed Billie. 'Come on, before they come back.'

Taking Billie by an elbow, I urged her across the road. She pulled gently from my grasp before we were halfway across, and jogged forward, then crouched again at the treeline. The bags hanging off my shoulders bounced uncomfortably as I jogged after her. They were an encumbrance, but if I ditched them it would give a clue to our pursuers as to where we had re-entered the woods. I should have dumped them out in the wedge of woodland, thrown them off the scent for a few minutes.

Further down the slope another engine roared. The vehicle was out of sight but its headlights flared between the trees. At least two cars were now on our tail, and it was apparent that having found our car stuck in the mud our pursuers had pushed on up the hill. Coming to the fork they had enough vehicles to take both ways. I tapped Billie on the shoulder, flicking my hand in the direction of the deep woods. Billie stood, and jogged bent over into the trees. The forest floor was thick with needles. They covered Billie's footfalls, but I could easily see the deep swathe as she kicked through them. Anybody with experience of tracking would immediately spot the trail if they stumbled across it, even in the dark. I backed into the woods trying to kick the needles back into place, but it was largely a fruitless task. I searched through the gloom for higher ground, rocks or even packed earth where we could tread without leaving a trail a blind man could follow.

A hundred yards in, Billie paused, waiting for me to catch up. She took a moment to adjust her pumps, emptying them of invading needles. Running in them must have been hell, and I again regretted not advising bringing sturdier shoes.

'Everything OK?' I asked.

'Apart from being hunted through the woods by a bunch of hired killers, you mean?' She smiled to show she wasn't over-troubled by the notion. But I noted that the smile wouldn't hold. She grew tight-lipped, less excitable than before. I knew that the initial flush of adrenalin would dissipate and with it she'd feel drained. Through the darkness I could barely make out a rocky feature in the terrain, but it was there. Billie followed my gaze, and without comment headed for it. It angled back towards the road and a crest in the hill, but it was better than working our way through the deep drifts of fir needles.

A car shot up the trail, going too fast for the conditions, but the driver probably didn't care about the depreciation of the vehicle he was driving. As it moved its headlights danced up and down among the trees. By now our pursuers had probably guessed we'd gone into the woods and were more concerned with cutting off our progress than anything. Lower on the slope a third vehicle joined the search, coming at a slower pace. It stopped and I heard the clunk-clunk of opening and closing doors. I could neither see nor hear the helicopter. I didn't believe it had left the area, only that it had continued its search along the other trail towards the cabin.

We were surrounded on three sides, with only the option left to us of heading east into the wild mountains. Had I been alone I would have taken it, but not when accompanied by Billie. My order of play would be to outdistance the noose our hunters were attempting to tighten, flank them and then take the fight back to them from an unexpected direction. But with Billie along, I couldn't do that. It would mean abandoning her while I went off to play seek and destroy, and I didn't trust that she'd stay safely hidden for long enough: not while they had greater numbers and an eye in the sky. Plus, I'd no clue about the terrain. For all I knew we could run into a bottle-necked canyon, or to the lip of a precipice, and then where could we go? At the moment our best allies were the darkness and stealth. Stay quiet, stay down, and with luck we'd foil our pursuers.

Arriving at the outcrop of earth, I found it scattered with large boulders. Fallen twigs and needles drifted at their bases but there was no other cover. We could set our backs to the larger boulders, hidden from one side, but it wouldn't put off a determined hunter who'd make a point of checking behind the rocks. Still, they offered momentary respite. I gestured at a huge boulder and Billie headed for it. She leaned against its mossy side while she again emptied her shoes of needles. Without asking I delved in her bag, and pulled out two T-shirts she'd packed. While she eyed me quizzically I knotted each at their necks, then crouched down, and pulled one after the other over her feet. I then bunched and tied off the tops around her ankles. She looked comical in her impromptu footwear, but it stopped her shoes being invaded at every step. 'Looks weird,' I whispered, 'but they'll help.'

I didn't expect that we could travel far before the cloth became worn and shredded, but then again I didn't think we'd be going much further in the meantime.

'We have to find somewhere to hide until they go past.'

'Then what?' Billie asked.

'We backtrack, try to avoid them until they give up.'

'What if they don't give up?'

'They will. If we manage to evade them they'll have no idea where we are and assume we've made it back to a road. If we stay hidden long enough they'll abandon the search here and start looking further afield. Hopefully by then we'll have found somewhere where we can get a signal and phone for help. If I can get hold of Rink I can organise extraction.'

Nearby was a storm-toppled tree. The trunk had snapped midway, and the upper half of the tree had fallen, and become wedged among its neighbours. The branches hung low to the ground; a pile of broken limbs and twigs lay scattered beneath. 'Over there,' I urged Billie.

The forest floor undulated like a series of waves on a balmy sea, and there was a natural depression beneath the fallen tree. I pulled aside some of the branches and Billie settled down in the hollow. I unhitched the bags off my shoulder and laid them next to her, then quickly rearranged the branches so that they were piled around her, concealing her from those coming up the trail. I moved to one side, crouching alongside an upright tree trunk, and took out my SIG just as the third vehicle came into view. I could tell from the shape that it was a large GMC Suburban, and through the backwash of its lights could see three figures inside. One of them was scanning the area with night vision binoculars.

I warned Billie to stay low and silent, and promised that I would protect her.

Everything went to hell in seconds.

When the shooter broke cover and we exchanged rounds, there was a small part of me that expected him to be one of the Jaeger brothers. Because he wasn't wearing spectacles, I hoped it was the other one referred to as Danny. But it was neither. It was some guy I'd never seen before. That's the way of many soldiers' deaths: they don't recognise the stranger behind the bullet that ends their life. I wondered briefly if he thought the same about me, but probably not.

He fell.

I fell too.

When I came round briefly I didn't give him a second's notice, but took it that he was lying dead or wounded beyond where Billie crouched over me with my knife. I lay on my back, peering up at her as she spat and screamed like a bobcat, cutting wildly at the air.

'I . . . I'm done,' I told her. 'Get away before the others come.'

Of course it was already too late for that. Figures stood around us, pitiless men with guns in their hands.

Billie shrieked savagely, launching herself at them as if thinking she could cut a way through them.

One of them grabbed Billie by an elbow and yanked the knife away. She struggled to break loose of his hold and was struck in the face for her trouble. As she slumped, I tried to struggle up, but I wasn't going anywhere. My extremities were numb. I felt crushed by an immense weight. Only my eyelids had the ability to move, but even that strength was fading.

Someone crouched, roughly patting me down.

'So who the hell is this guy?' someone asked.

'Doesn't matter now,' said another. 'Finish him, Danny.'

Those words sealed my fate. Death was coming and I tried to face it with resolution, but I could barely keep my eyes open.

A gun barrel caught a beam of moonlight, and it was enough to focus on.

A second flash blinded me.

Then there was nothing.

You don't hear the bullet that kills you.

18

I wasn't dead.

Part of me wished that I were because the pain was incredible, and I longed for release from it. It came in pulsing waves that wouldn't diminish, and the agony went on for an eternity. That, at least, was how it seemed. I can't be sure if it was hours or simply minutes, but after waking that next time and trying to roll over on to my belly, the effort only helped intensify the pain to a point where I felt as if molten magma was boiling from my every orifice. Scarlet flashes across my vision grew white, then blinked off and I knew nothing. When I next returned to some sort of cognisance I found myself at the edge of the muddy track, a dozen yards from where I'd fallen. I'd no recollection of having crawled there, but must have, and the trail of blood spatters and smears on the forest floor told that it had been a winding route. I was upright. No, on second thoughts I was only partly upright. My back was supported by a mossy rock, my legs splayed in an ungainly manner on the muddy verge, my boot heels digging into the hardpack of the trail.

The mist of last night was back, and my world was one that faded within a hundred yards on all sides. It was silvery grey. But a roseate glow overhead hinted that the sun was up. I'd no idea how long ago the sun had risen, but it can't have been long because it hadn't begun to burn off the mist or dew that clung to the grass my palms were pressed into. My arms propped me, but there was little feeling in them beyond pain. Blinking, I watched a trickle of blood run out of my left cuff and across the back of my hand. It was only one trickle of many that had previously dried on my hand. Hopefully the bleeding in my upper chest had stopped, and the movements I'd made on waking had only broken the scabby coagulation. I tried to lift my hands to check the wound, but couldn't without swaying and threatening to fall on my side. I sat there, taking in air, fighting the stabbing ache throughout my entire body.

I must have passed out again, because when next I eased open my eyelids it was nearing noon. The mist had disappeared, and the sun was a ball of fire hovering over the down slope to my left. It wasn't hot, but it seared my eyes when I tilted my head up. The tickling of its rays wasn't what roused me, but the distant sound of an engine. I wondered if somehow the Jaegers had realised that I'd beaten the odds and were on their way back to finish the job. In my current state they wouldn't have to try very hard.

I craned round as far as the pain would allow. There was no sign of the man I'd shot, so either he'd survived or his friends had taken him with them when they left. I decided it would be the latter because I was positive at least one of my bullets had hit his head. Then again . . .

I felt for the gun wound in my own skull.

There was no bullet hole, no gaping wound through which I could feel the mushy pulp that was left of my brain, just a sore spot and a large knot of swollen tissue. So I hadn't been shot in the head at the end? Thinking my wounds mortal, the gunman had used the butt of his weapon to rap me unconscious. I doubted it had been an act of mercy, but an oversight. I was alive, but there were no guarantees things would stay that way for long.

Peering down the trail, I expected to see a bottle-green van appear from the dappled shadows. It didn't, but then neither did any other vehicle. Something was there though, somewhere down the hill beyond where the road forked. Police perhaps, though I doubted it. My hope was that it was Rink, that somehow – beating odds in the billions – he'd managed to follow my trail from Baker's Hole to this muddy hole in the ground I currently sat in. Of course it couldn't be Rink: that was just my delirium offering false hope. The engine noise sounded as if it was getting closer, but who knew? The acoustics of the mountains had already proven unreliable, so it could be the last of Billie's hunting party moving away.

Billie!

Hell, I hadn't given the woman much thought throughout my misery of the last few hours.

Where was she?

I looked around, and being unable to find her didn't exactly make me feel much better. If I had discovered her lying close by she'd be dead, and that would be bad. But the alternative was that she'd been taken and God alone knew what she'd have to go through before she was finally put to death. Of that there was no doubt. The Jaegers, or those they worked for, would torture answers from her, and once they'd learned what they wanted then there would be only one outcome. They couldn't release her; she'd be buried in an unmarked grave in some desolate place.

Until then I'd been complacent about my lot. I'd sat, feeling the pain and the leaking blood, and it hadn't been enough to get me moving. But now that I had someone else to focus on I struggled to get to my feet.

I didn't make it

I ended up on my face in the road, and lay groaning at my inability to put one foot in front of the other.

'*Get up, goddamnit!*' The voice was Rink's but it was only in my head. '*Quit now and you die. You ready to die?*'

If the question had been posed earlier, I wouldn't have cared. I would have welcomed relief from the pain. But now I railed against death. It was more like frustration. I pawed at the dirt, tried to get my knees under me, and ended up rolling on my side. I blinked up at a patch of sky overhead. It was a narrow strip between the treetops.

'*I never took you for a quitter, Hunter.*' Rink's voice again.

'I'm not quitting. I just need to gather my strength.' I have no idea if I spoke out loud, or that I merely answered the imaginary berating of my friend.

'*The longer you lie there, the weaker you'll get. Now get your butt in gear, soldier. Move, see to your wounds, or you'll bleed out like a goddamn frog on a gig.*'

'I'm up, I'm up, stop going on like an old woman.' Surprisingly I had made it to my knees. I leaned forward, palms flat on the earth: the perfect position for purging my guts. It was many hours since I'd gorged myself on Billie's homemade stew, but you wouldn't think it. Perhaps through the chase and subsequent fight, followed by my hours of inactivity, my digestive system hadn't been working effectively, because I vomited a huge puddle of meat and vegetables that looked little different to when I'd spooned them down. It was unpleasant, but I felt a small sense of relief. There was no blood in the sick. I'd probably escaped large-scale internal damage. I was sick a second time, and this time it was mainly liquid, which was rapidly replaced by stringy drools of bile. My head banged repeatedly, as if it was a tambourine being beaten on by an over-zealous Hari Krishna. I wiped my mouth on the back of my jacket sleeve, then lifted tremulous fingers to the lump on my head. I hadn't been shot, but the whack of the gun butt had come close to cracking my skull.

'You've survived worse injuries. Get up, lame ass.'

I had been hurt worse in the past. I'd been shot before on a few occasions, one time to the point where I would have died if a colleague hadn't dragged me out of the sniper's sights and into the hands of the waiting medics. That time the bullet had gone right through my chest and out of my back, and there was no way I would have lived if not for the emergency surgery, blood transfusions and weeks in a hospital bed. Right there on the muddy trail there were no colleagues to drag me out of harm's way, or to give even the most rudimentary first aid. If I wanted to live, I had to save myself.

The head wound could wait.

So could the one in my gut, and the nick on my shoulder. They didn't trouble me the way the one in my chest did. The antiballistic vest I was wearing had stopped the bullet from entering my gut. The Kevlar had dispersed some of the kinetic force, but it still felt as if I'd been kicked in the belly by a horse due to the hydrostatic shock: if I lived, the next few days were going to be sore ones. I imagined that already I was sporting a black and blue bruise that would make even the slightest movement painful. I wasn't bleeding into my stomach, and until I took a leak I wouldn't know if the impact of the round had caused damage to my liver. I doubted it, because if I'd been bleeding internally I wouldn't have wakened from my swoon, I'd have continued to fade and fallen into a coma.

Crawling to the edge of the road I found the same mossy boulder I'd woken against, but this time parked my butt on top of it. My left arm was numb, but it still had movement. I hooked my jacket collar, helping while I unzipped the front with my right. It hurt like hell to shrug the jacket off my left shoulder, but I persevered. Rink's voice had faded, but had been replaced by my own self-berating. Jamming my jaw to my collarbone I could see the mess of blood on my shirt.

Enough had leaked from me that it had darkened the vest in a wide ring extending from under my left armpit almost to my sternum. Above and to the left of my heart, there was a hole in the bulletproof vest – which in this case was somewhat of an oxymoron – and some of the internal padding had puffed out around the edge. It was wet with blood, but I caught a glint of a second colour and was happy to note that it was the copper alloy base of a jacketed round. The vest hadn't saved me from injury, but had prevented full penetration of the bullet into my torso. The rear end of the bullet was wedged in the vest, and only a couple of millimetres of the tip must have made its way through to my flesh. Nevertheless, it still didn't mean that I hadn't suffered serious damage. If the bullet had fragmented, parts of the projectile could have penetrated deeper, spinning and tumbling and causing untold damage to soft tissue, bone and organs alike. But I thought that this bullet was a regular lead projectile jacketed in copper, and not an armour piercer containing tungsten or steel. It tells you something about the man when he's happy that he has been shot with a full metal jacket round and not a high-density, soft nose or hollow point – any of those would have gone right through the vest and killed me, no question.

I struggled with the Velcro straps and unhitched the vest. It sucked off me, the wetness of my bodily fluids causing a vacuum. I swear I felt the tip of the bullet extracting from my flesh, and it was with mixed feelings. The relief was huge, but the pain was enormous. I almost blacked out again. Blood began to pulse anew. My shirt was sopping, and I didn't bother pulling it off, just got my fingers in the bullet hole and yanked it apart. There was a shallow depression in my left pectoral muscle that looked far too small to have leaked all of that blood, but I knew that once I'd extracted the bullet the edges of the wound had puckered in on themselves, partly sealing it again. The flesh was sore and tender a good hand's span all around it, and there was deeper pain in my ribs and even in my left lung when I concentrated on breathing. Thankfully the wound wasn't mortal, the way I'd feared. I was lucky: those men that had taken Billie hadn't realised I was wearing a vest. They just saw the hole in my jacket, the blood and likely the delirium in my face and decided I'd minutes to live at most. Their mistake. I was happy to note I wasn't the only one to have made poor decisions last night.

Knowing that your next move won't be your last has a placebo effect. Strength I hadn't been aware of previously began to reach my hands. My numb legs began twitching in their urgency to get up and move. Not a bad idea, considering the engine noise had grown louder and was definitely approaching this time. Before I could do that I had to do something about the wound. If it opened again and I began bleeding then I'd be face-planting the ground again in no time. Our bags were gone, taken along with Billie and the guy I'd shot. I scratched through my jacket pockets but they'd been rifled, my wallet stolen. My outer clothing was filthy with mud and forest litter, none of it clean enough for a dressing. My shirt was saturated with blood. I pulled off my jacket, and checked the inner lining at the back. It was clean. My knife had been taken, so it was down to the strength of my fingers alone to rip the lining out. Ordinarily it would have been a task of seconds, but my limbs were still weak and the tough lining almost beat me. I had to nip the lining with my teeth – a painful job carrying a head wound – to get a hole opened up then insert my right fingers, stand on the sleeve with one foot and then throw myself backwards. A long strip of clean cloth came away. Once I'd got it going the rest ripped away with less effort. I tore off a clump of smaller strips and used them to dab away the blood from the chest wound. Once that was done, I folded a larger strip and pressed it over the bullet hole. Then came the difficult part. It took some contorting of my body, and much gritting of teeth to hold back the curses, but I managed to loop the impromptu bandage around my shoulder, back under my armpit and tie it off over the wadded cloth. With another rag I cleaned the blood from my shoulder wound, and found it was little more than a graze. I left that wound uncovered. It wasn't ideal, but it was all I had.

The engine noise was nearby, but there was still no sign of a vehicle. The driver had gone up the other trail. Now that I was thinking clearer, I'd discarded the idea that the car belonged to either the Jaegers or Rink; it simply had to belong to someone else, hunters or perhaps someone out for a hike in the hills. I doubted those in the vehicle were enemies, and more likely people who could help, but I couldn't take that chance. Leaving the vest unfastened down my left side in order to ease my breathing, I shrugged back into my jacket. Suffering from shock was still a firm possibility, and I needed the extra layer of clothing to keep warm, despite the sun being up now. I needed to replace fluids, too. Bleeding out, purging my stomach, all had conspired to dehydrate me, and helped weaken me, not to mention exacerbate my headache.

I wondered how far the people in the car would travel. Perhaps they were going to the cabin – which couldn't be too far away now – and there I'd get a chance at taking their vehicle, or at least items that I could use while I trekked out of the hills to the main road. I was uncomfortable at the idea of stealing, but when it was a case of needs must, then I'd just have to put my morals on a back burner. I had to make a decision: did I backtrack down the road, find the fork and the second route to the cabin, or did I forge through the woods to the second road? The second route was much shorter, but the going tougher in my present condition.

In the end, the decision was taken from me.

Before I could strike out in either direction, a figure materialised from out of the dappled shadows below me and stood eyeing me, as tense as a wild animal caught in the open. The person lifted something to his face, and I knew he was calling in backup. The engine noise halted. In seconds it roared again and I realised the driver was heading at speed to join the searcher on foot.

I looked for a weapon.

The mossy boulder was heavier than I was; I had my choice of small pebbles or rotted twigs.

My run of bad luck didn't appear to be getting any better.

19

The figure waited until the car was making its way up the trail towards us before taking a tentative step forward. I didn't run or try to hide. There was no point. Even if the newcomers were dangerous I'd have simply looked a fool trying to do so, so it was better that I stay put, conserve what energy I had left and wait for a more opportune moment to act. But it wasn't necessary, because with that one step the figure emerged from a deep pool of shadow and I instantly recognised his red coat. It was Adam, younger of the two private investigators I'd met the previous day. The SUV approaching was Adam's Escalade, and it stood to reason that the one driving it was his older partner, Noah Kirk. They'd had the presence of mind to bring the SUV as opposed to Noah's saloon with the sticky brakes, so maybe they weren't as inept as I'd first thought.

We'd parted on decent enough terms, and I thought I'd been forgiven for my strong-arm approach with them when first we'd met – even Noah had shrugged his shoulders and rubbed at his head when I apologised for clubbing him unconscious – so hopefully we could remain on good terms now. You never could tell. I'd taken it as fact that they would hang around the farm because they still had a job to do, but I wondered if they'd been got to by the Jaegers and if they were here to finish off what the Procrylon team hadn't. I didn't believe either man had it in them, even if it was only to clean up a crime scene and lose a corpse deeper in the woods. Still, I wanted to feel them out before fully relaxing my guard.

Noah pulled the Escalade alongside Adam and they conversed through the window. Adam turned and peered at me. I stood facing them, attempting to look as if I wasn't ready to drop. Trying to look tough. Adam raised an open palm to me. I lifted my chin, inviting them to come forward. The motion sent pain stabbing from my skull down the side of my neck into my chest wound. Static prickled along my hairline, and sweat flooded my face.

Noah drove the SUV slowly, following Adam as he approached on foot. The younger man could tell that I was hurt, his mouth hanging open at my dishevelled appearance. It hadn't occurred to me that the blood on my clothing and hands was also all over my face.

'What the hell happened?' Adam croaked as he stood ten feet distant, as if afraid to approach in case my condition was catching. He glanced at Noah, and I followed his gaze. The older guy looked equally shocked. Both stared back at me.

'It's not as bad as it looks,' I lied.

'You could have fooled me!'

I didn't reply to Adam. I still wasn't sure about their motive for trailing me to the mountains.

The door clunked as Noah got out of the SUV. He didn't move further, just stood there with one hand resting on the open door. I noticed that he'd taken my advice and strapped two fingers together. 'Man, you're a mess. How the hell are you still standing?'

I shrugged off his concern, but even that small action almost sent me reeling. I squeezed my hands into fists, concentrating on pushing back the blackness edging my vision. 'Never mind that. How'd you find me?'

Noah and Adam shared a glance, and Noah elected to tell the truth. 'We followed you here.'

'Last night?'

'Yeah. Last night.' Noah's mouth formed a tight grimace. He probably expected to be asked why the fuck they hadn't come to help sooner.

'You saw the guys chasing me and Billie, then?'

'We saw the first guy follow you from the farm.' Again Noah elected to take things no further.

'You watched what happened to him?' I eyed them both steadily in turn.

'We were back a-ways,' Adam said, 'so we didn't see what happened. We only got close enough to see after his car went down in the canyon.'

'I didn't hear you following us,' I said, thinking out loud.

'We parked out of sight in the mist and crept in,' Adam admitted. 'By then that guy's car had gone off the road and we saw you checking it out.'

So they'd hadn't actually witnessed our fight, my accidental killing of the man and then sending his car off the road, only the aftermath; and they'd misread it. That suited me. As far as they knew the guy had driven off the road in the mist. Either that or they weren't stupid enough to admit what they'd actually witnessed for fear I turned on them. If I was the type to do away with them to cover up my crime, there would have been little I could have done then, but I chose to make them no wiser. 'He tried to force us to stop; he wanted to take Billie.'

'We figured as much,' Noah said.

It went without saying that Noah and Adam had witnessed the team arrive at the farm earlier, the only reason they were in position to follow the guy who'd subsequently chased me and Billie. They must have set up surveillance on the SUV, watched it follow Billie and me and slipped in covertly on its tail. They must then have followed us to this part of the forest, only to be overtaken by those pursuing us.

It was as if Noah read my mind.

'We'd just pulled off the road when we saw that green panel van and a couple more SUVs converge on the trail at the bottom of the mountain. We kept our heads down, and looking at you it's probably best we did.'

He was right. If they'd shown themselves then the Procrylon team would have assumed they were assisting us and taken them out of the picture. I was sure that the Jaegers and their pals wouldn't have left any witnesses alive: considering what they planned for Billie.

'We were lucky not to be spotted by the dudes in the helo,' Adam put in. 'It buzzed us a couple times but it was too dark for them to spot us among the trees.'

'Looks like you weren't as lucky,' Noah put in. Finally he'd stepped away from the car, not too close, but near enough that he could see me clearly. 'Shit, man! You've been shot!'

Dumbly I followed his gaze to the bloody hole in my jacket. I poked a finger at it, but was careful to avoid pressing on the bandage beneath. 'More than once,' I said.

My admission was enough to galvanise them. They came towards me. Maybe it was simply mawkishness and they wanted a closer look at my injuries, or maybe they genuinely wanted to help. I held out a bloody palm to slow them down. There was something troubling me, and I still wasn't certain that Noah and Adam could be trusted. 'You say that you weren't spotted, and yet those bastards knew where me and Billie had gone . . .'

'What?' Noah said, offended by my unspoken suggestion. 'You think we told those guys where you were?'

Adam made a harsh sound in the back of his throat in support of his pal.

'How else could they have found us so quickly?'

'Hell, it doesn't take too much figuring out. It's not as if there are that many turn-offs from the highway between Baker's Hole and Hope End. Anybody with a map could have plotted where you'd got to in no time.' Previously Noah had looked ready to offer a steadying hand, but now he shoved his hands in his coat pockets.

'I just bet you were carrying a cell phone,' Adam put in. 'Guys who can source a helicopter and half a dozen vehicles in such short time can probably trace a cell phone signal.'

'No signal,' I pointed out, with a nod to the surrounding hills.

'Doesn't mean a thing,' Adam argued. 'The CIA can trace a signal even when your cell's turned off. As long as the battery and the SIM card are in the phone it can be located easily enough.'

He wasn't far wrong, but I didn't believe that was how the Jaegers had tracked us down so quickly.

Noah shook his head, as if he was thinking the same way. But then he squinted, and thumbed over his shoulder back down the trail. 'That's your rental stuck in the mud back there, right?'

'Yeah.' No point lying, not when they'd already followed the car here.

'I just bet it has an anti-theft device installed, some kind of transponder so that it can be located if stolen.' Noah gave a self-satisfied smile at the frown I wore. 'I guess that before that guy went off the road, he gave them your licence number, and they discovered it was a rental vehicle. Like Adam said, they're resourceful. Some hacker on their payroll probably got into the system and was able to lock on to the car's beacon.'

Noah had just won some respect, and I wasn't grudging about it. 'I hadn't thought of that.'

'You just thought the worst of us, even after we've risked our asses to come help you?'

'Forgive me,' I said, 'getting shot makes me grumpy.'

Adam snorted out a laugh. 'I wouldn't say you've been a barrel of laughs since we met you.'

I tried to smile at his wit, but couldn't. But maybe my attempt was enough for them because they came forward, Adam supporting my left elbow before I shrugged him off. 'That's the bad side,' I told him. Then to show my appreciation of his help I offered him my right elbow and he hooked it around his shoulder. They assisted me to their car, and good job that they did because I'm unsure if I'd have made it under my own steam. 'Do you have anything to drink? Water preferably.'

'Coffee,' Noah offered. 'Got a couple flasks of the stuff when I was in Hill End last night. Might not be hot now, but it'll still help warm you through.'

I was more concerned with rehydrating. Ordinarily caffeine was a diuretic, but there was plenty research that said the liquid content to caffeine ratio made a difference, and there was enough fluid to counteract any adverse effects in your normal cup of coffee. Plus, I liked coffee. 'Great,' I said. 'You got any sugar?'

Noah looked slightly abashed, but not because he had a sweet tooth. He owned up to a forgivable crime. 'I almost emptied the coffee shop of their sugar sachets. That boy over there can't get enough of the stuff. I've seen him suck the stuff direct from the packet.'

'Got to keep my energy up,' Adam said. 'It's cold and damp out in those woods.'

'I told him he's going to get diabetes if he's not careful,' Noah went on, and Adam muttered in denial, something about being healthy as a horse. 'Probably why I have to keep feeding you goddamn sugar cubes.'

It was all small talk as they loaded me in the back seat of Adam's Escalade. The pain in my chest was tremendous, but I diverted my attention to checking for the promised flasks of coffee. I ordinarily drank it black, with nothing. The sugar would help stave off the effects of shock, and maybe give me some of that energy that Adam talked about.

'You should lie down,' Adam said.

'Don't fuss over the man,' Noah scolded him. 'He knows where he's most comfortable.'

Sitting upright wasn't a matter of comfort for me, but an attempt at stopping any further bleeding. If I fell asleep, my wound opening while I slumbered, I'd likely bleed out long before I reached the kind of medical assistance I needed. Noah mentioned something about a doctor's surgery in Hill End.

'No doctors,' I said. 'Take me back to Billie's place.'

'You need a doctor,' Noah argued. 'In fact, we should take you somewhere with an ER, let alone a small town practice. You need that wound treated, and in case you need surgery . . .'

'It's not as bad as it looks,' I reiterated.

'Your head looks like it was hit by a mallet,' Adam said as he clambered in the driving position. 'What if you've a fractured skull?'

'I haven't. I wouldn't have lasted this long if there was any major damage.' Even to my own ears I didn't sound convincing. 'Look, guys, if you want to help, just take me to Billie's; there's stuff there that I can use.'

Noah gave up arguing, nodding at Adam to do as I asked, while he clambered in the front passenger seat. He passed back a thermos flask of coffee after twisting off the lid. I noted that though his first two fingers were strapped – legacy of me dislocating his index finger that time – but he seemed untroubled by pain. 'Cup?' he asked, offering the plastic cap.

'I'm fine with just the flask.' I only had one good hand at that moment, and would need Noah to pour for me if I elected to use the cup. I put the flask to my mouth and drank directly from it. The heat had gone out of the brew as Noah had warned, but it was still warm and went down easily. After being sick my throat was raw, but it was a mild sting at most, and getting the coffee down me far outweighed any discomfort. I barely tasted it. By the time we came to my abandoned rental car, and Adam negotiated a way past it with two wheels on the embankment on the opposite side of the road, I'd finished the first flask. I handed it to Noah, who offered the second thermos. 'Not just now,' I said. If I drank another litre on top of the first I'd probably be throwing my guts up again in no time. 'Some of that sugar wouldn't go amiss, though.'

'You should have dissolved it in the coffee, it would have got into your system faster,' Noah said as he hunted for the stash of stolen sachets.

'I'll do that with the next flask, but that isn't really why I want sugar.' Without further explanation, I shucked out of my right jacket sleeve and worked it off round my back, before easing out of the left sleeve. I'd left the bulletproof vest unfastened, so could still get at the impromptu bandage beneath my torn shirt. It was sodden with blood. 'Rip a good handful of those packets open, will you, and pass them back to me?'

Adam glanced frequently in the rear-view mirror, intrigued by what I planned. Noah could watch, but I wished the driver would keep his eyes on the road. 'Don't go running us off the trail, Adam,' I warned.

'What are you doing?' he asked, as I dragged aside the bloody bandage and disclosed the wound. I glanced in the mirror and watched his eyes pinch. He hissed in sympathy.

'Believe it or not,' I said, accepting some opened sachets from Noah, 'but sugar is one of the oldest antiseptics known to man. Honey's better, but I guess you didn't think to grab a jar when you were in Hill End, eh, Noah?'

I wasn't making stuff up. Sugar and honey had been employed as an effective antiseptic for thousands of years, and were even now endorsed by modern doctors and veterinarians to treat serious injuries where there was significant skin loss, or flesh and tendon damage, when pharmaceutical antiseptics had failed. The simple natural remedy could even relieve pain and help seal the wound, through the process of dehydration of the surrounding tissue. As a soldier I'd used sugar on my wounds in the past.

'Did you get the bullet out?' Noah asked.

'Yeah,' I said, 'and thankfully it was in one piece. No fragmentation, but that's not the only worry. Tiny bits of my clothing will have been pushed into my flesh when the bullet hit. They're too small to see, but they're there, and they can kill me if I don't get this clean. If I don't disinfect the wound now the fragments of cloth will cause infection and the wound will be running with pus in no time.'

'Jesus, spare me the gory details, will ya?' To give him his due, Noah didn't turn away and continued to tear open and pass back packets of sugar when I needed them. Adam on the other hand had seen enough. He kept his eyes on the road while I poured granules into the open wound until I had a sticky mound in place. Ideally I required a fresh bandage, clean gauze and such, but things would do for now. We'd be back at the farm soon enough. There I could better tend my wounds, and begin organising how I was going to get Billie back.

Despite needing to stave off my own death, Billie's liberation from her captors took priority.

20

We took extra care on our approach to the farm. Procrylon wanted Richard Womack, and taking Billie was only a side-project of their plan to capture him. It made sense that they would send someone back to guard the farm in case Richard turned up in the meantime. Yet it seemed that we'd beaten them to the idea, as we didn't spot anyone in hiding, and a quick scout of the farm showed no sign of trespassers. Noah and Adam had become my allies, and they moved without question for the house with me. The door was still locked, the way that Billie had left it.

'How do we get inside?' Adam wondered.

'How do you think?' I mimed kicking the door open.

'Won't Billie be pissed at us for breaking her door?'

I shared an incredulous glance with Noah, before saying, 'Believe me, a broken lock is the least of her worries right now.'

Adam grinned. 'Can I do it? I always wanted to kick open a door.'

God spare us from over-enthusiastic amateurs, I thought. But then I decided, why not? Let the guy have a little fun. I owed him that much. 'Kick it near the lock,' I advised.

Adam sucked in a breath, steadied himself then lifted his heel and rammed it into the door as he let out a Bruce Lee war cry. His screech was curtailed to a muttered curse as he staggered back from the resolute door. 'Hell, I almost put my knee out of joint. This ain't as easy as it looks in the movies.'

Noah shook his head in disbelief. 'Want me to do it?'

'I've got it,' Adam said, his youthful gusto undaunted. This time he stood a little further back, so that when he lifted his knee he could hop in, his entire weight behind the kick. The lock popped and the door flew inwards. 'See, I must've loosened it the first time,' Adam crowed.

Noah grunted something at Adam, but I didn't hear what he said. I was too busy checking for any sign we'd been heard or observed. Distantly birds broke from the trees, but that was in reaction to the sudden bangs, not because they'd been startled by anyone lurking in the treeline. 'One of you should move the Escalade,' I said. 'Get it out of sight otherwise they'll know someone's here.'

Adam stood with his hands fisted at his hips, a Superman pose. Maybe he was waiting for praise for kicking the door open; all he got was a curt order from Noah to move his ass, and he sulked off to shift the SUV out of sight. Noah offered me a shrug of shared bemusement.

Moving inside the house, I said, 'I haven't thanked you yet for helping me. I appreciate what you've done, but maybe you should get the kid out of here before those guys come back.'

'Adam isn't a kid, he's twenty-eight.'

'You could've fooled me,' I said.

'For all he comes across as a bit dim, he's a good guy.'

'No argument from me,' I said, making it to the kitchen. I perched on the same chair I'd sat at while eating dinner the evening before.

'What? That he's dim or a good guy?'

I only offered a smile, and Noah laughed into his chest.

Taking off my jacket, I put it aside. Then began unfastening the bulletproof vest.

'You want me to help with that?' Noah came forward without waiting, and helped lift it from me. Again it pulled and sucked at my wet shirt, and his assistance was a great help. While Noah put the vest to one side I conceded that it had been a good idea wearing it after all, despite only doing so to make a good impression on Billie: it had definitely saved my life. Noah crouched and inspected the vest.

'You were hit a few times, huh? Lucky that one to the gut didn't get through or I doubt we'd have found you alive and well back in the woods.'

'I'd have died for sure,' I agreed as I pulled off the remains of my T-shirt. The bandage was dark with blood, but I was pleased to note there were no fresh rivulets of red tracking down my body. The smaller cut on my shoulder had congealed.

'Who'd have thought a few sachets of sugar were worth their weight in gold?' Noah moved to the kitchen sink, turning on the taps to get the warm water running. He ducked down to the cupboards beneath and checked for anything useful. 'What do you need?'

'Nothing from under there.' At a push the bottles of bleach could come in handy, but I was hoping Billie had a stocked medicine cabinet in the bathroom. I asked Noah if he'd check, and I directed him to the stairs. 'First door on the left as you go up.'

Without question he complied, and it made me wonder why Noah and Adam were so selfless in offering their help. An insurance company, via their broker Chris Frieden, had employed them to find proof that Richard Womack was alive. Unlike those employed by Procrylon, they had very little stake in the matter. It was as Adam pointed out, they were on a retainer fee, and were paid one way or another. Basically they could hold their hands in the air, back off from the danger and still pick up a wage while 'enjoying a bit of hiking and camping at someone else's expense'. I had to consider the possibility that there was more to their story than they'd let on, but I didn't think so. The reality was that they were decent human beings, and helping came naturally to them. With that in mind I felt guiltier for dislocating his finger and then knocking Noah cold when first we met.

Adam backed in through the front door, while checking his surroundings. 'Maybe one of us should keep a look-out,' he said.

I was sitting bare-chested, covered in blood. Noah was upstairs rooting around Billie's medicine cabinet. Adam got it. 'That'd be me, then,' he sighed.

As he was about to leave I called him.

'Yeah?'

'Thank you,' I said.

He waited a second or two, as if mulling my words over, then a smile broke across his face. 'No problem,' he said. 'Actually it's the most excitement I've had in ages.'

He sloped outside, and I sat a moment longer, shaking my head in bemusement. A moment later my mild amusement faded; I was reminded again of how excitable Billie had grown when she'd first tasted real danger. Had I fallen into a nest of adrenalin junkies? In the past I'd often been asked why I did what I did. Some people assumed I enjoyed the violence, the constant sense of danger, and, yes, the adrenalin buzz, but there was more to it than that. Frankly, I chose to throw myself into the mouth of danger because I couldn't imagine doing anything else. Soldiering had been a part of me for too many years, officially and unofficially, and was both the *what* and *who* of Joe Hunter. In the past few years I'd considered retiring, and had even toyed with the idea of opening a coffee shop of all things. 'Joe's Joe', I would call it. I drank the stuff, a lot, and thought that the profits would be better returning to my own pocket. But I also knew that my business plan was a pipe dream, a non-starter.

Pushing up from the chair, I held on to the back for a moment while I waited for my head to stop spinning. I stumbled over to the sink, where Noah had left the hot water running, and fed in the plug. I leaned on the counter as I watched the water pooling, and thought how perhaps chaining myself to a small business enterprise might be preferable to being shot at on regular occasions. Teasing off the bandage, I found that the sugar had worked wonders. It was a sticky mess, but it had served to make the blood coagulate and the wound didn't look half as bad as before. But as I'd told Noah and Adam, the threat of infection troubled me most. I leaned over the sink to splash water over my chest, allowing the dried blood to sluice away. Some of the mess got on Billie's floor but, again, it was the least of her current problems. Washing away the mound of congealed blood and sugar set my wound to leaking again, but it was barely a trickle so I gritted my teeth, gripped the edges of the wound between my forefinger and thumb and squeezed. The pain wasn't bad, the area around the entry wound having grown numb. I squeezed some more, and exposed the rawness of the pulped flesh below the skin. Then, while I pressured the wound open, I poured more water on it with my other hand. I kept washing until I was fairly confident I'd cleansed the wound of foreign material. I repeated the process with my shoulder wound. By then Noah had come back down from the bathroom.

He was toting a first-aid kit, and a couple of bottles. 'Not much in the kit,' he announced, 'but I found some peroxide.'

'Ideal,' I said as he walked towards me. 'You mind rooting about and seeing if you can find Billie's sewing box?'

Again Noah didn't question my instructions. I finished washing, sluicing my hair and face, using the available bottle of hand wash I found beside the sink to lather into my hair. It smelled of tea tree oil and mint and set my skin tingling. By the time I was done, Noah was back. He'd found a needle and bobbin of black thread somewhere and stood with a sour look on his face as he held it out to me. When she'd last used the sewing kit Billie had left a length of thread in the needle: good job because I doubted either of us could have threaded it with our clumsy fingers. 'I'd offer to help, but I'm too squeamish,' Noah said.

'That's OK, I'd rather do it myself.'

Noah looked relieved. He kicked his heels as I towelled myself dry with a clean dishcloth I'd discovered under the counter.

'Where's Adam?' he wondered.

'Keeping watch.'

He merely nodded.

'Mind if I don't?' he ventured after a pause.

He didn't mean taking a stint on guard.

'If you can help me with the peroxide, you can do what you want after that.'

His face went a few shades paler, but he didn't back off. He began unscrewing the cap off one of the peroxide bottles as I retreated to the living room and lay back on the settee. I laid the cloth across my lower chest to catch most of the peroxide as Noah prepared himself. 'Pour it above the wound so that it flows over it,' I instructed, then did my thing to expose the pulpy flesh inside. I heard Noah fight down his gag reflex, but didn't bear witness because I'd already closed my eyes in anticipation.

I managed not to scream like a girl, but it was tough.

When I reopened my eyes I could barely see for the tears streaming from them. I told myself they watered because of the fumes, not because of the stinging pain. Noah was still alongside me. He'd brought over the first-aid kit. 'Gauze pads and bandages,' he said. 'Also there's some antiseptic cream.'

'Good. I'll have need of them,' I said. 'But first the nasty bit.'

I held out my hand for the threaded needle and Noah finally decided it was time to make himself scarce with a muttered curse. 'Goddamn Rambo.'

The wound would take only a couple of stitches to close it, a small blessing. But it wasn't a task I was looking forward to. I squeezed out some of the antiseptic cream first, and smeared it around the cut. Then I sat poised with the needle. Now or never, I told myself.

But I was wrong.

There was a clatter from outside, and I watched Noah tense. He glanced at me before his gaze returned to the front door where Adam walked inside, kind of puppet-like. His ungainly movement was down to the fact that a huge guy gripped him by the collar of his jacket, and had the tip of a blade poised under his chin.

21

'You took your time getting here,' I said.

Rink still held Adam's collar, but he lowered the sharp tip of his KABAR knife so that it wouldn't open the young man's throat if he slumped. Adam looked ready to collapse, his eyes rolling, tongue flicking at his lips. Rink took in a steady scan of the room, briefly lighting on Noah – discarding him as harmless – before settling on me. 'Looks like I missed a wild party, brother,' he said, eyeing the wound in my chest.

'I got tagged,' I explained, 'but it's not too bad.'

Rink doesn't miss much. 'Where's Billie Womack?'

I shook my head. Rink's eyes grew flint-hard.

'No,' I quickly rectified. 'She's not dead. Not yet.'

Rink lifted Adam another inch on to his toes. 'Who's this dude?'

'You can let him down, Rink. He's a friend.'

Rink again checked out Noah, who had not moved or said a word since watching Rink manhandle Adam inside. 'Take it he is too?'

'Yeah. I owe them both. They probably saved my life.'

Rink set Adam on his feet, and the young man would have fallen if there hadn't been a credenza nearby to lean against. 'Jesus Christ, I thought he was going to cut my head off,' he wheezed.

'I still might,' Rink growled.

Adam almost slumped again.

'He's kidding, don't listen to him,' I said and received a grandiose wink from my big friend as he slid away his knife.

Rink moved further inside the house, and I noticed that Noah and Adam gave him space; small tugs shifting around an ocean liner. They stared at Rink as if he was a force of nature, which wasn't far wrong. Or maybe it was the bright-coloured bowling shirt he wore. It was neon blue with decals in red and green across the chest and back. They were probably trying to figure out how such a giant, wearing colours reminiscent of a firework display, had managed to get so close without Adam spotting him. I wasn't surprised. I often believed that Rink's Japanese heritage came with the ninja gene.

'I take it these are the guys who you spotted watching Billie's shop?' Rink ventured a sniff in Adam's direction, and maybe he is part bloodhound too. 'You were right, brother, that one does smell like mushrooms.'

Adam frowned, took an indiscreet sniff of his own armpit.

'Yeah,' I said. 'These are the guys. We had our wires crossed at first, but things have untangled nicely. Noah, Adam, meet my friend, Rink.'

They nodded in greeting, but still looked wary.

'Relax, boys, I ain't gonna eat ya,' Rink drawled as he stood over me. 'Dammit, Hunter, I leave you alone for a coupla days and look at the mess you've gotten yourself in.'

'Stop moaning and give me a hand here, will you?' I offered him the threaded needle. He lifted one eyebrow, turning instead to Adam. 'Hey, kid. Why don'tcha go back outside and keep watch again, huh? And this time, keep your eyes *and* ears open.'

Adam offered no argument and sloped out the door. He was happy to escape for a few minutes, I guessed, giving him an opportunity to regain his composure. I held out the needle to Rink again. 'Want to do the honours?'

'I'd rather stand over here and watch you blubber like a little baby.' He crossed his arms over his expansive chest, offering a sly smile at my misery. Then he shook his head, snapped his fingers. 'Give it here. You never could darn your goddamn socks, let alone stitch your own hide.'

As Rink set to closing my wound, I distracted myself by bringing him up to speed on what had happened through the night. I managed not to cry out, which was a bonus. Noah assisted, handing over clean gauze and bandages, but it was Rink who fixed them. 'You were lucky,' he said as I tested my shoulder for movement.

'Not the way I saw things,' I admitted. 'Everything was going to shit, and fast.'

'That's what happens when you're shackled by rules.'

He was talking about Agent Cooper's instructions.

'Yeah,' I said. 'But it didn't take me long to break them.' I told him about the meathead whose neck I'd broken by accident. I didn't look directly at Noah, but was surreptitiously checking out his response. He hung his head momentarily but that was the extent of his shock. It told me that he, and Adam no doubt, had seen what happened on the mountain road, but had concluded that I was the lesser of two evils they should ally themselves to while chasing Richard Womack. Yes, Noah and Adam thought they could use me, but I didn't hold it against them. There was more than a little selflessness in their willingness to haul me to safety as well. Plus, I was obviously using them too.

Perhaps Noah had been thinking the same thing. 'So where do we all go from here?'

'We bring Billie home,' I said.

'Good plan,' Rink said, and he didn't sound the least sarcastic.

'I need to speak to Brandon Cooper,' I said.

'Yup. That'd be a start. And while you're at it, ask the frog-gigger why he hung you out to fucking dry.'

I already had my suspicions. His claim that the ATF couldn't be seen to be involved in protecting a suspect was bullshit. He'd more or less intimated that there was a mole in his organisation, and it had led to the murder of an undercover agent; putting in another undercover agent would have been a waste of time. But – despite me being his inside man to watch out for Richard Womack – it wasn't as if he was using me as a spy per se. I was supposedly a bodyguard for Billie, and any number of his own team could have performed the same role.

'But first,' Rink went on, 'you need to sleep, eat and pull yourself together.'

'I'm OK.'

'No. You're not. You're ready to drop, and I'd prefer it was on your own terms than me having to pick you up off the floor in the next ten minutes.'

'While I'm sleeping, Billie could be hurting,' I argued.

'Trust me, brother,' Rink said. 'Billie's a civilian. They've had her what, ten hours or more? By now they'll have learned everything they need to know from her. She's either sleeping things off or . . .'

'She's already dead,' I finished for him.

'Not necessarily,' Noah interjected. And he was right.

Rink nodded. 'If they intend using her to draw in her husband, they'll keep her alive. They'll be figuring a way to get their message out. It's not as if they can broadcast the fact they've kidnapped his missus on the TV news channels.'

'If it were you, how would you use her?' Noah wondered.

'I wouldn't,' I said. 'But I get what you mean. I'm not sure. But I'm guessing if Richard used to work for them they had some kind of communication network in place. Maybe they're trusting him to check in on his messages the way he used to.'

Rink grunted in agreement. 'We need Harvey's expertise on this. Joe, brother, go get your head down and leave it to me. I'll wake you as soon as we've got a direction to follow.'

I was loath to give in, but he was correct. Although I'd slept through the night, it hadn't been healthy. I'd passed out from my injuries, and it had done nothing for my fatigue. I required regular sleep. Now that my bullet wounds were cleaned and dressed, and liberally smeared with antiseptic cream I could ignore the dull throb. My head was still thumping from being pistol-whipped, but a handful of the painkillers from Billie's first-aid kit would deaden the pain, and probably put me into a deep sleep. 'The second you get a lead you wake me, OK?'

'Yup, you've got it.'

I knew he was being conservative with the truth, but wouldn't push it. I was dead on my feet and had to rest. Billie would need me firing on all cylinders if I'd any hope of bringing her safely home.

22

I woke on Billie's bed with no recollection of how I'd got there. Last I recalled was bedding down on the settee where I'd dozed last night before trouble came to the farm. At some point Rink, and possibly Noah or Adam, must have got me to my feet and steered me to the bedroom where I'd less chance of being disturbed while they went about their business in the living room. Either the drugs had affected me more than I thought or I'd been semi-delirious from my injuries. It didn't matter which, only that I woke feeling better than I had since the blazing gun battle in the forest. As I shifted there was some mild pain in my wounds, but not enough to keep me on my back much longer. Something else was more apparent than the hurt: I could smell Billie's perfume wafting off the throw and pillows as I adjusted my position. It was an intimate aroma and I was uncomfortable having invaded her private space without invitation.

I sat on the edge of the bed.

A faint qualm moved through my body; a gentle shivering I hoped wasn't the beginnings of a fever. But my flesh was cool and dry to the touch, and the shiver was simply down to the evening chill in the room. I was still wearing my jeans, but was bare-chested save for the bandages. My ripped and soiled Homer Simpson T-shirt had been consigned to the trashcan. I had a spare shirt in my bag, but it had been dumped back in the forest, or taken by those who'd left me for dead. I trusted that Rink had brought fresh clothing with him, and hoped he had something less gaudy than his usual attire. Muted conversation drifted from below, two voices, one of them Rink's Arkansas drawl. He'd have set one of the other guys on sentry duty. I took it there'd been no trouble while I slept. That thought made me wonder what time it was. The light beyond the drapes was fading and I'd already subliminally deduced it was evening due to the chill in the air. An alarm clock sat on a bedside cabinet, but apparently there'd been a power cut at some point because the LEDs flashed and said it was 2:17 a.m. I glanced around looking for a more reliable wind-up clock, but my gaze caught on something else. On the opposite wall was one of Billie's paintings. I recognised the style from her works of art displayed at her boutique in Hill End. I also recognised the landscape depicted in the painting as being the southern shore of Baker's Hole and the hills beyond. An indistinct figure in red stood beneath the trees at the lakeside. The dash of vibrant colour among the other muted shades held my gaze, and my thoughts, for a long time.

Rink came in the room, and I realised I'd been lost so far in thought that I hadn't heard him ascend the stairs. If he meant to be silent he would have been, but not under those circumstances. 'What you doing sitting there like a toad on a lump of driftwood?' he asked. 'I heard you up and about minutes ago.'

'Just gathering myself.' I indicated my state of semi-undress. 'Do you have anything I can put on?'

'Hell, you expect me to give you the shirt off my back?' He was joking, but that was his way.

'No thanks,' I quipped in return. 'I'd rather keep with the Tarzan look than be seen in that monstrosity.'

He shook his head in remorse. 'I finally have the opportunity to get you into a splash of colour and all I've spare is a grey undershirt.'

'Suits me fine.'

'It's in the bathroom waiting for you, with some spare socks and underwear. Thought you might want to shower before you present yourself to your adoring public.' He chuckled. 'Don't know what you did but those guys have a serious case of hero worship for you. I had to remind them that *actually* you got your ass kicked, so they should be lavishing all their adoration on someone else more deserving.' He slapped his own chest for emphasis.

'Arsehole,' I called him.

He grinned, flashing his pearly white teeth. 'It's nice to have the old Joe Hunter back. Now come on. Hit the shower and we'll see you downstairs. Grub's cooking, mate.' His last was a poor impression of my Brit accent, sounding more like John Lennon, but meant as a piss take.

'Did you get hold of Harvey?'

'He's on the case, buddy. Now come on, get up, lame ass.'

I chuckled at his final command.

'What?' he demanded.

'When I was back in the woods, almost dead, I dreamed about you.'

'Jeez, I don't wanna hear,' he said.

'Don't flatter yourself. It's just you used those same words then: "Get up, lame ass."'

'And they were as pertinent then as they are now. Do as you're told.'

Rink went back downstairs while I eased up from the bed. There was some creaking and groaning and not all of it from the mattress. Testing my footing, I found I could stand still without my brain doing loop-the-loops. I concentrated my vision, again zoning in on the figure in red in the painting. I guessed what it represented to Billie. The undefined, almost spectral figure was her daughter, Nicola. I just wondered what the girl was pointing at between her feet. Probably nothing, I decided, and headed for the shower.

23

Billie had lost all sense of time or place. It didn't help that she'd slept on and off on a number of occasions, with no real idea how long for: each nap could have been hours or indeed only a few seconds. The first she suspected had been much longer because it was an unnatural slumber, induced by a drug administered to her by one of her captors. As she'd been dragged from Joe Hunter's side she'd fought her captors, clawing at the face of one of the rough men. He'd slapped her across the mouth with the back of his hand. Perhaps he thought his disdainful smack would be enough, as if she was the browbeaten wife of a violent husband, but he didn't know Billie Womack. She'd smacked him back, and the full weight of her arm had been behind her clenched fist. The man had sworn savagely, covering his bleeding mouth while his friends laughed at his downfall. When next he struck her it was with his open palm and the force of his slap almost took her off her feet. She was positive he would have kicked her if one of the others hadn't intervened.

'She's no good to us if she can't speak,' a bespectacled man with a poorly set broken nose snapped. 'Hit her again and I'll do the same to you.'

Her attacker was immediately cowed, but he glared at her, his eyes furnace-bright. 'She's a fucking wild animal. Needs putting in her place or she'll cause more trouble.'

'Try to hurt me again and I'll show you how much trouble, you bastard,' Billie snarled.

The man who'd come to her rescue hadn't done so through pity. He grabbed her by her hair, twisting it savagely, and forced her to her knees. 'Hey, Danny, bring me that syringe.'

Another man approached, who looked like a younger version of the one holding her. His face was less beat up, and he didn't require glasses to squint down at her. From his pocket he took out a small leather case, enjoying the fear he induced in her as he took his own goddamn time about unzipping it. When a hypodermic syringe was handed over the first man was more perfunctory about his actions.

'Get that away from me,' Billie shrieked and reared away from the needle.

Her captor yanked back her head, exposing her throat where the collar of her sweatshirt gaped above the bulletproof vest. 'Hold still,' he growled and jabbed the needle into the muscles of her upper shoulder. Whatever kind of drug was administered remained a mystery to her, but its effect was absolute. Within seconds she drifted into a cold darkness where she had no sense of herself, never mind what was going on around her. Cognisance returned in swift snatches, though clouds of dirty cotton wool muffled these moments. She was aware of movement, of the buzzing of voices, the thrum of engines, but nothing made much sense. She thought that perhaps more of the knock-out drug had been administered to keep her docile while she was transported to her prison.

'Prison' was a misnomer. It wasn't a barred cell, dungeon or even fortified room she had finally woken in, but some sort of office cubicle. It was barely fifteen by fifteen feet in size, with blank walls, inexpensive maroon floor covering and a suspended ceiling. She had been positioned so that her back was to the single door. She'd given up craning her neck to check it out. The pale grey walls around her were discoloured where framed pictures or notices had hung for years.

Watermarks on the ceiling extended down the walls. On the thin carpet she could see where a desk had once stood, and there were track marks where some lazy person had wheeled their chair back and forward rather than take the trouble to stand and walk the few feet. She wondered if she was sitting in the same chair that had left the ghosts of its former movements.

She was seated in a standard office chair, brown faux leather over a fake chrome and plastic frame, atop four castor wheels. Her forearms were secured to the armrests with plastic lock-ties that dug into her flesh; her fingertips were numb and she feared that the blood flow to her extremities had been cut off. Her ankles were similarly secured to the pedestal, elevating her heels so that only her toes rested on the floor. Her bullet-proof vest had been removed at some point during her transportation to the room, as had her makeshift booties and pumps, and she sat now in only her sweats, with a thick nylon strap round her ribs secured at the back of the seat by Velcro fasteners. She wasn't totally restricted, and if she wished could probably wheel the chair around the room, but where would she go? She'd also considered tilting forward and getting her feet flat on the ground, but all she'd achieve then was carrying the chair on her back like the shell of some mutant turtle. Then what, try to open the door handle with her teeth? That'd be pointless seeing as she'd heard a key turned in the lock each time her captors came and went from the room.

There were only three options for release. One was that she somehow got loose from her bonds and armed herself with a piece of the broken chair, then fought her way clear next time her door was opened. She didn't fancy her odds with that idea. Once they'd extracted whatever information they were after, her captors could have a change of heart and allow her freedom. But she doubted that would happen: she'd seen their faces and knew what that meant. Lastly, someone could come to her rescue. Except the only person who knew that she'd been taken was lying dead in the forest. She thought of Joe Hunter and how he'd promised to protect her. Ultimately it had been a false promise, just like the ones her husband had always given her. Broken promises, she thought abstractedly, always ended up with dead men in Billie Womack's life.

Other people might grow despondent in the circumstances, but Billie wasn't the type to give in so easily. When she'd lost a child and found the fortitude to carry on, it would take more than abduction by a group of violent thugs to stop her in her tracks. There had to be another way out of her quandary, she just didn't know what it was yet. Trying to escape the room was probably not a good idea. Not when she had no clue where it was situated, or what kind of building surrounded it or how many people stood ready to stop her. Frankly she'd no clue either as to where she was in the country. While drugged she could have been driven for miles, and she also had some dim recollection of being inside the helicopter. She had been flown somewhere, and without knowing the direction, flight time or anything else she couldn't begin to guess. The blank walls of her prison gave no hint; there wasn't even a scrap of paper lying in view with some handy information printed on it. And when her captors had entered the room to check on her, they had refused to answer any of her questions. She was confident she was still in the US, but that was about it. Better that she wait and scheme. Sooner or later her captors would return and take her elsewhere in order to do whatever it was they planned for her. She'd been left in this room for no other reason than she was out of their hair and less of a problem for them. Those holding her were hired guns, simple as, and not really the ones who wished to press her for the whereabouts of Richard. She guessed that someone more important was coming to interrogate her, and her incarceration would end only when they arrived. When it was over with, she chose to think that her freedom would be under her own terms and not at the end of a gun barrel.

24

It was approximately eighteen hours after Billie's abduction before Agent Cooper returned my call. He made a poor attempt at apologising for his tardiness, stating that he hadn't recognised the number on his cell phone.

'That's because mine was taken along with everything else,' I said. Rink had loaned me his phone, and the space to speak in private. I'd walked out on to the porch, leaving him and the others inside. 'This is a friend's cell, store the number.'

'Wait up a minute, I'm not in a good place to speak.' In the background there was chatter, the noise of a busy workspace. Cooper muffled his cell, but I could hear him speaking quickly with someone else, before he came back on. There followed the swift rat-a-tat of his footsteps on hard flooring, and his breath had quickened. 'I'm just finding somewhere more private.'

'How about Hill End?' I suggested.

'I'm in Seattle,' he reminded me.

'So meet me halfway.' I was still at Billie's farm, but we'd planned on moving soon. Not because we feared an attack, but because while we were at the house we were no closer to finding Billie. I needed to get moving or I'd implode.

'I can't, Hunter. I've ongoing investigations here in the city. I told you this was an off-the-books job, I can't just up and leave my post whenever I please.' His voice was at a hush; he obviously hadn't found a private place to speak yet.

'If Richard had showed up you'd be burning rubber to get here,' I said. 'Doesn't an abducted woman merit the same response?'

'What the hell?'

'Billie,' I emphasised. 'She was taken.'

'How the hell did that happen?' He was strident, and it didn't seem to matter if he was overheard now or not.

'Those guys you warned us might be coming? They came.'

'Hold on.' There followed a muffled rattle and thump, then Cooper's voice was clearer. He'd hidden inside an office, or broom closet or whatever. 'OK, I can talk now. Start at the beginning and tell me what happened.'

'I haven't all day,' I said. 'So here's the important stuff: a group of well-armed and equipped men chased us into the woods. They shot me and took Billie. What's more important is how I'm going to get her back.'

'They shot you?'

'I'm good.'

Cooper swore under his breath. Then something dawned on him. 'You didn't kill any of them?'

'Only in self-defence.'

'Oh, Jesus . . .'

'Listen up. I tried the softly-softly approach. They almost killed me and they snatched Billie. Your way didn't work.' I waited a beat. 'Or maybe it did.'

Cooper's silence lasted. Finally he said, 'I don't understand what you mean.'

'Sure you do.'

He pretended to think again. 'Do you want to enlighten me, Hunter? I'm not happy with the way this conversation is heading.'

'You set us up, Cooper. Plain and simple.'

'Set you up? What the hell are you talking about?'

'This is all some elaborate game you're playing, and all you're interested in is winning. The big prize is getting your hands on Richard Womack and you don't care what you have to do as long as you get him.'

'How'd you come up with that absurd idea?'

I snorted in disdain. 'You might think I'm just dumb muscle to be manipulated. I'm not. You set all this up, Cooper. You brought me in to watch over Billie, to win her trust. But there was more to it than that: I'm expendable. If I happened to die in the line of duty, it'd be no big deal. In fact, if I were killed while trying to protect her, Billie would buy into the lie even more. She'd see my death as a huge sacrifice on her behalf, and being the one who'd sent me, her trust in you would strengthen. How's that for starters?'

Cooper laughed. 'Do you know how paranoid you sound?'

'Paranoia keeps me alive,' I replied sharply. 'What about the bulletproof vests?'

'What about them?' Even as his words came out I heard them falter and slow, as he understood where I was heading.

'See, it troubled me how quickly those goons caught up with us. We'd escaped the farm and ended up in the wilderness, but those guys knew exactly where we were. I almost bought into the idea that we might've been tracked because of an anti-theft beacon in my rental car, but it was too long a shot. So I got to thinking: what else could have led them to us? I knew it wasn't our cell phones because of the crappy reception, so it had to be something else. I've just cut an electronic bug out of the vest you supplied me. I bet that there was an identical one in Billie's vest too.'

'And?' Cooper said. 'That means I set you up? Jesus, it's standard practice to insert GPS tracking technology into anti-ballistic vests these days. Most close protection outfits use them. If the unimaginable happens and the client is abducted then their protection team can find them again. Hell, Hunter, I thought you'd have known that.'

'Like I said, I'm not dumb muscle. What's troubling me is how those assholes from Procrylon knew about the trackers, and how they were able to follow them. Are you suggesting they just randomly hit on the correct transmission? Bull shit.'

'It's not an impossible scenario,' Cooper said. 'Maybe they had the technology to sweep for signals and locked on to them. I'm betting there weren't many other transponders working out there in the wilderness.'

'Bollocks. It wasn't random chance. They were coming to snatch a woman from her bed, not take down a fucking terrorist cell. They learned about the GPS trackers after failing to find Billie at the farm, and came back prepared to hunt her down with the correct equipment. How would they even know she was bugged to start with unless someone told them about the vests?'

Cooper was silent again. When he came back on he'd mostly forgiven me for accusing him of being a treacherous bastard. 'I told you I was worried about a mole in the ATF. If you're right and you were tracked because of the beacons in your vests, someone in my agency must have given out the serial numbers. That's a worrying thought.'

'Think about how it feels from my end.'

'Yeah, I can see why you'd be pissed. But Hunter, you have to trust me. It wasn't me, man. I probably owe you my life. Without you my head would've been bashed in and I'm not the type to treat that debt lightly.' He left that thought hanging.

I stood looking out across the lake. The water was stippled by the breeze, and reflected the evening sky, though the first stars were disguised by highlights on the gentle waves. Beyond the lake the hills were a ridge of shadows, but still recognisable as those in the painting I'd recently viewed in Billie's room. Momentarily I found myself looking for the flash of a red coat, listening for the disconsolate moan of a lost girl as she pointed knowingly at something mysterious and intangible. I shook off a cold shiver that ran its finger up my spine. I could do nothing for the girl, and should concentrate on her lost mother.

'OK,' I said. 'So we're still friends. But do we stay that way?'

'What do you mean?'

'I'm going after Billie, but I need your help.'

'If she's been abducted we need to inform the FBI. It's in their jurisdiction now.'

'Not yet,' I said. 'This is on me. And it's on you, even if you aren't the one responsible for setting us up.'

'I can't do it, Hunter. I must follow official procedure—'

'Bringing me in wasn't procedure. Let's not change things now.'

'No way, I'm—'

'Going to listen to me,' I finished for him. 'Here's the thing, Cooper: those guys think I'm dead. They think I'm a rotting corpse out in the woods. They don't know I'm coming after them. Without your help I wouldn't know where to start look-ing, but the thing that led them to Billie can also lead us to her. Understand?'

'You want the codes for tracking her vest?'

'Think you can do that?'

'Easily enough. But what then? I can't sanction a private rescue mission, Hunter.'

'I'm not asking for permission.' I allowed that announce-ment to sink in. 'All I'm asking is that you keep the good guys out of the way, until I give you the green light.'

'What about the mission to find Richard Womack?'

'If Richard's still AWOL then it won't make a difference either way, but those guys didn't take Billie for nothing. I think they know more about his whereabouts than anyone. Maybe they already have him. We won't know until I take a look. If things work out then I get Billie, you get her husband and all that lovely cash you're so concerned about. You can't lose, Cooper. Even if the money has gone up in smoke, and Richard is a corpse, you will have Procrylon by the short and curlies when you show they were responsible for kidnapping Billie Womack. But to do that we need her back alive if she's going to bear witness in court. Let me get her out, my way, without having my hands tied by rules and regulations.'

'You said you weren't seeking my permission.'

'I'm not. I'm going with or without your help. It's just that you can speed the process along.'

I waited. Cooper could easily have told me to kiss his ass, and made an immediate call to the FBI. In fact he could have set the entire law enforcement world in my way if he wished. If he had there would have been nothing I could have done about it, but I knew that he was thinking more about a successful end to his mission than mine. I could hear him breathing, muttering an occasional curse, as he pretended to consider my proposed course of action, but finally he came back on. He told me an email address and log on details. 'That's a blind account. Log on via a proxy server. I'll leave a draft email for you with the details you need. Once you're done, delete the email, do not reply to it.'

'I know the process, don't worry.'

'I can't have this coming back on me.'

'It won't.' I hung up, and immediately thought about calling back. I needed weaponry. My gun had been taken along with everything else. Rink had flown in, and although he'd brought a knife buried in his checked luggage, he hadn't brought a firearm. I should also have asked Cooper about the Jaeger brothers. It paid to know my enemies, but I wasn't at a total loss. I already knew they were dangerous adversaries. And anything that Agent Cooper could say about them, my friend Harvey Lucas could tell me more. I trusted Harvey would also be able to source us the guns we'd need.

I headed inside to muster the gang.

25

The signal beacon from Billie's antiballistic vest emanated from a location very close to Joint Base Lewis-McChord, to the south of Tacoma, Washington. The JBLM was an amalgamated military installation comprising both US Army and Air Force garrisons, the primary training and mobilisation centre west of the Rocky Mountains, and during their time with the Rangers both Rink and Harvey Lucas had been deployed through the army base on a number of occasions, back when it was still called Fort Lewis, and transported out via the 62nd Airlift Wing stationed at McChord Air Force Base. The joint facility was huge, and took up most of the wedge of land formed by a rugged triangle bordered by the I-5, and Routes 510 and 507. As well as military personnel it also accommodated their families, support staff and medical and leisure facilities. Dozens if not hundreds of active and retired military men and women lived in the 'burbs surrounding JBLM, and in nearby Tacoma and Olympia. If we couldn't scratch up a couple of guns from all of those possible sources then we didn't deserve to be in the game. Rink and Noah Kirk were on such a mission, scaring up a few old contacts of Harvey.

I waited in a soulless room in a chain motel off Route 507, making a plan of action with Adam Sanderson. By then we were on full name terms. It made sense when we had become allies to know just who we were trusting our arses with, and that truth went both ways. Adam – for all he sounded as if he was an awed youth eager to hear war stories from a veteran – was more astute than I'd previously given him credit for. His naïve style of questioning got answers that direct demands would not have. I was warming to the young man and thought that after this we might stay friends. Only time would tell.

In the meantime it paid to have a younger guy on hand. Although Harvey had come through for us on tracing the signal from Billie's vest, he was half a continent away in Arkansas and there was only so much he could impart during a conference call when it came to handling the technology at our end. Adam had grown up in the new digital age, unlike this old analog dinosaur, and could achieve with a few deft taps and swipes of his hand what I'd take ages to figure out on an iPad. Piggybacking the motel's Wi-Fi service he'd logged on to a site on which a cursor currently blinked at the centre of a detailed satellite image of the nearby streets. Considering Procrylon's ties to the weapons development industry it made perfect sense that they would have holdings adjacent to the largest military base in the north-west corner of the country, but not so much that they'd take an abducted woman there. Then again, a quick check of the location's address had thrown up no direct ties to Procrylon, so I took it that ownership was probably registered under one of those shell companies that Agent Cooper mentioned they were fond of.

'It's a warehouse and distribution hub, logistics, that kind of thing. They have a fleet of trucks and also have a secondary property at the rail hub here.' Adam tapped the screen of his iPad and the satellite image zoomed in. He nipped and twisted, so that the picture displayed imagery at street level. I saw freight trains and engines lined up on tracks.

'Go back to the original location,' I urged him and Adam did his stuff. 'Zoom in again, like you just did.'

'There you go,' said Adam. The imagery was at street level again but now showed a large industrial complex consisting of at least a dozen red-brick buildings and steel sheet sheds, some interconnected by corridors and skywalks. As Adam manipulated the picture I saw rows of trucks lined up on a wide lot. They were bottle-green in colour.

'Can you get any closer?'

'Only so far. These pictures were recorded from the roads at the perimeter of the site, not actually from within the compound's fences. Because of its nature the site has privacy restrictions. It's not Area 51, so the satellite imagery hasn't been censored, but at street level this is as good as it gets.'

'Can you get another angle on it?'

'Yeah. Not a problem. What are you interested in?'

I pointed out a distant blur on the current view. Adam manipulated the map and brought up a scene from the opposite side of the complex. The object I'd originally noticed was now seen from a different angle and from a tad closer. 'Zoom in as best you can.'

'It's a helicopter,' Adam announced.

That's exactly what I'd thought. I couldn't swear on it, because I'd been unable to study the aircraft buzzing us overhead, but I was certain it was the same chopper conducting the sweep for Billie last night. Adam also knew there'd been a helicopter involved in the hunt. But he held up a cautionary finger. 'This stuff isn't real-time footage,' he explained. 'Could even be a few years old. The satellite imagery is contemporaneous, but not the street view.' As if to enforce his point, he came out of the close-up view and returned to the overhead mapping facility. He zoomed in, matching up from memory where he thought the helicopter had been parked. There was no chopper in evidence now, but there were the landing markings of a helipad. Good enough for me.

'Zoom out again,' I prompted. 'There's something I noticed inside the fence there.'

CCTV cameras were mounted on poles at regular intervals all around the site. Common practice, I supposed, but I made myself a silent bet that there were also other security measures in place. It was as Adam noted concerning the delicate nature of some of Procrylon's products; guarding them would require secretiveness but also a high level of security. 'Can you check out the company and find out who's supplying their security personnel?'

While he worked his wizardry, I sat on the edge of the bed. I'd slept, eaten and slaked my raging thirst, but still felt weak and a little shaky. The scalp wound wasn't giving me much trouble, more of an itch now than pain, the graze on my shoulder barely noticeable. My abdomen ached as if I'd done a thousand crunches, bearable discomfort, but the bullet wound to my upper chest still throbbed like a stubborn bastard despite the liberal amount of painkillers I'd downed. I breathed in and out slowly, settling myself and banishing the pain to a far corner of my mind. There would be time for the pain after I got Billie back. If I failed to do so, then it wouldn't matter, because I'd probably be beyond the pain's reach.

'PMCs.'

Adam's announcement caught me off guard, and I snapped open my eyes. I think I might have slept a few seconds. I blinked for clarity. My face felt rubbery and about twice its normal size.

'PMCs,' Adam repeated. 'Private military contractors.'

I knew what PMCs were, and wasn't at all surprised to learn that the Jaegers were ex-military men, now employed in the private security industry. These days there were more PMCs on the ground in many of the world's war zones than there were regular soldiers. Since it was forbidden by the United Nations

Mercenary Convention to employ 'mercenaries', the industry had gone through a radical change in image, but in my mind a new name designation didn't make a jot of difference. Call them PMCs or security contractors, they were still mercs to me. Most private military companies were reputable, and offered training, services and expertise in support of official armed forces. They were regularly assigned the task of protecting key personnel and premises, most often in hot zones. Those well-known private military companies – like Blackwater, or Xe Services or Academi as it had subsequently been rebranded – had to be above reproach, and the US Military Commissions Act forbade them to employ offensive force, though that wasn't always the case. In my opinion the decree was simply a piece of paper, waved in the air by the US military brass when they needed to sever any responsibility between them and the acts of deniable 'unlawful combatants'. I guessed that the company behind the Jaegers was flagrant in flouting governmental rules, the way in which they dealt with their customers.

Adam chuckled to himself, then grinned at me over his iPad.

'What's up?'

'I just realised something,' he said. 'Do you know what "jaeger" translates as?'

'Yeah.' It translated from German as 'hunter', and the irony wasn't lost on me.

'So do you think these Jaeger brothers are your Euro-trash cousins, or what?'

'I don't think they're even European. From their accents they're American, East Coast by the sound of things.'

'Kissing cousins at best,' Adam went on. He laughed again, then frowned as he tapped away at his tablet. 'Look here.'

I stood and joined him so that he could angle the iPad to enable me to see what was on the screen. He'd brought up an

employee manifest of the private military company working
on Procrylon's behalf. He opened separate windows so that
Erick and Daniel Jaeger stood shoulder to shoulder. The CVs
below their photographs were basic, stating age, vital statistics
and relative military experience. They'd both served in the US
Marine Corps, the elder brother Erick attaining the rank of
captain, while his kid brother only ascended to first sergeant.
Daniel's deference to Erick wasn't simply down to sibling
dynamics, but also to past military service. Both men had
served tours in Iraq, but had decamped to the PMC after the
military operation began scaling down in 2011. Both men, it
seemed, were still up for a fight. One thing I knew about
marines was that they were tough bastards, and wily oppo-
nents, and I should be wary of them. But more than that I
looked forward to meeting them again. Even through the fog
of delirium I could picture that gun coming down on my head,
and beyond it was the gloating face of Daniel Jaeger after his
big brother gave the order to bash my brains out. Made me
wonder what such heartless men were capable of when deal-
ing with a woman.

'How is it you didn't get into the PMC business?' Adam
wondered. 'With your military background I'd've thought it
would be the obvious step.'

'I was tempted. But the truth is I don't often see eye to eye
with some of the people who end up on The Circuit.'

I didn't expound. I was with a counter-terrorism unit code-
named Arrowsake for fourteen years, and some of those now
involved with the PMC circuit were the kind of people I once
fought against. Due to the changing political environment,
my unit had been disbanded, and part of me had welcomed it.
My relationship with Diane was in free fall, and I thought that
continuing with my soldiering career would be the death of
our marriage. Giving up my career hadn't saved it, and we'd

divorced not long after I'd returned to Civvy Street. Some might argue that in the intervening years I was still a soldier, just not in an official capacity, and was selling out my services any different than any other mercenary selling theirs? Despite the things I'd done, many of them violent, I'd always thought of myself as one of the good guys. There were moral standards I adhered to when taking on and accepting a job. Unlike the Jaegers I wouldn't be involved in the abduction of an innocent woman, no matter what the reward.

Soldiering should be an honourable pursuit, but there was a truth about why people became soldiers that wasn't always apparent. Basically there are few reasons why people enlist. Ambition motivates some, duty and family history others, some enlist because they've nowhere else to go and then there's the final group. They become soldiers because they have a need to kill, and if they can make a wage from doing what they enjoy then even better. Sometimes the reasons for enlisting overlapped, and sometimes they changed over time. I was of the group who had nowhere else to go, but I became a killer, though I never enjoyed it.

I wondered what path the Jaegers had followed. I guessed they came from a family with a military history, and brother followed brother into the services, as had their father and grandfather before them. Had they become soldiers through duty and family honour, before their sensibilities had been beaten and warped on the devil's anvil of war to a point where they had lost their original focus?

Whatever. Psychoanalysing wouldn't help. The Jaegers were scum now, and my enemies.

26

It was a different room, a different chair, but Billie's situation hadn't changed much in the last few hours. She was still a prisoner, in an abandoned office that doubled as a cell. While she'd been escorted from one holding room to the other she'd been allowed to visit the bathroom, but it had been difficult relieving herself while observed by stern-faced men who wouldn't allow her the privacy of closing the door behind her. They'd stood, barely making the effort to avert their gazes as she'd squatted over the bowl. What did they expect her to do, make an impromptu weapon out of balled toilet tissue? She assumed that their reticence to allow her out of their sight was because of the small window high up in the back wall of the cubicle. Maybe they expected her to try to make a break for it, but one brief glance had been enough to tell her it'd be a smaller woman who fit through that neat space. Hell, the last time she could have squeezed through that window was when she was a slip of a child Nicola's age. Bringing her daughter to mind had an instant effect on her, but not in an expected way. There was no melancholy or longing for her dead child, but anger. How dare these men treat a grieving mother this way? She'd given her guards a piece of her mind, vociferously shamed them into momentarily looking away while she struggled to get her pants around her knees and squat down.

After that they'd marched her in silence to the second room, where she was handed over to other men who'd strapped her down in a chair, again ensuring she had limited movement by way of zip-ties and Velcro straps. They left the room but stationed themselves outside. Billie could make out their shadows through the opaque ribbed glass in the door. A young, athletic-looking woman in a green uniform with the decal tags removed had come in, carrying a tray. She wasn't delivering Billie's supper. On the metal tray was a plastic bottle with a drinking straw, but there was no food. A nylon pouch took up the other side of the tray. The woman placed the tray on the floor, well out of range of Billie's feet, and picked up the bottle. She came forward, and without a word pressed the drinking straw to Billie's lips. Billie was tempted to spit the straw out in defiance, but she was as thirsty as hell. She sucked hungrily on tepid water that tasted like the warm plastic container it came in. Before she was finished the woman pulled the straw away. Billie was left feeling thirstier than ever. But she wasn't going to beg for more. 'You stinking bitch,' she said. 'Keep the water, you'll need it for next time you remember to douche.'

Billie eyed the woman, who raised a plucked eyebrow, then snorted under her breath at Billie's insolence. She turned and walked away without comment, leaving the tray and nylon pouch. Billie stared at the pouch as if it was a bomb on countdown to detonation.

The nylon pouch didn't explode, but she almost did. It took rigid self-control not to holler and rant, because she still had no idea what her captors were waiting for and her guards had refused her the slightest of clues. She was left to ponder and she was sure it had been for hours. This time she didn't sleep, and the time crawled by.

There was no mystery why she'd been snatched. The ATF agent, Cooper, had warned her that she might be the target for the people diligently chasing her husband. Joe Hunter had enforced the idea too. But what could she tell her captors?

The official police report said that Richard crashed his car, plummeting from a bridge into a deep ravine, killing both him and their daughter, Nicola. Billie knew that Richard was dead, even if his body had never been recovered from the river the way Nicola's had. She'd learned that a man resembling Richard had been spotted coming through Seattle-Tacoma Airport, red-flagged via a facial recognition program. The program must have been flawed, because it simply could not have been Richard. Of course, it wasn't Richard everyone was most interested in finding. It was the money he'd allegedly squirrelled away from the accounts of several shell companies, one of them involved in the illegal arms trade. Thirty million dollars was a large motivator, enough that the company would pay handsomely to anyone who could reunite it with its original owners. The armed men who'd killed Hunter, and snatched her, were simply stormtroopers, brutish men who did the grunt work, but she trusted there was someone behind them and it was he who wished to question Billie. What the hell did they hope to learn from her? If her husband had stolen money, then they wanted to find it. But it wasn't as if the cash was an actual tangible commodity, was it? The thirty million dollars they were concerned about was probably nothing more than a sequence of numbers lost in cyberspace. Did they expect Richard to have hoarded it somewhere, a massive mound of stacked dollar bills, and handed Billie his treasure map, 'X marks the spot' emblazoned over the location of the loot? It'd be funny if things weren't so damn serious.

She assumed that she was going to be dangled like a carrot, bait to draw in Richard. But he wouldn't be coming. So what would happen then: physical torture to force her into giving up the money's secret location? Little good that would do any of them, considering she had no clue. In fact the first she'd heard of her husband's alleged criminal activity was from

Agent Cooper. His infidelity wasn't the only secret that Richard had kept from her.

She looked again at the nylon pouch on the tray, and had a good idea what was within it. It wasn't unlike the pouch from which the thugs had pulled the needle to sedate her last night. However she didn't expect that this one held the same drug; why would they want to knock her out if they were looking for answers? She didn't think it was an incapacitant, and had a horrible feeling that there'd be no waking up from it. Placing the damn thing in her cell was tantamount to psychological torture. She knew enough about kidnap to know that seeing her abductors' faces was never a good thing; it meant they weren't concerned about witnesses because they planned on doing away with her after she was no longer useful.

Maybe she shouldn't be so adamant about his death when they asked if Richard was still alive. Hell, let them search the globe for him and she'd be happy to stick around while they were at it. The longer they were engaged in a wild goose chase, the longer she had to find a way out of her predicament.

Outside in the corridor there was a brief mutter of voices and the clip of heels on hard flooring. Through the grainy ribbed glass of the door she watched the shadows shift as one of her guards moved. A key rattled and the door was pushed open. The eldest of the two men responsible for drugging her last night stood in the threshold. He'd discarded his informal clothing and now wore pristine black slacks, a pale grey shirt and maroon tie, expertly knotted. His black leather shoes gleamed, buffed to mirror sheen. His spectacle lenses had been recently cleaned too, and were crystal-clear. He'd shaved and his skin was almost waxy, drawn taut across the lumpy planes of his face. Discounting the broken nose, the surly turn of his mouth, he didn't resemble a thug now, more a business executive. He studied her without comment before entering and stepping aside, making room for his superior.

Whomever Billie had expected, this wasn't he.

In fact the person that walked into her cell wasn't even a 'he'.

A forty-something woman, willowy and tall, entered and stood on high heels, her ankles touching, her hands clasped at her midriff. She wore a trouser suit, grey, over a pale lilac shirt and a thin gold chain encircled her swan-like neck. Her auburn hair hung in loose curls around her shoulders, but not in a haphazard fashion: hours and much expense had gone into her 'natural'-looking hairdo. She too resembled a high-powered executive, and the steel-grey glint of her gaze only added to the impression. She wasn't a pretty woman. She had an aquiline nose, a bulbous forehead and her mouth was too small, puckered like the painted mouth of a porcelain doll. For some reason Billie feared her more than she did the brutish men who guarded her.

27

Rink drove Adam Sanderson's SUV while I sat in the back, studying the ingress and egress points of the sprawling logistics hub. Our new friends were in Noah Kirk's sedan, parked discreetly in the parking lot of a gas station from where they could observe the front access gate to Route 507. At the front of the complex a slip road ran a couple of hundred yards parallel to the main route before converging with it, allowing traffic to gain and match speed before entering the highway. It was late, and the Spanaway McKenna highway was still busier than expected, but once we got off it and on to the surface roads around the site the traffic was much lighter. We followed East Gate Road, then took a left on an unmarked service road that followed the perimeter fence north, along the back end of the distribution complex. I recognised the view as the one showed to me earlier on Adam's iPad. I noted the tall poles and CCTV cameras, watching for areas where the arc of one camera sweep would meet that of the next. There were no apparent blind spots that I could tell, but I knew that it was largely down to whether or not those watching the camera feeds were alert or not. A raised sidewalk adjacent to the fence was a good sign. If there was a pedestrian right of way then it was highly unlikely that the fence was electrified, or that it was equipped with motion sensors. Someone walking their dog, or kids from the nearby housing project, could easily bump the fence, and set off alarms, and I guessed these inconveniences would've been taken into consideration. Any other security measures would be within the perimeter fence.

Approximately three hundred yards along, we came across a back entrance. It was probably only opened to allow fire trucks urgent access, but it didn't appear to have been used recently. Weeds grew along the bottom of the large gates, intertwining in the wire mesh, and the chain and padlock were rusty. CCTV cameras covered the gate, but I recognised a gap in the security net. The cameras angled down to cover the gates, but the next pole was a good hundred yards away and its cameras were pointed in the opposite direction. Whoever had last used the PTZ facility of the cameras had been tardy, forgetting to realign them to their original targets. I shared a nod with Rink, who'd also recognised a way inside. We didn't stop.

We followed the service trail to where it dead-ended at an undeveloped tract of land. Bushes and tall grass couldn't fully conceal the mounds of rubble and dirt, or the burned-out husk of a car, that had been dumped on the fallow ground. On the corner of the perimeter fence stood another CCTV pole, this one armed with two cameras to watch both directions where the fence took a right angle. A well-trodden footpath followed the fence back towards the distant highway and I guessed that people from the housing project used it as a short cut to the shops and services adjacent to the 507 rather than go all the way around the logistics hub.

'That could be our best way in,' Rink noted.

'Security will have grown complacent back here,' I said by way of agreement. If there were someone watching the cameras, they'd regularly see civilians wandering along the path next to the fence, possibly to a point where they barely registered them anymore.

'We doing this then, brother?'

'We have to,' I replied.

'We don't have to. You can still call Cooper and get the FBI on the case.'

'That'd be the sensible thing to do,' I said, but without conviction. 'But what if Billie isn't here? All we know is that the beacon from her vest is. It could have been removed the way mine has. Billie could have been moved since. If the FBI go in now and find nothing, that'll be it. Procrylon will know they're rumbled, and Billie will probably be dropped in a deep hole in the ground somewhere. Then both the FBI and ATF'll shut us out. Let's do as we agreed, Rink. We take a look, and if we can't get Billie out ourselves, then we'll call in Cooper.'

Rink shook his head, chuckling under his breath. 'You've no intention of calling Cooper.'

I sat quietly. He was right. But my reluctance to hand over the rescue attempt to the federal government had been taken out of my hands. Noah and Adam were under express instructions to call Cooper at the first hint of trouble. Cooper knew I was on the case and I trusted that he was waiting for the inevitable crap to hit the fan: even if he didn't have an armed response team on stand-by I expected he could call in the other members of his small task force. And if that wasn't the case, there was an entire battalion of soldiers little more than a stone's throw away that could be mobilised in a hurry.

'How are you bearing up, Joe?'

When Rink calls me by my given name it means he's concerned.

'Sore but capable,' I said.

He made a noise in his throat.

'I'm OK. Quit worrying.'

'Glad you agreed to wear that vest again,' Rink said.

'Yeah.' I smiled. 'It helps hold me together.'

Rink didn't have the luxury of a bulletproof vest, but that wasn't unusual. He had come through on gathering the necessary weapons we'd need, though. From Harvey's contacts he'd sourced us a couple of handguns, suppressors and ammunition, plus a Mossberg 590 pump-action shotgun, Rink's weapon of choice for when events grew nasty and loud. He'd brought with him an ammunition belt stuffed with three-inch magnum cartridges, enough firepower to drop a small army, or to breach as many locked doors as necessary. He'd forsaken his colourful shirt for a black sweatshirt now that things had grown serious, and his ever-present KABAR was tucked away in a sheath on his hip.

Rink performed a 'Y' turn in the road and headed back the direction we'd come. A little way down the service road he took a left and into the housing project. He tucked the SUV out of the way in a cul-de-sac. The car didn't look out of place, as there were others of its type parked on the driveways of at least two of the houses in near view. Most people had retired for the evening, but inside a few homes TVs still flickered. We sat a few minutes, and I went over the map of the logistics complex Adam had printed for us. I'd memorised the location of the last known signal from Billie's vest beacon, though it was unlikely that she'd still be in its vicinity. Also I'd taken note of the layout and configuration of the complex of buildings and warehouses, and tried to plot where Billie was most likely being held. It was a lottery, but I'd decided on an order of entry, and once inside I was hopeful of finding someone to point me to her. Rink had also plotted his actions. We weren't going in together; Rink was our backstop, our extraction man for when I got Billie away from her guards. He was going to run diversion and disruption tactics. In many ways his was the more dangerous job, because his was about thunder and destruction while mine should be subtler. Noah and Adam were non-combatants and our last resort for when the time came for escape and evasion.

Rink's cell vibrated. I'd handed it back to him earlier. He took it out and held it up so we could both hear. It was Noah calling.

'I don't know if it's important but a limo turned up a few minutes ago. We couldn't get eyes on the passenger but the guards at the gate stood to attention, and jumped to it pretty sharp when they recognised their visitor. The limo was ushered inside and directed over to that large administration building with the domed roof.'

We knew the building that Noah referred to, marking it out earlier as a probable location for Billie.

'A few minutes ago, you said?' Rink sounded displeased at the lapse in time.

'We thought it best to wait and see where it went before calling it in and keep you holding.' Noah's logic was sound. 'Still couldn't make out who was inside, but judging by the looks on the faces of the guards it was someone with clout, and not very likeable.'

'You did well,' I said.

Adam said something in the background, but his words were too muffled to hear. Noah came back on. 'You sure we can't be of more help to you guys?'

'You are being helpful,' I reminded them. 'Sit tight, and if things grow noisy, do as we agreed. Get Cooper and his gang over here quick like.'

'Stay frosty,' Rink reminded them, meaning they remain calm and alert. 'We're going silent now.' He switched off his cell, looked over at me. 'We should roll.'

'We're rolling,' I said and slipped out of the SUV.

28

'You know what we want from you, so make things easy on us all and tell us the truth.'

It wasn't the first time the woman had uttered similar words, but Billie knew that frustration was beginning to edge in and before long the reasonable tone would grow more threatening.

Billie was no longer in the cell.

After the arrival of the tall woman the man with the spectacles had come forward and snicked through her zip-ties with a knife, then forced her up and out of the room ahead of him. Billie had glanced down at the mysterious nylon pouch on the tray, wondering again what it held, before she was propelled out of the door and along a corridor. She was taken up a flight of stairs and into another corridor and another set of offices. Finally she was led to a corner room, with windows dominating two of the walls. Outside it was dark, and she could see the far-off lights of a city, or at least a large town. In the night sky the landing lights of aircraft blinked and were low enough over the horizon to hint at a nearby airport. She was seated at a desk and the newcomer had strolled round the other side and sat in a plush leather chair, crossing her long legs primly and placing her folded hands in her lap.

They'd left the uniformed guards behind on the lower floor, but it was apparent to all that the bespectacled man was enough of a threat to keep her under control. He positioned himself behind Billie, his arms folded loosely across his chest, while the tall woman studied her as if she was something distasteful and beneath her attention. They waited, and a minute or so later the other familiar man entered the room. Billie watched her guards' reflections in the windows behind the woman. As he had in the forest, the younger man presented the nylon pouch to his brother. Billie couldn't be sure, but she'd assumed that the men were siblings. They looked too alike to be otherwise.

'Stay with us, Danny,' the woman said and the younger man took up a position, leaning with his shoulders against the wall to Billie's left, arms also folded nonchalantly. He wore a firearm holstered on his left hip. Everyone was silent again, and Billie guessed it was a ploy to get her talking. She licked her lips, working up some moisture, but then settled back and folded her own arms in defiance, watching as the woman's doll mouth pinched tighter and colour blemished her cheeks.

'We are not unreasonable people,' the woman began.

'Aren't you? Tell that to the man your goons shot to death when they kidnapped me.'

'My goons?' The woman glanced past Billie at the brothers and smiled. The men laughed disparagingly at the insult, but Billie wasn't sure if it was her words or the woman's apparent pleasure they were responding to.

The woman went on. 'I heard that your friend was first to employ violence. My *goons* only responded in kind.'

'Well pardon me if I disagree,' Billie said.

'We won't hold it against you. Like I said, we're not unreasonable. We're happy to play nice if you're willing to work with us on our mutual problem.' The woman showed her teeth in a smile that held all the warmth of an attack dog's snarl. 'Answer our questions truthfully, make things easier for all of us, and we will find happy resolution.'

Billie stared at the woman. 'Are you for real?'

'Very much so.' The woman sat back, flicking imaginary lint off her thighs. 'And very much to be taken seriously.'

'I don't even know who you are.'

'You may call me Amanda. I represent the interests of a certain party keen on finding resolution to our mutual problem.'

'You're a merc like this lot?' Billie jerked her head at her stoic guards.

'A mercenary?' Amanda sneered. 'I take it you mean a soldier for hire. No, Mrs Womack, I'm no soldier; I'm something far more dangerous. You should take note of that.' She allowed her sneer to smooth out, again forming a congenial smile. 'You do understand why you're here?'

'I've guessed. Something to do with my dead husband, right?'

Amanda laughed at Billie's sarcasm, and it was a soft rasp. 'Something to the tune of thirty million dollars.'

'You probably know everything about me,' Billie said. 'If so, you know I'm an artist who barely scrapes a living from her work. If I knew anything about thirty million dollars, don't you think I'd have made a better life for myself?'

Amanda shook her head so softly it barely disturbed her curls. 'You've been our guest for . . .' she checked a watch on her wrist, 'the best part of twenty-two hours? In all that time you've barely said a word, or raised a complaint about your mistreatment. You strike me as being incredibly calm and patient. A self-controlled individual might have the presence of mind to inhibit her spending, in order not to raise suspicion about her actual wealth.'

Laughter crackled in Billie's throat. 'You think *I've* got your damn money?'

The woman leaned forward, placing her interlocked fingers on the table. 'Have you?'

'Don't be ridiculous.'

'It's a fair question, Mrs Womack. Like I said,' Amanda flipped open one hand, palm up. 'You know what we want from you, so make things easy on us all and tell us the truth.'

Gripping the arms of her chair, Billie also leaned forward. Behind her the bespectacled man moved slightly but Billie ignored his looming presence. 'You want the truth? Well here it is. My husband was a thief, a liar, and an adulterer. He *murdered* my daughter. He died and it's the only thing he ever did that made me happy. Do you think that's the kind of man who would leave me a nest egg of thirty million dollars? If you do then you're *fucking nuts*!'

Blinking slowly Amanda sat back in her chair. Billie still leaned forward, nodding in emphasis with jerky movements of her head, her eyeballs bulging. Amanda looked beyond Billie, offering a subtle nod. Billie felt the stirring of the air before the hand that clamped down on her right wrist. She tore her gaze from her inquisitor to look up and saw her angry face reflected in the lenses of the man's glasses. 'Get off me, you pig!'

The grip on her wrist was resolute. Billie attempted to twist away, but then the younger man – Danny – had hold of her opposite wrist.

'Erick,' Amanda said, 'put her hand on the desk please.'

'What are you doing?' Billie's cry was rhetorical, because it was apparent. The bespectacled man – Erick – forced her arm straight and held her hand on the desktop. Billie squirmed, but she was going nowhere, particularly now that Danny bunched his other hand in her collar and forced her down in the seat.

'Open your hand,' Amanda commanded.

'Go to hell!' Billie clenched her fist.

'Erick?'

Erick forced the tip of his thumb into the soft flesh at the juncture of Billie's thumb and index finger. A dull pain grew, then pulsed into white fire as Erick targeted the deep nerve. Billie croaked in agony, and her hand sprang open involuntarily. Erick mashed her hand to the desk, holding it in place while he looked at Amanda for further instruction.

'You know what to do, Erick,' the woman said.

'Ma'am,' he agreed, and wrapped his callused fingertips around Billie's pinky finger.

'Do you wish to try again?' the woman asked Billie. 'I did warn you that I was dangerous.'

'Torturing me won't make a difference. I don't know where the money is!'

'Erick.'

'Yes, ma'am.'

Billie screamed as Erick yanked her pinky back against the knuckle. She felt the tendons ripping, the cartilage popping. For an artist her hands were her living, but right then and there her career wasn't a consideration; all that mattered was the agony that washed over her like a wave of black ink. Erick released her finger, and Billie stared at it through watering eyes. She expected to see the digit malformed, at an unnatural angle, but her finger merely contracted on itself, hooking under her palm. It had been a shade from dislocation, but Erick was skilled at his job.

'We can keep this up all day,' Amanda said, 'or you can do as I ask and answer my questions truthfully. There are three answers I'm looking for: where is Richard Womack; how are you in contact with him – email, telephone, blind letter drop? – and lastly: where is the money?'

Billie's assaulted finger trembled and the shakes went right up her arm. The pain was replaced by numbness that also invaded her mind.

'Again, Erick.' The skin around Amanda's eyes crinkled.

The soldier forced Billie's pinky straight, wrapping it in his palm. Billie cried out in anticipation.

Amanda flashed a palm at him and Erick relaxed his grip. 'Are you ready to speak, Mrs Womack?'

'I can't tell you what I don't know,' Billie gasped.

'Then we'll take a different tack.' Amanda interlaced her hands once more and sat back, as if thinking, or more likely calculating. 'You were expecting us.'

Billie didn't understand the question, or indeed the statement. She looked up from her tormented hand and settled her gaze on the sharp planes of Amanda's face. Billie's mouth fell open, but no words followed.

'You had arranged protection. The man you were with when we found you. Who was he?'

'He was just a friend,' Billie said, unsure why she would lie.

'He was a skilled soldier,' Erick offered from behind.

'Not skilled enough,' Danny added and chuckled to himself.

Amanda ignored her men's input. 'He was there to protect you. He was armed, and had equipped you with a bulletproof vest. I say again, you were expecting us. Why would you prepare yourself like that if you'd nothing to hide?'

There was no point in lying, and perhaps it would be to her advantage to admit part of the truth. If her tormentors knew that Agent Cooper had approached her then maybe they'd be reluctant to kill her. 'I was warned that I might be in danger by an ATF agent.'

'He warned you specifically about us?'

'No.' Time for lies again. 'He said that I might be in danger from my husband. I told him it was ridiculous. My husband is dead, so what had I to fear. But the ATF was adamant, and sent the man you asked about to watch out for me.'

'He was a federal agent?'

'No. Freelance. Just like your men.'

'Tell me his name,' Amanda said.

'Why? He's dead.'

'Tell me.'

'He introduced himself as Joe Hunter. I'm not sure if it was his actual name. What does it matter if he's dead?'

Billie knew exactly why it mattered. Amanda was concerned that the death of Hunter might be traced back to the organisation she represented. Billie recognised the woman's concern as a possible advantage. Without any prompting she went on, 'I suppose when he doesn't contact the ATF, they'll begin looking for him, and for me.'

'They won't find you. Or your friend, Hunter.' Amanda smiled at her one-upmanship. 'We've already dispatched a recovery team. Hunter's body will disappear as completely as anything else we wish to disappear. The ATF are no concern of ours. They won't be coming to your assistance, Mrs Womack. Your only way out of this is to continue to be forthcoming with your answers. The sooner we get to the bottom of this, the better.'

'Am I the only one who believes Richard is dead?'

Amanda shrugged. 'Unlike your daughter's, his body was never found.'

'The police hypothesised that his corpse was preyed upon by wildlife. We have black bears and grizzlies: Richard's corpse was dragged from the river and eaten.'

Amanda's tongue clucked at the inanity of the scenario.

'Just because his remains haven't been found yet, it doesn't mean a thing. Sooner or later a hunter or hiker will stumble upon them. A few crushed bones, or tattered clothing, will be found and the case will finally be closed.' Billie went still. 'I hope he *was* still alive when the bears got him.'

'That's just cold,' Danny commented, and when Billie glanced at him she caught him grinning in admiration. She wondered if she could play that to her advantage; but no, the man was simply a sadist. He would probably prefer that he were the one allowed to twist her fingers to the point of dislocation instead of his brother.

'We have reason to believe that Richard is alive and well. We believe that he has been in contact with you, or that such communication is imminent.' Amanda pushed a curl over her ear, all the better to hear and judge the validity of Billie's reply. 'Where is he?'

'Jesus Christ, haven't you been listening to me?'

Ignoring the outburst, Amanda leaned closer. Her words came out calm and yet held more emphasis. 'Where is he?'

'I don't know,' Billie replied, also enunciating each word slowly and clearly.

Her mouth formed a tight slash as Amanda stared at Billie across the desk. She exhaled noisily through her nostrils, the skin at their edges going white. She directed her next words at Erick. 'You know what to do.'

'Ma'am.' Erick yanked Billie's pinky finger, and this time he didn't release it at the last second. Billie screamed. He held on to her arm with one hand while reaching to his belt where he'd hooked the small nylon pouch, and as painful as her hand was Billie attempted to wrest free. 'Hold her,' Erick told his brother.

Danny moved so that he was leaning over her shoulders, his chin nestled alongside her right ear, his arms extended to hold out both hers on the desk. Erick pulled a hypodermic syringe from the pouch, and Billie's fears were realised.

'No, no, no,' she said, while struggling to free herself. Danny's grip was remorseless.

Amanda smiled at the drama. 'Settle down, Mrs Womack. We're not about to kill you. It's anaesthetic in the syringe.

Erick is only going to give you a tiny shot to soothe your pain. Not because I wish to spare you the agony, but because my time is precious. I can't have you passing out each time we must punish you for your lies.'

29

Taking advantage of the right angle formed by the perimeter fence, and the gap of a few yards in the security net, I climbed inside the compound without raising any alarms – at any rate none that I was aware of. Barbed wire at the top of the fence wasn't enough to deter me, and I made it over with barely a scratch, though the pulling in my chest wound told me that I might have lost a stitch or two. Rink covered me until I was kneeling on the ground and could return the honours. He shoved his Mossberg under the fence and then swarmed over as lithe as an ape. Shotgun in hand, he moved aside so that we didn't offer a single target.

'There's still time to turn back,' he whispered.

'Call yourself a ranger?' I quipped.

I was referring back to the old adage that 'Rangers lead the way'. Rink however had another motto in mind. *Sua Sponte* meant 'Of their own accord' and recognised that rangers volunteered three times when joining the elite regiment: once for the Army, once for Airborne School, and finally for the Ranger Regiment itself. He offered a lopsided smile and said, 'I didn't volunteer for this shit.'

'*Utrinque Paratus*.' I quoted the motto of 1 Para, to which I'd belonged before we were both inducted into Arrowsake. 'Ready for anything, brother.'

'*Da mihi asimun*,' he growled, and it didn't take a scholar of Latin to understand where he told me to kiss. We both showed our teeth in a grin of camaraderie.

Then we were moving again. Rink went off at an angle, across the wide lot, his footfalls silent on the concrete paving. Large sulphur lights bathed the distant buildings in their yellow glow, but out on the grounds they only lent solidity to the darkness. Within seconds I could no longer see Rink. I went directly ahead, moving for the building I'd earlier earmarked on the map. Billie's vest was still there; she might not be, but it was a good starting point.

Even as I headed across the grounds I knew how reckless the mission was. Back in my Arrowsake days I had full logistical and technical support, and the manpower and equipment necessary to a successful mission. Now I had Rink, a couple of borrowed guns, and two untried allies in Noah and Adam. The odds were stacked against us. The sensible thing to do was allow Cooper his way and send in a full FBI tactical team, except this was a test of sorts. Things weren't ringing right with me, and I hoped I was wrong about everything. Hell, I'd been wrong enough in my actions over the past few days, so in some way this was also about vindicating myself.

As I jogged forward, my antiballistic vest bounced up and down with each step. The movement was marginal, but was enough to rub at the dressing on my chest wound. I felt heat and moisture and knew I was bleeding again, but it was hardly a concern. I wasn't bleeding out as before, and as long as the bullet hole didn't open all the way I shouldn't weaken from blood loss. My chest ached, but the pain only kept me focused on what I needed to do.

The buildings loomed overhead. Judging by the architecture and grounds the logistics hub had once been an airport, circa World War Two, but it had long been abandoned, then sold off to private enterprise a number of years later. Some of the red-brick buildings had been left to the elements, and were in ruins, while alongside them newer prefabricated buildings of steel and sheetrock had been erected. The latter were cavernous, with huge sliding doors large enough to allow access to freightliners, and even smaller aircraft. I was reminded of the business that Procrylon was in, and that they produced armament casings and carry boxes for the weapons and demolition industries. But it stood to reason that their fleet would require housing, and that a number of people on site would be innocent workers with no involvement in their nefarious activities. Collateral damage, a very real fear, was not something I could ignore.

The sulphurous lights gave the nearer structures a haunted-house feel, the blacked-out windows like the empty sockets in a row of yellowing skulls. Doors at ground level were open maws, ready to snap down on the unwary and carry you down to the gullet of hell. Jesus, my imagination was in overdrive. Shaking off the uncanny feelings, I avoided the nearest pools of light, sticking to the deep shadows, and headed for a service alley between two of the tall buildings. The structure with the domed roof was beyond them, and my true destination. I checked for CCTV cameras, but if there were any I couldn't see them. No alarms rang, no klaxons blared, so I felt confident I hadn't yet been spotted though that was certain to change.

If I had extended both arms I could have touched the walls of the buildings, they were so close together. I moved down the centre of the alley – less chance I'd bump up against something piled against a wall. I kept my handgun down by my side, finger off the trigger, but ready to snatch it up in an instant. In the alley I was almost invisible, but light at its far mouth would alert me to anyone entering the alley from that end. I occasionally glanced back to check nobody was sneaking up on me, but the darkness worked against me there. I moved on, confident that even if somebody was prowling up behind me they'd offer a warning before an attack: going up against pros meant that they sometimes fell foul of the ingrained rules and regulations whereas an out-and-out criminal wouldn't. No one challenged me, and I reached the end of the alley. I checked the way was clear before proceeding. There was a paved road, and beyond it a two-storey building with a flat roof. Behind its windows the dull glow of night lights could be seen, but it didn't appear anyone was at home. To my left the road was clear, while to my right a small fleet of vehicles was parked alongside the large building I crouched against. The vehicles were all bottle-green, some carrying company decals, others lacking identifiers, just like the van the Jaegers had arrived at Billie's farm in. There were no guards watching over the fleet.

I went directly across the road and on to a raised pavement, which descended in wide concrete steps to a walkway adjacent to the two-storey structure. A porch on steel poles warded rain off the entrance doors. I paused there, taking a glance inside the foyer, and saw it deserted. For all I knew Billie was inside, but I doubted it. I headed along a path that skirted the building and led to a patio of wide concrete slabs. Beyond it reared the tall red-brick building with its domed roof. Lights were on inside, and I watched two figures pass by windows on the lowest floor. They walked together, in conversation, one of them gesticulating to make a point. I couldn't tell if they were security or regular workers, but any of them had eyes to spot me. I crouched low, waited until they passed out of sight. Now that I was nearer my enemies, and stealth trumped accuracy, I took the opportunity to screw the suppressor on my gun. Then I went at a running crouch for the building, weighing up and discarding my next move until I settled on a bold idea. I moved along the side of the building, ducking beneath the level of each window until I reached the front. Pressing up close to the wall, I leaned out and checked Noah's earlier information. On a turning circle outside the front door was a sleek black limousine. Kicking his heels while he waited for the return of his passenger was a uniformed chauffeur. He'd placed his peaked cap on the hood of the limo, taking things easy while he got the chance. He'd lit up, and was smoking a cigarette as he ambled back and forward. Other stubs on the floor showed he'd been waiting a while, and probably had more time to kill. I took his measure.

He was a big guy in his late thirties, four inches taller than me, and broader across the back with thick arms. His square head sported a military buzz cut, but he lacked a soldier's bearing. He slouched, and there was a hitch in his walk that told of an old knee injury. Maybe he was an ex-footballer, or college wrestler now gone to seed, but still tough and imposing enough to work close protection for a company executive under minimum threat of attack. When he bent slightly to flick ash so it missed his polished shoes, his suit jacket swung open and I caught a glint of metal. It was possibly a pistol in a shoulder rig.

I took it that the chauffeur wasn't welcome inside the facility, or that he simply preferred to stay outside and satisfy his nicotine habit, and therefore should have no idea what went on beyond the doors. But he would be able to tell me who his absent passenger was, and if their late arrival was down to Billie Womack's capture. Even when the hired hands lacked interest in their bosses' business they couldn't help but overhear what they shouldn't.

My mind made up, I walked out boldly from the corner. There'd be dozens of people on site and he'd have no clue who I was, or that I was a threat. I concealed my handgun behind my hip as I came forward, checking once that there was nobody watching from the doorway. The chauffeur glanced at me, even tipped his head in a nod of greeting, and I almost felt bad about what I was about to do. He turned aside to discreetly flick ash again, and by the time he turned back I was already alongside him.

'Not one sound, buddy,' I warned as I jammed my handgun under his ribs.

'What?' He was too stunned to react effectively, and all he did was look once at the gun, and then at his half-finished cigarette that he held instinctively to one side.

'Didn't you hear me?' I whispered harshly, jabbing him again with the gun so my message was clear. I quickly leaned in and unsnapped his holster; it wasn't a gun at all, but a walkie-talkie radio. I took it anyway and threw it away beneath the limo. 'Over there. Now.'

With my gun pressed to his lower spine, I directed him towards the shadows of a nearby building. He went without fuss or complaint, as if I was the Smoking Police and he'd just been caught red-handed.

Happy that we'd gone unseen, I pressed him into the deep well of shadows caused by a recessed doorway. 'Don't try to be a hero,' I advised, 'and everything will end up fine.'

'Wh-what's this all about, mate?' Surprisingly the chauffeur had an antipodean accent: Australian or New Zealander, I couldn't tell.

'First we get things straight, so there's no confusion. I ask the questions, you answer. Understand?'

'What am I supposed to have done wrong?'

'Obviously you still don't understand. Let me make this clearer. I ask, you answer. Got it?' For emphasis I pushed the barrel of my gun under his sternum. 'And ditch that cigarette before you burn your fingers.'

He glanced down at the smouldering stump, then flicked it away like a reviled thing. I was more concerned that he might try to jam the damn thing in my eyes, or something equally desperate, than that he singe his fingers.

'Where's Billie Womack?'

'Who?'

I shook my head. I hadn't expected him to know but it was worth a try. 'Who did you bring here?'

'You mean Amanda Sheehan?'

'If that's her name, then yes. Who is she? More specifically what's her business here?'

'Beats me, mate; I only drive the car.'

'Loyalty to your employer's an admirable trait, but not right now. Tell me who she is and what she's doing here.'

The big guy glanced about, as if this was some kind of test. Perhaps he thought his future employment depended upon his next answer. 'Look, mate, I don't know. This is the first time I've driven for her. She's a frosty cow, that one. Some snotty high-flier with a stick up her hole. I just got a call, picked her up at the airport and brought her here. She barely spoke to me except to order me around like a dog.'

'You regularly do pick-ups for Procrylon, right?'

'Procrylon? That's the client, all right. But I don't work for them.'

From what I'd already deduced he was a freelance contractor, and probably worked regular pick-ups for a number of companies besides Procrylon Inc. It felt wrong terrorising the guy, but it was a case of needs must.

'On the way from the airport, did she make any phone calls or anything?'

He thought for a second. 'Yeah. But she made me close the privacy window.'

'So you didn't hear a thing?'

He smiled secretively. 'Those windows aren't soundproof,' he said, and almost looked ready to offer a conspiratorial wink. 'It's kind of entertaining listening when your passengers think they can't be overheard. Sometimes you hear some pretty juicy pillow talk, mate. One time this guy said . . .' His words trailed off at the look on my face. 'She was speaking about somebody called Richard. I haven't a clue what the conversation was about before you ask. Just heard her repeat that name a few times. Oh, yeah, and something about relying on her to get the job done.'

I nodded in contemplation. I'd learned all I could from him. Time to move on.

'Give me your jacket.'

'What?'

'Come on, you heard me.'

'You're stealing my jacket?'

'Borrowing it. Now do as I say and I promise you'll get it back.' I didn't tell him what state it might be in when it was returned. He huffed and puffed as he stripped it off. 'Good,' I said, and indicated a stand of trees beyond the turning circle on which his limo stood. I trusted that Rink was in place by now. 'There's a friend of mine in those trees and he has a rifle-scope on you. Walk to him, don't make a sound and we stay friends. Do you understand what you have to do?'

'Why don't you let me drive away, mate? I don't want to get involved in whatever's going on here. Jesus, I don't get paid enough for this kind of shit.'

I didn't trust him not to get in his car and start hitting the horn, but I didn't tell him that. 'Sorry, but I might need a loan of your car too.'

'Can I just ask something? Are you some kind of cop?'

'ATF,' I said, the lie coming easily enough. 'But before you start asking to see my ID, you don't think undercover agents are stupid enough to carry any, do you?'

'What if my car gets damaged?'

'You'll be fully compensated. That's if you're still around. Now do as I say, and no funny stuff. Raise any kind of alarm and we'll assume you're complicit with the criminals inside and you'll be taken down.'

The chauffeur stood and eyed me for a few seconds; he wore a whimsical smile. Perhaps he still thought this was some kind of test, or that he was the subject of a grandiose prank. I expected him to begin looking for the hidden camera crew. But instead he looked down at the jacket I'd taken from him. 'Is there any rule against me getting my cigarettes back, or do you want to borrow those as well?'

I genuinely hoped he didn't do anything stupid, because in the few minutes I'd spent with him I'd grown to like him. I dipped into the jacket pocket and came out with a pack of Marlboro and petrol lighter, and handed them over.

'Is it OK if I smoke while I walk? It'll look more natural, mate, y'know, if somebody sees me and wonders what I'm up to.'

'Go for it,' I said.

He sparked up and took a satisfying drag on his cigarette. Then he winked and walked away, doing exactly as I'd asked. I watched him go, shaking my head in mild bemusement. My first instinct had been to knock the guy cold with a well-aimed smack of my gun to his head, but things had worked out better for the lack of violence. Brandon Cooper would be pleased with me, but I doubted that would last. I quickly pulled on the jacket, getting a waft of aftershave lotion and cigarette smoke as I buttoned it up. The chauffeur was bigger than me, and heavier built, but wearing the bulletproof vest helped fill out his jacket. On close inspection the rest of my clothing would be a giveaway, but I only required the disguise for a short time. I walked back towards the limo and lifted the discarded peaked cap off the hood and sat it on my head. It rested low on my forehead, but again it helped disguise my face, and the vivid bruise that extended out from my hairline.

Placing my handgun in the jacket pocket, I checked again that the chauffeur was still walking away, and beyond him I saw a shadow rise up from among the stand of trees and coax him forward at the point of a shotgun. I wondered if Rink would play things cool, but really it wasn't a concern. I turned for the front door of the target building.

30

As I entered the domed building, a uniformed security guard sitting behind a podium glanced up at me once, took in my cap and jacket, then looked down again at what he was doing; he was messing about on an iPad, surfing the web or something, when he should have been on the alert. But his inattentiveness was to my advantage, so I wasn't complaining. By the time his brain figured out that there was something distinctively wrong about my appearance, I'd already covered the distance and laid one hand on top of the podium. It was of course holding my gun, and the barrel was now less than a foot from the shiny badge on the guard's shirt. Just below his badge was his heart.

'Keep your hands on the pad,' I warned, 'and away from the alarm.'

The bleary-eyed guard blinked at me and sat back, as if trying to decide if I was real or not. Judging by the dark blur of stubble on his chin he'd been on duty a number of hours already, but it would take only a second or two more before he realised I wasn't a sleep-deprivation-induced hallucination. He opened his mouth, and being so close I smelled the sour tang of his breath.

'Keep your mouth shut,' I said, even as I checked the podium for a concealed alarm button. There was a red switch resembling a doorbell fixed below its lip. The screens of two small CCTV monitors on the podium were each divided into about a dozen smaller screens, and I couldn't help feel that it'd take someone much sharper than this guy to spot anything untoward happening on any of them.

'What's going on?' the guard asked, and I glared at him, even as I pressed the gun to his side.

'Didn't I tell you to shut your mouth?'

He nodded, now wide awake.

Checking nobody else was around, I scanned the foyer area. Double doors allowed entry to the building proper, but behind and to the left of the podium was another door. Grasping the guard by his shirt collar, I told him to put aside the iPad, then I manhandled him to the door and pushed through. We were in a small storage room. Old office desks were packed shoulder to shoulder along one wall, supporting cardboard folders and ring binders stuffed with yellowing paperwork. One of the desks had been partly cleared to make way for the guard's supper: take-out cartons and greasy wrappers, a few disconsolate noodles sticking to the side of the desk, were all that remained of his meal. The room stank of shrimp.

'Sit down.' I pressed him into the chair where he'd recently sat to eat his food. He complied, too afraid to resist. 'You received a visitor earlier, a woman. Amanda Sheehan. Where is she now?'

'I don't know.'

'Don't lie to me.'

'I'm not.' His eyes goggled at the gun hovering only inches from his face. 'I didn't speak with her. She was met by one of my superiors and led away.'

'Inside this building or elsewhere?' I demanded.

'This one. Upstairs, I assume, that's where the conference suites are.'

I doubted very much that Billie would be held in a conference room, but then it was all guesswork and assumption on both our parts. I checked out his uniform. I considered and discarded the idea of a second disguise, while also under-standing something important about the guy's clothing. He worked for a different security company than the one tasked with guarding Procrylon's interests. His was the type of company that you'd see guarding a mall. He was scarcely more than a nightwatchman and would have little to do with what went on there. But I couldn't send him out to Rink the way I had the chauffeur.

'What do you know about another woman who was brought here?' I asked.

He wasn't a good enough actor to lie. His face told me he'd no idea what I was talking about. Billie had probably been delivered via a different entrance, particularly if the helicopter had transported her. The landing pad was on the far side of the building.

'OK,' I said. 'Here's what's going to happen. A woman has been kidnapped and is being held here against her will. I'm getting her out.'

The guy's face was washed of all colours. 'Hell, we should call the police.'

'No. We shouldn't. You're going to do your part though. You're going to sit here, stay quiet, and not try anything stupid.' I looked around and saw some coils of electrical conduit stacked on a shelf at the end of the storage closet. The guard followed my gaze, and opened his mouth to object. 'Sorry, pal, but I can't trust you to do that,' I said, and before he could argue against my plan, I slammed the butt of my gun against his head. He went out like the proverbial light, slump-ing from the chair and on to the floor.

I left him where he was, tying his wrists and ankles to the metal legs at opposite ends of the desk. Then I wadded some of the greasy papers, stuffed them into his mouth and tied them in place with his own belt as an impromptu gag. Nothing would hold him long, but I hoped that he'd have more sense than to get involved once the shooting started. With a single glance back at him, to check his breathing was slow and steady, I went out of the storage room to the podium. None of the screen views showed me where Billie was, but it showed plenty of activity throughout the building. I pulled the feeds on the cameras and was just coming out from behind the podium when a guard pushed through the double doors and squinted at me in confusion.

'Who're you?' he demanded.

This man wore the green PMC uniform I associated with Billie's abductors. He was tall, with thick hairy forearms, and an old scar on his left cheek that had also nicked a chunk of flesh off the end of his nose. His pale-blue eyes danced as he took in my appearance, and tried to decide what was wrong with it.

'I'm Miss Sheehan's driver,' I said. 'I was wondering if she was ready to leave yet.'

The man came forward, sure of himself.

'What the hell were you doing back there?'

'Sorry,' I said, 'I was wondering where the desk guy was. I was going to ask him about Miss Sheehan, and just took a look at the cameras to see if I could spot him.'

'You've no right to do that.' He was now only yards from me, and his perusal was growing sharper. He checked out the cap, the ill-fitting jacket, and then down at my jeans and boots, and reflexively his hand went for a sidearm holstered on his belt. The time for deception was over. I snatched the cap off my head and threw it at his face.

I followed the cap, flying at the guard while he was distracted, and rearing back from the impromptu missile. The cap pinwheeled off the side of his head. I grasped his gun hand, keeping it wedged on top of the butt of his pistol, keeping that packed in the holster even as I rammed a knee into his groin. He emitted a woof of air and began to buckle forward at the waist. My forehead met the bridge of his nose and made it look even uglier, now flattened as well as scarred. The guard verged on unconsciousness, but wasn't totally out of the fight. He swung in reaction and his left fist clumped off the side of my injured head, so that I wobbled a little. But then I got a leg behind his and forced my shoulder into his chest and he sprawled backwards. Immediately I followed, losing my grip on his hand but stamping down on his chest. Both his arms came up in reaction – without a hold on his gun – and I skipped to one side then volleyed his head as if it was a soccer ball. He lay still.

Ducking down by his side, I tugged his gun out of its holster and pushed it under the tail of my jacket and down my belt. Our violent interaction lasted seconds at most, but apparently it was time well spent, and good for my soul. For the first time in ages I felt my old self. Fuck the softly-softly approach, I decided, and pulled off the jacket and slung it aside. It was time to get on with what I was supposed to be good at.

31

'Should I have Erick break another of your fingers?' Amanda's question was delivered amiably, as if she promised a treat rather than further torment. She'd grown weary with Billie's continued denials, and had finally left her seat to prowl back and forth, her hands clasped behind her backside, while observing the work of her two male colleagues. Billie couldn't see her, because she was folded over the desk with Daniel still controlling her while his older brother twisted and manipulated her fingers in unnatural directions. Three times now the bespectacled man had broken digits, and three times he'd administered anaesthetic to dull the pain, if not the shock.

Billie had tried partial truths, veiled lies, denial, and outright fabrications, all to no avail. Amanda wanted to hear a different story from any she could or was prepared to tell. Billie wept with a mix of soul-sapping torment and rage verging on eruption, both intense emotions coming in alternating, and sometimes overlapping, waves. She was confused and belittled, and those states of mind were unwelcome, bitter reminders of her marriage to Richard. She hated that she'd been brought to tears, because she'd always believed she was a tougher individual than that, and her only consolation was that she cried out of frustration, of anger, more than she did weakness. Her captors knew that by damaging her hands they were attacking her future as an artist, and fear of what was to come was always worse than what had gone before. Through mangling her fingers, and destroying her ability to wield a paintbrush with the same dexterity and skill, they could force her into submission, where she would give up her deepest held secrets. They were wasting their fucking time! They could chop off both her hands, blind her, and what could she say that she hadn't already repeated a dozen times?

'Richard's dead and I know nothing about your damn money!' she howled yet again.

Apparently Amanda still didn't believe, because after Erick glanced in the woman's direction he bent to Billie's hands again, this time selecting the index finger of her right hand. Billie attempted to form a fist, but it was already too late and Erick forced her fingertip sideways against the knuckle. Billie experienced a liquid pop in the joint and the end of her finger stood out sideways. Perhaps she was beyond pain, or some of the localised painkiller had leached into her index finger by now. Erick wasn't finished. He snapped the fingertip back to its original position, and now a flash of red went across Billie's vision. She hissed an unladylike curse.

'No,' Amanda said, again sounding almost reasonable with her proclamation. 'No more painkillers for her. I think it's time we up the game, don't you agree, gentlemen?'

'You should give her to me for five minutes,' Daniel offered, 'and I'll have her singing like she's a goddamn pop star.'

While Daniel had controlled her, he'd been more than intimate in the way in which he'd kissed her neck, sucked her earlobe, and rubbed his hardening member against her side, so Billie had no doubt about how he planned on forcing questions from her. She was almost glad that Erick was there, because despite his sadistic nature he found his younger brother's sexual depravity distasteful and wasn't slow in saying so. 'Better idea if you do your job and hold her still, *goddammit*,' he snapped.

'I am doing my job,' Daniel said, 'just not gaining any job satisfaction from it. We could make this a whole lot more enjoyable for all of us if you let me take over.'

'Enough of that talk.' Erick sounded disgusted, but Billie had to wonder if the brothers' interaction was designed to torment her more. Good cop bad cop didn't even apply here. This was a case of bad cop worse cop. Erick proved her point when he took the end of her abused index finger against the opposite side of the joint as before and dislocated it again. Billie bit down on her bottom lip to halt a scream, and shuddered as her stomach spasmed.

'She's going to throw up,' Erick stated.

'Go fetch a bucket,' Daniel suggested. 'Don't worry; she'll be fine with me.'

Billie struggled to regain her composure. The last thing she wanted was for Erick to leave the room. Despite the monstrous skill of the man, Erick was the most human of the trio, and to some degree the only one she felt safe with. It hadn't gone unnoticed that Amanda had watched her torture with a certain amount of sadistic pleasure flitting across her hawkish face; she wouldn't put it past her to enjoy watching Billie raped. In fact, the bitch might even join in with her violation.

A knock at the door sounded, and it was a welcome distraction.

Being the only person able to without releasing their prisoner, Amanda went to the door and opened it a crack.

'Sorry about the intrusion, ma'am,' a male voice said, 'but I thought you'd want to hear this.'

'What is it?' Amanda snapped.

'The team sent to recover the body from the forest; they're back.'

It was apparent from the new arrival's tone that something was amiss. 'I take it there was a problem?' Amanda said.

Billie's ears pricked up.

'The body was gone,' the man announced.

'Probably bears,' Daniel said with a grunt of sarcasm for Billie.

Amanda must have hushed the messenger, because there was a scuff of feet and then the door closed as she joined him in the corridor. Billie listened hard, but couldn't make out anything worthwhile from their muffled conversation. While Amanda was outside, Erick relaxed his hold on her and stepped away. She tracked the man's gaze and saw a fleeting frown of worry as he looked at Daniel. 'You did finish that guy like I said?'

'He was shot in the chest, and then I broke his skull. No way anyone was going to get up and walk away from that.'

'Apparently he did,' Erick growled. 'You should have made sure, you idiot.'

Daniel's grip relaxed minutely as he peered back at his brother. For a moment Billie felt a space open between his body and hers, and if she was quick and determined enough she could twist out of his grasp and run for the door. What then? Amanda and another man were in the hall; even if she got past the brothers, she'd still be stopped. Better that she wait for another opportunity, one that she couldn't help feel was coming, because suddenly there was a different air of expectancy in the room, one that told her the brothers had grown anxious.

The door opened, Amanda's heels clopping as she entered, her steps fast and hard. She'd left the room for privacy, but apparently it didn't matter if Billie heard now, and that was not good news for her prospects of release.

'Erick! You told me that you tracked Mrs Womack via the distress beacon in the vest she was wearing?' Amanda made her questions sound like accusations, and for good reason.

'Did none of you think to disable the damn thing before you brought her here?'

Instead of answering her directly, Erick looked squarely at Daniel. 'Tell me that's not something else you fucked up, Danny.'

'Hey, man, not my problem.' Daniel released Billie to stand and face his accusers.

'Daniel's correct,' Amanda snapped. 'Who is in charge, Erick? Whose final responsibility is it to ensure his men don't neglect the small points?'

Erick didn't reply.

'I've just been informed that the body of this "Joe Hunter" is missing. Considering that Mrs Womack was wearing a bulletproof vest, and its tracker was used to find her, the team checked for the signal from Hunter's vest. It wasn't locatable. Do you know why? Because – even wounded – the man had the presence of mind to disable it. Unlike the incompetence shown here by you, Erick. When the team found that the beacon in Billie's vest was still sending out a signal, they thought it imperative that I know. Because it would be apparent to anyone with an ounce of intelligence that if we could trace it, then so could those looking to protect Billie.' Amanda's tirade had been delivered with venom. She had lost her cool, Billie understood, because she was suddenly afraid. The woman's fear was soothing for her. Hunter had survived? That meant that someone was probably looking for her then, and might not be far away. Billie felt hope rise and swell in her chest like a bubble, but Amanda popped it.

'We have to move her now,' the woman said.

'Yes,' Erick replied. 'Before we're all implicated in her abduction and torture.'

This last was meant to sound as dramatic as it had, because Erick wanted Amanda to understand that he wasn't prepared to take the fall for her, not when she was obviously so disrespectful of everything he'd done for her and for Procrylon.

'This has been a waste of our time and effort, anyway,' Erick went on. He looked down at Billie, and though his eyes twinkled behind the lenses of his glasses it wasn't through pity. 'I believe her. She doesn't have a clue about Richard or the money.'

Amanda huffed once in her chest. It was a sound of disappointment, but also of decision. 'Then she's no good to us. When you move her, lose her. And make sure that the job is carried out to the letter this time.' She turned her attention on Daniel. 'And you, go and ensure that damn beacon is disabled instantly. And hope that you haven't brought the FBI's Hostage Rescue Team down on our heads. Remember, Mrs Womack isn't the only person I can have buried without a trace.'

32

I moved through the same corridor I'd earlier watched the two workers walk along, before I'd entered the building. I had my silenced gun in my hand, and the spare in my belt. The PMC I'd taken it from was tied up in the same storage room as the security guard; he was still sound asleep. If the guard had wakened in the meantime he had the sense not to let on for fear of another smack around the head, and I'd left him to it. I'd considered plugging in and taking another quick scan of the security monitors, but without knowledge of the layout of the building to compare against the images, I wouldn't see anything useful to lead me to Billie. So I left them disabled and decided to simply follow my nose and my intuition deeper inside the building.

The lower floor of the main building was primarily offices and workspaces, and at this time of the evening deserted. I bypassed a bank of elevators, and headed for an adjacent staircase. It was too easy to get trapped inside an elevator. Stairwells could be dangerous areas too, but there was no alternative way of getting upstairs. The security guard let slip he thought that Amanda Sheehan could be found in one of the conference rooms up there, and I believed that where she was then so was Billie. Sheehan was quite obviously someone sent by Procrylon to turn the thumbscrews on their prisoner. I've fought and killed women before, but never out of choice. It was a dilemma having to go up against a woman now, but considering it was to free another woman I guessed the universe was balanced again. I had to be cautious of Sheehan, who hadn't arrived because she had a sweet disposition; she was some kind of professional torture artist. But more so I'd to be wary of the Jaeger brothers, since when it came to gunplay they'd be the ones I'd be up against, plus whatever sized private army they had at their backs. Once already they'd beaten me, and I didn't want history repeating.

I went up the stairs as if I had a right to be there. The number of personnel in such a large building, I doubted everyone was totally familiar with everyone else, and I wouldn't immediately be challenged. I hoped that I could find someone who wasn't on the direct payroll of either Procrylon or the private military company who'd give up information regarding Billie without my having to resort to threats or direct action, but maybe that was too much to ask. At the top I came to a set of double swing doors. Porthole-style windows allowed a view into another corridor, which was deserted. I went on through and padded down the hall, watching for signs on the walls for a hint of where to go. The rooms had numbered designations, but that was all. All were silent as I passed. Reaching another set of double doors I paused. From beyond them came the muted tones of conversation.

Taking a quick glance through a door window I spotted two figures standing outside a room, to which the door was standing open. Both wore the familiar green PMC uniform and had sidearms on their hips. One was a black man, the other an Asian. I didn't recognise either from my pursuers in the woods, but a third man exited the room and joined them and he was vaguely familiar. When the Jaegers had first arrived at Billie's farm they'd come with two helpers. One of those was now dead, but there was the last of the bunch. I knew him only from his shape and mannerisms as I'd never got a clean look at him through the mist that time as he closed in on the farm. Of anyone I'd seen up until now, this man offered most hope for a direct line to Billie. Hell, for all I knew, she could be in the very room he'd just come from. So could another dozen armed soldiers, but I couldn't allow what-ifs to slow me. Pulling the spare gun from my belt for extra effect, I immediately pushed through the door, a gun in each hand as I stalked forward.

'Nobody move,' I warned.

Of course my words had the opposite effect. The black man whose back had been presented to me turned at my voice, and the Asian also snapped his head round. Only the third man faced me head on and I watched him sway from side to side as his mind screamed for positive action while also cautioning against it. My boldness had thrown them off, and I was glad to see none of them reached for a weapon. I halted ten feet from them, and kept the guns levelled on the nearest men's chests. 'Dump your belts and kick them away from you. Quick about it.'

Three men against two guns. The PMCs shared little glances and nods. I could tell they were doing the maths. Anyone with sense would realise each of my guns held more than one bullet, and I was obviously the type with the balls to shoot as many times as necessary. Maybe they'd given their good sense the night off, because through some unspoken communication they all came to agreement. The idiots went for their guns.

My silenced handgun went off, the black man fell with a round through his throat and I adjusted my aim within a split second. The Asian didn't immediately go down, but he did stagger to one side, his hands going to the wound in his belly. I shot him again, and this time he did fall. By then the third man had cleared his holster and was lifting his sidearm. I aimed through the gap caused by his fallen comrades, but this time didn't go for a fatal target. My bullet passed through his wrist and splintered the door frame behind him. The man yelped in agony, collapsing to his knees as he grabbed at his injured arm. I moved in fast, checking both his comrades were out of the game, and kicked him over on to his back, even as I covered the doorway lest anyone should seek to join the fight. No one did, and there was no shout of alarm, so I quickly pushed away my spare gun in my belt and reached to take away the PMC's gun that hung precariously out of the holster. I tucked it into the small of my back too.

Two men were dead and another injured, and the most noise made was by the latter when he'd cried in agony. I didn't hear a corresponding shout of alarm, and the room he'd exited was still and silent. I doubted Billie was in there, but I had to check.

The injured man hugged his wounded wrist to his chest, glaring up at me from his prone position, and I gave him something to concentrate on. I aimed the suppressed muzzle of my gun directly at his face as I leaned in quickly and checked the room. It was a typical conference suite, with a large oblong table surrounded by chairs dominating the space. A couple other tables against one wall, an old-fashioned over-head projector and a water cooler completed the look. There was no sign of Billie, or anything to suggest she'd ever been there. I took it the trio had made an impromptu drinks stop at the water cooler during their rounds.

'Where's Billie Womack?' Hell, I was beginning to sound like a stuck record.

'I saw you die,' the man said.

'Obviously you didn't,' I said, and proved I was no ghost by placing the suppressor to his forehead. 'But you were there in the forest, sure enough. You know who I'm talking about; you were one of the bastards who took Billie. You also know exactly where she is now. Tell me.'

'You'll shoot me as soon as I tell you.'

'Maybe. But I'll shoot right now if you don't.'

'You'd murder an injured man?'

'In an instant,' I told him. But truth be told, I wouldn't. I'd resolved to take the fight to my enemies, though only where they were combatants and fair game. It was one thing shooting men with the same intention as I had, quite another an unarmed guy lying injured on the floor. But letting the man know that would be a huge mistake. Better that he believed I was a cold-blooded assassin. I dug the suppressor into the skin of his forehead. 'Do I need to give you a countdown?'

He'd screwed his eyelids tight, grimacing in pain. When he again looked up at me his gaze was pointed, resigned to his death. 'Quit the dramatics, will you? If you're going to shoot, shoot.'

'You're doing yourself no favours.'

'Fuck you.'

'Have it your way.' I didn't shoot. I grabbed his injured wrist and inserted my thumb in the bullet wound. Grinding my thumb into the splintered bones, I watched the guy change his mind about defying me. He bit down on his lips to stop from crying out, which was sensible of him. 'Ready to speak yet?'

'I . . . I'm ready.'

I withdrew my thumb. 'The question hasn't changed: where's Billie Womack?'

'She's not in this building.'

'I don't want to know where she isn't. C'mon. Spill.'

He jerked his head, and I thought it was to escape the gun, but it was actually a nod of direction. 'There's a sky bridge adjoining the next building across. You need to go that way. Billie's being held there.'

'Who has her? The Jaegers?'

He appeared surprised that I knew the names.

'The Jaegers, and then some.'

'How many?'

'Twenty, thirty, maybe more. I couldn't say. Maybe you'd best get yourself over there and find out.' He offered a sly smile that told me he didn't fancy my chances.

'You wouldn't be sending me on a wild goose chase . . .'

'Why would I? You're gonna kill me. If you decide not to be a punk-ass and let me live, well, whatever. I'm not going to be able to show my face around here anymore. Not if the Jaegers learn I sent you after them.'

'Trust me, I won't be wasting time carrying tales to them.'

He nodded. Professional gratitude.

'By the way, I'm no punk-ass.' I gave him the respect he was due. I kicked him hard in the head and sent him to sleep. By the time he woke up it wouldn't matter if he raised the alarm. And if he chose to join the fight, then so be it. Next time he would be fairer game.

Giving him no further thought, I headed past the conference room and found another short corridor. A set of double doors opened on to the promised skywalk. It was glassed in on three sides, though the windows and roof were semi-opaque with dirt and bird droppings, and underfoot the floor shuddered minutely with each step and made a thrumming noise. I didn't slow down, just kept going. The sound would be a feature to anyone familiar with the building. Reaching the far end I again paused at a set of double doors with porthole windows, and spied out what I was up against. I couldn't see a soul, but from somewhere below me voices rang out, and suddenly there was a new buzz of expectancy in the air. Doors banged, and there followed running footsteps, and more raised commands. I'd no idea how the news had got out, but they knew I was there. I pressed open the doors and entered the second building, looking immediately for passage down. Before I found a stairwell, I halted in my tracks.

In the distance a woman howled.

It was more a scream of rage than of fear.

It was followed instantly by a bleat of pain, and I threw all caution aside and plunged for the stairs down.

33

Billie went for Amanda Sheehan's eyes with the only weapons available to her: the nails of her left hand.

Her opportunity came after Danny left the room, stony-faced after hearing Amanda's proclamation about his future should he mess up again. Amanda had ignored him as he walked stiffly by; she'd said her piece and felt no need to reiterate it. Erick watched his brother go, and in those few seconds of inattentiveness Billie realised that she was neither being watched nor held. Her right hand was useless to her, twitching and shaking, and numb. She seethed like a kettle reaching boiling point, both at what had been done to her, and what was to come. She erupted out of her seat without warning, ducked past Erick who – apart from a narrowing of his eyelids – didn't react in time to stop her, and screeched a wild war cry as she went for the face of her tormentor. Amanda had been in the process of pulling out a cell phone, her attention on the screen, and it took her a second or two to understand she was the target of Billie's rage, and to react. The trouble for her was her reaction was wrong: instead of taking the fight to Billie, she attempted to escape backwards, and her heels caught on the threadbare carpet and she staggered against a wall. Billie was on her, and she clamped her nails on Amanda's bony face, her fingers curling over the dome of Amanda's forehead, while her thumb dug deep into her eye socket. Amanda cried shrilly, while Billie's scream rose and fell in pitch as she tore at the face of her enemy. Billie crashed up against her and both women went to the floor in an untidy heap, with Billie on top and never relinquishing her hold. In desperation, all Amanda could do was try to strike out at Billie's head, using the edge of her cell phone, without any conscious intention of doing so. Billie was beyond immediate pain, and she even tangled her broken fingers in Amanda's previously coiffed hair and twisted it into a tangle. She screamed and snarled like something wild, and then sank her teeth into Amanda's opposite cheek.

Seconds had passed, ample time for Erick to assist his boss, but he took his time walking over. He grasped Billie's hair and made a fist of his own, then reared back, and flung her on to her backside on the floor. Blood ran from Billie's lips, but it wasn't her own. She sat there, staring with volcanic heat in her gaze, as Amanda crawled to her knees, her hands going to the wounds on both sides of her face. Fearing that her looks had been permanently ruined, her stern, smug, sadistic traits of earlier were replaced by those of a vain woman. She cried into her hands, then dabbed at the wounds with her fingertips, and when she saw the glistening blood it didn't help. She fell over on to her right hip, then backed up to the wall. Surprisingly her accusations weren't immediately directed at Billie. 'You allowed her to attack me!' Amanda shrieked at Erick, her right eye screwed tight.

'Sorry, ma'am, she surprised us all.'

'You could have stopped her!'

'I did. Trust me, if I hadn't pulled her off you when I did your injuries wouldn't be as superficial.'

'Superficial? She's almost torn my eye out!' Amanda turned her ire on Billie. 'You bitch! I'll have you killed for that.'

Billie hadn't moved from where she'd landed on her backside. She smiled viciously. 'You were going to have me killed any way. What more can you do to me now?'

'You were going to be offered a clean bullet. Now I'm going to have you beaten to death. Slowly. Erick . . .'

Erick didn't move.

Billie laughed at the woman's pathetic threat. 'I bet you wouldn't try it yourself. Touch me and I'll finish ripping your face off, you whore.'

Amanda struggled to stand, to regain some vestige of dignity. It was difficult while blinking wildly, half blinded by blood and tears. Erick offered a steadying hand, but she slapped it away angrily, reaching instead for her dropped cell phone. She was horrified when she realised that her call had gone through and there was an open line, through which her superiors were listening. Her face an open book of dismay, she hit the end call button. She must contact her bosses with an update, to reassure them that everything was under control, but not in that room while Billie laughed as if she'd just heard the best joke ever.

'Erick! Shut her up now, goddamn it.'

'Yes, ma'am,' Erick said. He loomed over Billie where she still sat on the floor. Billie lifted her face to laugh in his.

'Quiet,' he said.

'Go to hell,' Billie replied.

'You got your licks in, but don't push your luck.'

'Touch me and I'll do the same to you as I did to that bitch,' Billie promised.

There were no second warnings from the PMC. Erick kicked her, his instep jarring her chin, slamming her teeth together, and knocking her flat on her back, unconscious.

34

Perhaps it was one of the two men from the foyer who I'd tied in the closet who raised the alarm, or maybe the guy I'd spared a few minutes ago. It didn't really matter, because sooner or later it was going to happen, and I'd been lucky to get as far as I had before the alarms started ringing. A recorded message played through amplified speakers, warning of an intruder alert. I heard corresponding shouts and running feet as the site went into lockdown mode and PMCs raced for their positions. I could continue to creep around, maybe even find a secure hiding spot, and avert detection for a while, but what was the purpose of that? I was there to snatch Billie out of the hands of her captors and couldn't do that if I was dug in like a tick. I'd always believed in forward momentum and decisive action. So I pressed on, and now put aside all thought of future consequences. Right then, right there, I was a man trying to save a woman from her abusers, and the laws of the lands meant nothing by comparison. If the PMCs came at me with deadly intent, they'd find me in a similar shoot-to-kill frame of mind.

My resolution was tested within seconds.

I'd reached the bottom of the stairs, and moved through another set of doors, finding myself in a storage area stacked high with crates and yellow plastic drums. On the drums were warnings about corrosive chemicals, and I steered away from them, placing myself near a stack of crates, just as two men in green PMC uniforms came in the same door I'd just entered by. They must have spotted me entering the storage room, and recognised me as an interloper, because they came in low, with their guns extended. They were decent soldiers, too, and had I been a few seconds slower in finding cover they would easily have taken me down. Instead, they were still sweeping their guns to and fro as they searched, while I bobbed out from behind the stacked crates at a ninety-degree angle to them. The nearest man caught movement in his peripheral vision and began his turn towards me, but by then my first shot was already on its way. He fell dead without ever fully laying eyes on me.

The second man fired and his bullets forced me down, as he too sought cover. He plunged behind a row of plastic drums while speaking frantically into a radio. Support was on the way and I couldn't afford to get trapped in the storage area. I took out a spare pistol, and propping both hands over the crates I unloaded on the plastic barrels. The sound was deafening, and even though I couldn't see clearly I could hear the puncturing of the drums, and chemicals splashing everywhere. My opponent had moved; he bobbed out a few yards distant and returned fire. Chips of wood almost blinded me, he came so close to taking off my head. I went down on my knees and then my belly and found a gap through the lower crates, firing again, but this time tracking the guard as he too tried to move for cover. My bullets tore through the drums, and at least one of them hit him. I heard a grunt and a clatter and believed he'd dropped the radio. I came up immediately and vaulted over the low stack of crates, ignoring the pulling in my chest. The man was swearing under his breath, and though I couldn't see him I pinpointed his position. I fired again, seeking gaps between the drums as I lunged forward and kicked the nearest drum over. The rim hit the man, and he struggled to get a good position on me. I swept up chemicals with the toe of my boot and the liquid splashed over his features. It wasn't acid in the conventional sense, so wasn't an immediate threat to him, but reaction forced his eyelids tight and his mouth pinched shut. While he was blinded, I shot him twice in the chest and he sank down.

I looked at him for the briefest of time. Like others I'd fought, it was long enough to tell I'd never seen him before in my life. Within seconds we'd become mortal enemies, and he had died. Such was the world that we moved in. I turned from him, running for the far end of the storage room, knowing that if I were pinned inside then the tight space would become a shooting gallery where I was the only sitting duck. I made the door and slipped into a service corridor just as the sound of running feet reached my ears. I plastered myself into a recessed doorway, out of sight as a guard running to back up the two I'd just killed pounded along the corridor. His adrenalin must have been racing because he showed no caution, heading directly for the door I'd just exited. I waited, holding my breath, my right elbow braced against the door behind me. He came into my line of sight for the briefest second, but it was long enough for me to shoot twice, the silenced rounds giving him no warning as they plunged into him. Then he was gone from view, but I heard him crumple and then slide on to the floor, his gun clattering. I came out behind him, and put another round through his skull. The slide stayed back on my gun, so I reached for his firearm. Before I'd been outgunned, but my collection was growing and his Colt M4 carbine was a welcome addition to my arsenal. This was the weapon of choice of the United States armed forces, lightweight for mobility and target acquisition, but with the potent firepower ability for most combat operations. The PMC hadn't got off a shot so I took it that the magazine was full, and on his webbing belt I found spare mags of 5.56 x 45 NATO rounds. So that I wasn't encumbered – I'd enough guns in my belt to contend with – I shoved one of the spare magazines down the front of my antiballistic vest, and another in my jacket pocket, and dumped the now depleted handgun and silencer.

I pulled and released the arming bolt on the carbine, and hit the selection switch to single shot. On fully automatic the magazine would be emptied in as little as one and a half seconds. Ferocious firepower by anybody's reckoning, but a waste of bullets. Then I paced along the corridor, listening, judging, trying desperately to hear another clue as to where Billie was. The corridor wasn't long, and it turned at a right angle to the left, forming little more than a vestibule where there was a bank of elevators. I moved past them, and through another door and into a larger storage or workroom. There were counters laid out along two sides and a broad counter down the centre like a kitchen island, on which were various scientific contraptions. The air stank of chemicals, and static electricity charged the air from the number of machines that blinked and whirred and whistled. If I'd to guess, I'd say I was in a laboratory, possibly where some of the research into Procrylon's acrylic polymer developments took form. Ordinarily this room should be heavily guarded against intruders, but with the alarms ringing and armed PMCs racing to secure the building, the civilian workers had quickly evacuated, and those tasked with guarding it had been the first responders I'd just shot down.

I moved through the room cautiously, and exited into another service corridor, again with a right-angled turn, this one to the right. I snuck a quick look around the corner and found an empty vestibule, but then noticed the ubiquitous swing doors that were a regular feature here. I crept to them and rather than peer through one of the porthole windows, I stayed near the wall and peeked through the slim gap up the edge of the nearest door. Beyond was another huge storage facility, this one stacked with steel and plastic drums, rows of metal shelves, shrink-wrapped boxes and packing crates.

The overhead lights suddenly dimmed, and somewhere a red alarm beacon flashed, causing shadows to strobe. Faintly I heard the recorded warning repeating. I moved into the room cautiously, ducking low, and moved among the rows of drums; I had gained the final quarter of the room when four armed men blocked any further progress. They weren't total amateurs either. They had positioned themselves either side of the exit doorway so that to advance would place me in their converging arcs of fire. Try to escape that way and I'd be holed like a sieve in seconds. My only saving grace was that they were unaware of my arrival. I kept my head down, but my relatively safe hiding place would be compromised if anyone crept in on me via the laboratory. I breathed in, holding the air in my lungs as I attempted to come up with a contingency plan.

To retreat meant losing ground I couldn't afford, and really wasn't an option. I could be returning to the killing grounds I'd just escaped if reinforcements had arrived. Best that I continue on, but to do that I had to first shatter the blockade ahead. My M4 carbine was a superior weapon to the hand-guns that the four men wielded, and I could probably drop a couple of them before the others got off a return shot. But it only took one of them to get a clear target and Billie's rescue attempt was over.

I crouched behind a stack of oil drums. Ordinarily the number of steel barrels would protect me, but I worried about their contents: for all I knew they were flammable and a stray spark from a ricochet would be enough to set off a chain reaction that would see me incinerated. A quick check of the nearest barrel didn't give any clues about what it contained; I could see no symbols, only faded writing in a foreign script I didn't recognise let alone understand. There was a chemical stink, but again it was too weak to define. Whatever, I didn't want to be splashed with the liquid inside. I belly-crawled to the left, toes and elbows, holding up the M4 so that it didn't rattle on the floor and give away my position.

The four men argued briefly. I only heard a couple of clear words, but they were enough to tell me that they were all nervous and trigger-happy. One of them urged his fellows to advance, but it sounded as if none of them was eager to go first. Couldn't say that I blamed them. They suspected I was out there in the warehouse, if not exactly where.

Coming up against a wall, I rose to a crouch and pressed my shoulder against it for support as I levelled my assault rifle over the top of a steel drum, this one empty and lacking a lid. The angle I presented had been cut down by fifty per cent, but then so had my choice of targets. The odds were more to my liking than before though: less chance of me being killed immediately. I aimed the carbine like a hunting rifle and lined it up with the furthest man on the right. As before I inhaled, then held my breath. My pulse was loud in my ears, but there was no transposition to my fingers and I held the barrel steady on its target. I waited.

A harsh whisper passed between the men. Perhaps one of the couple on the left took a look for me, but he was out of my line of sight. I waited some more. The whisperer said something else and this time the nearest man to my right poked his head out from his hiding place. He was an indistinct blur against the darker background. I could have killed him, but he wasn't my target of choice. I had to cut down the man at the rear right corner, then the one to front right. Do it in reverse order and the man furthest away would become more difficult to hit. Finally my target couldn't contain his inquisitiveness, and feeling protected by his buddies he stepped out and aimed a flashlight into the room, sweeping it towards the drums behind which I'd earlier hidden. Exhaling, I caressed the trigger, nice and gentle, and the beam of the flashlight swept the ceiling as its wielder went down on his back. In the brief flare of light I saw droplets of red in the air and knew that I'd scored a direct hit on the man's head. The lack of a death scream also confirmed it. Reaction to my gun's retort brought out the nearest man to the right, but he had not seen the muzzle flash and his bullets scorched the air a good ten feet across the room from me. I triple-tapped him. Two in centre mass, one a bit higher up. Throat or head, it didn't much matter, because he would be dead or close enough to it that he too was out of the fight.

Immediately I went to my knees, placing the steel drums between us, but with no intention of staying there. I knee-walked a few feet, then went down on my belly and squirmed across the floor so that I was a good twenty feet from my original position. There was no obstruction between the remaining two gunmen and me but they misconstrued my position, thinking me still braced up against the wall at their side. The back man couldn't fire for fear of hitting his pal in the spine, which meant only one of them could lean out and shoot at a time. Again I'd have preferred a line on the furthest man first, but I wouldn't turn down a gift either. From the left a man stepped out. He was small, wiry, a scarecrow's shadow against the darkness, but he presented more body mass than the other man as he raised his gun two-handed and fired along the wall at my imagined position. From my place on the ground I flipped the selector to fully auto and pulled the trigger. The flashes from my gun lit up the warehouse like a mad scientist's lab, and the third man span and went down in a series of strobing movements. Before he'd finished falling though, man number four was shooting, and this time he'd the advantage of having spotted me.

I held my prone position. He could see me, but I still made a poor target for a man with a handgun who was shooting on adrenalin and terror. A round struck the wall to my side and whined away into darkness. Another found the floor and skipped up dangerously close to my face. Despite my resolve I flinched and the move pulled the M4 up and high to the right as I fired back. I missed the gunman and he ducked back through a door into an adjoining room. The clicks and snaps of a man hurriedly re-arming his gun sounded.

I rolled to my left, placing steel drums between us again, though these were a few yards distant.

From behind me came the slap of feet and the clinks and bumps of reinforcements hurrying to the scene of our battle. There was no time for subtlety. No time for stalking the final gunman, or for getting into a cat and mouse chase. I had to move now. But if I ran for the exit he need only lean out and it would be first to fire that survived. At a crouch I ran to the drums and forced my shoulder against the one at the centre of the stack. It almost went over on its side at my first push. Told me the steel drum wasn't nearly full enough to offer much cover, but that wasn't my purpose. Placing down the M4, I got two palms on the rim and jostled it off the pallet on to the floor.

The clang of the drum striking ground brought out my quarry, and he fired. Rounds struck steel, but he'd fired at the stack of drums, not the one I crouched behind. Luckily for me they didn't prove as flammable as I'd feared. By the time I lifted my carbine he'd dipped back into the room. I stood and kicked the barrel over on its side, then placed my foot against it to line it up and pushed it into a roll towards the room he hid in.

As the barrel rolled, I fired into it. Ricochets whined and sparks blossomed.

I wanted the PMC to fear immolation. My plan worked. He didn't pop out of hiding again, but scurried further inside the room. The barrel rolled by the doorway without any detonation, and I gambled everything on the fact that my enemy had found something to hide behind and had anticipated the flash and spill of fiery liquid by covering his head with his arms. Any sane person with a regard for their life would react in a similar fashion. I sprinted past the doorway and didn't stop. I overtook the rolling drum, then dropped to the floor, swinging round and aiming my rifle at the doorway.

The man swore loudly when he realised he'd been fooled, and this was followed by a thud as he leaned against an item of furniture to help him stand. I waited for a three-count, and then saw the man's tentative check of the warehouse. From his hiding place he would likely make out the shape of the drum where it now rocked lazily as the liquid inside sloshed back and forth, and again I hoped that human nature would mean that the movement would draw his attention first. It did, and with it he fired. But I was three feet to the right and returned fire unhindered by his bullets. My rounds punched holes in his guts and groin and his handgun clattered on the floor. The man fell out of the room, sprawling in an ungainly heap on a level with me. Was he dead? Probably. But I shot him again to be sure.

I was only a few feet from him, and his dropped gun was much closer. I grabbed it up, ejected the magazine and inserted it in my waistband at the front. It was a bulk standard Glock 17, with a seventeen-round capacity, and I'd counted only three shots since he'd reloaded it. I couldn't tell if he'd had a full load to start with, but any spare ammunition was gratefully received. I dumped the gun, got up and went to the man at the far right corner. I liberated his ammunition too, plus the flashlight. Both could come in handy.

There was still no sign of the full power coming back on, but by now my eyesight had adjusted to the dimness and I hoped that the facility remained in near darkness. On the other hand, the vision of those hunting me would also have adapted to the dark. They were coming fast, unhindered by the lack of light, and with more familiarity with the layout of the building. I got up and ran for the exit. All sounds of pursuit came from my rear, but I'd be a fool to think that others hadn't positioned themselves between Billie and me.

It was difficult estimating the number of people in the facility. Not all of them would be armed, or even engaged in the hunt. But most were potential enemies. Even one of the civilian technicians or lab workers could try to brain me with a blunt object if they felt threatened. I'd killed, wounded, or at least immobilised ten fighters up until now, but the odds remained hugely against me – time and location too. For all I knew, Billie was too precious a hostage for them to allow me to get close to her, and even as I played at the fox in the henhouse, she was being moved elsewhere.

I wondered what the hell was keeping Cooper and his team. The instructions given to Noah and Adam were to call him at first hint of trouble. My first incursion had been tentative and largely silent, but surely it had grown obvious that the shit had hit the fan the moment the gunfire started in earnest. Cooper's team should have been on scene by now, but knowing any law enforcement group there was probably a heap of bureaucracy to wade through before they were allowed to mobilise. I could imagine plans and countermeasures being bandied around and was glad that I wasn't similarly hamstrung by procedure. It was one of the things that used to annoy me back when I was with Arrowsake: plans are all well and good but never last beyond first enemy contact. Hit hard, hit fast and hope for the best was always a credo of mine, though it never went down well with my superiors. In a way I was relieved that nobody was looking over my shoulder. What I had to do to save Billie would never be lawfully endorsed.

Another corridor stretched ahead of me, differentiated from the others by a lack of doors and adjoining offices, and by the fact that at the far end one emergency light had stayed on and offered dull yellow illumination to the walls and floor. It also showed a set of doors complete with push bars and wired windows. Beyond the semi-opaque glass was more light, but it dimmed and brightened and I guessed that further down the corridor beyond it, hunters moved with flashlights. I considered turning back and attempting to find another route, but instinctively knew that this was the only path to Billie's cell.

No one moved this side of the swing doors.

I rushed along the corridor, noting that it was simply an access passage alongside the laboratories and processing plant. The cinderblock wall to my left exuded coldness; most likely it was an exterior wall, or at least adjoined open loading bays. My location was precarious. There were defenders beyond the door I approached, and more moving in from behind. If I was stalled at the door I'd be wide open to a barrage of gunfire from behind, if I went through the doors I could very well be walking into a trap. Still the first scenario was more probable than the second, so I immediately went to the doors and planned to put them at my back before my hunters caught up.

The doors served no other purpose than as a necessary fire safety feature, to slow the spread of smoke and flames. They weren't locked, and a gentle push on one of the bars opened the right-hand door. As I pressed it open I held my breath, waiting for the inevitable storm of bullets. When they didn't come, I pushed open the door some more and went through quickly. Voices filtered down a corridor equally as long and featureless as the first, and there was a brief flare of light from a right-hand turn at the far end. But I felt confident I wasn't about to be discovered and paused to check the walls on this side of the fire doors. Hanging on slim chains were triangular wedges of wood. Though fire doors should be kept closed, day-to-day working practices dictated otherwise. The wedges had been left hanging in place to enable the doors to be chocked open while pallets and drums were moved along the corridors to the loading bays. Not that I planned jamming them open. Quite the opposite: I took down the wedges and pressed one under each door and forced them into place with a couple of kicks with my heel. The wood wouldn't hold back determined enemies for long, but at least I'd get a warning of their approach.

Satisfied that no immediate pursuit could follow, I padded along the corridor, my M4 up and targeting the far right corner. My rubber-soled boots made soft sucking noises on the linoleum flooring, but otherwise my run was quiet enough that I didn't alert those round the corner. I reached it and placed myself tight to the wall, then bent at the knees to offer a lower profile. I snuck a look along the next corridor. This one was partially full of stacked pallets, boxes and drums shrink-wrapped and ready for dispatch. A narrow walkway on the right, about two yards wide, was all that remained between the pallets and the wall. To go into such a tight space would be offering myself on a plate. The walkway was of course the fastest route along the corridor, and I weighed it up against a slower but safer way. I chose safer.

I crossed the corridor and pressed up against a pile of boxes stacked six feet tall. Standing on tiptoe I could see over the top of it, and a number of others, but my view was obscured about twenty yards ahead where another pallet was stacked higher with more steel drums. Checking the walkway again, it remained empty. Good enough. I clambered up on to the first stack, staying low and slow and progressing over it as silently as possible. The ceiling was lower here, barely two feet above my head. It would take an experienced soldier to check overhead, and I was confident that I was all but invisible in the shadows. I continued along, crawling from stack to stack of boxes until I reached the drums. There I'd need to take more care. The gap between the uppermost drums and the ceiling was barely enough to accommodate me, and I was now preparing to move over ringing steel barrels instead of sound-deadening cardboard. I held my carbine out ahead of me, placed it on the drums gently, and slithered snake-like into the gap. I lifted and moved my rifle, squirmed ahead, then repeated the manoeuvre. I'd almost reached the edge of the stack of drums when two figures came round the corner. They were indistinct behind the flaring beam of a flashlight, but I could tell enough about them that made my heart slump.

Only one of them was an armed PMC.

The figure to the right was a woman dressed in coveralls and a plastic cap.

She was a worker, a non-combatant, and call me old-fashioned but I'd never willingly harm her.

It made things difficult for taking out the armed guard.

If I'd had the choice I'd have scrunched down, remained silent and allowed the couple to pass, but that option was taken away from me. From back around the corner came the solid bangs of people attempting to force a way through the wedged fire doors.

The noise caused the two figures to halt almost directly beneath me. They were alert and nervous, but I saw how the man pressed a hand to the woman's elbow, urging her to stay put while he went on to investigate. If I allowed him to do so, he'd quickly realise it was his friends at the door and he'd pull out the wedges and allow them to come after me. Knowing I was responsible for locking the doors behind me, they'd come fast.

Squeezed between the ceiling and the uppermost drums, I wasn't in a great defensive position, with little manoeuvrability, so there wasn't room for finesse. I squirmed out and dropped to all fours, feeling the impact of the floor in my knees and elbows. The M4 I had to abandon on top of the stack, so I immediately went for one of the guns in my waistband even as I twisted towards the armed PMC. The woman's croak of alarm, the rustle of my clothing and subsequent thud on hitting the ground had already ensured he was turning towards me. The problem was, he was on his feet and steadier than my half-twisted-half-crouching posture allowed me to be. He also had a clear target while I was still trying to find mine.

He fired first.

35

He went for dead centre and struck bull's-eye.

Thankfully, that was what saved my life. His bullet struck my bulletproof vest, and this time the vest's integrity wasn't compromised. Still the impact felt as if my buddy, Rink, had kicked me, and sent a wave of red pain through my previous injuries. I staggered, and the air was pushed up from my lungs and made a high-pitched wheeze in my throat, but I managed to shoot on instinct. My bullet hit him in the side, just beneath his right armpit, and disappeared somewhere inside him. The nine mm round wasn't powerful enough to find an exit through his back and rattled around, breaking apart and pulping his innards. The PMC fell to his knees, shock shredding his resolve, and his gun hand drooped. I shot him again. There was no room for pity or remorse.

The woman screamed.

If she had run, I'd have probably allowed it. But she didn't. Maybe she was romantically tied to the man, or she simply felt a huge amount of loyalty to her fallen comrade, because she didn't make her escape. She jumped on my back, her left hand clawing at my face, seeking my eyes. With her right hand she clubbed at my head and shoulders with the flashlight. Light flashed behind my eyelids with each smack of the torch.

'Enough!'

My snarl wasn't sufficient to put the woman off.

I elbowed backwards and got her in the midriff. No shrinking violet, she held on, and if anything my strike infuriated her more.

'He's here,' she hollered as she tore at my forehead with her nails. 'He's here!'

From beyond the corner in the passage came the scrape of the fire doors being forced wider. A babble of voices rose, followed by the scuff and thud of a number of people forcing a way through the doors. The woman shouted to her friends one more time. I'd told her enough, and I meant it.

I ducked out of her grip, coming up alongside her, and with my left arm batted away her questing fingers. I got one look at her face, an oval blob swimming in the shadows beyond the flashlight beam. She was possibly pretty, but not then because her face was contorted with hatred. My gun was poised to shoot, but there was still that thread of caution that tethered me to my moral centre. I didn't pull the trigger. Instead I thrust my head forward and struck hers: forehead to forehead so that I didn't smash her face. The woman went down on her backside, stunned, arms and legs splayed, eyes rolling up in their sockets. The flashlight rattled from her numb fingers.

'I said *enough*, for fuck's sake!' I repeated as I rushed away from her, angrier with myself than at the woman.

I'd promised never to willingly make war on women or children, but there's something in the old adage that the female's the deadliest of the species. She'd torn stinging grooves in my forehead, and only luck had saved my vision. God help me if she hadn't worn her nails cut short. I'd killed women before, a fact I'm not proud of, but always in the heat of battle, and I was happy that this time I was able to neutralise an enemy without fatally wounding her. She'd have a sore head for a day or two, but should recover fully.

I left her sitting against the stack of pallets, holding her
face in her hands as she moaned in shock. Any stealth was
wasted now and I rushed along the narrow space between
the wall and stacks of drums and boxes. I held the handgun
ready, and had made ten or more paces before I remembered I'd left the M4 behind. It was too late to retrieve it. I
went round the next corner and found the corridor blocked
by a second set of doors. These too had been fitted against
the threat of fire, and again came with push bars. The glass
in the upper portions of the doors was grimy and I couldn't
see through it. But I'd no other recourse than go through,
this time at speed: shock and awe. I booted the doors open
and continued into the next corridor, having now negotiated
three turns and almost come back to where I'd started. Yet
here on the left there was an annexe to the building that
could not be accessed by way of my initial entry point via the
skywalk. The clamour of my entry had caused those inside
the annexe to fall silent, but it was fleeting. Voices called to
each other and there was a rumble of activity from within
the building. More voices joined the babble as those chasing
me came across the dazed woman. She didn't have to tell
them which way I'd gone.

No one presented themselves at the doorway into the
annexe. They could be setting up an ambush inside, but I
doubted it. The woman I'd head-butted had been dressed as a
worker, and I guessed that it was some of her workmates I
could hear scrambling for cover. I bore no ill will towards
them, and had no intention of harming them needlessly, but
some of Procrylon's hired mercs could be hiding among them,
ready to drop me if I went in. Yet I had to. I pulled the second
liberated pistol from my waistband and used it to press open
the door. The other gun led the way inside, and I crouched
behind it, offering the smallest target possible. No gunfire met

me and I moved on, placing myself behind a work counter. From the back right corner of the room came a bleat of alarm.

'I'm armed and will shoot if you try to stop me,' I called. 'Come out with your hands up and I'll allow you to leave.'

'Don't shoot,' a male voice answered.

'How many of you are there?'

'There are three of us. Don't shoot. We're no threat to you.'

'I'll be the judge of that. Come out, hands in the air.'

Frightened whispers echoed through the room. Outside, the slap of boots announced the arrival of my hunters at the fire doors.

'Now! I'm not going to ask again.'

Through the dimness I caught movement. Three indistinct figures rose up from behind a row of desks. Their hands sought the ceiling.

'Get over here,' I commanded.

I covered their approach with one gun; the other was aimed back at the door through which I'd entered.

'You said you'd let us go,' the elected spokesman pointed out.

'You're going to help me first. Get a hold of this counter.'

I arranged the trio of workers – two men and a woman – alongside the counter, then made them shove it up against the door. It was a flimsy barricade and wouldn't hold my pursuers for long, but the difference between no time and a few seconds could mean a lot for my continued existence.

'OK. Now. Go ahead of me. Lead the way to that door.'

'You said you'd let us go,' the spokesman said again, stuck on a loop of hope and fear.

'I will. But you must do as I say first. Now get moving.'

The talker was middle-aged. Squat build. Comb-over. Not your average hero image. But he was brave, and not to be underestimated. I made him usher his friends to the door at the far end, keeping my gun close to his spine should he decide to exercise some of that backbone.

He was brave, but he wasn't stupid. He had nothing to gain in trying to take me on, and to be honest I was glad that he didn't. I felt no animosity towards him or his co-workers; they were simply taking a wage and likely had no idea what those at the top of the company were involved in. Most likely they regarded me as a nutcase who'd invaded their workplace. The bad guy. I showed them they had the wrong impression of me as soon as we were through the next door.

'Are the offices that way?' I asked, aiming my gun along a narrow corridor that ended at a set of stairs.

'Yes,' he said. 'They're spread over two different floors above.'

'Good. You guys go that way.' I aimed down a second passage to our left. At the end a doleful gleam of red showed a heavy fire exit door that – by my reckoning – must lead outside. 'Get clear of here. There's going to be more fighting and I'd hate for any of you to get caught in the crossfire.'

Behind us the banging started as my pursuers tried to force a way into the workroom. The counter might not be the heaviest object, but it was causing problems. A few sturdy shoulders against the doors would soon have it pushed aside, though.

The second man and the woman had both moved gratefully for the exit, but the spokesman paused. He looked me over. Came to some kind of decision. 'You're not a cop,' he said.

'I'm not a criminal either.'

'You're looking for that woman, aren't you?'

His question surprised me.

'What do you know about her?'

'Nothing much. But I saw some of the security team leading a woman upstairs earlier. By the look of things she wasn't too keen on going up there. I was coming back from the restrooms and almost bumped into them. When the woman tried to say something one of the security men warned her to keep her mouth shut. Then he warned me to get back to work . . . asshole! I knew I should have said something.'

'Not much you could have said or done. Now, go on. Get out of here. And, hey!'

The man, who had started for the exit, turned and looked back.

'Thanks,' I said.

He lifted his eyebrows in reply, but that was all. Then he moved away. I heard him telling his friends to keep quiet and to close the door tightly behind them. Pressed by the security team, he'd tell them where I was, but I trusted him not to run directly to them. By the sound of things he had no love for Procrylon's PMC goons.

I headed for the stairs. Every step I took was placing me deeper in trouble. Once those chasing me followed upstairs the exits from the building would be closed down. It was nuts continuing like this; with no apparent escape route saving Billie might prove momentary at best. I couldn't back down now, though. I had to continue on and damn the consequences of my rash decision not to wait for Cooper's tactical team.

A one-man assault on such a heavily guarded facility was doomed to failure. Though, of course, that was what I hoped my enemies had decided. I was more optimistic. If I kept moving, hitting resistance hard and fast, then the situation would be more a series of small skirmishes. The odds of me winning every one of them was narrow, but better than if I stood my ground and went for a pitched battle against dozens of mercs.

The heat of battle was on me. I was up for the challenge. Something that could very well mean my violent death was the very thing that made me feel so *alive*.

The fact that I half-expected the Jaegers to be standing guard over Billie added speed to my legs too. I wanted my day with those sons of bitches. Twice already – if I counted the guy I'd fought on the mountain road – they'd attempted to kill me. Twice they'd failed. If I had my way, three times absolutely would not be the charm.

36

'This is no HRT assault, from the reports coming in it's only one goddamn man!' Daniel Jaeger sounded as if he was filled with mixed emotions. Partly he was relieved that his mistake over forgetting to cancel the beacon in Billie's vest hadn't led to this attack, but he was also maddened to hear that one man was responsible for taking down a quarter of their team already. Another part of him was excited at the prospect of engaging with such a worthy opponent, while yet another was annoyed: he suspected that the man had to be Joe Hunter, the person who'd been with Billie when she was taken, and the man Daniel was supposed to have finished off. Who else could it be?

'Get her out of here, Danny. I've called in the chopper, but if it hasn't come by the time you reach the helipad, take one of the vans.'

Daniel squinted at his older brother. 'You want me to play babysitter when there's an enemy to be killed?'

'I want you to do as I've ordered, soldier.'

Erick stared at his younger sibling, acting not as his big brother but as his commanding officer.

'This is bullshit, Erick. Any of the other guys can take the bitch out of here.'

'I don't want any of the others to do it, I want you to.'

'I'm better than any of those punks,' Daniel argued. 'You need me here. That dude is going through our team like a dose of salts, man!'

'That's exactly why I need you on Billie Womack. I need someone reliable. Now go. And don't make me repeat myself again.' Erick racked the slide on his automatic pistol. It wasn't a warning to his brother, but the clack was ominous enough to shut Daniel's mouth, cutting off his next retort.

Billie had listened to their interaction with mixed emotions. She was sore and frightened, and fearful for her life, but also overjoyed to hear that Joe had survived and had come looking for her. That was the type of man that Richard should have been: loyal. She knew that the chances of one man beating the insurmountable odds against him were slim, but she was also hopeful. There was something about Hunter that told her he could be relied on. Hell, he'd already put his life before hers, and she was sure he would do it again. When she'd watched him in her home that time while preparing a meal for him, it was with keener attention than mere curiosity or even attraction; she'd been weighing and evaluating him, and even then had recognised him as the kind of man she should have married. They were alike: they had a take-no-crap attitude, and were willing to fight and kill where necessary. She hadn't been lying when she'd told him she would willingly smash in Richard's brains given the opportunity, and after watching Joe break that big brute's neck with barely any effort, she knew Joe was capable of such uncompromising action too. In the forest, if he'd followed his natural instincts, he would have stopped these bastards before they'd got their hands on her, but back then Joe had been constrained by rules applied to him by the ATF agent, Cooper. She doubted he was hampered by rules now, judging by Daniel's proclamation, and was coming for her like a force of nature that could not be stopped.

Yet he was only one man.

He faced impossible odds, and even if he did fight his way through, what good would it serve if she had already been whisked away on a helicopter or in the back of a van? It was time to show these mercenaries, and that whore, Amanda, that they had made a huge mistake when thinking they could treat her like a simpering girl they could beat into submission. She had to buy some time for Joe to reach her.

Daniel kicked her in the thigh. 'Get up.'

Billie was still seated on her butt, except she'd been backed into one corner of the room. She'd been dragged there after being kicked into unconsciousness by Erick minutes ago, and propped up so that she didn't choke on the blood in her mouth. Neither man realised yet that she was awake, or that she was ready for them.

'Get up, bitch.' Daniel toed her again.

'Goddammit, Danny, just pick her up and drag her ass out of here.' Erick moved away, heading for the door. 'I'm going to make sure Sheehan gets out safely. Things are bad enough without her getting herself killed.'

'Couldn't happen to a better woman,' Daniel growled. 'Except maybe for this bitch here.'

Whether or not Erick was in agreement wasn't forthcoming because he left the room in a hurry. Billie hadn't heard Amanda go, but she thought that the sadistic whore had probably fled to find a mirror to check her injuries. Hell, it'd take more than scratches and bite marks to spoil that granite-faced visage. Billie felt like laughing at the image that flashed across her mind, one where Amanda leaned into a mirror moaning in self-loathing at how her cold beauty had been scarred. She held back the laughter, though, concentrating instead on play-ing possum, while at the same time moving something around in her hand for optimum positioning.

'Wake up!' Daniel smacked her across the jaw, not the pat of a well-meaning doctor either, but delivered stingingly by his callused palm. Billie moaned at the pain and it wasn't an act, though she made an effort to slowly blink and roll her head, then look up at her tormentor in fright. Daniel was bent at the waist, his hand lifted to slap again.

'Good. I've got your attention. Now get up before I make you.'

'I ... I can't.' Billie cradled her jaw in the cup of her left palm. Her right hand still jostled the item around, difficult to hold on to with her broken and dislocated fingers. But she got the slim object in the crease of her palm, and held it in place by pressure from her thumb, the hand's only undamaged digit.

'There's nothing wrong with your goddamn legs. Now move it, or I'll make you real sorry.'

'I can't. I think my jaw's broken.'

'It's not broken if you can still be so fucking insolent. Now get up before I smack that smart mouth of yours again.' Losing patience, Daniel leaned in to grasp her under her left armpit. It was what Billie had been waiting for. Her right hand swung in a sharp arch, and smacked against the side of Daniel's neck.

Daniel rocked back on his heels, a stunned expression on his face.

At first he must have thought Billie had punched him, because he could see both her hands were empty as she used them to push off from the wall. But then he felt with his fingers up the side of his neck and found the hypodermic syringe hanging from his flesh, the tip buried in his carotid artery. When she'd erupted from the table and gone for Amanda, the syringe had been knocked to the ground. As Erick dragged her unconscious body to the corner the syringe had caught in her clothing. It wasn't full, but there was still enough of the drug to compromise anyone.

Daniel grabbed the syringe and plucked it out, inspecting it and seeing that it had delivered its payload of anaesthetic directly into his system. 'Oh, you sneaky little tramp,' he said. He flung the syringe aside and took a step forward. 'Do you think that's going to stop me?'

'I'm sure it will,' Billie said.

Shot into his thigh or shoulder, the drug would have had little effect but the carotid artery fed directly to the brain. Even before he got to mouth another threat, Daniel swayed, then buckled to one knee. He gave a bellow of rage, but it barely left his chest.

'I told your brother not to touch me again,' Billie said. 'I warned him what would happen if he tried. I'm giving you the same warning.'

She moved alongside Daniel, and he tried to grab her, but his vision was already fading, and his groping fingers missed her by a mile. Billie crouched and slipped the sidearm from the holster on his belt. She was unfamiliar with the gun, but she'd shot other pistols before and this one was little different. She looked for a safety switch, before recalling that most modern firearms had integrated safety switches in the trigger mechanism. She pulled back the slide, arming the gun. Then she fed her trembling index finger through the trigger guard.

'Didn't you hear what I just said,' Billie demanded, 'about trying to touch me again?'

Daniel fell on to the flats of his hands and knees. He wasn't in a fit state to hear any warning, or to heed it if he did. Then again, Billie didn't expect him to. She expected him never to hear a thing again. She placed the gun to the nape of his skull, and though it was a struggle to make her numb finger work, she tugged on the trigger and the gun cracked sharply.

A splotch of blood hit the near wall. Billie's gaze strayed towards it. The wall was a dull beige colour, the crimson drop stark against it, reminiscent of the trademark brushstroke her art was known for. She cocked her head quizzically, staring for a long beat, then her gaze drifted down to the corpse lying at her feet and the glistening hole in its skull. Daniel's death barely moved her, and wasn't as satisfying as she expected. Never mind, there were still plenty of bullets left in the gun and her fingers were working better each passing second.

Gunshots rattled nearby.

Joe was getting closer.

She went to make things easier for him.

37

I came across Erick Jaeger and a phalanx of guards moving hurriedly through a foyer area at the far end of the building. Through glass doors I could see waiting vans, preparing to transport the group safely out of harm's way – perhaps far away, or then again maybe only as far as the helipad a few hundred yards off. I could hear the chatter of rotor blades, and guessed the chopper had been called in for a swift evacuation of the highest-ranking personnel – and Billie. But I couldn't see her. The only woman in the group was a tall, hawkish woman who dabbed at cuts on her cheeks and one eyelid. The woman was arguing that she had her own transportation on stand-by, and ordered Erick to call her driver, but the PMC was having none of it. Good job, because Amanda Sheehan's chauffeur was currently enjoying Rink's company.

Billie's absence was worrying.

I fully expected that she would be escorted out of the building along with those interrogating her, moved somewhere that wasn't the middle of a battle zone. But I was wrong.

A moment ago I heard the crack of a handgun. A single shot. An execution?

There was no knowing if that gunshot signified Billie's death, but I could think of no other reason for it. As I progressed through the annexe, I'd drawn the fight my way, so unless it was an accidental discharge by a nervous shooter, it had been done deliberately and for a specific reason. My guts clenched in regret. After all I'd done, all those I'd killed, I'd come too late. It was all for nothing if Billie was dead. No. Not for nothing. I'd tried my hardest and would continue to do so. If that now meant avenging her death, then Billie would not have died in vain. I readied both guns, about to lurch out from behind the door frame which hid me and cut down as many of her murderers as possible.

But Erick stopped, and he stared back thoughtfully. He mouthed words to himself, then turned to the group of six guards surrounding Amanda Sheehan. 'Get Miss Sheehan to the chopper. Wilkes, Bryant,' he indicated two of the PMCs, 'you're with me. We're going back for Danny.'

Sheehan twisted her face in anger. 'Worried that your brother has messed up again, Erick? Surely even he can handle one woman?'

'I told him to get Womack out, and he should have been here by now. Didn't you just hear that gunshot?'

'So he killed her. The problem's over.'

'No. His orders were to get her out, not shoot her. Something has happened.' Erick peered in the direction of a stairwell they'd recently come from. 'I'm going to check.'

'Leave him. Your priority is to get me safely away.' Sheehan was strident.

'You're safe with your detail. I'm going back for my brother. Wilkes, Bryant, on me.' Without waiting, Erick headed for the stairs followed by the two PMCs, while behind him Sheehan clenched her fists around the bloodied tissues.

'I'm recommending your immediate discharge after this, Captain Jaeger. You and your brother. You're both finished.'

Erick stopped, turned and faced his superior. 'Don't you get it, Sheehan? We're all finished. Procrylon's finished. You're finished. The best things to do now are to shut your fucking mouth, get in that chopper and go as far away from here as you can. Lose yourself, before you're burned along with the rest of us.'

Sheehan was horrified at the fatalism in Erick's warning. Perhaps it had just dawned on her that the entire operation was a complete disaster. What should have been a simple snatch and interrogation of a single woman had grown into a pitched battle, numerous casualties and a failure to learn anything she was supposed to. Those she worked for, whether it was the directors of Procrylon, or the private military company charged with protecting their assets, would deem her ultimately responsible for the massive cluster fuck. Erick wasn't kidding when he warned they would be burned, and going by their usual methods, it wouldn't be a case of a golden handshake by way of a healthy severance payoff from Procrylon – it would be a lead slug behind the ear or worse. Even if they escaped punishment from their employers, it had to be apparent by now that the weight of the law enforcement community would come down on them all after this. Her best bet would be to run for the hills, or some remote desert island, change her identity and keep her head low for many years.

If I had my way I'd stop her. She was as much an enemy as Erick and the rest of the faceless cadre I'd come to refer to as Procrylon. She was responsible for hurting Billie, possibly more than her hired mercs were. I was tempted again to step out and save some time by delivering the bullet to the skull she deserved. Yet I held back, again watching as Erick and his small team mounted the stairs. Then, as Sheehan and her detail pushed outside and climbed into the vans, I came out of hiding and followed hot on Erick's heels.

If Daniel had executed Billie, I needed to know. If such was the case, then I wasn't going to allow the younger Jaeger to leave this building alive. It made sense that his older brother would try to stop me, and there were only two ways that could end. He'd be dead or I would. But those were the cards that were dealt us, and we were both still in the game. If by some miracle Billie had survived, then we'd have to wait and see how the end played out.

38

Erick's shout of dismay gave a clue how things had gone down in Billie's holding room. I heard him call out to his brother, and it was the strangled croak of a concerned sibling, not that of a soldier-at-arms. I couldn't see the man, but his friends kept a respectful distance, and from the looks on their faces, the shakes of their heads, what Erick had found in the room wasn't good news. At least not for them. There were thumps and thuds, and I pictured the bespectacled man crouching over Daniel's corpse, trying to shake some life back into it. Erick's voice was too low to hear, but only for a brief spell. It was followed by an animalistic howl that grew in volume and erupted into savage rage. When he stormed out of the room, his firearm held aloft, head swivelling as he sought a target, I knew for certain that his brother was dead and that Billie was loose somewhere in the sprawling facility. Discounting the elevators, there was only the one way down, and none of us had stumbled upon Billie on the climb upstairs. She had fled deeper into the building, perhaps following the sounds of my gun battle with those on the lower floor of the annexe.

I was concealed at the corner of the stairwell, a couple of steps down, but able to lean out and spy on them. It was regrettable that I hadn't chosen this way inside the building to begin with. Had I done so, it would have been a quick run up one flight of stairs and I'd have found where Billie was being held, instead of having to fight my way through three buildings. Never mind, what was done was done. The reality was that my running battle had perhaps been for the best. It had put everyone in a mild state of panic and confusion, and had given Billie the opportunity to escape. Immediately storming the building via this route, things might have ended differently. Billie would be the one lying dead in that room, and who knew what would have become of the rest of us?

Erick was in my sights. The other two PMCs had their backs to me. I could kill them all and be done. Shooting someone in the back is seen as cowardice, but that's in a rose-tinted fantasy world. In the blood and guts arena of deadly combat you took the opportunities when you could, and to hell with the morality. I prepared to come out shooting.

Suddenly Erick wheeled away. He charged off and after a pause to gather their bearings, his backup detail followed. I mentally cursed, but waited as they raced along the corridor and disappeared deeper inside the building. Erick must have realised the same as me: Billie had gone in search of another way out, and with his superior knowledge of the layout of the building he was trying to cut off her escape route. Shit, I should have shot him the moment he poked his head out that door, but something had held me back. Maybe he deserved a moment of grief because, when all was said and done, Daniel was still his brother, and, despite the fact they were hard-nosed soldiers, uncompromising and tough, they would still share sibling love, and should be allowed at least a single tear of loss. But that was the only allowance I was going to make. I followed on their heels.

Erick moved without fear, good sense overridden by his need for vengeance. Plunging ahead, he neglected to watch his six, and towed along in his wake his friends made the same mistake. I followed within spitting distance and could have killed them in short order. Except it was better that I wait, follow to an appropriate exit and then do what needed doing. We went down a set of stairs, through some deserted work-spaces and into a corridor I recognised as one I'd been in earlier. There I'd traded bullets with a PMC and butted his girlfriend who tried to blind me with her nails. The corpse had been dragged away, but there was a wide swathe of blood. Footprints tracked away from us, and small, bare feet had formed them. The heel prints were faint, probably due to the fact the person was running, but I was reminded of the way that Billie bounced on the balls of her feet when she walked. Then again, who else would be running around barefoot except for an escaped prisoner?

I allowed Erick's party to draw ahead, then went to the stacked drums I'd crawled across earlier, and groped on top. I found the Colt M4 carbine I'd ditched there. The increased firepower was very welcome. Once the gun was back in my hands I followed the bloody footprints, and finally came to a set of exterior doors. They were chained and padlocked shut. The footprints were obliterated by then, but there was only one way Billie could have gone. Up and over the skywalk. I ran for the stairs that led up, even as I heard the repeated cracking of a handgun followed by a harsh shout from one of the PMCs. I powered up the stairs, careless of the racket I made, and charged to the entrance to the skywalk. Midway along it one of Erick's followers knelt with his back to me, with his pistol extended before him. He gripped his left shoulder with his left hand, and from the way he shivered I thought that he'd been hit. There was no sign of the others, or of Billie, but they had to be hot on her heels. I banged through the doors and into the glass-walled tunnel, the floor shuddering under my feet. The injured PMC looked behind him hopefully, fully expecting one of his buddies coming to his assistance. His wish was short-lived. If the idiot had laid aside his gun and surrendered that would have been it. He saw me, recognised me for an enemy, and his instinct was to twist round and engage. One of the glass panels to my left exploded in glittering chunks. I fired as I advanced, unloading a short burst from the M4 that tore the man's torso apart, and blasted more glass into the heavens. I didn't check my handiwork. No way was the PMC coming back from our exchange of rounds. Cold wind blasted through the broken window as I ran past him.

I had to assume that Erick and the remaining contractor heard our short gun battle, but I also trusted that Erick was focused on Billie and would continue to hunt her now he was so close. So I threw caution aside and continued running, retracing my steps from the skywalk, through the twists and turns of the corridor where I'd knocked out the PMC I first saw at Billie's farm, past the elevators and down the stairs to the ground floor. There was spent brass on the floor. A short exchange of rounds had taken place there, but the lack of bodies confirmed that nobody had died. I hurtled forward, past the numbered offices, and towards the foyer where I'd first entered. Before I reached the door to the foyer gunshots and gruff commands rang out. A woman shouted shrilly in denial. Billie had made it all the way to the exit, only to be cornered at the last second.

I didn't wait for the inevitable but went through the doors, my M4 ready to wreak havoc. Startled by the thunderclap as I kicked them open, a man turned to confront me, bringing up his gun. I shot him repeatedly, even as I ran past, and the PMC fell dead before I'd reached the podium with the CCTV monitors. I'd no interest in the video screens, only in the two figures that tussled wildly just behind it. Billie screeched like a cat as she clawed at Erick's face with her nails, knocking his glasses askew, but the bigger man got a hand at her throat and his pistol under her jaw. He spun her so her back was to me and I skidded to a halt, threatening with the carbine, but unable to do a thing. Billie's weapon lay empty on the floor at their feet.

'Back off,' Erick snarled at me. 'Or I'll shoot this bitch in the face.'

'Shoot her and you'll be dead the next second.'

Billie screamed a curse; throwing her body against Erick, and for a split second I waited for the crack of his gun. Erick knew what would happen if he shot her though, so instead he squeezed her throat tightly and Billie gagged, sinking at the knees, almost passing out. Erick grappled her closer, turning her so he could wrap an arm around her neck and position the muzzle of his gun under her ear. I searched for a clean shot, but wasn't confident I could get Erick before he killed Billie. He knew it too and offered a grimace of challenge.

'I don't know who the hell you are, buddy,' Erick said, 'but you've done pretty well here. You went through my men like goddamn Rambo. Trust me though: you aren't good enough. Drop your weapon or Billie dies.'

If I dropped my weapon she'd die anyway. There was no chance I'd relinquish it. 'You think Billie shot your brother, right?'

'What do you know about that?'

'I was there. It wasn't Billie who killed Danny, it was me.'

'Bullshit!'

'Do you really think an injured woman would be able to kill him? He was a fucking veteran, a soldier. I shot him. Then I gave Billie the gun and told her to run while I went to kill the rest of you.'

Under closer scrutiny my lie wouldn't hold water – if he demanded proof I couldn't tell him where Danny had been shot, head, body or anywhere else – but momentary doubt crossed Erick's face. Like most men he probably struggled to accept that a woman could be as deadly as Billie had proved. It made more sense that a soldier like me had killed his brother. Now his hatred for her was wavering and his jaw clenching as he weighed the possibilities that he was wrong. I was hoping that his anger would get the better of him, that he'd release Billie and come for me.

'I owed Danny,' I continued, adding layers of plausibility to my lie. 'He tried to kill me back in the forest. Almost smashed my brains in when I was lying there wounded. I wanted payback.'

Erick took the gun from Billie and aimed it at me. I shook my head, warning him what the outcome would be as I aimed the M4. I was loath to shoot but I wasn't going to die without getting off a round.

'Release the woman,' I said. 'Then we can go for it. What do you say, Erick? Want your revenge or not?'

'She's going nowhere.' Erick returned the gun to Billie's neck. But I could tell he was wavering. His eyelids pulsed, pinching in and out as he fought to control himself.

Maybe things would have gone the way I was pushing, except Billie spoiled everything. She again threw herself against Erick, trying to hit him with the back of her head, stamping her feet. 'I killed Daniel and I'm going to kill you, you bastard!' she screamed. 'I'll kill you the way I killed—'

Billie's outburst caused time to halt.

She'd almost finished her boast when suddenly she caught my eye and the admission caught in her throat. I watched her chest deflate, but it was only for a moment. Something snapped inside her, and she erupted into frenzy, reaching back to claw at Erick's face, while she screeched like something demented.

Time clicked back on, racing now to make up for the brief hiccup.

Erick twisted his head to avoid Billie's nails, while still trying to glare his hatred at me. He was going to do it. He would shoot and let the consequences be damned. I ran and threw myself at the podium, and it crashed into them. Erick staggered away and Billie spilled to the floor, still kicking and thrashing in unrestrained rage. The podium was tilted over and I went up it as if it was a ramp, and jammed my M4 under Erick's gun, just as he fired. The bullet scorched the air alongside my head. I didn't allow the close call to slow me, I powered into him, using the podium as a springboard, and we both smashed into the wall. I ground his wrist against the wall, but knew he'd never release the pistol so easily. I swung up the stock of the carbine and hit him under the jaw. It would have hurt like a bastard, but not under the circumstances, not in the heat of battle. Erick chopped at my face with his stiffened left hand. It felt as if a metal bar struck me, and blackness edged my vision. But I couldn't slow down or assess my latest injury: I slammed him with the carbine again and mashed the flesh of his lips against his teeth. It skidded off his jaw and under his throat. Then we were jammed together and slid along the wall, kicking and struggling.

'Billie! Get out of the fucking door!' I'd no idea where she was, my vision tunnelling, my hearing closing down to a single whoosh, and could only hope that for once she did I as bloody asked.

Erick finally dropped his sidearm, but only so he could get a grip on the barrel of my gun. I was carrying an injury that weakened me; he was strong. He forced the gun away from his throat, and I was struggling to hold on. I considered releasing my hold on the carbine to draw one of my handguns and give him a bellyful of lead, but if I did he'd yank the carbine away and turn it on me. So I made do with kneeing him in the groin. A waft of hot breath misted the lenses of his spectacles.

But he wasn't done. He wrapped a leg behind mine, and tripped me. We both went down on our sides, still struggling for control of the carbine.

Billie was there. She kicked at Erick, but her foot skipped off his forehead and hit mine. It was good of her to try to help, but not when she proved a hindrance.

'Outside, Billie! Now!'

While I was otherwise distracted Erick clubbed me in the ribs with his balled fist. The antiballistic vest saved me from any damage, but reminded me why my arms felt so weak. I'd ignored my chest injury throughout most of my running battle, but the sudden warm heat made sure it wouldn't be off my mind again soon. I couldn't go strength against strength with Erick, because it was a fight I would lose.

'They're coming!' Billie yelped. At first I didn't know what she meant – I was too intent on one thing: my enemy.

'You're fucked now,' Erick snarled, knowing too well to whom Billie referred. Reinforcements were on their way, drawn by the gunfire and the subsequent scuffle.

'Not yet,' I said, and finally let go of the carbine. I didn't relinquish my close hold on him though, pushing up against him, trapping him alongside the wall as I wormed my fingers up his face and under his glasses. I gouged at him with my fingernails, forcing him to screw his eyelids tight or be blinded. While he was blinkered like that I again drove a knee into his groin, and this time I got him good. But Erick still proved tougher than most. He kneed at me, banging my thighs painfully, then when he'd won a little room he kicked out, pushing me off him. That suited me; I wanted to disengage anyway. I quickly came up to one knee, going for a gun in my waistband. My hand found empty space, the damn guns having fallen out as we grappled on the floor. Just as Erick twisted the carbine in his grip, I spotted a gun lying yards away, and I dived for it.

As I did so, the doors burst wide and a group of uniformed PMCs charged into the foyer.

I got my hand to the grip of the gun, rolling over on to my butt to get a bead on Erick.

Another gun beat mine to the first shot.

39

I'd never heard a sweeter sound than the boom of Rink's Mossberg shotgun that turned the exit door to flying debris.

A moment later a fixture in the ceiling detonated in a glittering shower of sparks and chunks of plastic and glass that sent the newly arrived PMCs scuttling for cover. Erick also reacted to Rink's unexpected arrival by dropping low behind the overturned podium, so he didn't get to unload the M4 on me. Saying that I couldn't shoot him either, but I was happy enough with the outcome. I scrambled up and grabbed Billie by an arm and dragged her for the exit doors as Rink fired again, a succession of three blasts of buckshot that ensured our enemies were more concerned for their lives than ours. We were through the destroyed door in seconds, while Rink, leaning out from the door frame, discouraged immediate pursuit with another volley of shot, doling out the noise and thunder he'd promised. I took a quick look at my friend's face: it must have been hell for him holding his peace all that time, but extraction support had always been his part in our plan. Since I'd entered the complex little more than twenty minutes had passed, but I can guarantee to Rink it had felt an age. Rink shook his head in reproof at my tardiness. But then we were all sprinting together for the limousine that Rink had already got running.

It would be a fatal decision to get inside the car though. Already some of our pursuers were at the ruined doors and aiming their guns. I manhandled Billie around the hood and down behind the front wheel just as bullets began impacting the car. The limo wasn't the armoured variety favoured by politicians and high-risk business people and was a poor barrier against high-powered weapons, but it was all we had. Rink returned fire, pushing those in the doorway back inside. My handgun was almost out of ammo, but I found one of the spare mags I'd liberated and got it ready. Across the turning circle was the recessed doorway of another building, the same one where I'd first made the chauffeur strip off his uniform jacket. I briefly wondered what had become of the big guy, but it wasn't important, so concentrated on the next hare-brained move we could make. If Rink covered us, Billie and me could fall back to the building across the courtyard, and maybe find a way inside. I could then cover as Rink retreated and joined us, after which we could barricade ourselves in and wait for the cavalry to arrive. By now Noah or Adam must have alerted the authorities.

There was a cessation of gunfire.

'None of you are getting out of here alive.'

Erick's voice had come from within the foyer.

'Could say the same about you,' Rink retorted and, for good measure, blasted one of the windows into tinkling shards.

Guns cracked again, but nobody was showing their faces and their bullets didn't as much threaten us as they did the building across the way. Erick cursed, ordering a ceasefire. He called out again, 'You made the wrong enemies when you chose to come against us. You can't win. We've got you outgunned and outmanoeuvred. Lay down your guns.'

'Dream on,' Rink muttered and offered me a grandiose wink.

'Let us go, Erick,' I called. 'Enough people have died for Procrylon's greed. You don't have to join them if you just let us walk away.'

'You murdered my brother.'

I didn't say a thing. It wasn't the time for lies – or even the truth – as goading Erick was no longer a good idea. I looked once at Billie but she'd averted her face, although I didn't think it was through shame.

From a distance sounded the roar of engines.

'They've reinforcements coming,' I whispered to Rink. I doubted that the responding vehicles were Cooper's troops, because the engine sounds came from the side of the building where I'd earlier spotted the PMC fleet of vehicles. 'We can't get ourselves cornered here. Erick's after blood.'

'I'll show him the colour of his own blood if he pokes his head up for a second.' Rink's bluster was partly to reassure Billie. She was crouching down by my side now, her arms wrapped around her knees as she rocked back and forth, mouthing something under her breath.

'We have to move,' I said.

'Agreed.'

Erick shouted another warning, but I ignored the empty words. Instead I knelt in front of Billie, taking her shoulders in my hands. 'How badly are you hurt?'

'My hand . . .' She didn't elaborate.

She was barefooted, so she couldn't run far without the risk of seriously cutting herself, but it appeared she was going to have to. No. The other vehicles would run us all down in moments. There was nothing else for it. I reached and eased open the door of the limo. 'Can you still drive?'

Billie nodded eagerly. 'Even with a broken hand I could still shoot a gun.' Her eyes were feverish. 'I'm sure I can turn a steering wheel.'

'Good. Get in. When I tell you to, get out of here, but go slow and steady, we'll be covering you, but we need to get inside once we're clear of those front doors. Understand?'

Rink also nodded at my idea. He readied the shotgun as I helped Billie slide into the driver's position. I held her arm, studying her swollen fingers. The limousine was a European import, with a stick shift. There was no way she could handle the gears in that state. 'Billie, don't panic, OK. Just do as I said. Pull away, and get ready to move aside, because I'll take over the driving once we're moving.'

Erick hollered again, and from his terse delivery he was ready to assault our position if we didn't comply.

'Go,' I told Billie. She hit the gas and almost stalled the big car. But then the limo jerked backwards, and set off rolling at a steady clip. I moved with it, aiming over the roof alongside the open door and firing blind shots into the foyer, while Rink also pumped the shotgun and fired at the front of the building. There was a shout from inside and a couple of the PMCs crept out, looking for cover where there was none. I shot one in the thigh, then the slide locked open, my gun empty. Rink put the other man down for good. Then more PMCs including Erick were out of the door, fanning out to encircle us. I ducked, slapping in a fresh magazine, just as rifle rounds blatted off the car's roof and whined over my head. To my right, Rink's shotgun fired again, but then he was out of shells and with no opportunity to reload from his ammo belt. He threw himself inside the back of the limo, even as I eased in, pushing Billie across and down into the footwell on the passenger side. She blocked the gear stick, her clothing catching on it, and there followed a frantic few seconds while I pulled her sweat top clear. Rounds shattered the windscreen, throwing glass and shards of metal on us. Something hot nestled in my hair, but I hadn't time to worry about what it was. I hit the gas, reversing at speed. The PMCs chased us, and bullets began chewing into the luxury car. Any second and they'd get the tyres, or the engine, and we'd be going nowhere fast. I hit a handbrake skid, rammed the gearshift and hit the gas. We pulled away just as the first of three vans powered round the near corner and struck our back end. Fishtailing, I fought the wheel, then stomped the gas again and accelerated. The limousine was designed for a comfortable ride, not for high speed, and though it responded it was with a steady build-up rather than instantly. One of the other vans matched us speed for speed, and the driver fancied his chances of running us off the road and into the wall of the next building. He slewed the bigger vehicle into us, the sound of grinding metal a banshee's shriek. By then Rink had reloaded. He stuck the Mossberg out of his window and let the driver have a face full of shot. The van slewed again, but this time away, and with no hand at the wheel it did a half-turn before the wheels hit a kerb and the van went up and over a sidewalk into the front of a building. I'd have cheered if I hadn't checked my mirrors and seen the other two vans chasing us down. Distantly, Erick was clambering into another vehicle, this one a 4x4, to join the hunt. Billie raised her head but I pushed it back down.

'We're not out of this yet,' I told her. Then to my friend, 'Rink?'

'Yeah?'

'Call Noah. Tell him to move his arse.'

'Got ya!'

Up ahead, about four hundred yards distant, was the old gatehouse from when the logistics hub was part of the nearby wartime military installation. There was a brick guardhouse on one side and a wide brick pillar on the other. Vehicles were funnelled through a narrow gap with room for only one truck at a time. A steel barrier had been lowered. In movies you see cars smashing through them like they're balsa wood, but that wasn't the case in real life. If we collided with the barrier at speed it would take off the top of the car, and our heads along with it. I decelerated as we approached, going for a lower gear, allowing the stream of PMC vehicles to gain on us. Somebody leaned out the leading van and fired at us, but the bullets came nowhere near.

Fifty yards from the barrier, I hit the brakes, pulled down on the wheel and yelled something glib like 'Hold on to your hats!'

The limo skidded, the tyres juddering on the concrete paving, sending up smoke and the stink of burning rubber, and the back end began to spin towards the gatehouse. I hit an adjustment and the front found its trajectory again and we crashed side-on against the guardhouse. The back end of the car was well and truly crumpled now, but I didn't care. I hit the throttle, pulling clear of the building so that Billie and Rink could scramble out, while still blocking access to the exit. One of the vans was coming so fast that it had no hope of stopping, but that wasn't the driver's intent. I threw myself across the passenger seat as the heavier van impacted the side of the limousine and rammed it into the space between the guardhouse and pillar. Hell, the driver had unwittingly achieved for me what I'd been aiming to do. He'd blocked their way, so that they couldn't follow. I slid out the mangled car on to the road, then popped up and fired a few pot shots at the van's windscreen: whether I hit the driver or not didn't matter, it was about keeping his head down. I ducked under the barrier, and saw Rink and Billie running to my right. A decorative hedge had grown to about fifteen feet tall, and obscured them from the view of those still within the compound. I stood at the back corner of the guardhouse, but nobody came out to join the fight. The van door opened, and the driver, shaken but alive, staggered out and went to one knee, before scrambling for his life out of my firing line. I let him go.

My attention was caught by another roaring engine. This one I was happy to hear, and ran for Noah's sedan as he skidded to a halt alongside Rink and Billie. Adam was about to get out, waving a pistol, but Rink grabbed him by his collar and shoved him back inside, even as he steered Billie for the back seat. I joined them seconds later, and Noah peeled away before I'd even got the door fully shut.

We streaked past the front gate, and could see people swarming to get round the compacted limo, but the chase was over for now. One man watched us go, the ambient light striking highlights off the lenses of his glasses. I wished I could have ended things there and then with Erick, but so be it.

I'd've happily laid a bet that we'd still have our day.

40

As we fled northeast on Route 507, skirting the wetlands boundary of Joint Base Lewis/McChord, responding police and State Trooper vehicles sped past on the other side, heading for the logistics depot. There was no sign of the ATF or an FBI hostage rescue team, though Noah assured us that he'd called Agent Cooper at the sound of the first distant pop of gunfire. What could I say? I'd asked Cooper for the opportunity to rescue Billie myself, but I hadn't really expected total freedom to engage Procrylon in a personal war. Not for the first time I considered Cooper's hidden agenda in all that had happened.

I was in the back seat of Noah's sedan. Rink was on the opposite side, and Billie was scrunched between us. She was silent. Not weeping, not saying a word. She had to be in pain, shock, and a thousand emotions must have been playing havoc with her mind, so I let her be. Sometimes silence was the best healer. I wanted to call Cooper and ask him what the hell was going on, but not while Billie could overhear.

'Where do we go now?' Noah ventured. He was driving, his hands rigid on the steering wheel, foot heavy on the gas pedal.

'Back to the motel,' I said.

'It's too close,' Noah warned.

'And probably the last place anyone will think to look for us,' I replied. 'Once the police organise themselves they'll have roadblocks in place, helicopters in the sky. We'd be caught in no time. Better that we get our heads down, stay hidden until I can get Cooper organised and back on-side.'

I caught a glance from Rink, and he didn't need to say a thing.

He didn't trust Cooper any further than I did. But what exactly could we do? We couldn't take Billie to the police and demand their protection, not without the rest of us ending up in cells. As far as anyone knew, or needed to know, I was the only person who'd invaded the logistics depot to liberate a kidnapped woman. Rink, Noah and Adam remained unknown quantities and I hoped to keep things that way. What had been important before was getting Billie safely out of Procrylon's grasp, but now I also had to think about how I was going to escape prosecution. Too many people had seen me and lived. Not that I was too upset that some of them had survived: there was a mix of good and bad people in there, and I was happy that the decent folks had gone unharmed. I was remorseful about head-butting that woman, but under the circumstances things could have proved much worse for her. The PMCs I'd engaged were fair game; we were all soldiers and possible casualties of the war, but those that I'd spared were simply guys doing their jobs and I didn't regret that they were still around either. 'What happened to the chauffeur?' I asked Rink.

Rink chuckled to himself. 'He smoked a bunch of cigarettes, tried to regale me with a few humorous cabbie tales, then suggested I tie him up so that he didn't look as if he'd been consorting with the opposing team. He's safe, and happy. Think of the tales he'll tell his next fare?'

I was glad the big Australian's easy-going manner had won over Rink. Of everyone we'd come across at the logistics depot, he truly was an innocent party and it would have been a shame if Rink had been forced to do something nasty to him. The chauffeur's car was a write-off, so I hoped his insurance company paid out. If not, then there was some reparation coming from the ATF if I had any say in the matter. I also owed him a cap and suit jacket.

There were a couple of people I'd have liked to see well and truly stopped: Erick Jaeger and Amanda Sheehan. The latter I had no personal interest in: the ATF could deal with her. But Erick was another case in point. I fully expected that both of them would disappear off the radar for a while, but Erick would resurrect somewhere down the trail. He was a soldier with a soldier's sensibilities, and in that case he wouldn't take our conflict personally. But he was also a grieving brother who'd want revenge on the killer of Daniel – whoever that might be. If he decided that was me, then good, he'd find me waiting. If he went for Billie, then I'd also be waiting.

I checked on Billie. She was still quiet; sitting there with her broken fingers cupped in those of her other hand. She required medical attention, but for now it would have to be of the battlefield type. We couldn't go to a hospital, clinic or doctor's surgery because the cops would be on to us within minutes. Billie looked up at me. She offered a lop-sided smile. 'I can handle the pain,' she said, as if she'd read my mind.

'Jeezus,' Noah said from the front. 'Joe only dislocated one of my fingers and it hurt like hell. I don't know how you do it, Mrs Womack.'

'I'm tougher than I look,' Billie said.

She wasn't wrong. But then again it wasn't physical toughness that had seen her through her incarceration and torture. It was her state of mind. 'We'll get some ice on your hand once we're back at the motel. How are you otherwise, no other injuries we've missed?'

She showed me her left hand and the broken fingernails. One was pulled to the quick, bloody. 'I left one of my nails stuck in that Amanda bitch's face. But it was worth the pain.'

I hadn't yet learned the details of what had gone on, but now I knew from whom the scream had come that led me to Billie. She'd fought back against her captors even without the knowledge that I was coming for her. Her proactivity had allowed her to get hold of a gun and shoot Daniel Jaeger. I should have offered her kudos, but instead I said, 'We were all lucky to get out alive, and relatively uninjured. We can all pat each other on the back once this is over with.'

Over the top of Billie's head I caught another glance from Rink. This time there was definite confusion in it. I didn't offer an explanation, just nodded softly at him. Rink knew enough not to push, and we fell back to silence.

A few minutes later we arrived at the motel and Noah parked the car out of sight of the highway. If anyone at the logistics depot had spotted our getaway car it wouldn't matter, because I believed that everyone there would have been high-tailing it in the opposite direction to that of the responding police officers. Any that were mopped up and interrogated would plead ignorance of what had gone down, because to admit otherwise would be to implicate them in the kidnapping and torturing of a citizen. I felt confident that the car hadn't been in view of any working CCTV cameras, so we'd be safe enough from discovery for now.

Adam was first out of the car. He still had a sidearm down alongside his thigh and I spoke gruffly. 'Put that thing away, will you? Try to be a bit less conspicuous if you can.'

Adam was suitably abashed and quickly stuck the gun inside his coat.

'Hey, go easy on the kid, brother,' Rink said. 'If it weren't for these guys we'd still be running up the five-o-seven with half the cops in Tacoma after us.'

Rink was right. Noah and Adam could have left us behind, but they'd chosen to come and rescue us instead. I owed them more than my surliness. It had nothing to do with them, but something worried me and was weighing heavily on my mind. I waved the young man an apology, but he had the grace to shrug it off. 'You were right, Joe. It was stupid of me to wave a gun around like that where anyone could see.'

As it was there was nobody in sight. We were in darkness at the back of the parking lot, and most people staying in the motel had retired for the night. Our arrival hadn't caused any of the bedroom curtains to twitch. We headed inside the room we'd used earlier. Without asking him, Adam offered to go and fetch ice for Billie's hand from a machine he'd earlier visited in the lobby. When he returned it was also with an armful of Coca-Cola drinks, and some chocolate bars from a vending machine. We all needed the sugar rush and carbs.

'What are we going to do about the guns?' Noah wondered, once we'd settled in the sitting area.

'We need to hang on to them for now,' Rink replied. Like I did, Rink understood that things had not yet come to a head. Without adding anything more, he went to Billie who was sitting on the edge of the bed. Out of us all – and considering my mind was on other things – he was the appropriate person to administer field dressings and such to Billie's hands. Billie offered up her malformed right hand, but she didn't look at Rink; she eyed me steadily, with great interest. I found her scrutiny oddly unnerving and looked away. I asked to borrow Noah's cell phone.

'I've got to make a couple of private calls,' I announced.

Once out of the room, I walked away from the motel across the lot to the darkness alongside the parked car.

I must call Brandon Cooper, I thought.

After that, Harvey Lucas.

First I wanted to clear up the lies, and follow that by learning the truth.

41

We didn't bring Billie home to her farm. She stayed in Hill End with Noah and Adam watching over her, while Rink drove the two of us to Baker's Hole. It was a solemn drive. After I'd made the calls last night, I'd got Rink alone and told him what I'd learned, and also what I suspected. I hoped to God I was wrong, but the clenching in my guts was too intense to ignore.

Arriving at the farm, I went inside the house through the front door Adam had booted open, and upstairs to Billie's bedroom. I then joined Rink on the stoop and we walked out by the lake. As I stood on the shore, Rink silent alongside me, I held up the painting I'd taken down off Billie's bedroom wall. Then taking our bearings from the scene in the painting we visually marked the spot of interest on the opposite shore.

'X marks the spot, huh?' Rink said, but with no enthusiasm.

'C'mon, let's get going before Cooper arrives.' I put the painting down on the shore – a clue for the ATF agent to follow. I didn't need the painting as I'd memorised it in detail and could probably draw it again myself, not with Billie's artistic flair but a good copy.

We each shouldered garden spades and set off, following the curve of the lakeshore around its eastern end. It took us twenty minutes to find the general location we'd noted from the other side of the lake, and I lined us up on the natural landmarks I'd taken note of. 'It should be here somewhere,' I said.

Rink is an expert tracker. He sees things that would go unnoticed by your regular man, and what would appear a natural feature of the landscape would stand out to him like an explosion of colour. 'There's irregularity in the under-growth over there,' he said, indicating a low hummock of turf just beyond the pebble-strewn shore. I trusted his instincts and we moved together for the area he pointed out. It wasn't the hummock itself, but the depression in the ground in front. The grass and weed that had found purchase in the depression were darker, younger than the growth all around. Some of the rocks embedded in the earth were also darker in colour than those in the vicinity. Those rocks had once lain the other side up, and hadn't yet had time to fade the way their neighbours had. The earth had been disturbed there. It had been dug out, and then shovelled back into place. Over the years it had settled, sinking marginally lower than the ground nearby.

'You sure we should do this, brother?'

'It's the only way we're going to know for certain what's down there,' I said.

'Maybe it's best we never find out. It's not too late to walk away.'

Unfortunately, it was too late.

In my mind's eye I pictured the crimson stroke of colour in Billie's painting. The vibrant red depicted Nicola, her deceased daughter. In that painting – and others of Billie's if I'd had the time to study them – the dead girl pointed at the ground, at this very spot in the wilderness. Those paintings Billie had committed to canvas were both her way of paying homage to her daughter, and clues to the treasure everyone had been seeking in vain. Following the direction of Nicola's pointing finger, I settled the spade in the earth, stepped on it with one foot and pushed.

We only had to dig a few feet until we came across a galvanised steel barrel. I'd seen others like it in the shed on Billie's farm, next to her parked Jetta. We scraped away the soil, but left the barrel on its side, the lid untouched. By that time the crunch of approaching footsteps had alerted us to Agent Cooper's arrival and we stepped out of the hole and leaned on our spades. Cooper had come as I asked – alone – but I didn't doubt his ATF pals were waiting nearby. He held a pistol down by his thigh.

'Good of you to join us,' I said.

Cooper stopped fifteen feet away, his shoes sinking into gravel with a soft hiss. He didn't lift the pistol, but neither did he put it away.

'I'm surprised you'd doubted me,' he said.

When I'd phoned him the night before, he'd given a lame-arsed excuse about trying to round up a team of ATF agents to come to our assistance but had been too late to be of any help. By the time they'd arrived at the logistics depot it was a no-go area of cops and Feds and he'd backed off. When he'd enquired about Billie's welfare I told him she was safely in my care, and would stay that way without his help. He'd offered to come get her anyway, and to place her in protective custody. It was bullshit; he wasn't the least bit interested in Billie, only in what she could tell him. Still playing his game, he'd asked what I'd learned from her, and that was when I'd told him where and when to meet me, and I'd show him.

'I fully expected you to come.' I tapped the barrel with my spade and it rang dully. 'I promised I'd show you what I'd found. It's right here, Cooper.'

He couldn't keep the greed out of his face. He licked his lips, glancing from me to Rink and back again. Then he took a slow look at the surrounding hills, without ever fully losing sight of us. 'How the hell did you find it all the way out here? Billie must have finally told you the truth, right?'

'I've never been the best detective in the world, but even I was able to figure out the clues,' I said. 'And for the record, Billie wasn't lying. Only you were lying, Cooper.'

After I'd called Cooper I'd rung Harvey and had him check a few facts for me. Apparently Brandon Cooper was no longer an active ATF agent and hadn't been for months. He was simply another interested party in the hunt for Richard Womack, or more pertinently those missing millions of dollars. I should have checked his story earlier, and saved myself a whole heap of trouble. But there you go.

'You know, I should've known you were lying the first time we met and you told me that a facial recognition program had got a hit on Richard. If it had he wouldn't have progressed through border control without being detained. You knew that was bull, but to be fair it was reasonable enough for me to believe you at the time. You mentioned there was a mole in the ATF; that was true. But the mole was yours, he was feeding you intel, getting you the equipment you needed to put me in place, make your fantasy story ring true. You hoped that by having me stick close to Billie she'd finally relent and tell me where the money was, eh?'

Cooper's lips made a thin line. He had no need to lie any further, or to add the details of his fiendish plan like the bad guy in the final act of a mystery movie. All he need to do was allow that I was right and that would have suited me fine. But he felt that he must unburden himself, maybe to make room for all the cash he hoped to carry away from here. 'The ATF burned me, Hunter. After all my years of loyal service to them they kicked me loose, without as much as a kiss my ass. Well they got rid of me, but they couldn't take back what I knew up here.' He tapped his head with the barrel of his pistol. 'I knew about the Womack cold case and about the missing money. And, yeah, I wanted a piece of it.'

'So you dropped Procrylon the tip-off, and set me up as Billie's guardian, hoping to set us against each other, make everyone desperate and draw out the truth from Billie?'

He shrugged. 'Something like that.'

'You piece of crap,' Rink called him.

'Shut your pie hole,' Cooper said. 'This has nothing to do with you.'

Beside me I felt Rink coil like a spring. I shook my head gently at him and leaned on my spade handle again, eyeing Cooper. 'So was it you who told Procrylon about the beacons your ATF mole put in those bulletproof vests?'

'I had to give them a fighting chance, didn't I? If you'd driven Billie away they'd have had no hope of finding her again. I had to make sure that she was a prize that both of you would go after. If it's any consolation I never expected you to get shot, Hunter. I had faith in your abilities, and believed you'd get Billie safely out of the way, where she'd then feel indebted to you and tell you the truth about the money.' He looked down at the steel barrel I'd unearthed and smiled, but it was at his own ingenuity rather than mine. 'When you called me with the news that Billie had been taken, I admit I was a bit worried. Shit, for a second or two I even thought you were going to go along with my plan to call in the FBI. If you had, well, I guess everything would have gone to hell. But my suspicion played out; knowing your way of working, you'd want your chance to go after her yourself. I allowed you to talk me out of it and go along with your idea to rescue her. Luckily, everything worked out for the best, eh? My idea seems to have worked, even if it took a little longer than I anticipated.'

'Do you realise how many people died because of your greed?' I asked.

Cooper laughed at the inanity of my question. 'So a bunch of mercenaries and thugs died? Do I look as if I give a fuck?'

'Good people could have been hurt.'

'Good people *always* get hurt,' he said. 'You should know that.'

Sadly he was correct. But it didn't make it right.

He waved his gun in our general direction. 'Stand the barrel upright. I think it's time I got a look at all that lovely cash, don't you?'

I looked at Rink and he nodded. We left our spades buried in the loose soil, and each grabbed a hold of the barrel rim. It was heavy, and took effort to tug from the earth's embrace. We jostled it to an upright position, then stepped aside. But Cooper shook his head.

'One of you prise off the lid,' he ordered. He aimed his gun at my stomach. 'Rington, you do it.'

Rink fed his fingers into the groove between the lid and the barrel. He grunted in effort, but couldn't get the lid to move. 'I'll have to use the spade to lever it off,' he said.

'Go for it, but no funny business. If I see that shovel move even an inch in my direction, you'll be shovelling Hunter's guts into a grave alongside his corpse. Understand?'

'I get you, man. Lighten up, will ya?'

'Just get the damn lid off or I'll shoot you both and do it myself.'

Rink inserted the tip of his spade in the groove and pushed down on the handle.

'Cooper,' I warned. 'You might want to hold your breath.'

'What are you talking about?' Cooper took a step forward.

'I told you Billie was telling the truth. She said Richard was dead, and she meant it. She said that she knew nothing about the money, and she was telling the truth about that too.' I nodded at Rink, and he flicked off the lid with a final grunt of effort. 'Billie murdered her husband long before she heard anything about the money he had stolen.'

The stench of decomposition must have hit him at much the same time that Rink threw his weight against the barrel and toppled it towards Cooper. Richard Womack's semi-decomposed corpse spilled from the barrel, his fleshless skull still sporting matted black hair, and a huge indentation in the bone that had ended his life. Billie had once told me she would happily smash in Richard's skull given the chance, but she'd been replaying a happy memory rather than fantasising. Seeing a grinning skull staring back at him rather than bundles of cash was the last Cooper expected.

'The money's lost, Cooper,' I told him. 'It's just random numbers in cyberspace now.'

His dream of untold riches was dashed, and he sagged in defeat, a moan of dismay hissing out of him. For that briefest moment his attention was on his dissipating joy and off us. It was all I'd been waiting for. I snatched up my spade and hurled a pile of dirt in his face. He was blinded, some of the muck invading his mouth and nostrils, and easy game as I knocked the gun out of his hand. I was about to swing the shovel at his head, knock the fucker senseless, but Rink beat me to it. He snatched up the lid, swung it overarm, and the spinning metal disc struck Cooper smack in the middle of his face. He went over on his back, and lay there groaning, as I stooped down and picked up his gun. I was tempted to put a few rounds in his body for good measure, but instead I bent my head to the hidden microphone clipped inside my shirt and said, 'I hope you got all that on tape?'

'Loud and clear,' said a voice in my earpiece. Then tactical ATF agents moved in from the forest above us to effect the arrest of the rogue ex-agent. Unbeknown to Cooper a second team had already rounded up his pal, Ray Monaghan, who'd accompanied him when first he'd approached Billie at the farm. Monaghan was Cooper's mole – an active agent still inside the ATF – the man responsible for sourcing the equipment, and for ensuring the bulletproof vests could be traced when it had become necessary.

Once I'd learned from Harvey Lucas about Cooper's enforced retirement and bogus status, I'd got in touch with his old employers. In exchange for immunity from prosecution – something I'd demanded in writing from the director of the ATF himself – I'd promised them I'd give them Brandon Cooper, his mole, and the evidence they needed to bring down Procrylon, and to prosecute them for their part in the illegal arms trade. Their actions in their pursuit of Billie Womack, her subsequent kidnapping and torture, were enough for them to indict Amanda Sheehan at the very least, and from there those people on whose behalf she worked. Considering that we'd discovered she was highly placed in the company's management structure, it would give the ATF a doorway into their activities they'd never had access to before. Procrylon was finished. And now so was Brandon Cooper.

But they weren't the only ones I'd handed to the cops.

42

I'd grown uneasy about Billie Womack pretty early on after meeting her, even if I hadn't wanted to believe what my gut was telling me. It wasn't so much what she said as her reactions to danger and violence. She enjoyed it far too much for my liking, almost to a point where she had gleefulness in her expression when she should have been horrified. The first time she mentioned bashing in Richard's head, it had been delivered with such intent I should have worried for my own skull. Later, after I accidentally killed that dope on the mountain trail, she'd been filled with such excitement, admiration for what I'd done, that I could almost smell the sexual tension coming off her. She'd been turned on by the violence, and it had made me think back to the way in which she'd been watching me in her house while she thought my back was turned. She was studying me like a predatory insect, like the mantis that first satisfies its sexual desires before chewing off the head of its mate. I'd misconstrued her attention at first, and actually scolded myself for thinking of her in a sexual way. She'd offered other clues, but the most telling was the attack on Amanda Sheehan carried out with such vitriol and murderous intent, and then the cold-blooded shooting to death of Daniel Jaeger. Instead of making her escape as quickly as possible she'd gone off in search of further bloodshed, to a point where she'd almost got herself killed but had still been keen for a fight with Erick. Even during that desperate fight she couldn't help crowing, and had come so close to admitting to Richard's murder that it had almost stunned Erick and me into inactivity. Only after our escape from the logistics depot had she realised that she'd been so out of control I couldn't help but spot her psychopathic tendencies. In an effort at throwing me off, she'd sunk into silence, playing the hurt victim. But she couldn't help bragging about leaving a fingernail sticking in Amanda's face when I'd asked about injuries. Once all my suspicions had fallen into a row, I thought again about that painting, of how Nicola pointed at a desolate hole in the ground, and what its significance was, and deep in my heart I realised that I already knew.

After I'd taken the walk outside, made those telephone calls to Brandon Cooper and Harvey Lucas, I'd gone back to the motel room and taken Rink to one side. I told him my suspicions about both Cooper and Billie, and, give him his due, he hadn't questioned their validity. He'd asked Noah and Adam to join him outside while I spoke with Billie alone. Billie was no fool. She suspected what was coming, and she watched me from where she lay on the bed with a veiled expression on her face. She had an impromptu ice pack on her injured hand, cradling it with the other. I checked for hidden weapons lying close by, but there were none.

'Is there something wrong, Joe?'

'You tell me.'

'What do you want to know?'

'Tell me that you didn't intend to harm your daughter,' I said without preamble.

For the first time I saw genuine remorse in Billie's eyes. 'If I could change anything, it would be that my Nicola had to die.'

I felt sick. But I didn't let it show. If she thought she was having that effect on me it might encourage her darker side and I didn't want the situation to grow uglier than it already was.

'It wasn't Richard driving the car that went over the bridge, was it?' I said.

She shook her head. 'Richard was already dead by then.'

That explained why his body had never been found in the river. It was elsewhere, and it was Billie who'd been behind the wheel. I sat down on the bed, my back to her, because I didn't want her to see the disgust I felt for her. 'What happened, Billie?'

'He was cheating on me. He was threatening to leave me, and to take Nicola with him. I couldn't allow that.' She laughed to herself. 'By all accounts he was setting himself up with a nice little windfall, eh? All that cash he stole from Procrylon's accounts? He would have disappeared and I'd never have seen my daughter again.'

'You didn't know that then.'

'No, I didn't know about the money, but he told me he was leaving, and that I'd never find them.'

'You weren't going to allow it though.'

'No. I'd given that bastard the best years of my life; I wasn't going to let him dump me like a soiled rag when he was the one at fault. So, yeah, it's what you want to hear: I bashed his head in with a hammer from my dad's toolbox. I stuffed him in a steel drum, and drove him around the lake in my pick-up and buried him.' She waited for my reaction, but I felt it important to remain calm, non-committal. 'Can you really blame me, Joe? You're a man who will use violence when necessary. I've seen you use it, seen what you're prepared to do for what is right. We're alike in so many ways. Can you honestly say that you wouldn't have smashed in Richard's head if you were in my shoes?'

No, I wanted to say. Never. I was a violent man when pushed, but I wasn't a cold-blooded murderer, a fucking borderline psychopath, like her. I wondered that time about what made once-honourable men like the Jaegers become monsters, and decided that they had been pounded and shaped into something despicable on the devil's anvil. Well, warfare hadn't turned Billie into a monster; she'd been born that way. Instead of replying, I changed the subject. 'Why kill Nicola?'

She was silent for a moment, but for the creaking of the bed as she adjusted her position. I felt her left hand touch my back and it was an effort not to flinch away. 'Remorse, I guess. Call it what you want. I was broken, Joe. You must see that? I didn't know what to do and panicked. I thought the best thing for us all was if I ended it. I couldn't leave Nicola behind. I drove us off that bridge, but wouldn't you just know it? The barricade wasn't as weak as it looked and the car got stuck up in the support wires. As we hung there, I kind of came to my senses and realised the madness of what I'd been driven to by Richard. I climbed out, and was going to the other side of the car to help Nicola out when the damn wires gave way.'

I wasn't sure if what she was telling me was the entire truth, but she'd been forthright enough about everything else. I gave her a lifeline. 'So you tried to save Nicola?'

'Of course I did. But it was no good. The supports gave way before I could reach her and the car fell into the river. She died on impact, but was then washed away on the torrent. I would have looked for her, but again I panicked, I didn't know what to do, so I ran. I went home to my parents' old place. By the time the police arrived I'd showered and changed, and had got a plausible story in my mind. Why should I suffer for what that bastard Richard had pushed me to? I told them that Richard had left me and taken Nicola with him. They investigated me, but I fooled them. I got away with it, Joe.'

Jesus Christ. If she'd had the decency to sob I might have felt some pity for her, but she didn't. She ran her hand down my spine almost suggestively. I stood up, facing her. Billie lay down on the bed, staring back. 'You do understand, don't you, Joe?'

'No,' I said. 'I don't. And I don't believe Nicola's death was an accident. It was too convenient. You're a fighter, Billie, a survivor. Not the type to give in to suicidal urges, like you claim. There's a reason why Nicola had to die: I think that she either witnessed you killing her dad, or she figured it out.'

'Nicola always did have a wise head on young shoulders. I knew she didn't buy my story the way everyone else did.' She snorted scornfully. 'She didn't believe her dad would leave without her.'

'So before she could take her suspicions to anyone else you had to get rid of her.'

Billie only looked at me, and her silence spoke louder than any screamed confession.

'How could you murder your own child?'

'Richard was going to take her anyway,' Billie said, and her mouth turned up at one corner. I saw coldness in her soul that chilled me to the bone. 'Nicola wanted to go with him. Who am I to deny the wish of my child?'

I could no longer bear to look at her.

I called Rink and the fellas back inside. Told Adam to take out his pistol and watch her. Rink had already explained to them what was going on, but it didn't lessen the shock on the duo of private investigators' faces. The only consolation I could think of for them was that the payout on Richard's life insurance policy was now forfeit and the company employing them would be able to reclaim it from Billie's estate – they'd be getting their percentage after all. For Rink and me there'd be no payday, but right then it hadn't been a consideration.

We'd plotted how to catch Cooper, find the evidence of guilt we needed, and brought up the subject of Erick Jaeger.

'He's long gone,' Rink reassured me.

'He'll be back. Not today, maybe not for a while, but he'll come.'

'So when he does we'll be ready,' Rink said.

'Yeah.' I'd already made myself that promise.

I'd then gone outside again to organise the ATF to help them take down Brandon Cooper and Procrylon. I also told them they could collect the murderer of Richard and Nicola Womack at her art gallery in Hill End, where Noah and Adam would deliver her once we were finished at the lake. After that was done, all that was left to do was for me to avoid punching a few walls.

43

It isn't over until it's over.

Never has a truer word been said. And things with Erick Jaeger certainly weren't over with. Rink warned that he'd be coming; we both knew that it was inevitable. He'd a brother to avenge, and despite the truth coming out that Billie was his slayer, it wouldn't mean much. He couldn't get to her but there was still the next best thing: namely me. But that truism works both ways.

After all the hoo-ha was done with in Washington State, with deals and agreements struck – where not a little weight was added to my bargaining power by the intervention of a high-ranking CIA sub-division director who owed me a debt – we were released under our own recognisance with a promise to return to give evidence at the trials of Wilhelmina Womack, Brandon Cooper and those behind Procrylon Inc.'s illegal activities including Amanda Sheehan who'd been caught trying to flee the country on a false passport. Considering that the foreseeable future would be filled with court appearances, it was not a bad idea to return to Florida and make the most of our time there enjoying some rest and recuperation. Rink was hale and hearty, but me, I had some healing to do. Body, mind and spirit.

While Rink returned to his office in Tampa, primarily to catch up on the general state of play from Velasquez and McTeer and then to organise our coming workload, at his urging I retired to my beach house on the Gulf Coast to rest. The cold spell had passed. Or maybe it was just that the blue skies made the difference, instead of the interminable grey of the misty hills I'd been under for days. Simply the presence of a yellow sun gave a welcome lift to my heart. I shed my winter clothing in favour of board shorts and a T-shirt. I'd have foregone the shirt but for the ugliness of the semi-healed wounds on my body. My injuries had taken a toll, but worse was the state of my mind. Fatigue put me out for eighteen hours straight, and I awoke where I'd fallen asleep on a hammock on my deck with gulls wheeling in the morning sunshine. Their calls sent needles into my brain, but at least they weren't the red-hot pokers the shrill sounds would have inserted the day before. Still groggy, I stumbled inside and toileted, showered, then prepared breakfast and a much-needed coffee – I drink too much coffee for my sins, but I left the coffee maker dripping into the pot for later. Once the necessaries were seen to, I again wandered on to my deck, looking out across the water. The gulls had gone, and now only a solitary pelican skimmed the sea, appearing like some prehistoric pterosaur against the heat haze. I watched it glide along the coast until it was lost in the thermal waves. Then, barefoot, I went down to the shore and walked, following the pelican's direction. Step by step I built momentum until I was jogging, and then running.

It'd been a while since I'd last run the beach, but there was no time like the present. The going wasn't easy: there was lead in my thighs and a faint tremor in my chest, and I'd to ignore the thud of my pulse in my inner ears for fear it would morph into actual pain. But after a while something must have clicked in, as I was running without discomfort, and my mind emptied itself of all the questions and recriminations overwhelming it those past few days. At some point while I was in that Zen-like mindset I must have turned for home because before I was fully conscious of doing so I padded up on to my deck once again, to stand at the rail, hands fisted at my hips, peering out to sea while sweat poured off me and I regulated my breathing. I felt much better than I had. Until I turned around.

Usually I'm security-conscious. But I had to question myself: had I locked the door to my house before starting my run? As I set off I'd been distracted by thoughts of how easily I'd fallen for Billie's lies, and how long it had taken me to see through them. So perhaps I hadn't fully closed the door behind me – after all, this followed falling asleep on my hammock for eighteen hours, and wasn't it a good job that no enemy came upon me then while I was so vulnerable to attack?

The door into the open-plan kitchen stood ajar by a few inches. I might have neglected to drop the latch, and an errant breeze had nudged the door open, but I doubted it. Don't let it be said that I was a coward, but neither was I stupid. I took a step backwards.

'That's far enough, Hunter,' said a voice from my right. 'Your hands. Show me them.'

I turned to face Erick Jaeger where he'd stepped out from the corner of my house. He held a Glock 17, his gun hand supported by his opposite cupped palm. The gun was aimed at my centre mass, and this time I'd no bulletproof vest to save me. I held my open palms down by my sides. 'I'm unarmed,' I said.

His spectacle lenses reflected the sun as Erick eyed my damp shirt and bare feet. 'Lift your shirt.'

'You think I went running with a gun stuck down my shorts?'

'I'm taking no chances. Lift your shirt and turn around.'

I did as commanded. Erick nodded. 'OK. Now put your hands behind your neck. Lace your fingers together.'

I sniffed. 'Why? You want me helpless while you execute me?'

'Just do it.' Erick took a half step forward, but he wasn't ready to commit to entering lunging distance just yet. He jabbed the gun at me. 'Do it now.'

I complied. The position of my arms pulled at my chest wound, but it had sealed by now, and there was little worry it would open up again, discounting the threat of another bullet.

'Good. Now eyes front. Do not look at me.' Erick followed his perfunctory commands by moving quickly up and on to the deck. I faced away from him, but could see his reflection in the door as he closed in on me. I considered throwing my weight against him, taking him down, but knew it would be the last thing I ever did. He grabbed my interlaced fingers in his left fist and squeezed, even as he placed the muzzle of his Glock to my spine. 'Inside,' he grunted, and shoved to get me moving. I pressed the door open with my thigh, and moved into my kitchen. An archway led into my living room. Another figure waited inside. I didn't recognise him from the battle at the logistics hub, but didn't doubt this was another of the PMCs originally hired by Procrylon to protect their premises. It was a black man, tall and slim, his hair beginning to go grey. He'd a lined face, but I thought the wrinkles were down to hard experience rather than advanced years. The hands that clutched a pump-action shotgun looked young and strong as they aimed the gun at my chest. He stared at me, his eyes flat and expressionless.

'Down on your knees,' Erick snapped from behind.

'No,' I said.

Erick pushed the gun's muzzle against my nape. 'I said get on your goddamn knees.'

'I'm not doing it.'

'You don't have an option.' Erick pushed, but I resisted.

Opposite me the black guy shoved his shotgun forward, as if that added to the already considerable threat.

Bracing myself, I said, 'I'm not going down on my knees for you or anyone. If you're going to shoot me, then shoot and get it the fuck over with.'

Erick released my constricted fingers, but only so he could thrust his palm into the back of my skull. I feigned discomfort, moving my hands apart and half turning so I could brace my spine against the kitchen counter. Erick was now to my right, and his friend to my left. They couldn't get off a good clean shot for fear of possibly hitting one or the other. Erick quickly resolved that issue by shifting so that he again faced me. He didn't relinquish his aim at any time.

'You're a stubborn son of a bitch,' he said.

'So I've been told.'

'Even in the face of death?'

'Especially.'

Erick grunted, and couldn't help glancing at his companion to share a sneer.

'No one need die here today,' I said, relaxing my arms and allowing them to hang at my sides. 'You do know that we were all played, Erick? We both served people who didn't deserve our protection.'

'My brother didn't deserve to die.'

I thought of how Daniel had cracked me in the skull, fully intending to end my life, but didn't mention it. 'I didn't kill him. Despite what I told you at the time, it was a lie. I was only trying to protect the woman, who by the way it turned out was a murderous bitch.'

'So I heard.'

'Then you know I didn't shoot your brother.'

'Given the chance you would have. You tried to kill me. You *did* kill a bunch of my men.'

'They were trying to kill me at the time. Remember, I'm a stubborn son of a bitch when it comes to that kind of stuff.' I leaned my elbows on the counter, nonchalant enough to seem I was only bearing my weight. I nodded at the black guy, taking him into our circle. 'We're all soldiers; we all know the risks of warfare. Usually we don't take things personally.'

'*Usually* being the operative word,' Erick stated. 'But my brother was executed like a dog, and I take that very personally. You heard of that old expression "an eye for an eye"? Well, somebody has to pay.'

Why waste my breath arguing that Daniel was about to execute Billie when the tables were turned on him? It wasn't as if Erick would accept the knocks, make his apologies and leave. Funnily I felt no rancour for Erick though: if someone had murdered my brother then I'd want vengeance. In fact, someone had slain my brother and I'd shot his murderer in the head and watched him fall from a container ship on a storm-tossed sea. Erick wanted similar satisfaction. No, he wanted more. He should have shot me and had done with it, but he wanted me to suffer first. I'd heard how he'd tormented Billie, taking delight in her pain as he'd repeatedly dislocated her fingers. Maybe he planned a similar torture for me before serving the *coup de grâce*.

'Talking of eyes, maybe you should take off your glasses,' I said.

My comment came out of left field, and had the desired effect. Erick squinted behind his spectacles. 'What are you talking about?'

'It'd be unfair of me to hit a man wearing specs,' I went on.

Erick pulled back his head in incredulity. 'Are you fucking kidding me?'

'You think I'll go quietly?'

Erick raised his Glock, his mouth pulling into a wide sneer, and he exhaled a short grunt of disbelief. 'No, I expect you to beg for your life first.'

'Where did you learn such a cheesy line, from a villain in a James Bond movie?' Perhaps my laughter sounded forced, maybe a tad manic, because Erick glanced at his buddy and they shared a headshake at my madness.

It was what I'd been waiting for. I pivoted, sweeping my right forearm across my body, knocking aside Erick's gun. The black guy swore, and realigned his shotgun, but couldn't get off a clean shot for fear of severing Erick's arm and shoulder. I didn't stop swinging, before grasping the handle of the coffee pot and yanking it from the hot plate. I backhanded the scalding contents at the black guy, and he reared away, but not before his face, throat and upper chest were liberally splashed. He hollered more in surprise than agony, but that was about to follow. Erick had already recovered his senses, and was attempting to readjust his aim as I slammed the jug against the side of his face. The jug was formed of heat-proof, toughened glass, and didn't break. The dregs of hot coffee went up the side of Erick's head and into his hair. He cringed at the burning pain, his eyes screwing up involuntarily as coffee began pouring down his features. Blindly he fired, but I'd already dodged aside and his bullet put a hole in my kitchen wall. I backhanded the jug into the opposite side of his face and Erick went down on one knee. Before he could recover, I rammed my knee into his ribs and knocked him over on his side, even as I vaulted over him and grappled the man with the shotgun.

The black guy was scalded, and in agony, but his pain manifested itself in rage. His strength was almost unnatural as he wrestled with me for the gun. He yanked me bodily off my feet and tossed me across the central counter. I hit the floor rolling on my side and came back to my knees. But I had the shotgun in my grasp and brought it up, firing on instinct. The buckshot tore splinters of wood from the archway above the black man as he ran for his life towards the living room. I let him go, quickly swinging round, and covering Erick as he too came to his knees on the far side of the counter. He had his Glock up, but was blinking wildly, and had no real idea where I was. I pumped the shotgun to give him a clue. 'Drop the gun, Erick!'

From the living room came the drum of heavy feet, a meaty thud. I ignored what was happening there as I rose up, aiming the shotgun at Erick's chest. Erick swiped at his face with a forearm and his spectacles were knocked awry. He pulled them off and tossed them aside. His gun wasn't relinquished once.

'I said drop your fucking weapon!' I yelled again.

Erick squinted at me, his face contorting in disappointment. But then he held his Glock out to one side, allowed his fingers to unfold and dropped it with a clatter on the coffee-splattered floor. Maybe if it had only been me holding him under a weapon he'd have gone for broke, but my pals Velasquez and McTeer had rushed in through the open door from the decking, and both of them aimed handguns too.

The black guy was propelled through the arch, going to his hands and knees by the force of a push. He had a livid bruise growing on his forehead that matched the shape of the stock of the Mossberg shotgun Rink wielded as he strode into the kitchen. Erick looked at his pal, then shook his head in regret. I moved round the counter, never lowering my gun, until I stood a few feet before Erick, who, still on his knees, peered up at me. He swore under his breath as he checked out my friends all standing around us. 'You knew we were coming,' he said.

I rocked my head to one side. 'You took your time. Hell, how much setting up should a trap take? I lay out on that bloody hammock for long enough waiting for you to make your move, so there was nothing for it. I had to go for a run just to give you an opening to take.'

'I should've shot you when you first suggested it,' Erick said.

'Yeah, you should have. But you missed your opportunity.'

Rink offered a grin of his own. 'If you had, you wouldn't have walked outta here alive. Not pulling that trigger was the best decision you ever made, buddy.'

'So what happens now?' Erick returned his attention to me. 'You have me on my knees; are you going to execute me the way I planned for you?'

'I'm tempted,' I said.

But I also recalled Billie's words as she'd tried to vindicate her murderous actions. 'Can you really blame me, Joe?' she'd asked. 'You're a man who will use violence when necessary. I've seen you use it, seen what you're prepared to do for what is right.'

Right or wrong, executing Erick Jaeger in cold blood didn't fall into that category. Instead I exercised my civilian power of arrest. I gave McTeer a nod, and he took out his cell phone and punched in the number for the local ATF field office: Jaeger and his scalded friend could be added to the criminals I'd already sent their way.

THANKS

With grateful thanks to Luigi Bonomi, Alison Bonomi, Oliver Johnson, Anne Perry, Alice Wood and all the team at Hodder, and to all Joe Hunter readers new and old. This book would not be here without all your efforts.

JOE HUNTER

BRITAIN'S BEST VIGILANTE V AMERICA'S WORST CRIMINALS

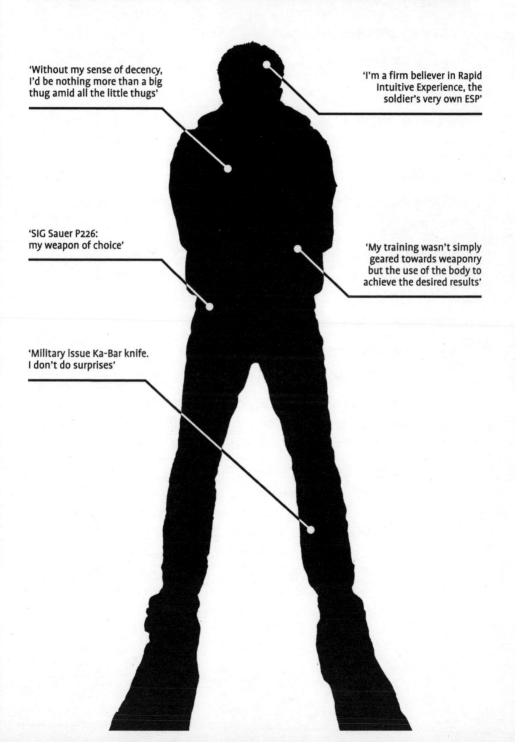

'Without my sense of decency, I'd be nothing more than a big thug amid all the little thugs'

'I'm a firm believer in Rapid Intuitive Experience, the soldier's very own ESP'

'SIG Sauer P226: my weapon of choice'

'My training wasn't simply geared towards weaponry but the use of the body to achieve the desired results'

'Military issue Ka-Bar knife. I don't do surprises'

CURRICULUM VITAE – JOE HUNTER

NAME: Joe Hunter.

DATE OF BIRTH: 8th August.

PLACE OF BIRTH: Manchester, England.

HOME: Mexico Beach, Florida, USA.

MARITAL STATUS: Divorced from Diane, who has now remarried.

CHILDREN: None.

OTHER DEPENDENTS: Two German shepherd dogs, Hector and Paris (currently residing with Diane).

PARENTS: Joe's father died when he was a child and his mother remarried. Both his mother and stepfather reside in Manchester.

SIBLINGS: Half-brother, John Telfer.

KNOWN ASSOCIATES: Jared 'Rink' Rington, Walter Hayes Conrad, Harvey Lucas.

EDUCATION: Secondary school education to 'O' level standard. Joe received further education and underwent self-teaching while in the British Army and Special Forces.

EMPLOYMENT HISTORY: Joined British Army at age 16. Transferred to the Parachute Regiment at age 19 and was drafted into an experimental coalition counterterrorism team code named 'ARROWSAKE' at age 20. As a sergeant, Joe headed his own unit comprising members from various Special Forces teams. Joe retired from 'ARROWSAKE' in 2004 when the unit was disbanded and has since then supported himself by working as a freelance security consultant.

HEIGHT: 5' 11".

WEIGHT: 13 stone.

BUILD: Athletic.

HAIR COLOUR/STYLE: Short brown hair with slight greying.

EYE COLOUR: Blue/brown.

APPEARANCE: Muscular but more lean than bulky, he has the appearance of a competitive athlete. His demeanour is generally calm and unhurried. Due to his background, Joe has the ability to blend with the general public when necessary, but when relaxed he tends to dress casually. He doesn't consider himself handsome, but women find him attractive. His eyes are his most striking feature and the colour appears to change dependent on his mood.

BLOOD TYPE: AB

MEDICAL HISTORY: Childhood complaints include measles and chicken pox. As an adult Joe has had no major medical conditions, but has been wounded on several occasions. Joe carries numerous scars including a bullet wound in his chest and various scars from knife and shrapnel wounds on his arms and legs. He has had various bone breakages, but none that have proven a continued disability.

RELIGION: Joe was raised in a Church of England environment, but is currently non-practising.

POLITICS: Joe has no political preferences and prefers morals and ethics.

CHARACTER: Joe can come over as a little aloof at times. He is a deep thinker who prefers only to speak when he has something important to say. He is very loyal to his family and friends. He dislikes injustice, hates bullies and will stand up to defend others in need of help.

MUSIC: Wide choice of music, but particularly enjoys vintage rhythm and blues.

MOVIES: Joe's favourite movie is 'It's a Wonderful Life'. It is a morality tale that resonates with his belief that a person's actions – good or bad – continually affect those around them.

BOOKS: When he was younger he enjoyed classic fiction by HP Lovecraft, RE Howard and Edgar Allan Poe, but currently reads a wide range of crime and suspense novels.

CIGARETTES: Smoked various brands but gave up.

ALCOHOL: Drinks only moderately and infrequently. Prefers beer to liquor.

DRUGS: Has been subjected to drugs during his military career, but has never personally taken any illegal drugs. Joe hates the influence that drugs have on the world and stands against those producing and supplying them.

HOBBIES: Fitness. Joe works out whenever he can with a combination of running, circuit training and martial arts.

SPECIAL SKILLS: As a soldier Joe gained many skills pertinent to his job, but also specialised in CQB (Close Quarter Battle), Point Shooting, Defensive Driving and in Urban Warfare Tactics. He is particularly adept with the handgun (usually a SIG Sauer P226) and with the knife (usually a military issue Ka-Bar).

CURRENT OCCUPATION: Joe describes himself as a security consultant and sometimes PI, but some people call him a vigilante.

CURRENT WHEREABOUTS: USA.

In the best books, the ending often comes as a shock.
Not just because of that one last twist in the tale,
but because you have been so absorbed in their world,
that coming back to the harsh light of reality is a jolt.

If that describes you now, then perhaps you should track down
some new leads, and find new suspense in other worlds.

Join us at www.hodder.co.uk, or follow us on
Twitter @hodderbooks, and you can tap in to a
community of fellow thrill-seekers.

Whether you want to find out more about this book,
or a particular author, watch trailers and interviews, have
the chance to win early limited editions, or simply browse
our expert readers' selection of the very best books,
we think you'll find what you're looking for.

And if you don't, that's the place to tell us what's missing.

We love what we do, and we'd love you to be part of it.

www.hodder.co.uk

 @hodderbooks

HodderBooks

HodderBooks